RIDING
SHOTGUN

C.J. PETIT

Printed in the United States of America

First Printing, 2021

ISBN: 9798513048398

CONTENTS

PROLOGUE

April 5, 1871
Lewiston, Idaho Territory

The clouds were still thick overhead, but the heavy rain that had soaked the town all morning had finally moved on. Townsfolk were going about their business more slowly because of the mud as four men rode down the sloppy main street. Not many of the residents took notice of the strangers because the main street was busier than normal now that the rain had stopped.

But one who did notice them was Deputy Sheriff Bill Lafferty. Otis Jacobsen had stopped him outside of the apothecary to complain about being overcharged when the riders passed by. He didn't see them until after they had ridden past and none of the four had so much as glanced at him. If they had, they would have noticed the shiny badge pinned to his dark brown vest.

After he'd spotted the four newcomers, Bill let Otis ramble on as he studied them more closely. One was riding a buckskin with white boots, which wasn't that unusual, but another was mounted on a tall gray roan with long black stockings. If they hadn't been together, Bill wouldn't have identified the riders.

He quickly said, "I'll tell the sheriff about it, Otis," then without waiting for a reply, he turned and headed back along the boardwalk.

Otis watched him leave and muttered, "You'd better."

Bill didn't look behind him until he had to cross the street. As he mucked his way to the jail, he noticed that three of the four men were dismounting in front of Martin's haberdashery. If the bank wasn't adjacent to the hat shop, Bill wouldn't have hurried so much. But when he was convinced that Ace Carr's gang was about to rob the bank, he tried to jog the last sixty feet.

Forty feet later, his right foot slipped, and he fell face forward into the mud. As the folks who witnessed his accident laughed, Bill scrambled to his feet and ignoring his thick brown coating, he mucked through the last twenty feet to the sheriff's office. Just before he opened the door, he looked once again down the street and only saw the one man still in the saddle. For that brief moment, their eyes met, and Bill knew that the Carr gang would be expecting them.

He burst into the jail, startling Sheriff Lyle Borden and fellow deputy Jim Winters.

They stared at him for a second or two before they burst into raucous laughter at his mud-covered appearance.

Bill ignored their laughter as he hurried to the desk and shouted, "Lyle, it's the Carr gang! They're gonna rob the bank!"

Lyle and Jim's merriment ended abruptly as both quickly stood and the sheriff asked, "Are you sure it's them?"

Bill nodded vigorously as he replied, "Yeah, I'm sure. One of 'em is out front in his saddle and the other three are probably already in the bank."

As the sheriff turned to the gun rack to grab a shotgun, Bill said, "The one on the horse saw me, boss. He's probably still watchin' the front of the jail."

Lyle's hand was still grasping the shotgun's barrel as he cursed under his breath.

He then turned and said, "I told them they shoulda put a back door in this place but it's too late now."

The sheriff switched his grip to a Winchester and yanked it free. He tossed another to Jim Winters and a third to muddy Bill Lafferty.

"The bank is far enough away that even if that one on the horse already has a bead on the front door, by the time I pass through, he'll probably miss his first shot. Jim, I want you to follow me no matter what happens. Bill, you come out right behind him. When we get past the door, we turn right and stay on the boardwalk as long as we can, so we don't slip in that mess. Don't run unless he starts shootin'. By the time we get through the door, the others will probably be leavin' the bank, so be prepared for anything. Alright?"

Both deputies nodded, but only Jim Winters cocked his Winchester's hammer.

Lyle didn't bother pulling on his hat as he approached the door. He took a deep breath and prepared himself for the expected gunfire. He yanked open the door then hurried out of the jail and turned onto the boardwalk. When he looked toward the bank, he was sure that the man on the horse spotted them, but still hadn't drawn his rifle.

When Jim and then Bill exited behind him, they were just as surprised as the sheriff that it had remained quiet. The three lawmen stared at the unmoving rider as he looked back at them.

Bill asked, "What do we do, boss?"

"Cock those Winchesters and follow me. Don't aim at that feller unless he makes a move."

As Sheriff Borden began walking toward the bank with his to deputies trailing, they studied the lookout and waited for him to pull his rifle.

The rider hadn't pulled his repeater because it wasn't necessary. What the lawmen didn't know was that the Carr gang now had five members, not four.

C.J. PETIT

The last recruit, Joe Hobart, was sitting astride his dark brown gelding just fifty feet west of the jail and had his cocked Winchester in his hands when the three lawmen exited. The lookout near the bank, Jack McFarland, smiled when he spotted the three badge toters leave the jail. As Joe brought his Winchester level behind the three lawmen, Jack finally ripped his from his scabbard.

As Sheriff Borden quickly began bringing his cocked Winchester level to aim at the rider, the echo of a rifle shot echoed through Lewiston. The sheriff spun to the boardwalk as blood gushed from his right upper bicep and his unfired Winchester plopped into the nearby mud. The main street of the town quickly turned into a battleground as the townsfolk hurried into the nearest building for protection. Even the three mounted citizen who could have pulled their pistols cleared the area.

After Joe fired, Jack McFarland aimed at Jim Winters and took his shot. He missed because Jim had quickly bent down to check on his wounded boss. Bill Lafferty had turned to face the unknown shooter and was about to fire when Joe squeezed his trigger for the second time. Bill felt the .44 slam into his left upper chest before he dropped to his knees. He still held his Winchester but dropped it to the boardwalk knowing he was no longer capable of using it. He yanked his Colt New Army pistol from his holster, cocked the hammer and fired. He was pulling back the hammer for a second shot knowing that it was highly unlikely that he'd hit the outlaw

6

when Joe's next .44 punched into his chest just a few inches below the first.

By the time Bill collapsed to the boardwalk, Jim Winters had fired at Jack McFarland. He missed and so did Jack's next shot. Deputy Winters glanced behind him and when he saw Bill lying face down on the boardwalk with a puddle of blood pooling around him, he knew he would soon die. He bolted past the sheriff as Joe Hobart fired at him. The .44 blasted a hole in the boardwalk near the sheriff's head, but Jim reached the nearby alley and ducked into its shadows where he stopped to think of what he should do.

Lyle's wound wasn't fatal, but he knew he was unable to do anything more than become a target, so he just played possum. As Jim raced past him and the bullet exploded through the wood just inches from his head, he'd almost popped to his feet. But then an eerie silence replaced the thunder of gunfire. He heard a horse's hooves squishing in the muck as the outlaw who'd shot him rode past. He held his breath and didn't let his eyes move knowing that the outlaw was probably inspecting his handiwork. He might still fire an insurance .44 into him, but Lyle had no other choice. He just prayed that both of his deputies were still alive.

Joe wasn't inspecting the sheriff and hadn't even given him a passing glance as he walked his gelding down the street. He was looking for the deputy who had escaped. He pulled up just before reaching the alley and just sat in his saddle. He didn't even set his sights on the alley's entrance. If the deputy was at the end of the alley and planning to fire, Joe wasn't about to give him a target. He just waved to Jack who waved back.

Inside the bank, Ace Carr, Hal Kingman and Frog Bouchard were about to finish the job. Ace was near the door with his cocked Colt Navy as Hal and Frog filled their saddlebags with the last of the silver from the cash drawers. He hadn't been worried about the gunfire echoing from the street because he was sure that Joe and Jack had done their part in the well-planned heist.

After Hal and Frog left the bank carrying their stuffed saddlebags over their shoulders, Ace remained standing near the door. They'd let him know when they were mounted and ready for him to leave.

Less than a minute later, he heard Jack yell, "Okay, boss!"

Ace loudly said, "You folks all stay inside. Anyone who sticks his nose out that door won't last long."

He then released his Colt's hammer, turned and slipped it back into his holster before he walked out of the bank.

Jim had finally decided to take a peek to see what was happening and stepped closer to the corner of Phillips Books and Periodicals. He was startled when he saw the mounted outlaw just fifty feet away and staring in his direction. He quickly ducked back into the security of the dark alley. His heart was pounding, and he expected to see the wood on the corner of the bookshop splintered by gunfire.

Instead of the crack of a Winchester, he heard Joe shout, "I'm gonna put a bullet into you if I see your face again! You better not have a gun pointed at me when I see you. If you wanna live, get on your belly and hug the ground!"

Jim felt like a coward as he dropped into the mud and waited for the man to pass but he didn't let his Winchester touch the ground. He was determined to prove his courage after the outlaw rode by. He'd stay on the ground for just a few more seconds then he'd get to his feet and shoot the bastard.

Joe had waited until the boss left the bank before making his threat. As he watched the rest of the gang ride away, he turned his horse away from the alley and headed for the next street where he turned left.

Jim didn't hear him leave and because the killer had warned him to not even look, he didn't know that Joe was gone. He suspected that the outlaw was still sitting on his horse hoping to get a clean shot.

It wasn't until he heard Sheriff Borden yell, "Jim, have you been hit?" that he slowly pulled himself out of the mud. He was so humiliated that he just stood frozen in the alley without replying.

Lyle's arm was still bleeding, and he needed to have it treated. But before he went back to check on Bill Lafferty, he again shouted, "Jim, I've been hit, so I gotta get fixed up. I need you! If you can walk, come out and help me with Bill!"

Jim reluctantly walked out of the alley and as he stepped onto the boardwalk and saw the sheriff's bloody wound, he felt even worse.

Lyle wasn't about to chastise his young deputy for his reaction, even if he didn't need Jim's help. The sheriff knew that the gang had them surrounded and if Jim hadn't bolted into the alley, there would be only one wounded lawman left to protect the town and the rest of Nez Perces County.

As his deputy slowly approached, Sheriff Borden said, "Jim, I need to get patched up, so you're in charge now."

Jim replied, "I'm not good enough to wear this badge, boss. I didn't stop any of 'em."

Lyle snapped, "For God's sake, Jim! I didn't slow 'em down either. You did the smart thing to get into the alley. If you didn't then the town would have no protection at all. Now, we got a job to do. You're a good man, Deputy Winters. I wouldn't have sworn you in if you weren't."

Jim didn't feel much better but understood that if he turned in his badge, he would be branded a coward. He had to cast off his shame and prove to the sheriff and the townsfolk that he was a lawman.

"Okay, boss. I'll do whatever you need. Can you make it to the doc's office on your own?"

"Yeah. First you need to have Bill's body taken off the boardwalk. Then send a telegram to Mitch Ward down in Salmon City and Harry Crenshaw in Pierce City. They rode south toward Lemhi County but they coulda turned east into Shoshone County."

"Yes, sir."

Lyle knew he had more instructions to give his only deputy, but he was beginning to get a little woozy, so he turned and headed for Doctor Edwards' office three blocks away. He only walked a half a block before two men arrived to help him. He was already so dizzy by then that he didn't even know who they were.

Jim didn't need to move Bill's body when the undertaker arrived and said that he'd arrange for everything. Deputy Winters then walked to the telegraph office and hoped that the gang continued riding south. He knew that if they reached Sheriff Mitch Ward's jurisdiction, they'd never leave unless they were returned to Lewiston in shackles.

CHAPTER 1

May 12, 1871
Salmon City, Idaho Territory

"I still think it was a lousy thing for Steve to do," Deputy Aaron Jackson said as he placed the seven of clubs below the eight of diamonds.

Sheriff Mitch Ward grinned and said, "They needed him more'n we did, Aaron."

Aaron searched for a red jack as he replied, "I know that, but I wouldn't go up there just 'cause it paid an extra ten dollars a month, Mitch. I like it here."

Pete Carter snickered then said, "You like Annabelle more'n you like the job, Aaron."

Aaron scooped up his cards as he said, "You're just jealous 'cause Annabelle's so pretty."

"I ain't jealous. My Nancy is just as pretty and so are my two girls. I'm just sayin' that Annabelle is the reason why you're stayin' put."

Deputy Jackson shuffled the cards and said, "She's the best reason. But even after we get hitched, I wouldn't want to take her away from her folks."

He then looked at his boss and asked, "Is that why you told Steve about it first, Mitch? Was it because he was unattached?"

Mitch shrugged and said, "I just reckoned that if I had to lose a deputy, I could get by without Steve."

Pete snickered before saying, "He wasn't that bad, Mitch."

"Maybe I just have a better opinion of you two, that's all."

Aaron was pleased and surprised by the sheriff's reply. Mitch wasn't the most talkative man in town and rarely expressed his thoughts, good or bad. The only time that he spoke more than a sentence or two was when it was necessary for the job. He'd correct their mistakes when necessary, but he never criticized or made light of what they'd done wrong. For him to mention that he had a good opinion of his two remaining deputies was monumental praise coming from Sheriff Mitchell D. Ward.

Pete asked, "Are you gonna hire another deputy, boss?"

"Yup."

Pete looked at Aaron and grinned as Aaron smiled back. Neither had expected more details from their boss.

Mitch stood and pulled on his faded blue cavalry hat then said, "You boys can head home," before he strode across the office floor and left the jail to do the evening rounds.

Aaron opened the top left-hand drawer and put away the cards before he said, "You heard the man, Pete. Let's lock this place up."

Pete grabbed his hat from its peg then waited for Aaron to do the same before they left the jail and Aaron locked the front door. As they walked west, Sheriff Ward was heading in the opposite direction. Most of the businesses were already closed for the day, so as he stepped along the boardwalk, Mitch either glanced through the window or turned the doorknob to make sure the owner had remembered to secure his shop.

By the time Aaron had entered Dennison's Boarding House and Pete had returned to his house on Apple Avenue, Mitch had reached the end of Main Street and crossed to the other side. He was about fifty feet away from the entrance to Salmon River Hotel when a guest stepped outside. Mitch hadn't seen the man before, which wasn't an immediate concern because he'd just left the hotel and had probably just arrived in town. He was probably just passing through. He did know that the stranger hadn't arrived on the stage because Mitch made a habit of greeting new arrivals when it rolled into the depot.

The visitor hadn't even looked to the east, so he didn't notice that the walking was behind him. But while Mitch didn't know him, he did recognize his mannerisms. The man had good measure of arrogance that was evident in the way he walked. He seemed to believe that he was in control even if he hadn't been to Salmon City before. He was almost strutting as he stepped along the boardwalk, but Mitch noticed his head shifting back and forth, but only barely. The stranger was evaluating the businesses on both sides of Main Street.

Once Sheriff Ward decided that the man wasn't visiting Salmon City to conduct any legitimate business, he figured that it was time to introduce himself. But caution was paramount, so he pulled his Smith & Wesson Model 3 from his holster without cocking the hammer. He increased his pace until he was just ten feet behind the stranger who must have finally realized someone was behind him. Just before Mitch announced his presence, the man quickly turned. He also automatically reached for his pistol but was startled to find that the man who'd been following him was not only the sheriff, but he already had had his pistol in his hand.

Ace quickly yanked his hand away from his Colt, then grinned as he said, "You scared me, Sheriff. I figured you might be some outlaw who was gonna rob me."

Mitch stared at the stranger for just a few seconds before he made a preliminary match to the wanted poster of the notorious Ace Carr.

"Let's head to my office."

"I was gonna have supper, Sheriff. Can't a man eat in peace in your town?"

"Later."

Ace nodded then turned to cross the street. As he stepped onto the dirt, he hoped that at least one of his boys would spot him being escorted to jail. He wasn't sure if the sheriff knew who he was yet and if he could continue to bluff the lawman long enough, then the sheriff wouldn't be expecting anyone to come to his rescue.

As Mitch followed his prisoner across the street, he glanced in both directions expecting the rest of the Carr gang to make an appearance. If they did, he'd put a .44 into their boss before facing the others. He doubted if he'd survive the gunfight, but he'd take put down as many as possible before he was unable to return fire.

It was a long and anxious walk back to the jail but when they stopped before the locked door, Mitch had Ace put his hands against the wall and removed his Colt. After shoving his pistol under the waist of his britches, Mitch patted him down and found a Colt Pocket pistol in a shoulder holster. He took the smaller pistol and slid it into his left pants pocket before stepping around the outlaw and unlocking the door.

After pushing the door open, he said, "Come inside."

Ace took his hands down and wanted to look back at the hotel to see if any of his men had stepped outside but didn't want to rouse the sheriff's suspicion.

He just continued his innocent charade and said, "You're makin' a big mistake, Sheriff. I ain't no outlaw."

Mitch just waved his Smith & Wesson's barrel toward the door and followed Ace as he entered the jail. Once inside, Mitch closed and locked the door then said, "Get into the first cell."

Ace quickly asked, "You're gonna put me in jail? I didn't do a damned thing, Sheriff. You ain't got cause to arrest me."

"Just get in there, mister."

Ace was annoyed that nothing seemed to be working in his favor. He'd been disarmed and the sheriff had even locked the jail's door. Even if his boys had seen him being led off, they wouldn't be able to free him short of using dynamite, and they didn't have any. After entering the cell, he watched as the sheriff closed and locked the door.

Mitch walked to the desk and set Ace's two Colts on its surface before pulling open the right-hand drawer and taking out the short stack of wanted posters. Ace's face peered back at him from the third one and even though it wasn't a great drawing, it was close enough for Mitch. He just needed a bit more confirmation.

He stepped close to the cell's bars and asked, "What's your name?"

"Fred. Fred Alberts."

"Okay, Fred. Where are you from and what are you doin' here?"

"I have a spread up near Millersburg and I was on my way to visit my brother. He's got a small ranch near Wilson's Creek."

"I don't recall any ranchers down that way named Alberts."

Ace was stalling for time as he replied, "It was his wife's place 'til he married her."

As Ace was inventing his lies, Mitch was studying him. While he certainly matched the vague description on the wanted poster and seemed to be quick on his feet, there was one thing that the outlaw chief couldn't hide.

Mitch then said, "That's a mighty nice hat you got, Fred. Mind if I take a look at it?"

Ace was taken aback but relieved when the sheriff seemed to have already abandoned the interrogation. He smiled and pulled off his dark gray Stetson, but as he held it out, he realized why the lawman had asked to see it.

Mitch grinned as he said, "You can put it back on now, Ace."

Ace cursed his streak of almost blonde hair that never changed color no matter how often it had been cut. He yanked his hat back on before he turned and sat down on the cot. His only hope now was his four partners. How they could spring him lose was the big question.

———

As Sheriff Ward had been searching Ace for a hidden gun, Hal Kingman and Jack McFarland were leaving Draper's Livery after checking on everyone's horses. Frog Bouchard and Joe Hobart were waiting for them in Comey's Saloon and Gambling Parlor.

When they spotted Mitch as he unlocked the door and followed their boss inside, they froze and Hal exclaimed, *"What happened? How did that sheriff get the drop on Ace?"*

Jack shook his head as he replied, "I got no idea. What should we do now?"

Hal quickly scanned the street before saying, "Let's find Joe and Frog and put our heads together. Maybe that sheriff doesn't know he's got Ace."

"That ain't likely, Hal. After killing that deputy and shootin' the sheriff last month up in Lewiston, I reckon they're all lookin' for us."

"We know he's got two deputies but don't know how many of 'em are in the jail right now. So, when we pass by the jail, you can take a quick look inside."

"Okay."

The two outlaws soon reached the boardwalk and Hal began talking about the weather, so when they passed the jail's window, Jack could be looking that way as he added his own comments.

———

Mitch was sitting behind the desk just watching the barred front window as he thought about what he'd do if the other gang members tried to free their boss. Less than two years ago, a lynch mob wanted to break down the doors to take his very guilty prisoner. While they had failed, the extensive damage and the fear that it might happen again provided a good reason to add an impressive array of protection to the jail. Not only were the windows protected with steel bars, but there were heavy blocking rails ready to be dropped across both the front and back doors. Both of the older, damaged doors had been replaced with thicker and denser wood as well. Mitch hadn't lowered the bars into place yet but could drop them quickly if necessary. As he watched, he was debating about leaving through the back door to let Aaron and Pete know about the situation and even regretted letting Steve Finch leave which he never thought possible.

He was still undecided when he saw two strangers pass by the window. They were trying very hard to appear disinterested as the one nearer the street looked inside. He didn't need to check his wanted posters to identify them as members of the Carr gang. He didn't bother turning around to see if Ace had recognized them, either. But seeing them made his decision unnecessary. He'd stay put and wait, but now he'd bar both doors in case they tried to break in.

Ace watched the sheriff drop the heavy bars to block the doors and wondered what the boys would do. He knew that they wouldn't abandon him, but he hoped that they'd play it smart. He wasn't wanted in Lemhi County, so if the law wanted to put him on trial, the sheriff would have to arrange to get him back to Lewiston. He knew that Nez Perces County wanted him, but their sheriff was still recovering. He guessed that the Lemhi County sheriff would take him to Lewiston for trial. It was just a question of how they'd move him. Even if he had a deputy with him when they made the long ride, his boys wouldn't much of a problem getting him loose. If they took the stagecoach it might be more problematic, but it was still a lot less secure than this fortress they called a jail.

———

Just a few blocks away, the four free members of his gang were discussing the unexpected problem.

Frog asked, "What do you wanna do, Hal?"

21

"I ain't sure yet."

Jack said, "The sheriff was sittin' by his lonesome in the jail, so we could wait for him to leave."

Hal looked at him as he said, "You saw that place. It'd be hard to break in and I don't reckon that sheriff is goin' anywhere 'til his deputies show up."

Joe Hobart asked, "Do you reckon he knows we're all in town, Hal?"

"I'm sure he does by now."

It was Jack who realized what Ace had already figured out.

He asked, "They can't hang him here; can they?"

Hal quickly replied, "That's right! He ain't wanted for nothin' in this county. They'll most likely bring him back on the stage to Lewiston. I can't see that sheriff ridin' two hundred miles."

Joe grinned as he said, "If we waited until they were almost to the Camas Plains, we could take that stage easy and then just disappear."

Hal nodded before saying, "All we need to know is when they're gonna be movin' him. We don't wanna start knockin' off stages without knowin'. Besides, I already figured out how to get it done without gettin' the boss shot while we're tryin' to spring him loose."

He then looked at Joe and said, "Joe, you don't stick out as much as the rest of us, so you're gonna be the one to find out when that sheriff is gonna move Ace to Lewiston. We're all gonna ride outta here, but you can set up a campsite just outside of town. We have to let that sheriff figure we're all gone. Now the next stage is gonna leave tomorrow, but he won't be ready yet. The next one he can take will be Tuesday, so just stop in for a beer and listen. Folks will be talkin' about it 'cause the boss is kinda famous. As soon as you hear when he's movin' Ace, let us know."

"Okay. Are you gonna be at the ranch?"

"We'll stop there but we'll meet you in Millersburg. If we're not there yet; just get a hotel room and wait for us to show up. Then we'll head past Mount Idaho and set up."

Joe grinned and said, "I'll get there as soon as I find out when they're movin' Ace."

Hal then explained his plan in detail. He was sure that even Ace couldn't have come up with anything better. By the time he finished, the others agreed with him. It was a good plan that couldn't fail.

———

The four men rode out of Salmon City heading north along the dark road less than an hour later, but Joe pulled off the road just three miles out of town to set up camp.

Mitch didn't light a lamp as he paced in the jail. He had returned to his earlier debate about leaving through the back door. If he did sneak out, he'd have to find one of his deputies quickly. He was about to leave when someone began to rap on the front door. He doubted if it was a member of Ace's gang but wasn't about to lift the blocking bar before finding out who was on the other side.

He walked to the door and shouted, "Who's there?"

Deputy Jackson yelled back, "It's Aaron, boss!"

Mitch quickly lifted the locking bar before unlocking the door. As he swung it open, Aaron stepped quickly past him. Mitch took advantage of the open doorway to step outside and scan the shadowed street before returning to the jail and closing the door.

He didn't lock it but turned to his deputy and asked, "How did you know I was thinkin' about lookin' for you?"

"I was having supper with Annabelle at Waldron's and Ed Johnson came up to our table and asked me who you arrested. He said he didn't recognize the feller but saw you take his guns. After I walked Annabelle home, I figured I'd see if you were still here."

"I was about to hunt for you or Pete. The man in the cell is Ace Carr. I'm pretty sure the rest of his gang is around, but I didn't want to give them a chance to free their boss, so I stayed put."

Aaron stared into the dark cell as he asked, "How'd you figure out it was him? He ain't one of those fellers that sticks out in a crowd."

"It doesn't matter. Now that you're here, you take the desk and bar both doors after I'm gone. I'll check around to see if I can find his gang. If I don't see any of 'em, I'll bring him his supper when I get back."

"Okay, boss."

Mitch grabbed his hat and pulled it on before leaving the jail. Once outside, he waited until he heard the heavy locking bar being lowered into its steel supports before walking to Draper's Livery. It was the one that was closest to the Salmon River Hotel where he'd spotted Ace.

Once he entered the livery, it didn't take long for him to realize that it didn't hold any strange horses. He was about to turn around to check the other two stables when he heard someone behind him.

He turned and saw Bud Rose leaving his small room carrying a lamp and asked, "Sorry to bother you, Bud. But has anyone taken their horses out in the last couple of hours?"

"Yup. Four fellers showed up, I reckon it was about an hour or so ago and seemed kinda in a rush. They took their friend's horse along, too."

"Did you see which way they rode off?"

"Yup. All of 'em headed north. Kinda odd to be leavin' after sundown; ain't it?"

"Not if you knew who they were, Bud. That was the Carr gang, and I got their boss locked in one of my cells."

Bud's eyes widened as he exclaimed, "Well, I'll be snookered! I coulda been killed!"

Mitch patted Bud on the shoulder before turning around and leaving the big barn. The four men might be gone, but he doubted if he'd seen the last of them. It was now just a question of when that would happen.

He headed for Millie's Café to have his supper rather than Waldron's Restaurant where Aaron had shared dinner with Annabelle. Millie's served bigger portions at lower prices but wasn't as fancy as Waldron's. Sheriff Mitch Ward didn't need to impress a young lady.

As he passed the jail, he glanced inside just to make sure everything was quiet. He was pleased that Aaron hadn't lit a lamp in his absence even though the other members of Ace's gang were out of town.

When he entered the café, he wasn't surprised when most of the diners' eyes turned towards him. He smiled then walked to the closest empty table where he took a seat and set his hat on the next chair.

Maddie McCall hurried across the floor then stopped and said, "I heard that you caught an outlaw, Mitch. Was he a bad one?"

"Yes, ma'am. I'll have to feed him, so if you can bring me the special, I'll take another one with me when I'm done."

Maddie was obviously disappointed that the sheriff hadn't identified the name of the bad man who was waiting for his supper but smiled at Mitch before she turned and headed back to the kitchen.

Mitch was sure that everyone else in the place wanted to know who was in the jail just as much as Maddie did, but he figured they'd all learn about it from Bud Rose soon enough. He'd send a telegram to Lyle Borden in the morning and already decided that he'd act as the shotgun rider on the stage that carried Ace back to Lewiston. While it was still possible that the other gang members might try to free their boss from the jail, he thought it was less likely now. That long stagecoach ride to Lewiston would be their best chance to keep him from hanging. Normally, the jurisdiction that issued the warrant would be responsible for transporting the prisoner, but after losing one deputy and with Sheriff Borden still recovering from his wound, that wasn't possible.

He wished that he had another deputy, but figured he'd leave Pete on his own for a few days. He'd want Aaron to ride inside the coach with Ace in shackles to protect any other passengers. He'd prefer that no one else would be on the

27

stage but knew that the Overland Stage Company wouldn't turn down any ticket buyers.

Maddie brought him a plate heavily loaded with thick pork chops and roasted potatoes five minutes later. After setting the plate and cutlery on the table, she added a smaller plate of fresh biscuits, a small bowl of butter and a large cup of steaming coffee.

"I'll bring you more coffee in a few minutes, Mitch," she said as she smiled down at him.

"Thank you, Maddie."

"I won't be bringing as much food for your prisoner."

Mitch smiled back and just as a verbal tip he said, "I'm sure that Ace Carr will take whatever I give him."

Maddie almost bounced onto her toes as she grinned then hurried away to tell the cook what Mitch had said.

The sheriff was still smiling as he began to eat his massive dinner. He figured that he may as well start the gossip chain from both ends of town.

———

Thirty minutes later, Aaron opened the jail door for his boss who was carrying a tray for his prisoner.

After closing the door, Mitch handed the tray to his deputy and said, "Let's go feed Ace."

Aaron brought the heavy tray to the cell and after sliding it through the wide slot near the floor, he sat in the chair behind the desk. Mitch struck a match, then lit the desk's lamp and perched his behind on the corner of the desktop.

Ace was studying his supper as Mitch studied the gang leader.

Without taking his eyes from his prisoner, Mitch said, "His gang was in town, but when I checked at Draper's, their horses were gone. Bud told me that they left about an hour ago and took Ace's horse with 'em."

Aaron quickly asked, "Do you reckon that they're comin' back?"

Mitch replied, "Maybe. But I don't figure we'll be seein' em anymore. I reckon that one of the other bad boys will take over the gang now that their old boss is gonna hang."

Aaron stared at Mitch because even he believed that they'd probably try to spring Ace loose.

But when Mitch saw the corners of Ace's mouth turn up slightly, he had his answer. He turned to Aaron and winked before pointing to his private office. Aaron understood, so when Mitch stood and walked past the cells, he followed.

29

Ace must have been satisfied that his food hadn't been poisoned, because he was eating before the two lawmen entered Mitch's small private office.

After Aaron closed the door and sat in one of the two chairs before the sheriff's desk, Mitch said, "I don't think Ace's boys are gonna try to break him outta here. They'll try to do that when we have to bring him to Lewiston for trial."

Deputy Jackson asked, "Are we gonna be takin' him?"

"Yup. We could just put him in his saddle and take him back when they don't expect it, but if one of 'em is watching the road, we'd be sitting ducks. I'm plannin' on ridin' shotgun on the next stage to Lewiston, so I can spot 'em fast and get ready. I'm gonna have Ace shackled in the coach but I still want you to guard him."

"We can't have any passengers in there, boss."

"I wish that was so, but it's not our call. I'll tell Hank Jones at Overland to warn any passengers, but if they still wanna come along, then we have to let 'em. But I do have one way to make it safer."

"How?"

"We kinda let word out that we'll be takin' next Friday's stage, then we leave on Tuesday. By the time they figure it out, we'll be in Lewiston."

"What if they're watchin' all of the stages?"

Mitch shrugged then replied, "Then we'll deal with 'em if they show up."

Aaron nodded as he envisioned the long ride to Lewiston and after almost a minute of silence, he asked, "What about the overnight stops at Millersburg and the Camas Prairie way station? They could hit us when we're sleepin'."

"We can use Kent Thompson's jail in Millersburg. He's only got one old deputy, but at least he's got a decent cell. But one of us will hafta stay on watch at the way station."

Aaron wished that there was a better way to get Ace Carr to Lewiston, but his boss had already explained why using the stagecoach was their best choice. He was impressed that Mitch had talked so much, too. He didn't need to ask why Pete would stay behind and he'd be the one to be guarding the gang leader. He may be planning to marry Annabelle, but Pete was already responsible for his wife and two little girls.

He asked, "Are you gonna stay with him tonight or do you want me to stick around, boss?"

"I'll watch him tonight. Can you stop by Pete's house and let him know what's goin' on?"

"I'll do that, Mitch," Aaron replied before standing and leaving his private office.

Mitch was still reviewing his decision to use the stage. If it had been a shorter trip, even a hundred miles or so, he'd just tie Ace down in his saddle and leave on his own. He was used to escorting prisoners without any support, but this was different. There were around two hundred miles between Salmon City and Lewiston and somewhere along the way, there would be four men determined to kill him to free their leader.

As he left his office to return to the front desk, he just hoped that there were no passengers on board the stagecoach. But if someone came along, and he trusted the man, maybe he'd let him have the shotgun. He wasn't planning to use the scattergun, anyway. He'd bring Goldie, his three revolvers and a couple of boxes of spare .44 rimfire cartridges for his Winchester and one box of Smith & Wesson cartridges for his Model 3. If he couldn't stop four outlaws with his own firepower, then he didn't deserve to wear the badge.

CHAPTER 2

Mitch was bleary-eyed when Pete Carter unlocked the door and entered the jail early the next morning carrying Ace's breakfast. He'd napped at the desk rather than use the cot in the empty cell. Ace had complained about having to use the chamber pot rather than being escorted to the privy, but Mitch wasn't about to let him out of the cell for any reason until they put him in shackles and led him to the stage depot.

Pete brought the tray to the cell and slid it through the slot before walking to the desk and taking off his hat.

Mitch stood, then stretched and arched his back as he said, "Thanks for showin' up early, Pete."

"You look like you tied one on at Comey's last night, Mitch."

The sheriff walked stiffly away from the desk to let Pete take over and said, "I imagine so."

"You need to get some sleep, boss. Aaron will be here soon, at least for a little while. He's takin' Annabelle to lunch. I'll stick around 'til you come back."

Mitch nodded then pulled his old blue hat from the peg and waved to Aaron before leaving the office. Once outside in the bright spring sun, he checked the traffic just out of habit. He

33

didn't expect to see anyone pointing a gun at him, but he was ready if it happened.

He turned and began walking east. He'd send the telegram to Lyle Borden letting him know about Ace's capture. He'd inform Lyle that he would return the gang leader for trial but to let him know if he would rather handle it himself.

Ten minutes later he was heading east again after sending the message. He included his planned date of departure to let Lyle know when they'd be arriving in Lewiston. He'd also asked the telegrapher to tell anyone who asked that he would be moving Ace on Friday.

He soon turned at the intersection with Meadow Street to go to house. He bought the excessively large house more than two years ago when he decided he just wanted some privacy. At least that was the excuse he gave to himself and anyone who asked. He didn't want to admit the real purpose for making the purchase because it was embarrassing. But he had the money even before collecting a large reward for capturing the Gallagher brothers. The house had been on the market for more than six months, so he was able to buy it for a very reasonable price.

He still ate most of his meals at the café and had to pay widowed Donna Brown to keep it clean. But he did appreciate not having to listen to folks making all sorts of noises in the adjacent rooms when he'd stayed at the boarding house.

He soon headed down the nice walkway of #19. After entering his home, he hung his hat on the fancy coat rack then passed through the foyer, the parlor and then entered the long hallway. He'd make himself some coffee and a quick breakfast before getting some sleep.

His lack of sleep was making it difficult for him to think straight. He blamed part of it on his advancing years. Granted, he may just have turned thirty-two in April, but he felt much older. He'd lived a hard life and it was taking its toll. He didn't expect to see fifty if he kept pushing himself this way, but he didn't worry about the future. Worrying about it didn't alter what would happen.

Yet despite the many difficulties he'd faced, Mitch only had one regret. The lone reason for his disappointment was the same one that had driven him to buy the house. He was convinced that when his end did come, if it wasn't caused by some outlaw's slug, he'd be alone in his big bed when he breathed his last.

He shook his head to clear his cobwebs and to stop feeling sorry for himself. It never served any useful purpose.

It was an hour later when Mitch pulled off his jacket, gunbelt and then his boots before stretching out on top of the four-poster's quilts. He was asleep in less than five minutes.

———

Lyle Borden still had his right arm in a sling when Bill Bishop entered the office and handed him a telegram.

As he read the message, the delivery boy asked, "Are you gonna send one back, Sheriff?"

Lyle nodded then replied, "Yup. I'll need you to write it, Billy. Can you do that for me?"

"Yes, sir. I'm good at spellin'."

Lyle grinned then said, "I'd have one of my deputies write it, but they've already gone home for the day. Here's what I want you to write."

After dictating his brief reply, the sheriff checked Billy's spelling, made two corrections then sent him on his way. He then stood and took his hat from the desk and left his office to go home for the day. He'd tell Steve and Jim tomorrow if he saw them or Monday if he didn't. He expected that they'd hear about Mitch Ward's capture of Ace Carr before sunset anyway.

As he walked to his house, he was pleased that Ace would soon be tried in his courthouse but wished that he knew where the other four gang members were.

———

Pete was in the locked jail guarding a surprisingly quiet Ace Carr while Aaron was spending time with Annabelle Gruber in her family's parlor. Aaron had hoped for a pleasant Saturday afternoon with her, but those hopes were dashed after he told her that he wouldn't be attending her eighteenth birthday party on Wednesday. He had expected her to react badly but was pleased when she didn't seem to be upset at all.

She did surprise him when she asked, "Are you going to guard him by all the way to Lewiston by yourself?"

"No, Mitch is gonna ride shotgun. But I'm gonna be inside cuffed to the outlaw 'cause he trusts me. This Ace Carr character is the boss of a tough gang, and the sheriff reckons that they might try to spring him loose while we're takin' him to Lewiston."

Her temper flared just momentarily before she asked, "If they want him in Lewiston, why doesn't their sheriff come down here and get him?"

"Um…remember I told you about why Steve took the job up there? Well, their sheriff is still laid up and they only have two deputies."

"So, Mitch is going to risk his life and leave just one deputy to guard the town for a few days while they have two deputies up there just twiddling their thumbs. That's stupid, Aaron!"

"No…no, it isn't. Lewiston is a much bigger town and it's right on the border with Oregon Territory, too. So, they get a lot more problems than we do. Mitch never does anything stupid, Annabelle."

"Then why did he buy that big house when he's not even married? He needs a woman to keep him happy and he's not even looking."

Aaron didn't know why Mitch bought the place either, but it wasn't his concern, especially not now. He'd been telling his friends that he and Annabelle were going to be married, but he hadn't even proposed yet. When Mitch told him that he'd be guarding Ace, he had forgotten about her birthday but then thought that she would be impressed with his bravery. She didn't seem to be pleased at all and now the idea of asking her to marry him seemed like a pipe dream. He needed to bail himself out of his rapidly sinking future with Annabelle.

So, in an attempt to recover, he smiled and said, "You're right, Annabelle. That is kinda stupid. But I'll make it up to you. I promise. When I'm in Lewiston, I'll buy you a special birthday present."

Annabelle smiled and asked, "How special?"

Aaron thought he was back on track and replied, "Very special. I already had somethin' in mind, but I couldn't find it here. I was gonna buy you another present that wasn't so special when Mitch told me that I was goin' to Lewiston with him. I knew you'd be disappointed, but I was kinda glad 'cause I knew I'd probably find it up there."

"Well, alright. But it had better be really nice, Aaron. A lot of other men are interested in visiting me."

38

Aaron's stomach plummeted when she mentioned the possibility of other competitors. Aaron had no idea what he'd buy for Annabelle when they got to Lewiston, but it would probably cost him most of his forty-dollar-a-month salary.

"Don't let anyone start visitin' you, Annabelle. Please."

Annabelle smiled coyly then said, "I'll hold them off until you to come back from Lewiston, Aaron."

Deputy Jackson returned her smile but wasn't happy with the way things were going. The rest of the afternoon's conversation didn't bolster his confidence either. They talked about suggested gifts and what Mitch expected the Carr gang might do. She seemed more concerned about Mitch than what might happened to him which was more than just mildly depressing. As he left her house two hours later, he wasn't sure he'd be able to win her even if he returned from Lewiston with a diamond necklace costing more than a full year's salary.

After Aaron returned to his room at the boarding house, Annabelle was joined by her sister and two brothers. She told them about the special gift that Aaron was going to give her after he returned from Lewiston. While her sister was excited about the gift, her older brothers were much more intrigued with the possibility that Tuesday's stagecoach to Lewiston might be attacked by Ace Carr's gang. So, when they asked, Annabelle passed along everything that Aaron had told her about the dangerous journey.

———

Mitch's eyes popped open, and he wasn't sure what time it was. He swung his legs off the bed and rubbed his eyes before looking out the nearest window. The sun was still shining, so he hadn't slept too long. He stretched then pulled on his boots and headed to the bathroom. After washing and scraping off his thick stubble, Mitch walked to the large kitchen and restarted the fire. He slid the half-full coffeepot onto a hot plate before he walked out the back door and stood on the wide porch. He guessed that it was somewhere between two and three o'clock.

He said, "I put it at 2:37 P.M. on Saturday, the thirteenth of May of the year 1871."

Mitch snickered then reentered the house, passed through the kitchen and headed down the long hallway to the parlor. When he reached the fancy room, he looked at the grandfather clock in the corner.

He smiled and said, "Well, grandpa, you're tellin' me it's 2:42, and I reckon your guess is better than mine."

He strode across the polished floor and the large rug before reaching the clock. He opened the glass face and wound the clock to keep it running for another eight days. He'd want to wind it before leaving on the stage, so it would still be accurate when he returned the following Monday. He wished somebody would build a railroad between Salmon City and Lewiston but knew that it wouldn't happen for at least ten years. The Northern Pacific had already planned its route, and it would pass through Lewiston. But it would be coming through Missoula in Montana Territory, so Salmon City would still need the Overland Stagecoach Company to provide passenger service.

He shook his head as he headed back to the kitchen. That railroad would be going to Oregon City, too. If he hadn't left the big town after his boss and mentor, Sheriff Abe Croaker had been killed, he'd be able to watch those rails arrive. But he didn't regret leaving. He knew he'd never be their sheriff and seriously disliked Abe's replacement. He thought he'd be able to land a position as deputy sheriff in Lewiston, but when he arrived, he found that they didn't have any openings.

Then Lyle Borden told him that Lemhi County needed a new sheriff, so he took the next stage to Salmon City. The powers that be seemed impressed with his years as a deputy sheriff, so they appointed him the new county sheriff over the protests of two of the three deputies. Steve Finch hadn't complained, but Mitch soon wished he had. Within a year, he had replaced the complainers with Pete and then Aaron. Both were much younger than the deputies they replaced, but Mitch was able to mold them into good lawmen.

He had a cup of hot, bitter coffee with two of Mrs. Brown's biscuits. Even though she was ten years older than he was and had two married children, he knew that there were whispers that she was doing more than just cleaning his house

41

and baking biscuits for him. He just let the tongues wag knowing that the more he protested the accuracy of the rumors, the louder the gossip would become.

After buckling his gunbelt around his waist, he donned his light jacket and pulled on his hat. The jacket's left pocket held his first cartridge pistol, a small .22 caliber Smith & Wesson Model 1. It had seven cylinders but would need all of them to put a bad man down. He bought the gun because it was innovative and didn't need to use percussion caps. He'd never needed to use the pistol for anything other than target practice and plinking but liked it well enough to buy another Smith & Wesson offering. He bought the Model 1 ½, which oddly enough, was released after they had introduced the larger Model 2.

It fired the same powerful .32 caliber round as the Model 2 and despite losing one chamber from the larger pistol, Mitch found it to be very effective. While it didn't have the stopping power of his .44 caliber Colt Navy, it could be reloaded much faster. He had a special holster made for his second Smith & Wesson which he kept in his jacket's right pocket. The holster had eight cartridge loops sewn onto the side for spare cartridges.

Both of his first two Smith & Wessons were reloaded in the same unique manner. When the pistol was empty, all it took was a quick release of a latch and the barrel would tilt up and away from the cylinder. After sliding the cylinder from its center post, he'd turn it upside down and any brass that didn't fall free would be pushed out by quickly forcing the recalcitrant empties out using the extraction post. After dropping in fresh cartridges, the cylinder was returned to the center post, the barrel was swung back down, and it was ready to fire. It took longer to explain the process than to actually do it.

But when Smith & Wesson came out with the Model 3 just two years ago, Mitch was one of their first customers. He ordered it before it even went into production. It was the same size as his older Colt and used .44 caliber cartridges. Unfortunately, it didn't use the .44 Henry rimfires that his Winchester fired. Smith & Wesson made their own centerfire cartridges. The fastest way to tell them apart even in the dark, was by the blunt nose of the Winchester's bullet. The Smith & Wesson had a rounded bullet. It was even faster to reload than Smith & Wesson's earlier models.

The new version's barrel broke down rather than up and the empty brass was ejected automatically. He could reload the pistol in less than thirty seconds. He heard that Colt and Remington were both close to developing cartridge pistols, but he wasn't about to change his loyalty. The Model 3 added one more significant improvement. It had a trigger guard like the Colt percussion pistols. He thought it was Smith & Wesson's first offering that looked like a serious gun.

While he doubted that the Model 1 would ever be anything more than a nuisance to outlaws, he still kept it with him. He just didn't bother carrying any spare .22 caliber ammunition. He didn't expect to engage an angry squirrel in a shootout.

After he was fully armed, Mitch left his house and headed back to the jail to relieve Pete. He'd watch Ace overnight again, but he'd get some sleep in the other cell now that he was reasonably confident that his gang wasn't going to return.

When he entered the jail, Pete yanked his feet from the desk so awkwardly that he almost flipped the chair over backwards.

Mitch didn't laugh but couldn't keep a grin from his face as he hung his hat on one of the empty pegs.

Deputy Carter was smiling sheepishly as he said, "I didn't expect you so soon, boss."

"I reckon not."

Mitch looked at Ace who was stretched out on the cell's cot with his eyes closed and asked, "Any problems?"

"Nope. Ace has been a model prisoner."

"On your way home, hunt down Aaron and tell him he can take over in the mornin'. You take the day off."

"Are you sure, Mitch?"

"Yup."

"I'm sure Nancy will appreciate it."

44

Mitch nodded as he sat behind the desk and watched Pete grab his hat then hurry out of the jail. He wouldn't lock the door until he returned from evening rounds but decided not to bother with the locking bar. The back door's bar was still down, so he'd just leave it.

He pulled the small stack of papers from the desk tray and was surprised to find a telegram on top. Pete must have been in a hurry to get home because it hadn't been opened. He pulled out the message out of its envelope, expecting it to be the reply from Lyle Borden. It was a response from his fellow sheriff, and Mitch smiled as he read it.

As he read the short message, he didn't have to be clairvoyant to imagine Lyle's relief when he read the telegram letting him know that Ace had been captured and would soon be delivered to his jurisdiction. He was sure that Sheriff Borden was as annoyed as he was that the others were still at large. While he wished he had all five of them in his jail, Mitch hoped that they stayed out of sight until he dropped off their boss. He was still uneasy with his decision to move him via the stagecoach but knew it was his only real choice. He just wished that Ace had committed a crime in his jurisdiction so he could be tried and hanged in Salmon City.

He glanced behind him and suspected that Ace wasn't napping. He was probably trying to figure out how his boys would keep him from walking up the gallows' steps in Lewiston.

―――

Mitch hadn't had any visitors for the rest of the day before he locked the door to begin his evening rounds. He knew that he could have skipped the security check, but it wasn't his nature to cut corners just because it was convenient.

After he ensured that all of the businesses were locked up, he entered Millie's Café and walked to his usual table. He took a seat and within seconds Maddie McCall magically appeared.

"Do you want the special again, Mitch?" she asked.

"Yes, ma'am. And I'll need one for my prisoner, too."

"I know. I'm sure you'll be glad to get him out of your jail."

Mitch nodded then smiled until Maddie turned and walked away to get his dinner.

―――

As he carried Ace's supper back to the jail, Mitch passed Comey's Saloon and Gambling Parlor. It seemed noisier than usual for a Saturday night, and that was pretty loud. He continued along the boardwalk and hoped that nobody started a brawl.

Inside the large saloon, Annabelle's two brothers, Art and Jason, were sitting at a table enjoying a night out with their friends. They were telling Jack Croft and Abner Shackleford how nervous Deputy Aaron was when he told their sister that he going to miss her eighteenth birthday party.

Art laughed then loudly said, "He told her he'd buy her somethin' special when he gets to Lewiston on Thursday. I figure he'd have to buy her a pair of white stallions and a fancy carriage to get in her good graces again."

With the raucous background noise, Jason had to shout, "I reckon that our lonely deputy ain't got a chance with Annabelle no matter what he buys her."

Jack Croft snickered then said, "Maybe I should start seein' Annabelle."

The Gruber brothers and Abner looked at Joe for a few seconds before they burst into laughter. Jack just grinned knowing that Annabelle wasn't about to give him so much as a glance. He considered himself pretty lucky just to be her brothers' friend.

As they laughed, Joe Hobart finished his beer then rose from his nearby table and left the saloon. As Ace was eating his barely warm dinner, Joe was riding out of Salmon City heading north. He wouldn't reach Millersburg tonight, but tomorrow he'd meet with the others to let them know that their boss would be on Tuesday's stage. He knew that Hal had come up with a good plan but still had concerns knowing that Sheriff Ward would be riding shotgun with his deadly Winchester.

———

After emptying and rinsing out the chamber pot, Mitch returned to the jail, slid it into Ace's cell, then blew out the lamp before entering his own cell. He removed his gunbelt and slid it under the cot before sitting down and pulling off his boots. He stretched out and looked through the bars at Ace Carr. He hadn't said a single word since the initial interrogation when he claimed to be an innocent visitor. While Mitch appreciated the lack of conversation, he wished that he could get the gang leader to give him even a hint of what he expected his gang might do.

He closed his eyes and followed a mental map of the route to Lewiston. The northwest route paralleled the Salmon River almost all the way to Millersburg before the river and road parted company. The mountains stayed on the eastern side of the road until they reached the smaller town, then after leaving Millersburg, it wound its way through some more mountains before it passed Mount Idaho and entered the wide Camas Prairie. The prairie wasn't nearly large enough to be confused with the Great Plains. While it was flat and covered with prairie grass, mountains were always visible and there were more creeks crisscrossing the land.

Mitch figured that if the gang was planning to stop the stage to spring their boss, it would be somewhere between Millersburg and the Camas Prairie way station. Even if he was right, that left more than sixty miles of potential ambush sites.

He'd travelled the road fairly often and tried to picture that long stretch of highway. While there were too many places that would serve as good spots to rob a stage, Ace's gang would need much more than a just a few boulders or trees to successfully free their boss. They might not know when he was bringing Ace to Lewiston, but they would definitely expect that Mitch would be riding shotgun on the stage. So, they'd have to hide four riders and try to avoid his Winchester when they made their attempt. None of them would want to die just to help out their leader, no matter how loyal they were. Survival was their top priority.

Mitch wished that he knew more about the other four members of the Carr gang. *Were any of them smart enough to devise a well-designed plan to free Ace?* Ace Carr was their boss because he was the brains of the outfit, not because he was the most ruthless. To be able to kill him and Aaron without getting their boss or any of themselves killed would be a difficult task. Mitch had to assume that one of them had the knowhow to come up with such a plan. It was up to him to figure it out before they left Salmon City and then come up with a way to stop it.

———

Aaron showed up at the jail around eight o'clock the next morning and was surprised to find the front door already open. He entered carrying their prisoner's breakfast with him and smiled at Sheriff Ward who was sitting at the desk.

49

"Mornin', boss."

"Mornin', Aaron."

After Deputy Jackson slid the tray through the slot to a silent Ace Carr, he took off his hat and hung it on a peg as he watched the gang leader pick up his breakfast then sit down on the cot.

"Did he say anything, Mitch?"

The sheriff was taking his own pistol-packed jacket from its peg as he replied, "Nope."

Aaron sat down behind the desk and asked, "Are we still leavin' on Tuesday's stage?"

Mitch donned his jacket then his hat as he answered, "Yup."

"Annabelle wasn't happy when I told her I'd miss her eighteenth birthday. I gotta find her a nice present while we're in Lewiston."

"I reckon so."

Mitch glanced at Ace who was chowing down then said, "I'll be back before four o'clock."

"Okay, boss."

Sheriff Ward nodded then turned and left the jail, closing the door behind him. Even though he hadn't even had a cup of coffee yet and it was Sunday, he headed west down the boardwalk to do his morning rounds. But as he'd checked the doors on his evening rounds and all of the businesses were closed, it was a few minutes faster than those on weeknights.

After his long loop through town and greeting churchgoers as they passed, he turned down Meadow Street and soon entered his house. He wasn't tired, but he sure could use a hot cup of coffee. He hadn't even been paying attention when Aaron said he'd told Annabelle that he'd miss her birthday. If he had, he would have suspected that the word was out about Tuesday's departure.

———

He returned to the jail well before four o'clock to relieve Aaron. His young deputy told him that their prisoner hadn't spoken a single word all day, but Mitch would only have been surprised if Ace had begun talking.

Three hours later, he'd finished his evening rounds, had his dinner and fed his prisoner. While the gang leader still hadn't uttered a sound, when Mitch slid his tray through the slot, Ace smiled. It wasn't an attempt to appear friendly. It was more like a warning that his captor would never get him to Lewiston. Mitch took note but didn't give Ace any indication that he'd understood the meaning of his slight smile.

Ace may not have known how his boys would spring him loose, but if he'd been in the hotel room in Millersburg where

51

they were meeting to discuss Hal's plan, he would have probably done more than just smile.

CHAPTER 3

Aaron was explaining his social difficulties with Annabelle to his fellow deputy when Mitch left the office the next morning to visit Hank Jones, the depot manager for the Overland Stagecoach Company. For the second time he didn't pay attention to what he considered unimportant chatter. He had serious issues on his mind.

The Monday morning street traffic was already making crossing to the street to the depot a dangerous proposition. He had to dodge two riders and a buckboard as he trotted to the north side of the roadway. The stage he'd be taking tomorrow would be arriving from Lewiston late this afternoon, so Hank shouldn't be busy. Mitch wanted to talk to him before anyone arrived to buy a ticket for tomorrow's run.

He turned into the open doorway and found Hank talking to Wally Arnold, his farrier.

Hank smiled when he saw Mitch and said, "Mornin', Mitch. I reckon you're here to tell me you'll be makin' use of our service to Lewiston tomorrow."

Mitch grimaced but figured it no longer mattered because it was only one day before they left Salmon City.

"Yup. I'll have Ace shackled and Aaron will be inside keepin' an eye on him. I'll ride shotgun, so Ed can take a few days off. Has anyone bought a ticket for tomorrow's run?"

"Miss Cohen is the only one so far. She bought it on Friday."

Mitch felt a chill run down his spine. Of all the people in Salmon City to be on the stage, it had to be her.

After he'd recovered from Hank's revelation, he asked, "Did she say why she was headin' to Lewiston?"

"Yes, sir. She said she was seein' the folks at St. Anne's for a job."

"She's leavin' Salmon City?" Mitch asked with wide eyes.

"I reckon so. I didn't ask, but I figured after Doc Walsh died, she wasn't able to work here anymore."

Mitch nodded then said, "Well, if anyone else shows up to buy a ticket, let 'em know that we'll be movin' Ace tomorrow and I'm expectin' his gang is gonna try to keep him from gettin' to Lewiston. Okay?"

Hank hesitated for a few seconds before saying, "I'll tell Jimmy when he gets in this afternoon."

"Tell him I'll do what I can to stop 'em if they try."

"He ain't got any choice, Mitch. It's his job."

"I reckon I'd better go talk to Esther Cohen. I really don't want her in the coach tomorrow."

"Good luck gettin' her to change her mind, Sheriff."

Mitch shrugged then left the depot and stepped onto the boardwalk. He removed his faded blue hat, ran his fingers through his light brown hair then pulled it back on. He didn't have to ask anyone where to find Esther Cohen. But he was just as concerned that she would be permanently leaving as he was about having her in the same coach with Ace Carr.

He turned west and headed for Doctor John Walsh's house on Third Street. Esther had been his nurse and lived in a room in the doctor's house. She'd arrived in Salmon City almost three years ago after Doc Walsh's wife died. His wife had been acting as his nurse for thirty-one years and most folks figured the doctor would give up his practice when she passed away. But he'd written a letter to the territorial hospital in Boise letting them know that he needed a nurse.

Surprisingly, even though she lived in the doctor's home, not one whisper entered the gossip chain. It wasn't because of Doctor Walsh's advanced age or poor health that no one suggested immoral behavior. It was that the elderly physician was well respected and a pillar of St. Michael's Catholic church.

As he walked toward Third Street, there was a reason that Mitch was surprised that Esther was leaving town even after

Doctor Walsh died. The other physician in town, the much younger Doctor Ernst Brandt needed a real nurse. His wife assisted him for some jobs but wasn't qualified to be a nurse by a long stretch. Ellie Brandt didn't even like seeing blood.

After Hank told him that Esther was leaving to find employment in Lewiston, he guessed that even if the doctor wanted to hire Miss Cohen, his wife had probably vehemently opposed it. Ellie wasn't a bad-looking or evil-tempered woman, but she faded in comparison to Esther Cohen.

He turned down Third Street and had to cross to the western side to reach #21. As he stepped onto the porch, he hoped that Esther hadn't gone to do some last-minute shopping.

Mitch removed his hat and knocked on the heavy oak door. As he waited, he wondered if Doc Walsh had any relatives. If not, maybe the doctor named Esther as his heir. If he did, then it might be enough incentive to keep her in town.

When the door opened, he smiled and said, "Hello, Esther. Can I talk to you for a minute?"

Esther's big brown eyes sparkled as she smiled back and said, "Of course. But it would be a record if you spoke to me for a whole minute."

As Mitch entered, he felt the tops of his ears burn and suspected their shade now matched the red glow of a dying fire as well.

Once in the doctor's waiting area, he sat down and waited for Esther to take a seat.

"Um…Esther, I…you heard about me arrestin' Ace Carr; didn't you?"

"The whole town heard about it. I assume that you're here to tell me that you'll be bringing him to Lewiston on tomorrow's stage."

Mitch was momentarily put off stride by her reply, but quickly recovered and said, "Yes, ma'am. I'm worried about his gang tryin' to free him. I was hopin' that the only passengers would be my deputy and Ace. I talked to Hank Jones over at the depot and he told me that you already bought a ticket."

"I did, and before you ask, I can't delay my departure. I have an interview scheduled at Saint Anne's on Friday morning."

"Can't you send 'em a telegram and make a new appointment?"

"There is another nurse applying for the job and I don't want to lose the opportunity. I'm sure that you'll be able to protect me."

Mitch was already convinced that he wouldn't be able to get her to reschedule her appointment, so he asked, "If you don't mind my askin'; why are you leavin'? I figured Doc Brandt would ask you to work for him after Doc Walsh died. I know Ellie Brandt isn't a nurse or even good enough to be a midwife. Is it because she's afraid you might take her place altogether?"

Esther stared at Mitch for a few seconds before she smiled then laughed lightly.

As she shook her head she replied, "No, I'm sure that's not the reason. I didn't even ask Doctor Brandt for a position. To be honest, I was surprised that St. Anne's even offered me an interview."

"Why is that? You're a fine nurse, Esther and coulda been a doctor yourself. I reckon you even know more about medicine than Doc Brandt does. When I had needed patchin' up, I went to see Doc Walsh, but you were the one to fix the damage."

"A knife wound on your left forearm, another on the right side of your chest and one gunshot to your left calf. At least you've gone almost a year without having to need another repair."

Mitch nodded as he said, "But you didn't say why Doc Brandt wasn't gonna hire you or why you were surprised that the folks up at St. Anne's wanted to see you."

Esther's eyebrows rose slightly as she asked, "Do you really have no idea why they wouldn't, Mitch?"

Mitch shook his head, still puzzled by Esther's apparent difficulty in finding a new position.

"It's the same reason that I was so anxious to leave my old job in Boise. They didn't want me there, either."

Mitch blurted, "But I don't want you to leave!"

Esther was startled and Mitch was embarrassed at his unexpected utterance.

He tried to recover by saying, "I'm sorry, Esther. I meant to say that the folks in Salmon City don't want you to leave."

"That's not true either, Mitch. But if I tell you why Doctor Brandt wouldn't dare hire me, maybe you'll understand why I believe that they'll be relieved when I do leave."

Mitch avoided another verbal blunder by just nodding.

Esther tilted her head slightly as she said, "It's quite obvious, Mitch. My first name is Esther, and my surname is Cohen. Think about it for a minute."

Mitch still didn't understand but after a few seconds, he shrugged and replied, "So? It's a good name."

Esther rolled her eyes as she exclaimed, "I'm Jewish, Mitch! I'm surprised that you still haven't figured it out."

Mitch quickly said, "I knew that when you first got here. But you're tellin' me that folks don't want to hire you as a nurse 'cause you're Jewish?"

"That's the reason. My heritage makes a lot of people uncomfortable, Mitch."

"That's plum stupid. But I wasn't one of 'em, Esther."

"I never would have guessed otherwise, Mitch. But until now, I doubt if you've spoken more than five hundred words to me over the past three years. If you didn't speak to me because I was Jewish, then what was the reason?"

Mitch wrung his hat as he looked at the waiting room floor. He could almost feel her brown eyes boring into him as he searched for the right words.

"I don't say much to most folks, but I reckon I said a lot less to you. It ain't that your Jewish, it's because, well, it's just that you're so smart and pretty and…well, I'm not."

Esther was astonished by his answer. She had known Sheriff Ward for almost three years and considered him to be as good a man as she ever hoped to meet. Whenever they'd talked, it had been almost a monologue. But even those one-sided conversations were important to her. She was pleased just to have someone actually listen to what she was saying and appeared to be interested. But the longer those talks remained more like soliloquies, the more she began to believe that the sheriff was only being polite. While even that was better than what she'd come to expect, she wished that he was more talkative. And now, just as she was leaving Salmon City, she discovered that he wasn't avoiding her for the usual reason at all.

"I think that you're much smarter than you believe, Mitch. And I'm sure that no man wants to be called pretty, either. But in my eyes, you're a very handsome man."

Mitch didn't dare raise his eyes as he blushed.

After almost a minute of silent discomfort, it was Sheriff Ward and not an embarrassed Mitch who finally looked at Esther and asked, "I'd really appreciate it if you sent a message to St. Anne's and made a new appointment, Esther."

"I need a job, Mitch. Besides, if you're on the stage, we can talk more."

"But I'm gonna be up top ridin' shotgun."

"There are two overnight stops on the way; aren't there?"

"Yes, ma'am. But I'd feel a lot better if you weren't comin'."

"I'm sure we'll arrive safely."

Mitch then asked, "What about this house? Did Doc Walsh have any relatives?"

"His nephew is arriving in a couple of weeks. It's another reason I need to go to Lewiston."

Mitch could only nod as he was already well out of his element. What he had expected to be a short visit to convince Esther to at least postpone her trip to Lewiston had morphed into something much different.

He stood then said, "I gotta head back to the office. I reckon I'll see you tomorrow."

Esther stood and smiled as she replied, "You will. I'm glad that you stopped by and broke your habit of silence, Mitch."

Despite his discomfort, Mitch smiled back as he said, "It's kinda new to me, Esther."

He ventured one last look into her probing brown eyes before he turned and walked to the foyer.

After leaving the house and closing the door behind him, Mitch stepped onto the porch and blew out his breath before pulling his hat back on. Now he had even more concerns about tomorrow's stagecoach trip.

He trotted down the porch steps and soon reached Third Street. As he strode toward Main Street, he hoped that Ace's gang wasn't even going to try to stop the stage. It was possible that his number two man, Hal Kingman, might take the opportunity to move to the top spot. He decided that when he returned to the jail, he'd push Ace a bit to see if it was a possibility. But before he even reached the intersection, he suspected that Ace wasn't going to talk no matter what. He decided to use a bit of playacting to see if a palace coup was likely.

———

Esther returned to her bedroom to finish packing. She had been taken by surprise when Mitch had explained his reason for not talking to her. She'd been so accustomed to being an outcast, if not worse, that she hadn't even suspected the real reason why the highly respected sheriff had seemed so reticent to speak to her.

As she continued emptying her dresser drawer and placing her clothes into her second travel bag, Esther reviewed her decision to go to Lewiston. She had enough savings to last more than a year if she stayed, *but what would she do if she did?* She had already planned to continue her journey into Oregon if St. Anne's hired the other nurse, but now wasn't sure she would find any employment there either. She wasn't going to change her name to hide her heritage, either.

Before she finished packing, Esther decided to use the three-day stagecoach trip to get to know Mitch better now that he was talking to her. Maybe by then, he'd be less self-conscious, and he'd be able to open up even more.

She smiled as she closed the travel bag when she recalled how embarrassed Mitch had been after telling her that she was smart and pretty. He hadn't even spoken to her when she'd sutured his wounds, but now she understood why he hadn't. The man who'd faced those knife-wielding and gun-toting troublemakers and had been involved in more than a dozen shootouts since she'd known him was apparently more afraid of her than those armed and dangerous men.

————

When Mitch returned to the office, he hung his hat then took a seat next to the front desk.

Aaron asked, "Did anybody buy a ticket yet?"

"Yup. Miss Cohen will be in the coach."

Pete asked, "Are you gonna ask her to wait 'til the next one?"

"I already tried."

Aaron said, "I kinda figured she might be leavin' town after Doc Walsh died."

Mitch quickly changed the subject by saying, "I don't figure we're gonna bump into Ace's boys now anyway."

"Why not? Did you hear somethin'?" asked Deputy Jackson.

"Yup. I hear Hal Kingman took over already. Four men matchin' their descriptions held up the Outta The Way Saloon up in Millersburg yesterday. They musta figured they would get along fine without him."

Pete snickered then said, "I reckon that you're still gonna ride shotgun."

"Yup."

As he'd told his big lie, Mitch watched Ace's reaction. The outlaw wasn't even looking their way, but even as he lay on his cot, Mitch could see a smile form on his face. It was enough to convince Mitch that the gang leader was confident in his men's loyalty. While it still didn't mean that they'd be waiting for the stage somewhere along the long route, it made it more likely that he'd be seeing the four outlaws. He'd probably find them set up on Wednesday when the stagecoach neared the Camas Plains.

––––––––

Mitch left the jail to return to his house to have lunch and pack his saddlebags for tomorrow. Even though he would be riding shotgun, he'd leave the Overland's scattergun in its holder attached to the footwell. He'd keep his Winchester '66 in his hands. The repeater was called Yellowboy by most shooters, but Mitch named his Goldie because he thought the common moniker wasn't flattering to the outstanding rifle.

When he headed back to the office ninety minutes later, his stuffed saddlebags were hung over his shoulder, and he gripped Goldie in his left hand. He was still adding more details to the plan to safely get Ace Carr to Lewiston, but in his gut, he felt that it didn't matter how prepared he was, those four bastards would still surprise him.

As he opened the door, he was surprised to see both of his deputies standing at the cell and Aaron was talking to the gang leader. He stopped in mid-sentence when he heard the sheriff enter.

Aaron quickly said, "I was tellin' Ace here how we're gonna shackle him tomorrow."

Mitch set his saddlebags on the floor near the desk and said, "We don't need to tell him a damned thing."

Deputy Jackson looked at Deputy Carter as he replied, "Yes, sir."

After hanging his hat and laying Goldie on the desktop, Mitch sat in the big chair and said, "I'll take over until you boys show up. I want you both here at sunrise. Pete, you stop at Millie's and pick up a couple of breakfasts. Aaron, you come here, and we'll get Ace ready."

Aaron nodded as Pete replied, "Okay, Mitch," but neither deputy moved as they looked expectantly at their boss.

Mitch snapped, "I musta not been clear enough. Skedaddle!"

Deputies Jackson and Carter raced across the room, snatched their hats from the wall pegs and were out of the jail twelve seconds after being told to vamoose.

Mitch smiled as he leaned back in the chair and wondered what else Aaron had told Ace Carr. He knew it probably didn't matter now, but he wished that they'd just let him stew in ignorant silence.

Mitch opened the right-hand drawer and pulled out the wanted posters on the five gang members. He wanted to study each detail to get a better idea of what to expect when he met them again. Hopefully, that would be after Ace swung.

He started with the man who was laying on his cot in the cell behind him. He had concentrated so much on the face the last time he'd seen it that he hadn't noticed some interesting details. One that struck him as funny was the reason he probably used Ace as a moniker. When he was a born, his parents had named him Cecil. Mitch had never met another man with that name, but if he had, he imagined that he'd be a clerk or maybe a barber. Cecil Carr probably had spent his boyhood fighting bullies who taunted him about his name until he became the biggest bully of them all.

Another surprise was that the poster proclaimed that Ace had attended college. He was an inch shorter than Mitch at five feet and eleven inches but weighed twenty pounds less at 170. The outlaw life didn't allow for regular meals.

He flipped to Ace's number two man, Halford Kingman. Hal was average in most aspects. The only thing that marked him was that he wore his hair long and had an equally impressive mustache but no beard.

Jack McFarland would be the easiest to spot. He was the tallest of the bunch and stood two inches taller than Mitch but weighed ten pounds less. He wore a full beard, but other than his height, his most notable feature was that he was left-handed.

Frog Bouchard's Christian name wasn't listed on the poster, but he would be almost as easily identified as Jack McFarland. While he wasn't abnormally short at five feet and seven inches, Frog wore a two-gun rig and had a reputation as a deadly marksman with both hands. Mitch hoped he never was within pistol range to find out how good he was.

The last member of the missing four was the newest and also the most innocuous. Joe Hobart was average height and weight with brown hair and eyes. He carried a pistol but had killed two men with his pair of deadly daggers.

Mitch had been shot four times and stabbed or sliced on five occasions. While two of the bullets had come closer to ending his life, the sensation of having a razor-sharp blade slide through his skin gave him the willies. A stab was like a gunshot, but those slices were downright creepy.

After committing each of the outlaws' profiles to memory, he returned them to the desk drawer. While he hoped that he didn't see any of them on the journey to Lewiston, he couldn't avoid adding up the total of the posted rewards. He'd get five hundred dollars for capturing Ace, and the other four would add another sixteen hundred. That was a lot of money and would more than double his bank account. He may not be a bounty hunter, but if he was given rewards for keeping the folks safe, Mitch wasn't going to complain.

———

Six hours later, Mitch pulled the empty food tray from the slot at the bottom of the cell and left it on the table near the gun rack. Ace still hadn't spoken, not even to complain about the delay in removing the used chamber pot. It wasn't unintentional. Despite the foul odor filling the jail, Mitch wanted to see if the obnoxious smell could get Ace talking.

After blowing out the lamp, Mitch walked to his cell and after pulling off his boots, he stretched out on the cot. There was no point in reviewing his plans again, so he relived his startling visit with Esther.

It was almost three years ago, in June of '68 when he watched the stage from Boise arrive. It only ran once a week, and he made it a point to check for any newcomers. After it pulled up, the driver and shotgun rider dropped to the ground and headed into the depot. He didn't know if there were any passengers because their luggage would be in the boot. He approached the stage and as the door opened, he was instantly smitten. But he was also surprised when the dark-haired young woman with the dark brown eyes looked back at him and began to step down. She was the only passenger, yet the driver hadn't opened the door and offered his hand to aid her exit. They normally did that for all unaccompanied woman passengers, but made a point of helping handsome young women and she was well beyond just handsome.

He had hurried to the side of the stagecoach and did the driver's job by offering his hand and helping her to the ground. He'd apologized for the stagecoach driver and Esther had smiled and thanked him. He forgot about the driver and shotgun rider as he carried her travel bags to the boarding house. He only introduced himself and let her do all the talking as they walked along the boardwalk. He was pleased to learn that she was going to be Doc Walsh's new nurse and was impressed with her bearing and perfect use of the English language.

As he returned to the jail, Mitch was already in awe of Esther Cohen and knew that he wasn't in her league. He had expected that she'd be married before autumn arrived.

That hadn't happened and he couldn't understand it. As the months passed, he thought that maybe it was because she was determined to stay unmarried so she could continue her nursing career. He didn't mind and although he tried to talk to her over the next almost-three years, every time he met her, he just passed a few irrelevant comments while she would speak eloquently about many different subjects.

Even when she was treating his wounds, he said almost nothing while she told him what she was doing with great detail. She also spoke on other topics which interested her and demonstrated her sharp mind even more. Even though he promised himself to say more each time they talked, whenever he heard Esther clearly enunciate each word and use some that he didn't understand, he was reminded of his ignorance and unworthiness.

But he had become accustomed to having her in Salmon City and all he could do was act as if she was just another citizen. Then Doc Walsh died, and he assumed that she would work with Doctor Brandt. Now Esther might be leaving to take a nursing position in Lewiston. She said that they could talk more during the two overnight stops, but Mitch wasn't sure that he'd be able to reach anything approaching the level of confidence he had when dealing with troublemakers or just normal citizens.

As he closed his eyes to get some sleep, he hoped that Esther wouldn't distract him from doing his job while riding shotgun on tomorrow's stage.

CHAPTER 4

Sheriff Ward hadn't slept well at all and by the time the sun rose, he had already washed, shaved and dressed. While Ace remained asleep in his cell, he donned gunbelt and his pistol-laden jacket, then sat behind the desk to wait for his deputies. The shackles that would keep the gang leader from escaping were lying on the desktop. The leg irons were fairly simple in design with just a pin locking each steel band. The cuffs for the wrists were similar in design and had a chain linked to another wrist cuff for guard. While they weren't exactly secure, it would keep the prisoner from making any sudden moves.

When they stopped in Millersburg, he'd leave Ace in Marshal Ken Thompson's jail. If the marshal or his old deputy volunteered, they could keep an eye on him overnight. If not, Mitch would have Aaron stay in the small jail.

If they made it to the Camas Prairie way station without encountering Ace's gang, then he'd bind his prisoner with rope and use the shackles to attach him to something heavy. He hadn't been to the way station in a while, but it was a well-built structure and if he stored Ace in one of the inside rooms, the gang would have to come through the front door to get him out. But he thought that the way station was probably the most likely place for the gang to spring their plan.

As he sat watching the front door, Mitch thought that if he was Hal Kingman, he'd wait until after midnight and send Joe Hobart in to silence any guards with his knives before sneaking into the way station. It would be almost a new moon that night, so it wouldn't be hard to get close enough to slice the guard's throat. Mitch shivered at the thought as he rubbed his neck. But if they didn't run into Ace's boys before reaching the way station, he still planned to be the one guarding the front door.

His hand was still rubbing his precious throat when the door opened, and Pete entered balancing a heavy tray.

Mitch bounced to his feet, trotted to his deputy and relieved him of his welcomed burden.

"Aaron is on his way, boss. I saw him just before I opened the door."

"Okay."

He set the tray on the desk and after moving his breakfast to the desk, he poured both cups full of coffee, then slid the tray through the cell's slot.

Before Mitch took a single bite, Aaron entered the jail and asked, "Do you want me to start gettin' Ace ready, Mitch?"

"Not yet."

As his two deputies talked, Mitch attacked his breakfast. The stage wouldn't leave without him and his prisoner, but he didn't want them to delay their scheduled departure. He was also hopefully anxious to see if Esther had changed her mind but doubted if she suddenly decided to miss the appointment. He hadn't given her any reason to stay and wasn't sure if she would even if he had asked.

After wolfing down his breakfast, Mitch stood then carried the leg irons and cuffs to Ace's cell. Aaron unlocked the door and Mitch had him stand guard with his Colt drawn and pointed at the gang leader. He suspected that Ace wasn't about to do anything rash as he seemed convinced that his boys wouldn't let the sheriff and his young deputy get him to Lewiston.

Twenty minutes later, Aaron and Pete escorted the heavily chained prisoner out of the jail and headed to the Overland depot. Mitch was walking a few feet behind them with his heavy saddlebags over his right shoulder, a coil of rope over his left and carrying Goldie. His two older Smith & Wessons were in his jacket pockets and the Model 3 was in his holster. In addition to the eight .32s on the larger model's holster, he had another box of the cartridges in his saddlebags along with two boxes of the .44 Henry rimfires Goldie and one of the Smith & Wesson centerfires for his Model 3. In addition to his guns, he carried one large knife on the left side of his gunbelt. Despite all of his firepower, Mitch still felt uneasy not knowing where the four gang members were or if they knew their boss would soon be on his way to Lewiston.

74

Mitch could see the stage already in place in front of the depot, but Al Crenshaw wasn't in the driver's seat yet. As they neared the coach, he looked for Esther and soon spotted her waiting on the boardwalk. She must have seen them approaching because she was already looking back at him and smiling. He smiled back as he followed Ace across the street but wasn't very pleased when he knew she hadn't changed her mind.

He had Pete and Aaron load their prisoner into the coach on the street side and after Aaron climbed in behind Ace, he checked that his young deputy was positioned correctly.

He then turned to Deputy Carter and said, "Okay, Pete. We'll see you in a few days."

Pete nodded, replied, "Okay, boss," then walked away.

Mitch then stepped around the back of the coach and onto the boardwalk. He glanced inside and saw Al Crenshaw talking to Hank Jones before he approached Esther.

"Good morning, Mitch. Are you still going to be riding up top?"

"Yes, ma'am. My deputy is cuffed to the prisoner, so you should be safe. But you should sit as far away as you can."

"That was my intention."

75

Mitch was thinking of offering her the use of his Model 1 and almost reached into his jacket's left pocket before he figured she might shoot herself accidentally.

She smiled and said, "Then I reckon you oughta help me enter the coach, Sheriff."

For just a moment, Mitch thought that she might be making fun of him, but her smile seemed so warm that he immediately dismissed the notion.

He returned her smile and opened the door before offering his hand. She took a firm grasp and climbed inside.

He watched until she slid to the far end of the seat then said, "Aaron, if I see the other four Carr boys, I'll pound four times on the side of the coach. Okay?"

Aaron had to lean past Ace before he replied, "Okay, boss."

Mitch clambered up the side of the stagecoach and sat on the far right side of the driver's seat. He removed his saddlebags and the coil of rope and set them on the roof behind him. As Al Crenshaw left the depot, he glanced at the shotgun's stock as it protruded from the leather holder nearby. He knew that it contained two shells loaded with buckshot, but he would only use it if he wasn't able to stop those four outlaws with Goldie. He knew that each of them had his own Winchester, but Mitch would be firing from a much more stable shooting platform. If he spotted them more than a hundred yards out, they'd never get close to the coach.

76

Al soon climbed up the other side and after taking a seat, he asked, "You all set, Mitch?"

"Yup."

Al grinned then released the handbrake and snapped the reins. The four-horse team lurched forward, and the coach headed west down Main Street. Just four minutes later, they left Salmon City behind.

As the stage rocked along the road, Mitch began scanning the landscape ahead just to get into the habit. He'd never ridden shotgun before but appreciated the added visibility provided by the higher viewpoint. The downside was that he had no control over the route or the timing. Maybe he should have taken Ace back to Lewiston on horseback despite the length of the journey. But if he had, he probably never would have known that Esther was leaving town.

He had Goldie in his hands as the coach raced along the dry road leaving a cloud of dust in its wake. Its speed would change as the stage ascended and descended passes and had to slow as it forded streams and passed around sharp curves. It was the curves that provided the biggest danger. By the time they rounded the sharp bends, he might find four shooters just fifty yards away. He still didn't think they'd try to ambush the stage, at least not as they would if they were just carrying out a robbery. Hal Kingman wouldn't take the risk of shooting Ace. Mitch believed that their best option would be a night raid at the Camas Prairie way station.

The stage had been on the road for more than two hours when Mitch pulled the canteen from its hook on the side of the footwell and unscrewed the cap. He handed it to Al and waited until he'd taken a few long swallows and gave it back before satisfying his thirst. He replaced the cap and hung it on its hook. This one was for the driver and shotgun rider. There were two more full canteens in the cabin for the passengers.

He and Al hadn't passed a word since the stage started rolling, but neither man seemed to mind. Mitch was still wondering why Esther had used words like 'reckon' and 'oughta' before he assisted her into the coach. He'd never heard her use them before, and he had listened to her much more than she'd heard him speak. When they stopped in Millersburg, maybe he'd ask her. They should reach the town by mid-afternoon. Passengers stayed at the Millersburg Hotel and their rooms' cost was included in their ticket price. Where he stayed depended on whether Marshal Thompson would be able to guard Ace for the night.

He continued to watch for a possible ambush as the stage bounced along the rough roadway. It would be better when they began started their descent to the Camas Plains shortly after noon tomorrow. This was the shortest leg of the journey, the fifty miles from Salmon City to Millersburg. But it took almost as much time as the final leg, the flatter seventy miles from the Camas Plains way station to Lewiston. Tomorrow the stage would take about the same time to travel the sixty miles to the way station. The first half would be slower because of the difficult terrain, but then they'd reach the Camas Plains and pick up the pace. He just hoped that they'd be able to board the coach for that last day.

———

Inside the cabin, Esther was sleeping with her head supported by the corner of the coach. Aaron was fighting to stay awake and even though Ace's eyes were closed, Aaron didn't think he was sleeping.

He hadn't spoken to Esther since she entered the stagecoach but noticed that she had extracted a smile from his boss. More than that, Mitch had actually spoken more than a few syllables to her. He'd watched the sheriff help her into the coach and swore that his boss seemed pleased to be holding her hand.

She was certainly a handsome woman, but she was at least five years older than he was and she wasn't Annabelle, either. But even if she was his age and he wasn't smitten with Annabelle, there was that other, unspoken reason why he could never consider visiting Esther Cohen. He was just surprised that Mitch didn't seem bothered by it. Maybe he didn't know, which would be hard to believe. But even if he didn't, Aaron wasn't about to tell him. It wasn't his business.

Ace wasn't sleeping but wasn't worrying about facing a jury in Lewiston as he sat with his eyes closed. He didn't know how Hal would keep that from happening but trusted his number two man to get it done. But whatever plan Hal devised, Ace

79

was confident that the sheriff would never even get him past the Camas Plains way station. By then, Sheriff Ward and his deputy would be dead.

He didn't care what happened to the Jew woman who was sleeping a few feet away, either. Just like Aaron, he had noticed the sheriff's interest in her and thought it was funny. When he'd told his deputies that Esther Cohen would be on the stage, he imagined that she was a white-haired old gnome. But even though he admitted that she was very attractive, he still didn't see her as a woman. If his boys wanted her after freeing him, he'd let them enjoy her. Once they were done, he'd tell them of her Jewish heritage. Ace still had his eyes closed as he smiled.

———

Esther woke up just after noon and opened her large handbag. She removed a paper sack and looked at Aaron.

"Would you like a beef sandwich. Deputy?"

Aaron was hungry, but just shook his head.

Esther wasn't about to offer one to the outlaw, even if he was awake. She slid one of her sandwiches from the bag and took a bite as she looked out the window. She wished that Mitch was linked to the prisoner and the deputy was riding shotgun. While she understood his reasoning for taking the shotgun rider's place, she knew that if he'd been sitting on the leather seat across from her, he would have gratefully accepted the sandwich. She might even get him to finally start talking to her. Even if it was just a few more words now and then, it would make the trip much more pleasant.

After finishing her sandwich, she took down one of the canteens, removed the cap and washed down her lunch. She almost offered the open canteen to the deputy just to watch his reaction but just screwed the cap back in place before hanging it back on its hook. She doubted if he'd even use the same canteen when he did need to quench his thirst. But there was no point in reminding herself of her lifelong situation.

She hadn't even noticed the problem when she was a girl. She never went to school for a single day because her parents had been concerned about how she would be treated by the other students and maybe the teachers. Everything she learned was from her parents, including her well-honed medical skills. It was only after her mother died and her father passed away two years later that she began to realize why they had wanted to keep her so isolated. If it hadn't been for her exceptional medial training, she probably would have had to engage in a much less reputable line of work to survive. But even though she knew more than most of the doctors she assisted, she still wasn't accepted.

It wasn't until she was hired by Doctor Walsh that she finally found someone who appreciated her as a person as well as a talented nurse. Then she met Mitch Ward and despite his shyness, he hadn't treated her any differently than anyone else. She hated to admit that she was almost pleased when he'd been wounded.

The first time, when he'd been stabbed, she was surprised when he'd come to Doctor Walsh's office rather than Doctor Brandt's. By then, Doctor Walsh was already in poor health, and she was seeing most of his diminishing number of patients. When the doctor told Mitch that his nurse would be suturing his wound, she'd expected him to turn around and leave. But he'd smiled before laying down on the examination table. He barely spoken while she had closed the long cut. Even when she asked a question, his answer would be a simple "Yes, ma'am," or "No, ma'am."

Now he was just a few feet above her head and hidden by an inch of pine while she sat across from a sullen deputy and a sleeping outlaw. She slid the paper sack and its untouched sandwich back into her purse. She wondered what Mitch was having for lunch, but knew the stage wasn't going to stop until it reached Millersburg. If there had been a narrow window to the driver's seat, she would offer him the sandwich.

―――――

She shouldn't have worried. Just after she'd returned the paper bag to her purse, Mitch pulled his saddlebags from the roof and opened the left side. He took out his own paper sack and handed Al a ham sandwich before taking out the second one. He didn't crumple the paper bag but folded it and returned it to the saddlebag for reuse.

He and Al made short work of the sandwiches before Mitch grabbed the canteen. After they drank it dry, he returned it to its hook as the coach entered a right-hand curve.

Mitch had Goldie in his hands by the time the coach straightened out again but didn't find any outlaws waiting on the other side. He would have been shocked if he had. About twenty minutes ago, they had to slow and pull far to the right side of the road when they passed a small train of three freight wagons headed for Salmon City. He had waved at the freighters before they returned to the center of the road. Seeing the heavy wagons meant that the road ahead was probably clear all the way to Millersburg.

Now that he was less concerned about a possible ambush, he turned to driver and asked, "Al, did anyone in Millersburg buy a ticket to Lewiston before you left there?"

Al was startled when Mitch asked, so he didn't answer right away. When he did, he shook his head and replied, "Not yet, but I reckon somebody coulda bought one yesterday or this mornin'."

Mitch nodded as he ended the brief conversation. Until he discovered that Esther was going to be in the stagecoach with Ace, he had hoped that no one would board the stage in Millersburg. Now he hoped that a couple of burly, well-armed men would be waiting to make the trip. He'd find out soon enough. Millersburg should come into view within an hour. They'd already crossed the bridge over Wood's Creek, so after they topped the next mountain pass, the town should appear on the horizon. It would still be a good hour away, but it would be a welcome sight for many reasons.

————

Mitch wasn't far off in his estimate as Millersburg appeared just an hour and fifteen minutes later. Al had to slow the stage as it began its long descent. Mitch hadn't heard any noise from the cabin and hoped that Aaron hadn't fallen asleep. He understood that the combination of rhythmic motion and sounds combined with the warm temperature would make it difficult to stay alert, but he still expected his deputy to avoid the temptation to nap.

He hadn't heard anyone talking either, which surprised him. He expected that even though Aaron was smitten with Annabelle Gruber, it would have been difficult to ignore such an attractive young woman sitting nearby. Even if Aaron was as awestruck with Esther had he had been, he thought that she would try to engage his deputy in spirited conversation.

It hadn't taken a stab wound for Mitch to understand that Esther was a very well-educated woman with definite opinions which she was more than happy to express. He added the unexpected silence to the other questions he would ask her when they arrived in Millersburg. Of course, that depended on whether he'd be able to spend time with her or if he would need to join Ace in the marshal's small jail.

In the cabin, Aaron was alert, but only because he'd just awakened from a short nap. He was horrified when he realized he'd drifted off and quickly slapped his Colt's grip to make sure it was still there. He was relieved when his palm felt the hard wooden grips before he pulled his left wrist to his chest and felt the chain yank it back.

Ace looked at the deputy and didn't even smile before he glanced at Esther and closed his eyes.

After eating her sandwich lunch, Esther hadn't fallen asleep again. She spent most of the time watching the scenery pass by. She could see the Salmon River in the distance but didn't know how much farther it was to Millersburg. She'd been told by the depot manager that the stage arrived in the town around three o'clock, but she didn't have a watch. When she wasn't watching the river flow past, she looked at the sleeping deputy and the resting outlaw. She wondered why a man who was facing almost certain death in just a few days could appear so calm. She didn't believe that the killer had made his peace with God. She agreed with Mitch that he probably expected that his fate wasn't in the hands of a jury but in his gang's loyalty.

When Aaron's eyes reopened, he looked out the window and was just as uncertain as Esther about their location. He just stared at the passing mountains as the stage continued its long descent into Millersburg.

———

When they were about a mile away from the town, Mitch thought about banging the side of the stage a few times to see if Aaron was awake. But he decided against it because if he had to warn his deputy when he spotted the gang, he didn't want Aaron to believe it was just another joke.

He did lean over the side and shout, "Millersburg in five minutes!"

Inside the cabin, only Esther reacted to Mitch's loud announcement. She moved her handbag onto her lap and ran her fingers through her long black hair. She was one of the few women who not only wore her hair long but didn't wear a hat unless it was cold or raining. It wasn't a mark of rebellion, but just a way of honoring her mother who had worn her hair long and avoided wearing any form of head covering.

As the stage slowed before entering Millersburg, Mitch asked, "Al, can you pull up near the jail so I can unload Ace?"

Al nodded as he replied, "Sure thing, Mitch."

When Al pulled the coach to a stop, Mitch left Goldie, the rope and saddlebags on the roof before he quickly climbed down. He opened the door and smiled at Esther before looking at Aaron.

"Aaron, let's get Ace into a cell before the stage goes to the depot."

"Okay, boss."

Ace stood and had to awkwardly follow the attached deputy as they vacated the cabin. Mitch helped Ace down and after Aaron stepped to the ground, Mitch looked up and said, "We'll be back in a few minutes, Al."

Al waved before Mitch and Aaron escorted Ace onto the boardwalk and entered Marshal Kent Thompson's jail.

The marshal was rising from his chair as they marched Ace across the floor.

He glanced at the prisoner before asking, "Are you needin' my jail for the night, Mitch?"

"Yup. This is Ace Carr. I'm takin' him to Lewiston but don't know where the other four members of his gang are. Can you watch him for the night, or do you want me to take care of it?"

"I'll have Tom stick around. He'll be okay."

Mitch nodded but wasn't sure if old Deputy Marshal Tom Wilkerson was up to it. He was a good man but was over fifty years old and tended to nap even during the day. If Mitch didn't expect the gang to do anything until tomorrow night, then he might have decided to stay in the jail himself. But he was almost certain that even if the gang knew he was in Millersburg that they wouldn't make their move tonight.

After removing Ace's shackles, then locking him in the cell, Mitch and Aaron left the jail. Once on the boardwalk, Aaron said, "I'm gonna get my travel bag and head to the hotel, boss."

"If I don't see you later, I'll meet you here at sunrise tomorrow."

"Yes, sir."

They walked to the stage and as Mitch climbed to the driver's seat, Aaron walked in back and opened the boot while Al watched. Mitch was going to tell him that his deputy was getting his travel bag, but it wasn't necessary as Aaron pulled it free and waved as he walked away from the coach.

Al glanced at him, then shrugged and snapped the reins. The coach jerked and then rolled the two blocks to the Overland depot where it stopped for the night. Mitch threw his saddlebags over his shoulder but left the rope on the roof before he grabbed Goldie and clambered down the side.

He was surprised that Esther hadn't already left the cabin as he opened the door.

Esther smiled as she said, "I've been waiting for you to assist my perilous exit, Sheriff Ward."

Mitch took her hand as he replied, "I'm kinda surprised that you didn't try it on your own, Miss Cohen."

She was laughing as she stepped down then walked to the back of the coach to retrieve her bags.

88

After Al set them on the ground, Mitch picked both of the large travel bags in his free hand, which seemed to have surprised Esther. But she didn't say anything before they stepped onto the boardwalk and headed for the nearby hotel.

They only walked a few feet before she asked, "Are you going to have to watch your prisoner tonight, Mitch?"

"No, ma'am. The marshal's deputy will do that. I'm plannin' on gettin' a good night's sleep."

"Mitch, may I ask you something?"

"If you reckon that I can answer it, then go ahead."

She briefly smiled before she asked, "When I watched the outlaw, he seemed awfully relaxed for a man who was facing the noose. Do you believe he's so calm because he knows that his gang will try to free him?"

Mitch was impressed that she had reached that conclusion, but not at all surprised. But he would have been shocked if his deputy had noticed.

"That's what I think. I expect they'll take their shot either tomorrow around noon before we enter the Camas Plains or late tomorrow night when everybody's asleep in the way station. That's why I didn't want you to come along."

"I still have to meet with the staff at St. Anne's, Mitch. Can I do anything to help?"

For the second time, Mitch considered offering her the .22 caliber Smith & Wesson in his left-hand jacket pocket. This time, he decided to ask her.

"Have you ever shot a pistol, Esther?"

"No. Are you planning to give me one?"

"Maybe. I'm still kinda on the fence about it. I have a small pistol in my jacket pocket you can use. It's easy to fire, but it's not a powerful gun. It can stop somebody from hurtin' you, but it won't put 'em down."

"I appreciate your offer, Mitch. But I don't think I'd be able to appear very threatening to anyone who might want to harm me."

Mitch smiled as they neared the hotel and replied, "I guess I'm the only feller who's afraid of you."

She stopped and turned towards him then waited when he had to back up a step.

"Why are you afraid of me, Mitch?"

"I guess afraid ain't the right word. It's just that I'm kinda worried about feelin' like a fool when I talk to you."

"That's not possible. I would never see you that way."

Mitch was growing more uncomfortable, so rather than continue the conversation, he said, "Let's get our rooms."

Esther had been surprised that he'd talked as much as he had and believed that soon, she could convince him to say even more.

They entered the small hotel and after registering, the clerk gave them two adjacent rooms. Mitch assumed that the man behind the desk expected them to share one of the two beds but didn't care what he thought. He carried Esther's bags down the hall and waited for her to open the door. After she entered, he followed inside and set her bags on the floor.

As he started to leave, Esther asked, "Will you escort me to dinner, Mitch? I've never been to Millersburg before."

Mitch turned and smiled as he replied, "I was gonna ask you, but I've got to drop Goldie and my saddlebags in my room."

"Goldie?"

"My Winchester. Most men call it Yellowboy 'cause of the brass, but I call mine Goldie."

She laughed lightly before saying, "I can understand why you would prefer that name. Will you knock on my door when you're ready?"

"It won't take me long. I guess it's around four o'clock, so do you want me to come by in an hour or so? I reckon you must be pretty hungry."

"I'm famished. But if it's alright with you, can we sit out in the lobby and talk for a while?"

Mitch still had his two questions about the silence in the cabin and her use of 'reckon' and 'oughta', so he nodded and replied, "That's fine. I'll be back shortly."

As he turned and left her room, Esther quickly began unpacking one of her bags. She had placed her trip necessities in one bag and what she might need after she arrived in Lewiston in the other.

Mitch entered his room next door and set his saddlebags on the dresser then leaned Goldie against the outer wall. He still felt a bit uncomfortable around Esther, but it wasn't nearly as bad as it had been when he'd talked to her yesterday. While she said that he didn't appear foolish when he spoke, he still wanted to avoid torturing the language as much as he usually did.

He took off his hat, then slowly walked out of his room and closed the door. He took just two steps down the hallway when he noticed that Esther's door was already open and two steps after that, he found her standing just behind the doorway.

"I thought you would need more time to unpack," he said carefully.

She stepped into the hallway, and as she closed her door, she replied, "I separated my things to make it faster."

92

"That was smart."

She smiled before she took his arm which almost made Mitch hop an inch off the floor. But after regaining his senses, they walked down the hallway and entered the small lobby. There were only two chairs and a couch, and the chairs were occupied by an elderly couple. The old man was reading a newspaper and his wife was knitting. Mitch wished that they had decided to sit together or just stayed in their room as he and Esther walked to the unoccupied couch.

When she took her seat, he was grateful that she hadn't sat in the center of the couch. If she had, he doubted if he'd even be able to speak a single word. After he sat down, he glanced at the desk clerk who was either not interested or feigning disinterest.

He was hoping that Esther would start the conversation, but she just looked at him with her soft brown eyes which unsettled him. When he met her in her room's doorway, he had reviewed each word before speaking. It was much slower and now he worried about sounding like a first-year student trying to read McGuffey's Reader aloud in front of the class. He'd never even had a year of schooling but knew how hard it would be.

Shortly after he'd taken the job, he had been a guest at the Salmon City school and the teacher had told one of the young boys had to read *The Song of Hiawatha* to show the sheriff how much he learned. The boy read it in a slow monotone and

Mitch felt bad for him. He did what he could to help him when he interrupted his torture by saying how one line reminded him of a shootout that he had with an outlaw pretending to be an Indian. It was all fiction, of course, but the class and even their teacher were mesmerized. It was the longest he'd ever talked but because he was making it up as he went, he hadn't noticed. Now he hoped that he didn't appear as anguished as that boy as he recited Longfellow's epic poem.

He carefully asked, "Esther, I didn't hear anyone talking in the stagecoach for the entire trip. That was…unusual because I know you enjoy conversation. Why was it quiet?"

Mitch thought he'd done reasonably well except for his pause before 'unusual', but apparently Esther noticed because she smiled a bit more as she watched him ask his question.

"I only enjoy talking when I have someone who wants to have a conversation, Mitch. I wasn't about to start one with your prisoner and your deputy was apparently not interested in anything I had to say."

"But I didn't talk much. Even when you were…um…sewing my wounds."

This time, Mitch knew he had struggled and almost blushed.

Esther noticed his discomfort but didn't mention it before she replied, "No, you barely spoke a word as I fixed you up. The first time you needed a wound sutured, I began to talk to keep your mind off of what I was doing. All you said while I closed your wound was 'yes, ma'am', or 'no, ma'am,' or an occasional, 'maybe'. Yet you seemed interested in what I said. That wasn't an act; was it?"

He replied, "No, it wasn't. I can recall what you talked about during each of those visits almost word-for-word," then when he finished his brief answer, he let out his breath.

Esther almost patted him on the shoulder and told him not to worry about what he was saying, but she correctly assumed that he wouldn't hear a word she spoke if he felt her fingers touch him.

"Do you know that I almost hoped that you'd be shot again just so I could talk to you again? I was ashamed of myself for even having the thought, but I was just so lonely."

Mitch snapped, "That ain't right, Esther," and grimaced at his verbal faux pas.

Esther quickly said, "Until I met Doctor Walsh, I didn't realize just how much I missed normal conversation. But he was still mourning the recent loss of his wife, so when we talked, it was either about patients or his wife. Then you arrived with your knife wound and I could talk about things that interested me."

"Didn't other men, um, want to talk to you before they knew you were Jewish?"

As soon as he'd finished asking the question, Mitch was mortified with how it must have sounded and was about to beg her forgiveness when she began to answer without a hint of anger.

"Yes, they would talk to me, usually before they knew my name. But even then, all they talked about was themselves. I'm sure that many of them would be willing to overlook my heritage if I would let them visit me in my room at the hospital. Some were even married doctors, by the way. It didn't take me long to realize that none of them wanted to hear what I had to say. I suppose I could have ignored their intentions, but I wasn't about to bring shame to my parents. But you were different. I'll admit that I assumed you were just being polite, but even that was a wonderful change."

Mitch carefully replied, "I wasn't being polite, Esther. After you repaired my wounds, I felt like a coward for not even telling you how good you were at nursing. All I did was say 'thank you, ma'am,' before I left."

"I understood that when you talked to me yesterday, and it made me very happy."

He looked at her and almost said something that he was sure would offend her.

Instead, he asked, "Why did you talk like me this morning? You said 'reckon' and 'oughta', and I never heard you use those words before. For just a second, I thought you might be making fun of how I talked, but I knew you wouldn't do that."

She smiled as she replied, "I was just trying to let you understand that you don't have to worry about how you spoke. When you try to be more careful, as you are right now, you seem very uncomfortable. I don't want you to be someone other than yourself, Mitch."

Mitch smiled as he looked down at his faded blue hat he held tightly in his hands and said, "I am kinda watchin' what I say and it's makin' me say things that don't come out right. I just didn't wanna sound so…I was gonna say stupid, but you'd tell me I'm wrong. So, I'll just say ignorant. I didn't even go to school, and you sound like you went to college."

Esther laughed then said, "Hardly. I never set foot in a classroom. I was taught at home by my parents."

He quickly looked up at her as he said, "Really? You musta had smart folks."

"I did. But if you never went to school, how did you learn to read and write? I assume you couldn't function as a sheriff if you couldn't."

"I could always read and write. I don't know how, but I just did. I had to find some old books to figure out how to cypher, but it all made sense, too."

"That's amazing, Mitch. You're probably a lot smarter than I am."

Mitch blushed as he shook his head and said, "I don't reckon that's so, Esther. But I appreciate you lettin' me know that it's okay to not worry about how I talk."

She changed the subject entirely when she asked, "Where's your deputy? Didn't he get a room at this hotel? It's the only one in Millersburg; isn't it?"

Mitch had totally forgotten about Aaron after watching him leave with his travel bag. He hadn't seen his deputy since and even if he'd walked the two blocks, he should have reached the hotel while he and Esther were getting their rooms.

"I reckon he mighta headed over to the saloon to have a beer before comin' to the hotel. I hope he doesn't overdo it. I need him to be alert tomorrow."

"I'm sure he'll be fine. Besides, we'll have you riding shotgun."

Mitch grinned as he said, "Maybe I should call it ridin' Winchester. I don't plan to be pullin' that scattergun."

"Are you a good shot with Goldie?"

Mitch was pleased that she remembered what he called his repeater and replied, "Yes, ma'am. I'm not braggin' or anything, but I know I'm a lot better than most shooters. I can put seven out of ten shots into an eight-inch target at a hundred yards. And the ones that are off don't miss by more than an inch or so."

"What about your pistol?"

Mitch smoothly pulled his Model 3 from its holster and said, "A pistol ain't as accurate as a rifle 'cause of the shorter barrel. My Smith & Wesson is different than the Colts and Remingtons that most men carry 'cause it uses a cartridge. The others all need to be loaded with balls and caps, so it takes a lot longer to reload. I heard that Colt and Remington are both gonna come out with their own cartridge pistols soon, and some boys already have their ball and cap revolvers modified to use cartridges, but I like my Smith & Wessons. Let me show you how it reloads."

Esther was grinning as Mitch cracked open his pistol and explained how if he did it quickly, the cartridges would be ejected all over the floor. As he rambled on about his gun, she was astonished by his exuberance as much as by the length of his description. On Monday, she'd been amazed to hear him talk as much as he had, but now he was positively garrulous. She knew that it was because he was in his element, but more importantly, it meant that he was no longer afraid of her.

After holstering his pistol, he looked at Esther's smiling face and, even a few minutes ago, he would have blushed when he saw her studying him.

Now he simply returned her smile and said, "I'm not gonna bore you by showin' you my other two Smith & Wessons."

She didn't see another pistol at his waist, so she asked, "Did you leave them in your room?"

"No, ma'am. They're older and much smaller models that look really different. I keep 'em in my jacket pockets."

"Oh, that's right. You offered one to me earlier; didn't you?"

"Yes, ma'am. If you change your mind, you can still borrow it."

"No, that's alright. You can use it much better than I could anyway."

"I hope I never have to use the .22 for more'n shootin' varmints."

Esther smiled as she said, "I reckon not."

Mitch laughed then asked, "Do you want to head over to the diner, Esther?"

"I know it's early, but I believe that you'll want to check on your prisoner before turning in."

Mitch stood and replied, "Yes, ma'am."

He surprised himself when he offered Esther his arm as she rose from the couch. She smiled as she took his arm before they strolled across the lobby to the doorway.

————

Mitch had guessed correctly that Aaron had wandered to the saloon to have a beer or two. He also took advantage of their minimal dining services to have a late lunch and early supper. He was still sore after having stayed attached to Ace for that long ride. He hoped that there would be another passenger for tomorrow's leg to help pass the time.

As he sipped his second beer, Aaron wondered what his boss was doing with Miss Cohen. He'd never seen Mitch spend any time with a woman before even though many of the ladies in town showed an interest. Even Annabelle had mentioned that she had tried to attract his attention. Now, of all the women in town, Sheriff Ward seemed to be attracted to the Jewish nurse. It was baffling.

He finished his beer then grabbed his hat and travel bag before heading for the door. Once on the boardwalk, he stopped, pulled his hat on and turned right to get his hotel room.

He had just entered the lobby and almost walked into the elderly woman's chair when he spotted a very attractive young woman sitting on the couch reading. She looked up from her book and her bright blue eyes weakened his knees as she smiled.

Aaron slowly walked to the reception desk and asked for a room.

It didn't take great detective work for the clerk to identify him as the sheriff's deputy. The LEMHI COUNTY DEPUTY SHERIFF badge on his vest was a good clue. He grabbed a key and waited for the young lawman to sign the register.

Aaron almost forgot why he was standing at the counter before he sheepishly accepted the key and added his name to the register. After he signed, he looked at the name above Mitch's and read Grace Dubois. He had no doubt that it belonged to the beautiful apparition sitting just behind him. He was even more pleased when he hadn't seen an entry for a Mister Dubois. If the other two chairs hadn't been occupied, he might have used one to start a pleasant conversation. But he didn't want to appear to be so impolite as to join her on the couch. So, he picked up his travel bag and headed for his room. Maybe he'd meet her again later. There weren't many guests in the hotel and his boss seemed occupied. Not once did he think of Annabelle.

———

As they approached the diner, Esther read the eatery's name and was grinning as she asked, "Is there some reason it's called The Widows' Kitchen?"

"Yes, ma'am."

She was going to ask Mitch to expand his reply when he opened the door and let her enter. After following her into the diner, she walked to the closest table and sat down before Mitch joined her. They were the only customers.

He had barely taken off his hat when a middle-aged waitress arrived wearing a soiled pinkish apron and a grin.

Mitch smiled and said, "Howdy, Mary."

"Why, if it isn't our county's protector himself. How long as it been since you stopped by, Mitch?"

"I figure it's been four months and twenty-one days, Mary. I was kinda stuck here when that blizzard hit."

"That's right! You had just captured the Roberts brothers a few miles north of town. Well, you captured one and buried the other one."

As she listened, Esther was very impressed. Not with his capture of the Roberts brothers, but by Mitch's almost instant computation of the elapsed time since his last visit.

Mary then said, "This is the first time you shared a table with anyone, especially a handsome young lady, Mitch."

He looked at Esther as he said, "Mary, I'd like you to meet Esther Cohen."

Esther smiled and said, "It's nice to meet you."

"It's nice to meet you too, Esther. Call me Mary. You're a very lucky woman, but I reckon you already know that."

As Mitch blushed, Mary patted him on the shoulder, winked at Esther, then turned and headed for the kitchen.

Esther smiled at his reaction and said, "I should have corrected her."

"It's okay. Mary's a good woman but says what's on her mind even if it's wrong."

"They didn't ask for our order."

"Nope. They always bring me the special, so I reckon that's what they'll be settin' on our table shortly."

She nodded then asked, "Can you tell me why the diner is named The Widows' Kitchen?"

"Mary's last name is Ludden, and she used to live here with her husband Wallace. He was a butcher. Anyway, before I even left Oregon City, he died from pneumonia. After sellin' his butcher shop, Mary had their house made into a diner. Her sister Alice, who is a widow too, came down from Lewiston to help. Between the two of 'em, they're doin' pretty good."

Esther nodded then said, "They couldn't have given it a better name. I noticed that when you answered Mary's question about how long it's been since your last visit, you quickly gave her the exact number of days. That was amazing. How do you do that?"

Mitch shrugged as he replied, "Beats me. It just kinda pops into my head. Once I read about cypherin', it just happens."

She was about to test him with a more complex math problem when Mary exited the kitchen carrying a tray. She was followed by another woman who was younger, but obviously her sister. Alice had another tray in her hands.

After setting the trays down on the neighboring table, the sisters began moving everything from the trays to their table.

When the trays were empty, Alice smiled at Mitch and said, "Mary told me that you weren't alone, Mitch, and I had to see it for myself."

She then turned her laughing eyes to Esther and said, "After seeing you, I can understand why he finally decided not to remain a recluse."

Esther glanced at Mitch who wasn't blushing this time and said, "I'm taking the stage to Lewiston and Mitch is riding shotgun because of his prisoner."

Alice seemed disappointed before Mary said, "We already heard about how he captured that Ace Carr."

Mitch quickly asked, "How do you know about it, Mary?"

"Just a little while ago, Kent Thompson stopped by and told us he had to feed the outlaw. Should he have kept quiet about it?"

"No, it's okay now. I was kinda worried that word had already leaked out that he was on today's stage. I figure that his four boys might want to keep him from reachin' Lewiston, so I wanted to keep 'em in the dark."

"I hope you don't meet up with those killers. Well, you and Miss Cohen enjoy your supper."

"We'll do that. Thank you, Mary and you too, Alice."

Then Mary looked at Esther and said, "Just so you don't worry, that's roast turkey underneath the gravy, Esther."

Before Esther could reply, the sisters smiled and as they turned to leave, they both winked at Esther before bustling back to their kitchen.

Esther watched them disappear then looked back at Mitch and said, "I'm not a practicing Jew, so I wouldn't object if it had been roast pork, Mitch. I'm just surprised that they were still so nice to me after figuring out that I was Jewish."

Mitch was already chewing his first bite of gravy-coated turkey, so he had to swallow before replying, "Alice and Mary are good ladies, Esther."

Esther cut her turkey breast as she said, "Most of the people that ignore me are good people."

Mitch didn't comment as he continued to eat. He knew all of those good people in Salmon City and until he spoke to Esther on Monday, he didn't even notice that she felt ostracized. He believed that those who expressed their distaste after discovering her Jewish heritage were in the minority, but Esther seemed to expect it of everyone.

Esther had a very different opinion. While she accepted Mitch's judgement of the sisters' character, she believed that they seemed to accept her so readily because they believed that she was more than just a passenger on the same stage. She attributed their kindness to having Mitch share her table.

They continued to eat in silence for almost a minute before Esther said, "Was it one of the Roberts brothers who shot you in the leg?"

"No, ma'am. It wasn't for lack of tryin'. They just weren't very good shots."

She sipped her coffee before saying, "You had other scars before I sutured your first knife wound. Two of them were gunshot wounds. Because I did all the talking when I was closing your new ones, I never asked about the ones that were already there. Can you tell me about them?"

Mitch swallowed then replied, "There are seven old ones altogether. I started collectin' 'em before I even wore a badge."

107

"How old were you when you received the first one?"

"I was twelve, but it wasn't a bullet or a knife that needed fixin'. It was a brandin' iron."

Esther was horrified at the thought of a young Mitch being branded yet couldn't imagine that she'd missed seeing the massive damage that would have been left by a glowing piece of steel used to mark cattle.

Mitch had picked up a biscuit when he saw Esther's reaction and quickly said, "It wasn't hot, Esther. Well, it was hot, but not hot enough to burn my hide."

"Then why did it need to be sutured?"

Mitch wished he hadn't mentioned the first wound, but replied, "The other boys wanted to brand me, but they were too anxious. When it didn't burn my skin, they got mad and just hit my butt with the edge of the brand. I guess they were satisfied when I started bleedin'."

"What did your parents do about it?"

Mitch took a bite of the biscuit and chewed slowly. He'd opened up a window to memories that he had kept in a dark area of his mind and needed to slam it closed again.

"It was my fault, Esther. I kinda provoked those fellers. What about your folks? Why don't you tell me about them?"

Esther understood that it wasn't his usual reluctance to talk that made Mitch to change the topic but decided not to ask again.

She began to talk about her physician father and nurse mother as Mitch listened. She mixed her life's story with bites of turkey dinner and sips of coffee.

Before they finished, other diners arrived and waved at Mitch and smiled at Esther before sitting at their tables. Mary and Alice were trotting in and out of the kitchen serving their new customers. So, after their plates were empty, Mitch dropped a dollar on the table then stood and as Esther rose from her chair, he picked up his hat.

After leaving the diner, Mitch pulled his old blue hat back on and offered Esther his arm.

Esther was relieved as she took his arm as she expected that he might be brooding after telling her about the branding iron incident. He'd just listened for the rest of the meal as she talked, and she wouldn't have given it a second thought just a few days ago. But after their few genuine conversations, his return to silence had become a concern.

As they walked back to the hotel, Mitch was far from brooding. He was curious about Aaron. Even if he'd gone to the saloon, he had expected him to show up at the diner.

Esther asked, "Are you going to the jail now?"

"Yes, ma'am. I need to find my lost deputy, too. So, if he's not with Ace, then I'll probably head over to the saloon to see if he's havin' a beer."

"Are you going to have one even if he's not there?"

He grinned as he replied, "Nope. I'm not fond of any kind of liquor. It's not 'cause I object to drinkin', it's just that it kinda upsets my stomach."

"So, what is your big vice, Mitch?"

"Are you askin' about the ones they list in the Bible, Esther?"

"Not necessarily."

"I reckon my worst one is sloth. I'm a lazy cuss."

"Now that surprises me. I never would have thought of you that way. Since I've known you, it seems that your deputies are much more inactive than you are. I can't recall a single incident where you weren't involved."

"They're both young fellers without much experience. I'm teachin' 'em so they don't make the kinda mistakes I made when I started."

"Yes, they're young, but you're not that old yourself, Mitch."

"I reckon I'm eight years older than you, Esther."

"I doubt if you're thirty-six years old, Mitch."

Mitch looked at her and said, "I figured you were around twenty-four."

"I'll celebrate my twenty-eighth birthday on the eleventh of January. How old will you be on your next birthday?"

"I'll be thirty-three on the twelfth of April. I reckon I just feel a lot older."

"I thought you'd just passed thirty. And you probably feel older because you are as far from slothful as any man I've ever met."

"I reckon you that's only 'cause you ain't met many."

"Probably not as many as you have, but it's still quite a large sample."

"Maybe I oughta start usin' tobacco to have a vice you can see."

"I hope not. But you'd need to start by tomorrow if you expect me to witness your new bad habit."

Mitch didn't reply. He'd almost forgotten the reason she was even on the stage. But when she'd reminded him of her appointment on Friday, he realized that he would probably be returning to Salmon City with Aaron as his only companion.

Esther was a bit disappointed when Mitch hadn't reacted to her remark. But after a few seconds, she accepted it as consistent with his character. She was very pleased that he had seemed to be more open. They could talk more tomorrow night at the way station and maybe by then, he'd tell her about his life, and she might understand him even better.

When they reached the hotel, Mitch said, "I'll see you in the mornin', Esther. I won't be able to take you to breakfast 'cause I've got to get Ace ready."

"I'll see you at the depot."

Mitch just nodded and smiled before he turned and headed for the jail.

Esther watched him leave and decided to sit in the lobby for a while. When she entered the hotel, she found the small lobby empty and took a seat on the couch. Luckily, the elderly gentleman had left his newspaper behind, so she picked up the three-day-old copy of *The Salmon City Leader* and began reading. Not surprisingly, the big news was of the county sheriff's capture of Ace Carr. It made for very interesting reading, and she wondered how much of what she read was accurate. She'd ask Mitch tomorrow night.

————

Mitch soon entered the jail and found Deputy Marshal Tom Wilkerson sitting at the desk cleaning a shotgun.

When the old deputy looked up, Mitch said, "Evenin', Tom. Have you seen my lost deputy?"

Tom grinned as he shook his head and replied, "Nope. I reckon you might find him over at the saloon or The Widows' Kitchen."

"I just left the kitchen, so I'll check the saloon before headin' back to the hotel. Has your guest given you any trouble?"

"Nope."

"You need any help tonight?"

"No, sir. My boss is gonna bring us some supper shortly then he's takin' over."

"Tell him that I appreciate it and I'll stop by real early to get him ready to move. Maybe I'll even have my deputy with me."

Tom chuckled as Mitch waved and left the jail. If he didn't find Aaron in the saloon, he'd return to the hotel and ask the clerk for his room number. He wanted to make sure that Aaron was sober and would be sharp for tomorrow's leg. While he still expected that a night attack at the way station was more likely, the probability that the gang would try to free Ace before the stage reached the Camas Plains was almost as high.

He soon stepped into the almost empty saloon and after a quick scan, turned around and headed back to the hotel. While he had confessed to the sin of sloth to Esther, he knew that he

113

was far from lazy but had latched onto the failing because it was the first one that came to mind. She had surprised him by noticing that he never sent either of his young deputies to handle a problem on their own. While it was true that he was training them to be good lawmen, the real reason why he dealt with all of the dangerous trouble was also his vice. He enjoyed the satisfaction he gained when he stopped bad men or kept good men from doing bad things. While he didn't care about the attention or praise that invariably followed, he admitted to the sin of pride for doing a good job.

As he turned to enter the hotel, he hoped to instill that same sense of pride into his two deputies. Aaron's absence emphasized the need.

He'd just opened the door when he spotted Esther sitting on the couch reading a newspaper. She immediately looked over the top of the pages and smiled.

Mitch closed the door and walked to the couch where he took a seat as she folded the newspaper and set it back on the empty chair.

She then asked, "I assume that you didn't find your wandering deputy."

"No, ma'am. I was just about to ask the clerk for his room number."

"Can you talk with me for a little while before going to look for him?"

"How about if I find him first?"

"Only if you don't intend to go to your room and hide."

Mitch smiled as he stood and said, "No, ma'am."

"If you're not back in five minutes, Sheriff Ward, I will enter your room without knocking."

"I reckon you would, Miss Cohen."

Mitch stepped to the desk and before he even asked, the clerk said, "He's in room eight."

Mitch nodded and didn't comment on the clerk's eavesdropping before he walked to the hallway and soon reached room eight. He knocked on the door and almost immediately heard Aaron's footsteps on the other side.

When he opened the door, Aaron said, "I was gonna come and talk to you, boss, but I kinda fell asleep."

As he entered, Mitch replied, "You seem a bit outta sorts. Did you get any supper?"

Aaron closed the door and after Mitch took the small room's only chair, he sat on his bed.

"I had a couple of sandwiches while I was havin' a beer."

"Why don't you head over to The Widows' Kitchen and have some real food? Tomorrow we need to be at the jail real early to get Ace ready to go and you might not get any breakfast."

"Okay. Are you comin'?"

"Nope. I already ate."

Aaron paused before he asked, "Did you have anybody with ya?"

Mitch stood before saying, "Yup," then walked past Aaron, opened the door and left the room.

After his boss closed the door, Aaron shook his head. *What was going on between Mitch and that woman?*

Mitch entered the lobby and reached that woman a few seconds later then sat down on the couch beside her.

She said, "I assume you found him."

"Yes, ma'am. He said he was takin' a nap and had some sandwiches at the saloon, but I told him to head over to the diner and get a full supper. I want him to be prepared for anything tomorrow."

"I hope you're wrong, Mitch."

"So, do I."

Before Esther could start the conversation, Aaron walked quickly past and just nodded at them before pulling on his hat and leaving the hotel.

"I don't believe that your deputy is pleased to see you sitting with me, Mitch."

While Mitch was sure that Esther was right, especially after watching Aaron's face when he told his deputy that he hadn't dined alone.

But he smiled and said, "I reckon he's just jealous, Esther."

Esther laughed before saying, "If he was interested, he had his chance to talk to me during the long hours that we spent in the coach today, Mitch."

Mitch began to say, "Maybe he was…he coulda…" then after he failed to find any obvious excuse for Aaron's behavior, he finished his aborted sentence by saying, "I guess I didn't do a good job teachin' him."

"There are some things that can't be taught, Mitch."

He slowly said, "Maybe. But I don't figure this is one of 'em. You're a better person than anyone else I ever met, Esther. You should be treated with respect and courtesy because of the who you are and what you do. Nobody should be treated poorly just because of their names or what they believe."

Mitch suddenly realized he was close to preaching, so he quickly stopped before he got carried away.

Esther wasn't surprised by his viewpoint on fairness, but she was almost stunned when he'd revealed his opinion of her.

Before she could even comment, Mitch flushed and said, "Sorry, Esther. I was close to gettin' preachy. I shoulda been standin' on a pulpit or a soapbox."

"That's okay."

Mitch glanced at the desk clerk and considered strongly suggesting that was impolite to eavesdrop on guests' conversations but knew it was just a passing thought.

Esther asked, "Are you going to wait for your deputy to return?"

"I reckon not. He might head over to the saloon when he's done eatin'. I should go to my room to get ready for tomorrow."

She'd noticed his brief, but noticeably displeased look at the desk clerk and understood why he wanted to leave. She didn't believe that he needed to spend a couple of hours in preparation, nor did she think he wanted to avoid her company.

So, when Mitch stood, she rose as well. They ignored the clerk as they walked to the hallway and Mitch wasn't surprised that she had left the lobby with him. But when they reached her room, he was expecting her to open the door, yet she continued walking beside him.

Mitch glanced at her, but she was looking down the hallway when they reached his room. He wasn't sure if she was going to use the washroom at the end of the hallway until he stopped and opened his door.

He was about to enter when he turned to ask her about her intentions when she just looked up at him, smiled and stepped past him. He stood in the doorway and watched as she pulled out the lone chair in the room and sat down. She didn't say a word as she looked back at him with her big brown eyes, obviously expecting him to react.

Mitch thought he'd shock her when he closed the door, but after it clicked shut, she didn't even lose her smile.

So, he stepped to his bed and sat down before saying, "I figure you want to talk without havin' a nosy desk clerk listenin' to every word."

"I thought that was why you wanted to leave early. Was I wrong?"

"Nope. I was close to headin' over there and lettin' him know it wasn't polite."

"Do you want me to leave?"

Mitch hesitated before softly answering, "No."

"Thank you, Mitch."

Mitch nodded and wondered what she had to say. He hadn't even realized that he'd told her that she was the best person he'd ever met because he'd been so irritated with Aaron's behavior.

She said, "I've known you for almost three years, Mitch. I may have heard all the stories about you but didn't know you any better than anyone else in the county, and probably EVEN less. We've talked a lot since you came to warn me about the danger of taking the stage, but there is still so much I don't know. I told you my life story at the diner, but all I know about yours is that some boys tried to brand you when you were twelve. I thought you might just be ashamed of your past. But after you just told me that we should only judge people by who they are and what they do, I don't understand why you won't tell me about your life. You weren't an outlaw in Oregon City; were you?"

"No. I wasn't an outlaw, but I wasn't exactly an angel, either."

"But I heard that you say that you were a deputy sheriff there before you came to Salmon City."

"I was. I was a Clackamas County deputy sheriff for more than three years. I was even younger than Aaron when I put

120

on the badge. It was when I was younger that I was a troublemaker."

"Can you tell me about it?"

"Alright. Remember when you asked me what my parents did when those boys tried to brand my behind?"

As Esther nodded, Mitch continued, saying, "I couldn't answer 'cause I never knew my parents. I don't even know how I got to Oregon City. I grew up on what they called a school farm about four miles southwest of town, but it was more like an orphanage and reform school but only for boys. They had a few women there to raise the young boys, but I figured out later that they earned extra pay from the guards who kept us in line. They weren't called guards, though. The man who ran the place called them teachers.

"They used us for labor once we were big enough. Of course, what they figured was big enough wasn't what most folks would consider very big. I started workin' before I was five. I didn't know how odd it was that I could read even when I learned that most of the guards and none of the other boys could. Whenever I saw tins with writin' on 'em or anything else with letters, I enjoyed figurin' out what the word meant.

"I was seven when I made the mistake of tellin' another boy I thought was my friend about it and that made everything worse. I was still one of the smaller kids and took my share of beatings from the big boys, but after they found out I could read and was startin' to write, they came at me real hard. I figured if I didn't talk much, they'd leave me alone. It helped a little, so I learned to keep my mouth shut. The guards didn't care what they did to me, either. If they beat me to death, it was one less kid they had to watch and feed.

"It went that way for a while, but I kept readin' and writin' just 'cause I didn't want 'em to win. I was gettin' bigger, too. But when I figured out how to cypher, that seemed to really make 'em mad. That was when they cornered me and were gonna burn my hide. I was kinda lucky all they did was cut me."

Esther was shaken by his story, but quickly asked, "Who sutured your wound?"

"One of the small kids who liked me. He was bawlin' all the time he was sewin', but I kept tellin' him it didn't hurt. But he figured I was just tryin' to make him feel better, so he kept cryin'."

Esther wasn't about to ask him to show her the scar left by a young boy's attempt at suturing a large wound.

Mitch took a deep breath before saying, "After it healed, I turned into bit of a bully myself. I was tired of bein' tortured by the big boys, and now I was big enough to fight back."

"You didn't beat the smaller boys; did you?"

"Sometimes. Some of 'em began to look to me for protection, so even if the boy who was causing them trouble was smaller than me, I'd stop it."

"That's not being a bully, Mitch."

Mitch shrugged then resumed his story.

"When I was fourteen, I was almost as big as I am now, and I got to be pretty full of myself. The other bullies were either gone or afraid of me. I was the big boss and enjoyed the title. But I went too far just a couple of months before my fifteenth birthday.

"I was out in the fields pulling weeds when one of the guards walked up behind me. He told me to get on my knees and dig a hole where the weed had sprouted to make sure it was all gone. I knew he was just tellin' me that to make me look bad and I told him so. He slapped me, which hadn't happened for a long time, and I automatically raised my fist.

"That set him off even after I opened my hand. As I turned away, he hit me on the right side of my chest with his hickory club. I fell and was rollin' around on the ground in pain when he got ready to kick me where no boy or man wants to be kicked.

"I already had my knees bent because of the pain, so all I had to do was straighten my leg really fast. I caught him in his left knee, and he screamed before he fell to the ground just a few feet away. He dropped his club, so I got to my feet before he did and grabbed it. I was so mad that I wanted to slam it into his head. I raised it over my head and just as I was gonna hit him, I looked at his face and saw fear in his eyes. I don't know why it stopped me from hittin' him, but it did. I dropped the club and hurried back to the dormitory. I grabbed my extra clothes and left the farm before the other guards came after me."

"Did they catch you?"

Mitch shook his head as he replied, "Nope. I'm not even sure they even looked for me. They were probably just happy to get rid of me a year early. So, I walked to Oregon City and began doin' odd jobs but had to steal sometimes to get by. I did that for more than two years and thought about leavin', but never had enough money to even buy a horse."

"Where did you live?"

"I found an abandoned cabin about a mile north of town. It was pretty small and in bad shape, but it kept out most of the wind."

"How did you become a deputy?"

Mitch smiled then answered, "Like I said, I was stealin' to keep alive and was gettin' pretty good at it. I was sure that Sheriff Croaker knew about me, but I couldn't figure out why he hadn't arrested me yet. I reckoned it was because I never took that much, and he had serious crimes to worry about.

"When I was seventeen, I was in the corral at Julip's Livery talkin' to a handsome buckskin gelding when the horse looked away. I turned and saw the sheriff staring at me as he leaned on the barn door. He said that if I planned on stealin' the horse, he'd have to hunt me down and shoot me. I told him I'd never think of stealin' somethin' as valuable as a horse. He grinned and asked me to come to the jail. I thought he was gonna arrest me for just bein' in the corral or maybe for stealin' somethin' else. I figured my luck had run out.

"But when we got there, he sat me down and told me that he'd been watching me for a while. He'd even heard the story about why I'd left the work farm because the guard had filed charges. He said he took the report but threw it out after the guard left. By then, I thought he just wanted to tell me to stop stealin', which would mean I'd have to leave town. He mighta been headin' that way because he started tellin' me how impressed he was with my ability as a thief.

"As he was talkin', I noticed a wanted poster on his desk and snickered. He asked me what was funny, and I pointed out that they'd misspelled 'homicide' when they added an extra 'm'. He was surprised that I could read and after he had me read a few more posters, he had me add up the rewards. I guess he was surprised that I didn't even ask for a pencil to do the cypherin'.

"That was when he told me that he was gonna tell me to stop annoying the folks with my stealin'. But once he found that I could read and write, he decided I could help him a lot more. He had two deputies, but neither of 'em could read. So, he asked me if I'd work as a jailer. I could live in the jail, and they'd pay me twenty dollars a month. I'd even get to eat at the diner for free.

"So, I began working at the jail. It took a while for the folks to get used to me bein' there, and his deputies weren't happy about it either. But the sheriff did much more than give me a place to stay and put money in my pocket. He began teachin' me how to be a good man and what it took to be a lawman."

"Were you still as untalkative even with the sheriff teaching you?"

"Yup. Sheriff Croaker didn't talk much either, so it kinda became a habit."

"When did you become a deputy?"

"I was given the badge just before I turned twenty, but by then, I was doin' more than his real deputies were. One of 'em left to take a job in Portland, so Sheriff Croaker swore me in. The other deputy was still annoyed havin' me around 'cause he was ten years older and still a deputy. He figured the sheriff was settin' me up to take over when he retired. He was already approaching fifty when I put on the badge.

"I kept learnin' and gettin' better over the next three years and we added a third deputy who was still older than me. Then things kind crashed down on the tenth of June in '62. I was in the jail keepin' and eye on one of our regulars when I heard a gunshot. I grabbed the shotgun and hurried outside. When I saw a bunch of fellers runnin' out of the saloon, I headed that way. When I got there, I found Sheriff Croaker on the floor. He was already dead and so was the man who shot him. It was just a barroom argument that Abe tried to stop when one of 'em pulled his pistol and shot Abe. Before he died, Abe put a bullet into the feller.

"After I carried his body to the mortician, I didn't want to stay in Oregon City anymore, even if they asked me to be sheriff. As it turned out, they didn't even ask. They appointed the old deputy. He was probably expectin' me to get mad, but I just shook his hand, handed him my badge and headed east. I figured that I'd find work as a deputy in Lewiston 'cause it was the territorial capital and I knew Sheriff Borden. They didn't have any openings, but Sheriff Borden told me that they really needed a new sheriff in Lemhi County. He said that even though I was still pretty young, he knew I was better qualified than the deputies they had. He even wrote me a nice letter of recommendation.

"So, I headed to Salmon City, showed them the letter and spent a whole day with the county commissioners. The three deputies who were in line for the job weren't happy, so two of 'em left after a while. Steve Finch was the youngest and the only one who stayed, and he works for Lyle now. I hired Pete to replace the first one who left then a hired Aaron after that. Now you know more about me than anyone else in the territory."

Esther nodded as she said, "Thank you for telling me, Mitch. After you told me that you were troublemaker, I expected much worse."

"It felt worse when I was sneakin' around Oregon City and takin' things that weren't mine."

"We all do things we're not proud of when we're young. But I think it's part of growing up."

"I find it hard to believe that you'd do anything worse than sayin', 'oh, darn!'."

Esther laughed before replying, "I've done much worse. Trust me."

"I won't ask what you did. Not that it'd make me think less of you."

She was about to ask him just what he did think of her when he glanced at the closed door and said, "I should at least open the door, Esther."

"Why? Are you worried that your deputy might think you were bedding a Jewess?"

Mitch was startled and stared at her with wide eyes before she grinned.

"I was just poking fun at you for suggesting that the closed door might damage my reputation. It won't affect my standing in the community at all, but it might cause raised eyebrows when you return to Salmon City."

"When I first took this job eight years ago, I didn't care what those kinda folks thought, and I still don't. Abe Croaker taught me that. He said they're the ones who would rather think bad about others just to make themselves feel better."

"He was probably right. May I ask you something that has puzzled me for a while?"

"Whatever it is, it can't be worse than what I've already told you."

"It's about your house. When someone mentioned that you'd bought that big place, I thought it was a just a silly rumor. Then I discovered that it was true. You live alone and had to hire Mrs. Brown to keep it clean. I was just wondering why you bought it."

"I was expectin' you to ask me if the rumors were true about Mrs. Brown warmin' my bed."

"I heard that gossip but gave it no credence. I was just wondering why you would have bought such a large house."

Mitch felt like an outlaw being pressured to confess his crime as Esther sat just a few feet away waiting for his answer.

"Um…it was such a bargain that I couldn't pass it up."

"Do you really expect me to believe that you'd enjoy living in that mausoleum by yourself?"

"I was already lookin' for a place, and I was able to get the big house for just a little more. I figured if it didn't work out, I could sell it when I got a good offer."

She knew he had been living in the house for more than two years and he could have already sold it to a number of newcomers. While she was certain that he hadn't given her the real reason, she didn't want to make him uncomfortable again. He'd just told her his life story that he had probably never revealed to anyone else, so she decided to quit while she was ahead.

She smiled and said, "I suppose I'll let you start preparing for tomorrow. I know that I probably won't see you before I board the coach, but I'll bring you some breakfast."

He rose from the mattress as he replied, "Thank you, Esther. You don't have to bring anything for Aaron. He hasn't earned your courtesy."

She stood and said, "I'll think about it."

Mitch walked with her to the doorway and after swinging the door open, he said, "I'll see you in the mornin'."

"Can we have another long conversation at the way station?"

"I'll look forward to it."

She smiled, then quickly stepped into the hallway and turned toward her room. After he heard her door close, Mitch closed his door and walked to the chair and sat down. Not only had he never told anyone his life history before; he was sure that he had never spoken this much at one sitting in his entire life. But it wasn't just the length that made it special. Just telling Esther had filled holes in his soul that he didn't even know existed. He tried to remember the last time he'd actually enjoyed a conversation and couldn't think of one.

Now he only hoped that they'd have another, even more interesting chat tomorrow night after arriving at the way station. If they reached the Camas Plains way station safely, he'd have Aaron take the early watch so he could spend more time with Esther. After she retired for the night, he'd take over guard duty. He expected that Ace's boys would arrive after midnight if they hadn't already made their attempt to free their boss before they entered the flatlands.

———

Aaron hadn't even thought about returning to the saloon after having a very filling meal at The Widows' Kitchen. He might have paid the bar a visit if he hadn't seen the stunning blonde sitting in the hotel lobby. After finishing his supper, he walked quickly back to the hotel with the hope of seeing her again. He hoped that the old folks weren't there, or even worse, he didn't want to see Mitch with the nurse.

When he entered the lobby, he was disappointed to find it empty, so he headed for the hallway. As he passed the nurse's room, he wondered if his boss was inside. He grinned and decided to see if Mitch was in his room.

Mitch had his saddlebags open and was moving his boxes of ammunition to the inside behind his spare clothes. He would keep them over his shoulder tomorrow and didn't want the boxes' sharp corners jamming into his ribs. He had just tied down the leather flaps when loud knocking on his door made him jerk. He left his saddlebags on the bed and headed for the door. He was certain that he'd find Aaron on the other side and had a good idea what had made him decide to pay a visit.

He swung it open, and Aaron smiled as he said, "Howdy, Mitch. I just wanted to let you know that I had a big dinner and didn't go back to the saloon. I'll be in good shape for tomorrow."

"Okay."

Aaron continued to grin as he glanced past his boss and saw the empty room.

"I guess I'll head to my room now, boss. See ya in the mornin'."

"Early."

"Yes, sir."

Aaron turned and stepped away from the doorway before Mitch closed it and returned to his bed. After moving the saddlebags to the top of the small dresser, he took off his jacket and draped it over one of the brass hooks on the door next to his hat. He then unbuckled his gunbelt and hung it from the last open hook.

He returned to the bed, sat down and pulled off his boots. After stretching out on the bed, he wished that he'd left Aaron to mind the jail and brought Pete along. He was only a year older than Aaron but was much closer to being a fully qualified lawman. Mitch gave much of the credit to his wife, Nancy. Being a father gave him an even greater sense of responsibility.

But as he thought about Pete's family, he wondered if he should have told Esther the reason why he'd bought the house. She seemed to like him more than he could have hoped and even overlooked his abuse of the language. He knew she wouldn't lie to him but wondered if she hadn't been a bit obtuse when she said that she'd learned everything from her parents. Even after she'd explained that her father was a doctor and her mother a nurse, he suspected that she must have been tutored as well. She still seemed so much smarter than he was.

Before he drifted off to sleep, he hoped that Ace's gang hadn't discovered that they were moving their boss on this stage, and he'd be able to convince her to cancel the interview at St. Anne's.

CHAPTER 5

The sun had been up for more than an hour when Mitch knocked on Aaron's door. He'd already washed and shaved and had expected that his deputy would soon leave his room.

After another two sessions of door-pounding, Aaron finally shouted, "I'm up, boss!"

Mitch was sure that he'd woken all of the hotel's other guests, but he needed to have Aaron meet him at the jail.

He hadn't seen anyone else moving yet and guessed it was getting close to seven o'clock. He had enough time get some breakfast but wanted to make sure Ace was ready to be moved.

As he crossed the lobby, he tossed his key onto the desk and headed for the front door. After stepping into the chilly late spring morning, he took a deep breath before stepping down onto the boardwalk.

Before he went to the jail, Mitch headed to the depot to talk to the manager, and if he was lucky, Al Crenshaw. The driver and shotgun rider stayed in a room in back of the depot, so Al should be awake by now. They'd have to harness the team and prepare the stage for the journey to the way station. While the scheduled departure was for eight o'clock, they would leave as soon as the last passenger was in the coach. He wanted to have Ace shackled to Aaron and in the stagecoach by seven-thirty.

When he entered the depot, he found Al talking to Jasper Simmons, the Millersburg depot manager. Both men turned when they heard Mitch walk into the room.

Al grinned as he said, "You got another passenger, Mitch."

"That's good news. Can he handle a shotgun?"

Jasper and Al started laughing which puzzled Mitch for just a few seconds. Then he rolled his eyes and asked, "Is it another woman?"

Al replied, "Yup. A real looker, too. I don't reckon she's gonna be able to shoot anything but the breeze."

"Does she have to leave today?"

"Yup. Jasper was tellin' me that she needs to head back to Lewiston to tell her brother about their aunt dyin'. She only got here a couple of days ago."

"Alright."

"Sorry, Mitch. But I'll have the team hitched up in a little while and we'll be ready as soon as the two ladies and your bad boy and deputy are sittin' pretty in my coach."

Mitch just nodded before he turned and walked out of the depot. He wished the stage was out front already so he could put Goldie and his saddlebags on top until he boarded.

He soon entered the jail and was pleased to find Ace eating his breakfast already. Marshal Thompson stood and met Mitch in the center of the small office.

Mitch shook his hand and said, "Thanks, Kent. We'll get him outta your hair when he's finished."

"He gave me less trouble than those drunks we pick up from the saloon. He ain't said a word all night. I coulda slept in my own bed."

"I reckon so."

"You want a cup of coffee, Mitch?"

"I sure would."

He set Goldie against the desk as the marshal poured two cups of coffee from the pot that he had sitting on the heat stove.

As he sipped the scalding hot brew, Mitch studied his prisoner. His level of confidence in the belief that Ace expected he would soon be a free man kicked up a notch. No outlaw facing the noose ever stayed quiet as he sat in his cell. Mitch didn't think that Ace was any different than the others but was convinced that his boys would find a way to get him loose.

He set his saddlebags on the floor and sat in front of the desk while Marshal Thompson returned to his seat on the other side. Neither man spoke as Mitch waited for Aaron. If he didn't show up soon, he and Kent would put him in chains. But he wasn't going to cuff himself to the outlaw leader. He needed to have his hands free in case he was wrong about when they would make their play.

Aaron entered the office before Mitch finished his coffee. He stood and after setting his cup on the desk, he and Aaron followed Marshal Thompson to the cell. After he opened the door, he removed his Model 3 from his holster and wordlessly handed it to Aaron.

Ace just watched silently as Sheriff Ward secured the leg irons around his ankles then closed the cuffs over his wrists. When Mitch held the other end of the chained cuffs out to Aaron, his deputy gave him back his pistol and secured himself to the other end of Ace's shackles.

Once his prisoner was ready, Mitch said, "Thanks again, Kent. I'll stop by on the way back and let you know what happens to Ace in Lewiston."

Marshal Thompson grinned as he replied, "I reckon I got a pretty good notion of what that'll be, Mitch."

Mitch nodded then let Aaron lead Ace out of the cell before he followed a few feet behind. He grabbed Goldie and hung his saddlebags over his shoulder before he stepped in front of them to reach the doorway first. He had Aaron hold up then stepped outside to scan the street. After checking both directions, he waved Aaron out and once they reached the boardwalk, he resumed his trailing position. He soon noticed that the coach was now out front, and the team was in harness but didn't see the new blond passenger or Esther which was a good thing. It was better to get Ace inside before they showed up.

After helping Ace and Aaron into the cabin, Mitch watched them settle into the front seat. Ace was at the window near the depot, which left enough room for another passenger on Aaron's right, but Mitch would tell Esther to sit on the other end and the other woman passenger to leave a gap in front of Ace. She'd be facing Aaron, and Mitch didn't think his young deputy would object if she was the looker that Al had professed her to be. Besides, she probably wasn't Jewish, so he wouldn't hesitate to chat with her.

Al walked out after Ace was uncomfortably seated and said, "As soon as the ladies arrive, we'll be ready to roll. We already moved their bags into the boot, too. Do you still figure Ace's boys are gonna try and spring him loose?"

"I'm positive they'll try somethin'. I think the most likely place is the way station after midnight, but they could be waitin' for us just after we pass Mount Idaho, too."

"Why there?"

"It might be sooner, but I reckon that the curve around Mount Idaho before we head down into Camas Plains would give 'em their best shot."

"I hope you're as good with that Winchester as everybody says you are."

"Me, too."

Mitch had been looking west along the boardwalk and spotted a blonde woman leaving the hotel. As she stepped toward the depot, he had to admit she was a very pretty young woman. She was wearing a white blouse and a dark green skirt and had a matching green scarf draped over her shoulders. Even her large handbag was a dark green. She must believe that shade of green accented her bright blonde hair. She was obviously very aware of the effect she had on males of the species just by the way she carried herself. But Mitch thought she overdid it and must consider herself on par with Venus. She didn't wear an excessive amount of makeup but wore enough to give her the look of an expensive working girl.

But even as he made his assessment, he caught sight of Esther approaching the hotel entrance just a hundred feet behind the blonde. He smiled as he contrasted the two women. Esther was dark haired, taller, and much more elegant. She was more beautiful than pretty and was the epitome of class. She was dressed more conservatively which amplified the differences between them. She wore a cream-colored dress with darker brown accents and had a tan wool jacket to keep herself warm. Her uncovered long black hair made her look almost like an Indian woman, but he suspected that if she was, she might have been treated better.

She was carrying her purse in her left hand and a paper sack in her right. He had a good idea of what she had in the bag, so she must have dropped off her travel bags and gone to The Widows' Kitchen to have breakfast while he was waiting for Aaron in the jail.

He had to shift his eyes away from Esther when the young blonde neared the coach.

She smiled at him and asked, "You're Sheriff Ward; aren't you?"

"Yes, ma'am."

"My name is Grace Dubois. I heard that you are escorting a notorious outlaw in my stagecoach, Sheriff."

"Yes, ma'am. He's sittin' inside with my deputy. For your protection, I'd appreciate it if you sat across from my deputy."

"Alright. Are you sure I shouldn't sit on the other side next to your deputy?"

"That would keep my deputy from reachin' his pistol if the prisoner tried to escape."

"Oh. Do you think that he might try that?"

"Yes, ma'am. Before you board, could you stay here for a minute? We have another passenger coming and she's almost here."

She turned and looked behind her as Esther approached then stopped next to Grace and held out the paper bag.

"Here's your breakfast, Mitch. I didn't even have to ask to have it prepared. Mary and Alice asked me where you were and after I told them, they said you needed a good breakfast for today's trip."

Mitch accepted the heavy paper sack and replied, "Thanks, Esther. I'll be sure to thank Alice and Mary on our way back."

"'Our way back', Sheriff Ward?" she asked with a smile.

"Um…you know, me and Aaron."

She laughed then said, "I'm sure."

"Anyway, I told Miss Dubois that I want her to sit across from Aaron, and I'd prefer that you sit on the left side of the seat near the window. I want to leave an empty space across from Ace."

"Alright."

Mitch nodded and said, "It's a long ride to the way station, so if you see my deputy noddin' off like he did yesterday, give him a wakeup kick."

Esther glanced at Grace and said, "I don't think you need to worry about Aaron napping this time."

Grace giggled before saying, "I was in the lobby yesterday when he walked past. Judging by the look on his face, I'd be surprised if he even closed his eyes for a second."

Mitch didn't take his eyes from Esther as he said, "I reckon you're right, miss."

Mitch then handed Goldie to Al before climbing up the side of the stage to the driver's seat. Jasper Simmons had been waiting for the sheriff to finish talking before helping Esther and then Grace into the coach.

Al waited until he figured the women were settled then snapped the reins and the stage began rolling out of Millersburg.

Inside the cabin, Aaron was stunned when the blonde woman from the hotel entered the cabin after Esther. He was also immensely pleased when she sat directly in front of him and didn't realize her seating choice was at the direction of his boss. It wouldn't matter anyway. For the next eight or nine hours, he'd be able to get acquainted with the blonde goddess.

Esther avoided smiling when she watched Aaron's reaction. He was staring at her seating partner without any attempt at polite reservation. When she glanced at Miss Dubois, Esther could tell that she was far from being insulted. She seemed to be thrilled with the impact she was having on Deputy Jackson.

She then looked at Ace Carr and was surprised to find that his eyes were already closed. She thought it was odd, even for a man who would probably be condemned to death in a few days. He must have seen the blonde enter the cabin, yet unlike the deputy, he seemed disinterested.

She then looked out the window and watched the last of Millersburg's buildings pass by. Mary and Alice had also given her a smaller bag with two turkey sandwiches for lunch which she had in her voluminous purse. She hadn't looked inside Mitch's bag, but wouldn't have been surprised if it didn't contain a love note. The sisters seemed very fond of Sheriff Ward.

She smiled and thought, "And for good reason."

———

Twenty-four miles ahead of the stagecoach, just on the other side of the curve around Mount Idaho, Hal Kingman sat on a rock going over the plan one last time.

"I reckon the stage should be here in about three more hours or so. Jack, I want you to set up watch from behind that outcrop I told you about. As soon as you pick it up, get back

143

here and we'll mount up. We gotta catch that stage before it reaches the curve. Do you all understand?"

The three outlaws nodded and acknowledged his directions. They were sure that in just a few more hours, they'd be returning to their hideout with Ace.

They'd been planning to rob the Salmon City Bank using the same strategy that they'd used in Lewiston when Ace had been captured. If they had been successful, then Sheriff Ward and his deputies would be dead and that would leave Lemhi County wide open. They could have emptied the bank at their leisure.

As far as Hal was concerned, Ace's capture was only an unexpected delay. After they killed the sheriff and his deputy while they freed him, they could return to Salmon City to finish the job.

———

Once they were on the open road, Al let the team control their path as he grinned at Mitch and said, "I told ya she was a real looker."

"Yeah, you did say that."

"You don't think so?"

Mitch shrugged as he kept focus on the road ahead. Even though he doubted if the gang would dare to make their attempt this close to town, he wasn't about to lessen his vigilance.

"Are you gonna carry that Winchester all the way to the way station?"

"Yup."

Al snickered then shook his head and focused on the team.

Mitch had set the bag with his breakfast on the seat between them but still had his saddlebags over his shoulder. With the boxes of ammunition padded by his clothes, he was able to use it as a cushion. It wasn't just for added comfort, either. If he had to engage the gang, it would give him a slightly more stable firing position. He had to take every advantage he could if he needed to outshoot four killers. His coil of old rope was still on the roof behind him, and he planned to use it to bind Ace when they arrived at the way station. It had been Sheriff Croaker who'd told him that it was better to use a worn rope to bind prisoners because the knots were tighter.

Until he'd told Esther about Abe, Mitch realized that he hadn't thought about his mentor that much over the past couple of years. He assumed it was just the way the mind worked but was determined not to let the old sheriff's memories completely fade away. Maybe he'd name his first son after the man who had been a father to him. Of course, he couldn't have any children at all on his own. But now for the first time since Esther had stepped off the stage almost three years ago, he realized that she might agree to marry him. He smiled when imagined her reaction when asked her if they should name their firstborn son Abraham. She might think he was having a bit of fun.

He had always believed that he wasn't even good enough to talk to her. When he bought the big house two years ago, it had been a more of a fantasy than a belief that one day she would share it with him. But even as he moved into the place, he felt foolish for having that impossible dream. Yet he kept that vaporous hope alive each time he entered the house and began fantasizing about having her living with him. He envisioned her in the kitchen and almost painfully, imagined her with him in their bedroom.

Until he'd spoken to her on Monday, it had been ethereal at best. But now it seemed within reach. He just had to ensure that he got her safely to Lewiston and that St. Anne's hired the other nurse. Then he'd ask her if she'd be willing to return to Salmon City with him and change that impossible dream into reality.

A sudden loud thump as the coach's front wheels crossed a rut in the road reminded him that he was woolgathering. He cursed himself as he studied the landscape ahead. He knew it well and didn't need mile markers to know that they were already six miles away from Millersburg. In less than three hours, they'd reach Mount Idaho.

He set Goldie between his legs and held the Winchester with his knees as he opened the paper sack. He pulled out a massive sandwich wrapped in butcher paper.

There was another one left in the bag, so he turned to the driver and asked, "Did you want one of my sandwiches for breakfast, Al?"

"Nope. I had a big breakfast, and my lunch is in my satchel in the footwell. I reckon Mary and Alice made 'em special for you anyway."

Mitch grinned as he peeled back the butcher paper and took a big bite of the thick bacon and fried egg sandwich.

———

Just a few feet beneath and behind them, Grace shed her heavy scarf and smiled at Aaron.

"Hello. My name is Grace Dubois."

Aaron was immensely pleased that she had introduced herself and quickly replied, "It's a great pleasure to meet you, Miss Dubois. I'm Lemhi County Deputy Sheriff Aaron Jackson. Please call me Aaron."

"Thank you, Aaron. I'd consider it an honor if you'd call me Grace."

Aaron's smile was close to splitting his face as he said, "I'm the one who's honored, Grace. I saw you in the hotel lobby yesterday but didn't want to disturb you."

"I watched you pass by and wished that you had stopped to talk. I arrived just a couple of days ago and found my beloved Aunt Mabel had already passed away before I even arrived. I didn't know anyone in Millersburg, and I wished that I had company."

"I'm sorry for your loss, Grace."

Then Aaron asked, "Why didn't your husband accompany you?"

Grace smiled as she replied, "I'm not married, Aaron."

"That's a big surprise, Grace. I gotta admit that it's a pleasant surprise, though."

Grace said, "My father kept an eye on me as if I was a prisoner. He died last year. and this is the first time I've been out of Lewiston. But now, it looks as if it was almost fate that made me take this stage."

"So, do I."

Aaron wished he could shed the cuffs binding him to Ace and move to the seat open seat beside Grace but had to worship her across the short gap. But when they reached the way station, Mitch could handle Ace and he'd have more time to spend with Grace.

Esther had been listening to their chatter as she watched the mountains pass by. The ones outside her window were shorter than the ones on the other side, but she didn't want to watch the flirtatious banter going on next to her. Hearing it was bad enough.

As annoying as it was, Esther still picked up some of what Grace has said. It seemed odd that a pretty young woman would be traveling alone. She didn't count herself as a young woman anymore. At least she'd already left her home and had more real-life experience than her blonde companion. She also found it hard to believe that even if Grace's father was as protective as she claimed, he could have controlled every minute of her life. He would have had to sleep and go to work, and Grace could have had a number of boyfriends without her father's knowledge.

But Grace wasn't her problem. If Aaron was interested, he would have to figure it out. When they arrived in Lewiston, Esther wouldn't be surprised to discover that Grace was far from the innocent maiden she appeared to be. She could even be a working girl but would command a high price for her services.

She watched the mountains and pine trees pass but glanced to her right to see if the outlaw chief was still pretending to be asleep. She found his eyes still closed then turned back to stare out her window. If Ace had been looking at Grace, Esther would have been more relaxed. She picked up her large purse and took out her small book of poems. Her mother had given it to her when she was fourteen after Esther had been able to recite John Milton's *On His Blindness* without pause or a single error.

———

Mitch had finished his filling sandwich then crumpled the butcher paper and stuffed it back into the sack to absorb some of the grease that would leak out of the other sandwich before he consumed it for lunch. He had some beef jerky and hard tack in his saddlebags, but the second bacon and egg sandwich would be a marked improvement. He set the paper bag on the seat, took the full canteen from its hook and washed down the sandwich. He offered the open canteen to Al who shook his head before closing it and returning it to its hook. Mitch finally released Goldie from his knees' grip and felt better having the repeater in his hands.

He knew that as long as they had mountains on both sides of the road, which would last until they reached White Bird Creek, it wouldn't be possible for the four men to set up an ambush. They could have left two men afoot in the rocks to try to pick off him and Al, but that was an iffy proposition at best. He still examined each of the potential ambush sites just in case Hal Kingman wasn't as smart as his boss.

There were three other creeks they had to ford before reaching White Bird Creek. The first was too small to earn a name. Then in rapid succession, about a mile apart, came Pioneer Creek and the much wider Slate Creek. Pioneer, Slate and White Bird Creeks all would cause the stage to slow before it entered the water. But only the terrain around White Bird Creek provided good protection for an ambush. Yet even those rocks and trees couldn't hide four horses. He still believed that Ace's boys would be waiting on the other side of Mount Idaho, unless they were planning to make their move while everyone was sleeping at the way station.

When he'd read Ace's wanted poster, he'd been surprised when he noticed that Ace had attended college. During their brief conversation on the boardwalk before he marched him to his jail, Ace spoke more like he did than a well-educated man. Either he was trying to blend in, or the wanted poster was wrong. He knew that Ace would never tell him one way or the other before he was hanged, but they had to get him to Lewiston first.

———

It was still late in the morning when the stagecoach approached the small, unnamed creek. They hadn't met any traffic heading south, but that wasn't unexpected. Any freight wagons leaving Lewiston wouldn't even have reached the way station yet.

Inside the coach, Aaron and Grace had continued their extended introductory conversation. Aaron had been doing most of the talking as he tried to impress Grace. He paid no attention whatsoever to Ace who had only shifted his position a couple of times. He'd opened his eyes for a few minutes, but Aaron didn't notice.

Grace had asked him about the gang leader bound to him with the handcuff's chain and told him that she was relieved to have Aaron there to protect her. She even expressed her admiration for his bravery, which almost made Esther gag.

But even as Esther spent most of her time looking out the window, she couldn't miss how Aaron was eagerly listening to each word she spoke and seemed to sit a little straighter and taller when she praised him. She couldn't avoid comparing Aaron's reaction to Mitch's when she'd told him that she thought he was smart and handsome. Mitch had blushed and didn't even seem to believe her. She could imagine what his response would be if she told him that he was brave.

She smiled as her mind heard him say, "I'm just doin' my job, ma'am."

———

After crossing the narrow stream, they rounded a gentle curve and Mitch spotted Pioneer Creek ahead. There were a few hiding spots on the other side, so he focused on those as he shifted in his seat to get more comfortable.

Al soon slowed the team and let the horses drink when they entered the creek.

As they dipped their muzzles into the cold water, Al turned to Mitch and said, "I figure I'll let 'em drink their fill here, then we won't need to stop at White Bird. That's only about five miles from Mount Idaho where you reckon those boys will be waitin'."

"Thanks, Al."

After Al thought the animals were satisfied, he snapped the reins and the stage rolled slowly through the creek and after reaching the other bank it began to pick up speed again.

Just fifteen minutes later, they had to slow again before entering the wider Slate Creek. It was just another three miles to White Bird Creek and soon after that, they'd follow that big curve around Mount Idaho. Mitch hoped to see the Camas Plains stretched out before him without having to fight off four killers.

As they crossed Slate Creek, Mitch quietly asked himself, "Where are you settin' up, Hal?"

————

Hal Kingman, Frog Bouchard and Joe Hobart were almost exactly where Mitch expected them to be. But they weren't hiding behind any of the good ambush sites nearby. They were just sitting in their saddles waiting for Jack McFarland to trot around the curve to let them know that the stage was coming.

Joe was holding the reins to Jack's horse after Frog handed them over so he could roll a smoke.

Just as Frog lit up his cigarette, Jack came racing into view and didn't have to shout. There was only one reason for him to leave his observation post. The stage was approaching White Bird Creek.

———

Mitch was growing anxious when White Bird Creek came into sight. He didn't do anything as foolish as cocking Goldie's hammer, but he did do something that didn't seem to make much sense. He pulled his coil of rope from the roof and hung it over his left shoulder.

Al noticed and asked, "Are you plannin' on hangin' Ace out here, Mitch?"

"Nope. Just wanted to balance my saddlebags some."

Al snickered and shook his head. He had no idea what Mitch meant, but it sounded like the sheriff did, so it didn't matter what he thought.

———

Esther was still watching out her window as they approached White Bird Creek, so she didn't see Grace take down one of the canteens.

Grace smiled at Aaron as she unscrewed the cap and then lifted the full canteen to her lips. The canteen slipped slightly, and a gush of water splashed onto her white blouse.

"Oh, my!" she exclaimed as she quickly turned the canteen upright and handed it to Aaron.

Aaron held the canteen in his right hand and said, "I'd offer you my handkerchief if I wasn't tied down, Grace."

Grace smiled as she pulled her large green handbag onto her lap and said, "Thank you, Aaron, but I'll use my own."

Esther had been startled when Grace had reacted to her accident, but once she saw her hand the offending canteen to Aaron, she just resumed watching the outside landscape pass by. She suspected that Grace hadn't accidentally spilled the water but wanted to give Aaron a better view.

Aaron was definitely intrigued when Grace's blouse became translucent and clung to her skin.

As Grace opened her handbag to retrieve her handkerchief, she looked at Aaron's greedy eyes and smiled as she asked, "Would you close your eyes for a minute so I can dry myself?"

155

He may have been hoping that she'd let him watch but wasn't about to deny her request. So, he nodded and closed his eyes. He then was able to let his imagination fill in what his eyes could no longer reveal.

Grace glanced at Esther before she reached into her handbag and smiled at Ace who seemed to have been awakened by her exclamation.

When her hand left her handbag, it wasn't holding a handkerchief. There was a Colt New Army pistol in her grip and after setting her handbag on the seat, she leaned forward and hammered the barrel onto Aaron's head. He never opened his eyes as he slumped forward before Ace stopped him from falling to the floor.

Ace had masked the sound of the loud thump by coughing, so Esther never even knew that Aaron was now unconscious. She was still looking out her window when Grace slammed the Colt's barrel onto the back of her head. She fell against the side of the seat and Grace had to catch her to keep her from falling onto the aisle. It wasn't because she was worried about Esther. She needed to keep the driver and Sheriff Ward from being alerted if Esther fell against the door and sprung it open.

Once Esther and Aaron were no longer a problem, Grace quickly began releasing Ace from his shackles. The stagecoach had just crossed White Bird Creek when Ace Carr became a free man.

Ace kissed Grace and quietly said, "I was kinda surprised to see you, Jane. I almost gave you away when I spotted you gettin' into the stage. Is Hal waitin'?"

She nodded as she smiled and replied, "He's got the boys just on the other side of Mount Idaho. He said to give you the big Colt and you could use it and the deputy's pistol to shoot the sheriff and the driver through the wood. He said he'd stop the stage before it reached the curve."

"That's a real good plan. Let's make it happen."

She smiled and handed him the large Colt and as Ace ripped Aaron's pistol from his holster, she reached into her purse and pulled out a Colt Pocket revolver with a four-inch barrel.

Ace grinned and said, "That's my girl."

She then slid to the other side of the seat to give Ace the center so he could eliminate the two men on the driver's seat.

———

Mitch had no idea that the escape plan that Hal had devised had already begun as he continued to study the landscape for possible ambush sites. If someone had added that Ace had a blonde girlfriend to his wanted poster, he wouldn't have even let Jane Newsome, a.k.a. Grace Dubois, onto the stage.

So, as the stagecoach reached its normal speed, he watched the road ahead and could already see it disappear around the base of Mount Idaho.

He was still focused ahead when a .44 blasted through the driver's seat just two inches from his left elbow. He didn't even notice the second slug punch through the seat on the other side and then into the right side of Al's chest before he stood and swung away from the seat. He grabbed onto the side rail as more bullets ripped through the driver's seat including where he'd just been sitting. For just a moment, he glanced at Al and saw blood gushing from his side, then he lost his balance and tumbled from the rocking stagecoach.

He slammed into the ground but was lucky because he hit the outer edge of the berm rather than any of the nearby rocks. It still hurt when he landed then rolled down the side of the road into a grassy depression. He was stunned and had no idea what had happened as he lay on the ground.

————

Ace's second shots had been nearer the edge, so while the one he'd aimed where Mitch had been sitting, his second shot under the driver's position buried itself into Al's left butt cheek, but it wasn't even necessary. All it did was to increase his blood loss. The first bullet was lodged in his chest, and he was struggling to breathe. Al was able to keep control of the team as it raced toward the curve, but after seeing Mitch fall, he knew he had no protection.

It was then that he spotted four riders racing towards him and he realized that he was going to die. He was already growing dizzy, so he used his last bit of energy to snap the reins to get the team to move even faster and try to blow the outlaws off the road. He finally fell onto his right side, squashing Mitch's leftover sandwich as the coach rocketed down the road.

Hal had expected the stagecoach to slow, not go faster, but he stuck to his plan because he had no other choice. It would never make the curve at that speed. It had to be stopped.

"Let's stop that coach, boys!" he shouted as he set his gelding into a fast trot toward the onrushing stage.

They split up into two columns on each side of the road as the gap rapidly closed. Just before the team reached them, they all turned their horses around and set them to a canter, which was still slower than the racing stagecoach.

As the team neared them, Hal dropped back slightly and soon grabbed the harness. Jack McFarland took hold of the other side, and the team began to slow. It took more than another mile of travel to bring the stagecoach to a full stop.

The moment the wheels stopped turning, Ace bounded out of the stage.

He grinned at Hal and shouted, "You did a great job, Hal! I reckon I'll be drivin' the stage after I shove that driver's carcass off the seat."

"Where's Ward?"

"I got him first. He fell off a couple of miles back. The deputy's still out like a light inside, but he won't be for long."

Hal started to ask if Ace wanted one of them to put a .44 into the deputy when a sharp crack sounded from the coach's cabin.

Ace smiled and said, "That's my girl."

Hal glanced at the stagecoach and asked, "Jane shot him?"

"Sounds like it. Why don't you drag that dead deputy outta there?"

"Okay, boss."

Hal walked to the coach, opened the door and after seeing the bullet hole in Aaron's forehead, he smiled at Jane and said, "Nice shot. Ace asked me to get him outta there."

"Good. I don't want to have to look at him all the way to the ranch."

"Are you stayin' in the coach?"

"I have to keep an eye on that Jew woman."

After a long look at Esther, Hal said, "She is one mighty handsome Jew woman, Jane."

"Then you can be the first one to have her, Hal. Now can you please drag that body out of here?"

Hal nodded and grabbed hold of Aaron's corpse and yanked it out of the cabin. Once it was on the ground, he continued pulling it across the road until it was out of the way. He was about to return to his horse when Jane hurled the manacles and then the leg irons onto the road.

When Hal turned to look at her, Jane said, "I'm sure Ace would appreciate it if you left them on the deputy."

Hal leaned down, snatched the shackles then carried them to Aaron's body and dropped them onto his chest. He didn't look back at the coach before walking quickly to his horse and stepping into the saddle.

Ace was already in the driver's seat and had shoved Al's bloody body to the ground before he took the reins. He'd need a clean pair of britches when they got to their hideout because he was sitting in the driver's blood. When the men began moving, he cracked the reins, and the stage resumed its journey away from Millersburg. It was never going to reach the Camas Plains way station. By tomorrow, the stagecoach would be nothing but cinders and ash.

The stage had just begun to roll when Ace noticed the paper bag that had been knocked into the footwell when he'd dumped the driver's body. He was curious about its contents, so he reached down and picked it up. The wonderful odor

161

gave him his answer before he even opened it. Less than two minutes later, he tossed the empty bag into the wind and enjoyed the aftertaste.

———

Mitch still didn't know what had happened in the cabin but didn't waste time to think about it. He had to hunt down Goldie and was relieved to find his Winchester just a few feet away and apparently undamaged. He would have preferred to take a shot to make sure it was fully functional but had to be satisfied by working the lever. After a .44 popped out of the ejection gate, he released the hammer and picked up the unfired cartridge. After rubbing it clean on his britches, he dropped it into his pants pocket before collecting his saddlebags and the coil of rope. He looked down at his old blue hat and decided to leave it and buy a new one when he returned. He couldn't let any doubt of a return to Salmon City creep into his mind. He didn't want to return alone, either. He had to find Esther. He assumed that Aaron was already dead.

After he reached the road, he spotted the stage and riders heading away in the distance. They'd disappear around the curve soon, so, despite his banged-up muscles, he began jogging.

He didn't care if they spotted him. He even hoped that they would. He was confident that he could kill each one of them before they put a single slug into him. But he wasn't worried about himself as he trotted along the road. He was only concerned about Esther. He wasn't sure if she was still alive, but all he could do was hope that she was unharmed. If she was still alive, he was sure the outlaws wouldn't take long to make her wish she wasn't. He couldn't allow that to happen. He just had no idea how he could do it.

He soon spotted Al's body in the road ahead. It didn't take him long to realize that he was dead. He couldn't help Al but would slide his body from the road and leave a flag to let the next stage or wagon know what had happened. He knew that the way station would send someone to investigate the overdue stage, but they wouldn't start worrying until the sun was down. By then, he had to figure out how to take down the entire Carr gang.

Before he reached Al's body, he spotted Aaron's lying just off the road with the iron restraints laid across his chest. He felt sick knowing that he'd failed to prepare for the attack but immediately set it aside. He had work to do and decided to deal with Al first.

He walked to Al's body, then quickly dragged him over the edge of the road. There was a stand of river birch nearby, so he hurried to the trees and picked up one of its discarded branches from the ground. River birches shed branches like hounds shed fur.

He returned to the body, jammed the branch into the ground, then opened his saddlebags and pulled out one of his two towels. After tying it to the end of the branch, he made sure it wasn't going to blow away before he pulled a stubby pencil and his small notebook from his shirt pockets. He wrote a minimal explanation, then ripped the page from the notebook and stuck it in Al's shirt pocket leaving the upper third exposed.

He then folded Al's arms across his chest and said, "I'll make 'em pay for what they did to you, Al. I'll get your stage to Lewiston, too. It'll be late, but I'll get it there."

He crossed the road to Aaron's body then took a knee and tossed the manacles aside before slowly removing the badge from his deputy's chest and slid it into his right pants pocket. He stood, took hold of his arms then dragged it back across the road and laid it beside Al's body. After folding his arms across his chest, Mitch stood and looked down at the two dead men but had no more words to say. He turned and after reaching the roadway, he began jogging again.

———

As the stagecoach passed around the curve, Esther's eyes fluttered. She was utterly confused, and her head was pounding. She tried to focus but the world was spinning before her eyes.

She was still trying to orient herself when she heard Grace say, "Welcome back, Esther. Have a nice nap?"

Esther closed her eyes again before turning and slowly reopening them again. The dark cabin helped with her dizziness, but she was still completely baffled.

Jane said, "It's just you and me in here now. I tried to hit the deputy in the head hard enough so I wouldn't have to waste a bullet but had to shoot him anyway. I was close to shooting you too, but I didn't want to spoil the boys' fun."

Esther turned toward the voice and asked, "What are you talking about?"

"I suppose I should tell you the bad news. At least it's bad for you. It's good news for me and Ace, though."

Her answer didn't help Esther understand anything. It only made things even more confusing.

When Esther didn't say anything, Jane said, "I'm not some silly girl named Grace Dubois. My real name is Jane Newsome and I've been Ace's girlfriend since I was sixteen. He's driving the stagecoach now and we're heading to our nice little hideaway."

Esther's mind was trying to make sense of what she had just heard but there was only one thing that prompted an immediate question.

"Where's Mitch?"

"That's the rest of my good news. Your sheriff boyfriend is lying dead on the ground a few miles back. Ace shot him and the driver through the stagecoach wall. See the new holes up there? You can even see blood dripping through some of them."

Esther tried to keep everything from dancing as she looked above the front seat. She could see bouncing spots of light but nothing distinct. But they were enough to make her believe that Mitch was dead. Her almost useless eyes filled with tears before she covered them with her hands.

Jane laughed then said, "Now isn't this a surprise. You actually seem to be fond of the dead sheriff. You don't really think that he'd marry a Jew, do you?"

Esther didn't bother to reply as she was overcome by the anguish of her loss. Just a few days ago, Mitch had barely been able to talk to her, but now, just as she was sure that she loved him and he loved her, he was dead. She'd never be able to tell him how she felt, nor would she hear his voice again. She no longer cared what Jane or Grace said or did. But if those four bastards came near her, she'd use her medical expertise to make them suffer in ways that they wouldn't expect.

The coach continued its descent toward the Camas Plains. The four outriders had no idea that the sheriff they believed to be dead was just three miles behind them and the man driving the stage never bothered looking back. If Ace had taken the time to look at the bullet holes he'd created in the other side of the driver's seat, he would have noticed the lack of blood. But he was so relieved at being a free man again and looking forward to spending the night with Jane that he didn't even think about Sheriff Mitchell Ward.

Esther's disorientation was fading, but she wasn't about to let Jane know it. She had stopped crying, but kept her eyes closed. She also decided not to give up hope. She needed to believe that Mitch wasn't dead. He may be injured and lying by the side of the road, but he couldn't be dead.

As she sat with her eyes closed, she would occasionally roll her head slightly to give Jane the impression that she was still dizzy. She was using the time to figure out a way to escape from the stage. But even if she made it out the door, she knew she wouldn't get far before she was shot. It would probably be Jane who did pulled the trigger because Esther now believed she was even worse than the prostitute that she had imagined her to be just a short time ago. She was a cold-hearted killer just like her boyfriend and the other four.

When she thought of Jane being Ace's girlfriend, Esther wondered if there were more women at the gang's hideout, wherever that was. But Jane's earlier comment about the boys needing their fun now sent chills down her back. Jane was probably the only woman at their place and none of the men would dare touch her as she was Ace's property. She shook off the fear by concentrating on how she would defend herself.

167

It was a much more acceptable way to pass the time as the coach rolled on.

———

When Mitch lost sight of the stage, he slowed to a fast walk to catch his breath. He hadn't even noticed that the coil of rope was still hung over his left shoulder, or he would probably have tossed it aside. He had no idea how he'd be able to catch the fast-moving stage, but he wasn't going to rest until he had a plan.

His first step was to reach the curve which would give him a long-distance view of the Camas Plains. He'd be able to see the stagecoach and watch where it goes. He already had a good guess that he hoped was better than his earlier one about where the gang would spring their trap. He still couldn't understand how Ace had managed to surprise Aaron. He was sure that his deputy had been distracted by the blonde woman, but he couldn't imagine how Ace could subdue Aaron with Esther watching. He expected that he would have heard at least one scream when Ace made his move. *But how did he know that his gang was waiting?* There was only one possible way he could have known. It also answered his first question about the lack of any kind of warning before those .44s blasted through the driver's seat.

He was still walking quickly toward the curve when he added the blonde woman to Ace's side of the ledger. If she hadn't been the sweet young thing she pretended to be, but had been hired by Hal Kingman to help Ace, it made the escape more plausible. Then another clue he'd overlooked popped into his mind. Those first shots blasted through the seat at the same time. Ace must have had two pistols and only the blonde could have provided the second.

He was less than a mile from the curve when he had a clearer picture of what had probably happened. As angry he was about his failure, he was even more concerned about Esther. He had to figure out a way to kill them all before they hurt her. He wasn't going to be treat the blonde bitch and differently either.

———

The stagecoach was about halfway down its long descent to level ground when Ace decided to ask Jane whether she had killed the Jew woman. He turned to yell down to her, but when he put his right hand onto the driver's seat, he caught a splinter in his thumb. He cursed and yanked his hand away.

But after he extracted the long splinter, he looked back at the other side of the seat and realized that he didn't see a single drop of blood on that half.

He exclaimed, "Son of a bitch!" before he shouted, "Hold up, Hal!"

As he pulled back on the reins, Hal and the others slowed their horses. When they were all stopped on the descending roadway, Hal walked his horse closer to the coach and loudly asked, "What's wrong, boss?"

"There ain't any blood where the sheriff was sittin'. He might be alive."

"I saw him fall, Ace."

"I wanna make sure he's dead. Send somebody up there to check on him while the rest of us keep goin'. He can catch up later."

Hal nodded then pointed to Frog Bouchard and said, "Frog, you got them twin Colts. You just head back to where that sheriff landed and put some .44s into his carcass to make the boss happy."

Frog grinned as he asked, "Can I have his guns, Hal?"

"Take anything he's got then come to the ranch and show 'em to Ace so he can sleep better."

Frog snickered then set his charcoal gray gelding to a medium trot as he passed the coach.

Soon the stage was racing back down the incline following the three riders as Frog rode uphill.

Inside the cabin, Esther still pretended to be disoriented, but had been close to cheering when she heard Ace yell that Mitch hadn't been shot. Yet as pleased as she was with that possibility, she was still concerned. He could have been badly injured by the fall, and now the outlaw who was riding back to the spot where he'd fallen could do what Ace had failed to do.

But on the other hand, if Mitch hadn't been hurt, he might spot the outlaw first. After he used Goldie to kill him, he'd have a horse and be able to follow them much faster than he could if he was on foot. It was all just conjecture, but she was determined to focus on the positive. With her eyes still closed and her head lolling every so often, she imagined Mitch putting bullets into every one of those five curs and their one bitch.

———

Mitch cursed his lack of stamina as he had to slow down. But he was almost to the curve and should soon be able to see the stagecoach out on the Camas Plains.

The way station was still more than thirty miles away and he was sure that the gang wasn't intending to reach it. While they could pretend that they were the scheduled run, it would be a risky situation because they didn't know who might be at the way station.

There were two turnoffs shortly after the road leveled onto the Camas Plains. One turned south toward the Salmon River and ended just twelve miles later in the tiny town of White Bird, which was in his county. The other was just a mile before that intersection and headed northeast. That road wasn't used very often. Fifty miles after the turnoff, it reached Elk City which was about the same size as Millersburg. About halfway to Elk

City, the road had to cross the Clearwater River. He'd used the ferry a couple of times and suspected that was the road they would probably take.

The Camas Plains were beginning to spread before his eyes when he heard hoofbeats and stopped in his tracks. He quickly realized that Ace had decided to send someone back to make sure he was dead. He'd expected someone to come back to look for his body as soon as they'd stopped the stage, but now he needed to get out of sight.

He hurried to the other side of the road near Mount Idaho and soon reached a jutting slab of granite. He shrugged off the rope and his saddlebags and cocked Goldie's hammer. He was sure that Ace and the others would hear his gunshot but didn't think it would matter. He figured that they'd be expecting to hear at least one when the man he sent back to check on him put a few rounds into the hopefully injured lawman.

Mitch hoped it was only one because as good as he was with his Winchester, he couldn't expect to be lucky enough to put down two or more without getting return fire.

He stayed pressed against the rock for what seemed like an eternity as the hoofbeats grew louder. Now he was pretty sure it was a lone rider and decided to fire more than one shot even if he killed the outlaw with his first .44. He hoped he could identify the man before he squeezed Goldie's trigger but was committed to the shot.

Frog didn't believe that the sheriff was even alive. He was just hoping that the lawman carried a bunch of cash with him. He would have needed some money when he got to Lewiston, so maybe he'd have up to a hundred bucks in his pockets. Even if he didn't have much cash, Frog heard that Ward had one of those Smith & Wesson cartridge pistols and that was almost as good.

As he reached the curve, he was smiling in anticipation of what he might find. He'd soon find something that he hadn't expected.

Mitch knew the rider was almost there. He didn't have his finger on the trigger because he'd learned early in his lawman career that it wasn't a good idea.

The hoofbeats were growing even louder and Mitch prepared to step onto the road and put the man's back in his sights. He wasn't going to give him a warning, either.

Frog soon exited the curve and looked at the road laid out before him. He didn't see anyone moving but noticed a fluttering flag of sorts in the distance. He mistakenly believed that the sheriff was still alive but so badly injured that he couldn't walk. He'd made the flag, so he'd be found and rescued.

He laughed and as he pulled his right-hand Colt, he loudly said, "I'm just gonna help you get to hell, Sheriff."

Mitch was grateful when he heard Frog's loud declaration as it branded him as one of Ace's men. There had been the small chance that the man was an innocent traveler.

As soon as Frog passed, Mitch took two long strides into the road and quickly aimed Goldie at the outlaw who was only twenty-five yards away. He let his sight settle, then squeezed his trigger.

Frog was still grinning when Mitch's .44 slammed into the left side of his back just two inches above his heart. He rocked in the saddle and didn't even have time to turn when Mitch's second shot punched into the other side of his back.

He dropped his Colt then slowly tipped over the left side of his saddle and dropped awkwardly to the ground. Mitch was sure he was dead after watching how he hit the ground, but still ran towards him. He wasn't worried about the outlaw but didn't want his horse to run off.

He soon caught up with the gelding and took his reins. He led him back to Frog's body and while still keeping a grip on the reins, he reached down and unbuckled his two-gun rig. He didn't care about the Colts, but still retrieved Frog's fallen New Army. Before he returned it to the holster, he pointed it in the air and began firing. He stopped after four then returned it to the empty holster. He rolled the gunbelt and put it in Frog's saddlebags. He hoped that if Ace and his three remaining men heard the shots and would appreciate their partner's enthusiasm.

He took Frog's hat and pulled it on but left Frog where he was so whoever passed by was more likely to stop. He then led the gelding back to where he'd left his saddlebags and rope. He quickly checked the contents of the outlaw's saddlebags before he hung his over the top and tied them down before hanging his coil of rope on the side. He mounted and wished that Frog had been taller but left the stirrups where they were for now.

Before he started the gelding moving, he removed Frog's Winchester from his scabbard and slid Goldie inside. He pushed Frog's repeater into his bedroll behind the saddle then started the horse toward the curve at a walk.

He'd only taken Frog's hat in case he was spotted. At the distance he expected to see them, he was sure they couldn't notice the five-inch difference between his and Frog's height. His jacket wasn't that much of a different shade than Frog's so he was confident that none of them would realize that their partner was the one who was now dead.

———

The stage had already taken its right turn toward Elk City as Mitch had anticipated, but none of them had heard the gunfire. They were moving quickly and the pounding of the twenty-eight combined hooves of the team and riders' horses drowned out any distant sounds.

Jane thought that Esther wouldn't regain consciousness before they reached the ranch and was getting annoyed with Esther's silent head-spinning. She was so irritated that she almost wanted to shoot her but knew that Hal and the others wouldn't be pleased if she did.

So, she turned to the window and yelled, "Ace, let me outta here!"

Ace laughed and shouted, "You boys keep ridin' while I let Jane come up here!"

As the three riders continued at their same fast pace, Ace pulled the stagecoach to a stop and waited for Jane to join him. He didn't even think about Esther as he waited for his woman to take the seat beside him.

Once she climbed onto the driver's seat, Jane slid close to Ace and let him know how happy she was to have him back. He let the reins drop as he expressed his appreciation. The stage didn't move for almost five minutes before the gang leader finally released Jane, then retrieved and snapped the reins. It wasn't moving as quickly as the three riders, who were already more than a mile ahead.

As soon she felt the familiar rocking motion, Esther opened her eyes and couldn't believe they'd left her alone. She had expected Jane to return at any moment, so had continued her mock dizziness. But once the stage started moving again, she knew that she finally had her opportunity to escape. She'd heard Ace yell to his men to keep riding, so she knew she had to get away soon.

Esther looked at the passing ground and all she saw was prairie grass. It wasn't ideal, but she didn't have a lot of options. She slowly opened the door and took a peek up at the driver's seat. She could see Ace's left arm and shoulder, but not his head.

She took a firm grip on her purse, then hurled herself from the coach. She tried to cushion her fall, but still landed on her left knee and felt a sharp pain rocket up her leg before she rolled into the nearby tall stalks of grass. She hadn't uttered a sound but believed that Ace would have heard her hit the ground or feel the coach lurch when she jumped.

So, as soon as she stopped rolling, Esther looked at the disappearing coach and expected to see it come to a sudden stop. But it didn't. She watched as it continued down the road as if nothing had changed. She kept it in view for another five minutes until it was almost a mile away before she realized that they didn't know she'd escaped.

While she wasn't sure if they even cared, Esther wasn't about to wait around to find out. But as she began to stand, another stab of pain from her left knee reminded her that walking or crawling wasn't an option, at least not for a while.

Esther rolled onto her back and stared at the late afternoon sky overhead. She had no water but had the bag with the two turkey sandwiches in her purse.

They'd turned off the main road a good two miles back and she'd never get there with her knee injury. She didn't know where the outlaws would take the stagecoach, but once they reached their hideout and opened the door, they'd know she'd escaped. Then she'd have to worry about them finding her.

She had no other choice but to stay flat and out of sight. After sunset, if her knee was feeling better, she'd try to walk to the main road. She knew she couldn't make it all the way to the way station, but there was bound to be more traffic soon. Maybe Mitch had killed the outlaw they'd sent to kill him, and he would be looking for her. It was her best hope, and it soothed her mind as she closed her eyes. She'd depend on her hearing to let her know if anyone was coming.

But now that she was free, Esther had another urgent issue. She slid her dress to her waist and painfully wiggled her underpants to her knees to relieve herself. After soaking the prairie, she gritted her teeth, lifted her back from the ground and crabbed a few feet to her left before collapsing onto her back again. After pulling her bloomers up and her dress down, she felt much better, but hoped that the odor didn't attract any coyotes or wolves. They would still be better than the animals who were sitting on the stagecoach driver's seat or riding their horses.

———

When Mitch rounded the curve, the late afternoon sun allowed him a good view of the distant stagecoach as it churned up dust on the eastbound road to Elk City. What puzzled him at first was when he spotted the riders a good distance out front. Then as he continued to watch, he noticed that there were two specks on the driver's seat. It was too far away to identify either of them, but because he was on Frog's horse and there were three riders, he assumed that one of them was Ace. He didn't think that Esther had suddenly turned outlaw, so that left the blonde. If that was so, then maybe she hadn't been hired for the job. She was probably just another gang member who served a very different purpose. Then again, there may have been another gang member or two who hadn't earned wanted posters yet. He didn't think it was likely because there were no spare horses behind the stagecoach and no self-respecting outlaw would ride double if it wasn't necessary.

He set the gelding at a fast trot as he made his descent to the Camas Plains. Now that he was on horseback, he knew that he had a good chance to catch up to the gang before they settled into their hideout. He should reach the eastbound road in less than an hour. By then, he'd lose sight of the coach, but he'd be able to follow their trail easily. His biggest concern was for Esther. He had to stop them from hurting her but had to avoid hitting her with an errant shot, so he couldn't just open fire at the stagecoach.

179

He was still watching the stagecoach when he saw a large object leave the stage and wondered if they had discarded something. He felt his stomach twist when he realized it was probably a body. It had to be Esther, and he prayed that she was still alive. He'd try to find the her when he made the turn. It appeared to be about two miles from the main road.

Mitch now had another mystery. If there were no spare horses and the blonde was on the driver's seat with Ace, *who was left to toss her from the stage?* As the gelding kept its fast downhill pace, Mitch realized there was only one very hopeful explanation for what he'd witnessed. If they hadn't bound Esther and the blonde was riding up top with Ace, then Esther could have escaped. He just found it hard to believe that they could be so careless as to leave her alone, but as the gap between the stagecoach and where she'd jumped grew, Mitch knew he needed to get to that spot before they realized she was gone.

———

By the time Mitch was approaching the turnoff, the three riders were still a couple of miles ahead of the stagecoach.

Hal looked behind him and snickered before saying, "I reckon the boss is glad to see Jane."

Jack asked, "What are we gonna do with the Jew woman?"

Hal looked at him with raised eyebrows then laughed before replying, "You gotta be kiddin', Jack! You didn't see her but I'm tellin' ya that she's worth havin'. I ain't never had no Jew woman before. I wonder if they're different where it counts."

"I reckon not. But I was askin' about what we were gonna do with her after that? We can't keep her on the ranch. Sooner or later, she's gonna run."

Joe said, "I reckon she'll be joinin' her sheriff boyfriend in a day or so."

Hal shook his head as he replied, "That's a real waste, Joe. It's too bad she ain't a Christian. She sure is fine lookin' woman. She's even easier on the eyes than Jane, but don't go tellin' Ace or Jane I said that."

Joe grinned as he said, "I'm kinda surprised Jane didn't put a slug into her after shootin' the deputy."

Jack shook his head while saying, "For such a pretty young thing, Jane sure is a viper inside."

Hal shrugged then said, "She's Ace's woman, so she can be whatever she wants. We'll be reachin' the ranch pretty soon. When we get there, we gotta make room in the barn for the stagecoach."

Neither Joe nor Jack replied as they looked ahead. They'd soon spot the boulders which marked the entrance to their almost invisible ranch hideout.

———

After turning off the main road, Mitch slowed the gelding. He had lost sight of the stagecoach much earlier after he'd reached level ground. If Esther had escaped, when they discovered she was no longer in the cabin, they might come back. What was worrisome was that Esther was nowhere to be seen. He could understand why she'd try to stay hidden in the prairie grass for a few minutes after escaping, but she should be on her feet by now.

He focused mainly to the north side of the road but mixed in the occasional glance to the east in case they did come back.

Esther still had her eyes closed as she listened for the sounds of an approaching rider. Her knee was still painful and there was a painful lump on the top of her head courtesy of the blonde bitch. She was thirsty, hungry and the only wall against becoming fatalistic was the hope that Mitch was still alive.

Then she heard the faint sound of hooves approaching. She almost shouted her relief, but quickly realized it might be the man they called Frog returning after killing Mitch. She opened her eyes and just turned her head toward the road. The grass limited her vision, but she thought she could see enough to identify Mitch and his faded blue hat.

Mitch was just fifty yards away when she'd opened her eyes, but didn't see her hidden among the thick, tall grass. It didn't help that her clothing also made for good camouflage. If she'd dressed like Jane, he would probably have spotted her no matter how tall the grass was.

He knew she had to be close and slowed the horse to a walk. Then he began studying the ground on the left side of the road searching for disturbed ground.

As he passed Esther, all she could see was Frog's hat, so she closed her eyes again believing that the outlaw had done what he'd been ordered to do.

Mitch didn't see where she landed but when he lifted his eyes just past the road's edge, he pulled the gelding to a stop. He'd almost missed the path of flattened grass. He stood in his short stirrups and followed the disturbed growth. When he spotted Esther's shoes, he was elated, but it only lasted a few seconds. She wasn't moving.

He quickly dropped to the ground and took the horse's reins before walking off the road. Just as he was about to call her name, her right foot moved just enough to let him know that she wasn't dead.

He let go of the reins and trotted the last twenty feet.

Esther had heard the horse stop and wasn't surprised to hear the outlaw coming. She pretended to be dead so she could take him by surprise, but then her foot betrayed her just before he arrived.

She ignored her painful left knee as she quickly sat up and opened her eyes to defy the killer. But as her eyelids parted, she thought her mind was playing an unforgivable joke on her. Then her ears joined in the illusion.

"Esther!" Mitch exclaimed before he dropped to his knees beside her.

Esther reached to touch his face as she asked, "Mitch?"

Mitch grinned as he took her hand and replied, "Yes, ma'am."

"But how…that man…they said…all those bullets."

"I'll tell you later. Are you hurt?"

"My knee is painful and probably swelling. I have a bump on my head from a pistol barrel. But other than that, I'm okay."

"Let's get you outta here in case they come back. You can tell me what happened when we're mounted on Frog's horse."

"Okay."

Mitch snatched her purse from the ground and set it on her lap. Then he put his left arm behind her back before sliding his right beneath her thighs. He slowly stood and lifted her from the prairie which let her left knee bend.

Esther grunted from the pain, but then rested her head on Mitch's shoulder as he carried her back to the horse. It was only a few seconds, but despite the pain, Esther found the sensation incredibly soothing.

When Mitch stopped beside the gelding, he said, "I'm gonna stand you up until I get in the saddle. Okay?"

She raised her head from his shoulder and replied, "Alright. Can I hold onto something?"

"Take hold of the bridle."

"Okay."

Mitch carefully lowered her legs to the ground. Once she was standing with most of her weight on her right leg, he waited until she had a good grip on the bridle.

He picked up her fallen purse again and hung it over Goldie's stock before asking, "Are you ready?"

"Yes, sir."

Mitch stepped into the stirrup and swung his leg high and wide to get past Frog's Winchester. Once in the seat, Mitch took Esther's free hand, then after she released her grip on the bridle, he took her other hand.

"I'll support your weight, so go ahead and step on my left foot."

He lifted her as she placed her right foot on his left and just three seconds later, she was sitting in front of Mitch with her arm around his waist. Her left knee was angrily protesting, but she didn't care.

Mitch wheeled the gelding back to the road, took one more look to the east then turned the horse in the other direction.

"Are we going to the way station?"

"No, ma'am. That's a good four-hour ride. We'll turn left on the road to the way station. There's another turnoff that heads southwest to the town of White Bird. The town is about fifteen miles away, but the Ferguson ranch is only about five. We can get there in less than an hour."

"What will we do when we get there?"

"I'll have Earl Ferguson and his missus take care of you for a day or so and have them send one of their ranch hands to the way station to let 'em know what happened."

"You're going to go after the gang; aren't you?"

"It's my job, Esther. How did they do it? I found Aaron's body."

"The last thing I remember was that the blonde woman, whose real name is Jane Newsome, spilled some water on her blouse then asked Aaron to close his eyes while she dried herself. I thought she was flirting, so I looked away. Then everything went dark, so I didn't see or hear anything. After I came to, Jane said that she shot him after she had knocked him out but didn't tell me much more than that. I'm sorry, Mitch."

"You don't have to apologize. I'm the one who screwed up. I shoulda checked her purse. I didn't even suspect that they had a woman in the gang."

"I didn't suspect her either, Mitch. But I think she's just as vicious as any of them."

"It still eats at me."

"Could I have some water? How did you manage to stay alive? Are you hurt at all?"

As he reached for the canteen, he replied, "Just a few bruises."

He managed to unscrew the cap while reaching around Esther before handing it to her.

As she began to quench her thirst, Mitch told her what had happened after that first bullet erupted through the driver's seat. After she was satisfied, she wasn't able to replace the cap as she tightly gripped Mitch but just held onto the open canteen as he continued.

He told her about finding Al, creating the flag and writing the note. He told her how he'd shot Frog but left his body in the road as a stronger message. He almost finished when they turned onto the southwest road.

She handed Mitch the canteen and as he took a few swallows, she asked, "Are you at least going to wait until the morning to go after them?"

He wrapped his arms around her, screwed the cap back on, then hung the canteen in place before saying, "I can't wait.

They'll be expectin' Frog to show up. If I don't get there in a few hours, they'll figure out that I musta killed him. Then they'll be waitin' for me."

"But you don't even know where they are, Mitch! How can you find them in the dark?"

"Before I even left Frog in the road, I noticed that he wasn't carryin' any food in his saddlebags. That meant that they didn't have to eat while they were waitin' for the stage. They can skip a meal or two, but I figure that they didn't have to ride very far to set up their ambush. I know this end of Nez Perces County pretty well and in the direction that they were headed, there is at least one abandoned farm and a couple of failed ranches. I'm sure they're usin' one of 'em as a hideout. They wouldn't ride the twenty-five miles to the Clearwater River and take the ferry."

"But it's going to be dark pretty soon."

"I'll be able to follow that coach's tracks even by the light of the sliver of a moon. At least now I won't have to worry about who's inside their hideout. I'm really glad you escaped, Esther."

She looked up at him and said, "I'd ask you to wait for help, but you wouldn't wait even if I asked; would you?"

"Nope. I let 'em get away once and I got Aaron killed. I don't want anyone else to get hurt because of my mistakes."

"If I didn't have my bad knee, I'd ask to come along. I may not be able to shoot a gun, but you might need me to repair some new holes."

Mitch smiled as he said, "I don't expect to get any more of 'em, ma'am. I intend to make a few, though."

Before she could reply, Mitch said, "There's the Ferguson's ranch house."

Esther looked to the front and spotted the low house among four other buildings. One was a barn, but she didn't know what the others were.

"Do you know the Fergusons?"

"I suppose you're only askin' if they're gonna be upset 'cause you're not a Christian."

"Sort of."

"Well, I don't know 'em well enough to tell you one way or the other for sure. But I do know that they're good folks, and I'm sure that they'll feed you and give you a bed for the night."

"I guess that's all I should expect."

"You should expect a lot more from folks, Esther. You're as close to a perfect person as I ever met, and they should be honored to have you as a guest."

"Do you really think of me that way, Mitch?"

Mitch paused before replying, "Yes, ma'am. I always have and you've never done anything to change my opinion for the worse."

"I'm not perfect, Mitch. You just haven't spent enough time with me to discover my many flaws."

Mitch wanted to say something more meaningful as they approached the access road. But he would soon leave her with the Fergusons and might not see her again, so he decided to let it remain unsaid until he returned.

All he did say was, "Maybe."

Esther looked at his face in the waning sunlight and wasn't sure how to respond to his terse reply. She had hoped that he would have told her that he wanted to spend more time with her to find those flaws. But she realized that she was probably expecting too much. Mitch had been almost transformed over the past few days, and she needed to give him more time. Now she worried that their time together would be measured in minutes, not years.

After the short ride down the access road, Mitch pulled up then carefully lowered Esther to the ground. After she took hold of the horse's bridle, he dismounted. He didn't carry her but acted as her crutch as they climbed the three steps onto the ranch house's porch.

He was about to call out when the door opened and Earl Ferguson quickly asked, "What happened, Mitch?"

"I'll tell you after we get inside, and Esther gets to sit down."

Earl stepped back and said, "Come on in."

After Mitch helped Esther through the doorway, Earl closed the door and shouted, "Maggie, Sheriff Ward's here with a lady!"

As his wife hurried from the kitchen, Mitch lowered Esther onto a cushioned chair then turned to the ranch owner.

He rapidly said, "I was takin' Ace Carr up to Lewiston for trial when his gang sprung him lose. They killed Al Crenshaw, who was drivin', then tried to kill me, but missed. I fell off the coach and they killed my deputy and knocked out Miss Cohen. I was gonna track 'em down on foot, but they sent one back to make sure I was dead. I shot him and took his horse. I need you and Maggie to take care of Esther while I go after them. I should be back by tomorrow afternoon."

Maggie stepped beside her husband and had heard most of what Mitch had told him. She looked at Esther, who was still covered in dust before she moved a chair close to hers and sat down.

Before Earl could ask a question, Mitch held up his hand and said, "Esther can tell you what happened, but I need to get movin'. She hurt her knee when she jumped out of the stage and her head has a big lump from a pistol barrel, so she's kinda hobbled."

Earl replied, "Don't worry. We'll take good care of her, Mitch."

"Thanks, Earl. Can you send someone to the Camas Plains way station to let 'em know what happened? They can send a telegram to Sheriff Borden in Lewiston and another one to my deputy, Pete Carter, back in Salmon City. I left my deputy and Al Crenshaw's bodies off the road but marked the spot with a flag."

"I'll send my top hand to the way station shortly. Do you need a fresh horse?"

Mitch thought about it for just a few seconds before replying, "I appreciate the offer, Earl, but I don't want to waste the time."

Earl shook his hand as he said, "Good luck, Mitch. I'm glad you're our sheriff, and I hope you're still wearing that badge for another thirty years."

Mitch smiled and said, "I'd be satisfied with another day right now, Earl."

He was about to leave when he looked at Esther and found her big brown eyes already focused on him.

He removed Frog's hat and stepped closer before he took a knee beside the chair.

Esther thought he was going to propose, but what he said was almost as good.

He leaned close and whispered, "I only bought that big house 'cause I was hopin' that you'd share it with me."

She wanted to kiss him, but he quickly stood, smiled at her then waved to Earl and Maggie before stepping out the door.

After he left, Maggie smiled at Esther and said, "I think our sheriff is smitten with you, Esther. Let's move you to the kitchen and get you fed. Then we'll let you rest in one of our spare bedrooms."

Esther was still gazing at the closed door as she nodded. She slowly stood and Earl helped her down the hallway behind Maggie. Mitch's whispered revelation would have filled her with ecstasy last night, but now it only added to her fear of what might happen to him in the next few hours.

CHAPTER 6

Once outside, Mitch spent a few minutes adjusting the stirrups to Frog's saddle. He slid Frog's Winchester out of the bedroll and carried it and Esther's purse to the porch. He opened the door slightly, glanced inside then put her purse onto the floor and leaned the carbine against the wall before closing the door. He didn't see any advantage to having Frog's Winchester. If he couldn't do the job with Goldie and his Smith & Wessons, then he wasn't as good a shot as he believed.

The gelding wasn't in bad shape which added to his belief that the gang's hideout was on this side of the Clearwater River. But he led it to the nearby trough and let it have some water while he filled the canteen at the pump. When he mounted, he wished he'd grabbed that last sandwich from the driver's seat. He had enough jerky and hard tack to keep his hunger at bay, but Mary and Alice's creation was equal to a full meal.

He set the gelding to a fast trot and soon turned right on the road. Soon, the sun would be setting, and he wanted to find where they'd taken the stagecoach as quickly as possible. As he rode, he tried to figure out how long they'd wait before they began to suspect that Frog had failed. He soon calculated about two hours after he found where they turned off the road. Until then, if they spotted him in the dim moonlight, they'd probably think he was Frog. But they might leave their hideout sooner when they discovered the empty stagecoach.

———

The three riders had already unsaddled their horses and left them in the barn. Hal and Jack were in front of the house waiting for the stage while Joe was in the kitchen firing up the cookstove. Joe did most of the cooking because Jane refused to be treated like a housewife. He wasn't a bad cook, so no one complained, including Joe. He even seemed to enjoy it.

When Hal turned the team down the access road, he spotted Hal and Jack but didn't wave.

He hugged Jane and said, "I can't wait to get you into bed. You already got me primed."

"That's why I'm here, Ace. But can we get something to eat first? I'm starving!"

"I suppose I can hold off long for a little while. Maybe I'll use that woman we got in the coach while you're eatin'."

Jane stared at him and was almost ready to slap him when he laughed. She smiled as she leaned over, kissed him and let him have a few gropes to let him know that no other woman could ever take her place.

Hal turned to Jack and said, "Jane sure is a piece of work. One minute she's a whore and before you know it, she's a snarling witch who won't blink an eye before she shoves a butcher knife into your gut."

Jack snickered then replied, "You got that right. She may be one pretty woman, but I wouldn't wanna turn my back on her."

"I feel that way, too. But watchin' what she's doin' to Ace makes me kinda anxious to drag that dark-haired woman outta the coach, throw her to the ground and take her right there."

Jack nodded then said, "I'll watch and when you're finished, it'll be my turn. Joe can have her when he finishes feedin' us."

Both outlaws turned their attention back to the approaching stage. The wheels had barely stopped turning when Hal trotted past the team and yanked open the door. It took him a few seconds to realize that it was empty.

He slammed the door then looked at Ace who was stepping down and shouted, "*Where the hell is she?*"

Ace hung onto the side of the stagecoach as he sharply asked, "She ain't there?"

Hal took a step toward Ace as he reached the ground and angrily replied, "No, she ain't."

Ace helped Jane down, looked at her and asked, "Do you know when she coulda jumped out?"

Jane glared at Hal for a couple of seconds before turning her blue eyes back to Ace and answering, "I have no idea. I didn't hear her leave and I thought she was too dizzy to go anywhere."

Ace looked at Hal and said, "Even if she ain't hurt, she can't get very far. There's no place for her to go within twenty miles. But I don't think she's worth huntin' down."

"That's easy for you to say, boss. You got Jane. I was really lookin' forward to spendin' some time with her. Jack was anxious and I'm sure Joe wanted to have some fun with her, too."

Ace put his hand around Jane's waist as he said, "If you and Jack wanna saddle your horses and go lookin' for her in the dark, be my guest. I'm gonna have some chow and then me and Jane are gonna get reacquainted. I think you should fill your belly before you go anywhere. Besides, Frog might find her on his way back."

Hal grumbled, "Maybe. But he'd probably spoil her first and I should be the one to do that."

Jane smiled and said, "That's only if she's a virgin, Hal. From what I heard; I imagine she spread her legs for Sheriff Ward back in Millersburg if not earlier."

She laughed then guided Ace away from the stagecoach.

Hal was far from mollified as he and Jack led the team and the attached stagecoach to the barn.

―――――

The sun disappeared below the horizon just as Mitch reached the location where he'd found Esther. He used the last vestige of sunlight to let his eyes follow the stagecoach's ruts as they faded away into the distance. Now he'd have to ride slower as he had to depend on the weak moonlight to illuminate the tracks.

While he knew that the first of the abandoned ranches was less than an hour's ride away, he had to be prepared to run into some of Ace's men who might be searching for Esther. It was also possible that there was another place they could use for a base that he didn't know about.

He was still focused down the eastbound road as the horse plodded along. Goldie was still snug in its scabbard, but he was confident that his excellent night vision would give him enough warning to get his Winchester ready to fire. He wasn't that hungry but figured he didn't know when he'd find the gang's hideout and didn't want any complaints from his stomach at an inopportune time.

Mitch kept his eyes focused on the ruts as he reached behind him and opened his right saddlebag. He rummaged past his boxes of cartridges and spare clothes until he reached his leather pouch of beef jerky. After pulling it free, he began ripping the salty beef strips with his teeth. He ate four large pieces before returning the pouch to the saddlebag and taking the canteen from the left side of the saddle.

He drank more than he needed because he wasn't sure when he'd get another opportunity. But it was still more than half-full when he replaced it. As the continued to ride into the deepening darkness, he tried to devise a rudimentary strategy. The horse probably carried him for another two miles before he realized that it wasn't possible. While he knew about the abandoned properties, he hadn't visited any of them.

But when he'd been trying to build his strategy, he recalled that one of those empty ranches had an unusual access road. Most ranch and farm access roads were easily visible from the nearest roadway. But the one about eight or nine miles further down this road was an oddity. Either the original ranch owner wanted his privacy, or he assumed that Mother Nature had planned the gateway to his new spread. Whatever his reason, when he built his ranch, he started his access road between a pair of enormous, jagged boulders. The gap was wide enough to allow two wagons to pass through side-by-side. He had originally laid a log across them and posted his ranch's name on a board nailed to the log. He couldn't remember the name of the place, but it didn't matter. He wished that he could recall if the log was still there but suspected that if Ace decided to use the abandoned buildings as his hideaway, he wasn't about to advertise its location. The ranch's ranch house and barn weren't visible from the road unless a rider knew where to look, at least when approaching from the west as he was now. Between the trees and a small hill, only small sections of the ranch house and the barn could be spotted from the road before reaching the access road.

The tracks soon passed the first abandoned ranch. The next one was a derelict farm on the north side of the road. He should reach its access road in twenty minutes and was sure that Ace's gang wasn't using it as their hideout. There was one more failed ranch on the left a couple of miles past the farm before he reached the hidden access road. The more he thought about it, the more he became convinced that he'd find Ace and his three men and one woman at the ranch. He wondered if Ace had fixed it up and wouldn't be surprised.

Over the past four years, the Carr gang did most of their damage in Sheriff Borden's Nez Perces County. The line separating his county from Lemhi County was just five miles behind him, so technically, he was out of his jurisdiction. He didn't think that Lyle Borden would complain. Their jurisdictions were fluid which was why he was so familiar with this road.

His confidence in finding them increased his anxious anticipation as he passed the empty farm. He was so convinced that he was nearing their hideout that he expected to see the shadows of approaching outlaws at any moment.

―――――

By the time they'd unharnessed the horses and returned to the house, Hal and Jack had decided to wait another hour for Frog to return. If he didn't come back by then, they'd saddle their horses and ride west. They planned to ride as far as the main north-south road before turning back but hoped to find the woman more than Frog.

They entered the kitchen and found Ace, Jane and Joe already eating, so each of them grabbed a plate and scooped spiced beans from the pot and then slid some baked ham from the platter before taking their seats at the table.

Before he took a bite, Hal said, "If Frog ain't back in an hour or so, me and Jack are gonna ride down to the main road to look for him."

Jane smiled as she said, "But you're really looking for the Jew woman; aren't you?"

Hal didn't answer but cut a large piece of ham from his plate and rammed it into his mouth while Jane giggled.

Jack said, "Watchin' you and Ace got us all fired up, Jane. So, you're damned straight we wanna find her."

Jane was still grinning when she asked, "Do you want to see if she's different from normal women, Jack?"

Before Jack could reply, Hal swallowed and snapped, "You know she's the same, Jane. You're just jealous 'cause she's prettier than you and has bigger titties."

Jane's smile vanished as she snarled, "It's not what a woman has on top that makes her a woman, Jack. It's how she uses what she has below her waist. That Jew woman probably doesn't even know what she has down there."

Before either Hal or Jack could say another word, Ace exclaimed, "Enough! I don't care if you boys stay or go. It don't matter to me whether you wanna go look for her or Frog. Just quit insultin' Jane."

"Sorry, boss," Hal said without a hint of sincerity.

"Don't apologize to me. You offended Jane. Tell her you're sorry for what you said."

Hal's jaw muscles bulged as he looked at Ace's girlfriend and said, "Sorry, Jane. I didn't mean nothin'"

Jane knew that Hal wasn't sorry at all but was enormously pleased that Ace had forced it out of him.

She smiled and said, "I accept your apology, Hal."

He nodded then continued eating as Jack looked at him for a few seconds before digging into his food. Hal was more annoyed that Jane had smiled than he would have been if she'd slapped him.

———

Earl had dispatched two of his men to the way station rather than one just in case they bumped into any of Carr's gang. He'd also sent his two youngest hands south with a wagon to retrieve the deputy and driver's bodies and take them to

Millersburg. He didn't give them instructions about what to do with the outlaw's remains.

Esther had already finished her much-appreciated dinner and after giving herself a sponge bath had changed into one of Maggie's nightdresses. Maggie was sitting in a chair beside the bed as Esther rested comfortably. Her purse was sitting on the night table.

Esther smiled and said, "Thank you for your kindness, Maggie."

"You're more than welcome, Esther. Your knee doesn't look too bad. How does it feel?"

"Not nearly as bad as it did before. I don't think it's serious and the small amount of swelling should be gone by tomorrow."

"I think that you've got yourself a very good man, Esther. I don't know the sheriff as well as you do, but everyone in the county appreciates his integrity and good nature. I wish he'd waited until morning and for more men to join him, but I'm not surprised that he decided to chase after those killers tonight."

Esther didn't comment on Maggie's assumption that Mitch was her man or that she knew him well, but replied, "I would have been surprised if he stayed. He blames himself for letting Ace Carr escape and for his deputy's death. Now I only hope that he doesn't let that guilt push him into making a mistake."

"I'm sure he'll be careful. Tomorrow, we'll probably watch him drive the stagecoach down our access road without a scratch."

Then after a pause, she asked, "You aren't going to continue to Lewiston; are you?"

"No. I have a house in Salmon City waiting for me now."

Maggie smiled as she stood, then patted Esther's shoulder as she said, "At least now everyone will know why the sheriff bought such a big house."

She then blew out the lamp before she left the bedroom.

Esther was sure that Maggie hadn't overheard what Mitch had whispered to her, so she was surprised that even this far from Salmon City, people heard about the almost empty big house. After Maggie closed the door, Esther closed her eyes and prayed that everything Maggie had said would come true.

————

Mitch slowly walked the gelding to the closer of the enormous boulders and pulled up. He sat in the saddle for a minute or so listening for any unnatural sounds. When he was satisfied that no one was coming, he tapped his heels and the horse stepped past the first boulder and didn't even need guidance before he began turning right. The horse wanted to join his friends waiting in the corral.

When Mitch spotted light in the distance, he pulled the horse to a stop again to study the layout. In the dim light of the waning moon, he could barely make out the roof of a barn. But the light coming from the ranch house's windows helped him to estimate the range. It was about six hundred yards away, so after the brief reconnaissance, he wheeled the horse around and passed back between the boulders. He glanced overhead, didn't see the log then turned west to hide behind one of the large rocks.

He dismounted and led the gelding to a nearby bush he couldn't identify in the dark and tied him off. He then slid Goldie from the scabbard, took one box of the Winchester .44 cartridges from his saddlebags, dropped it into his left jacket pocket with his Model 1 and walked back to the gap.

He stood in the center of the two massive boulders and watched the distant ranch house. He suspected that it wouldn't be long before someone rode towards him to hunt for either Esther or Frog. He hoped when he spotted them, that there would be two of them and they would come down that access road and not cut across the open ground. If they headed straight for him, he wouldn't hesitate to fire without warning. Once he eliminated them both, it would only leave Ace, his blonde devil, and one more man inside the ranch house.

He didn't care if the three in the house heard the gunfire. In fact, it would be to his advantage if they did. They'd know they were being hunted and who was doing the hunting. Let them feel fear for a change. How he dealt with the last three would depend on whether they took the offense or decided to defend the ranch house. All of the male outlaws were wanted dead or alive, but he wasn't about to give the female criminal a free pass. She'd killed Aaron in cold blood when it wasn't even necessary.

———

As Mitch stood in the dark at the end of the access road, Hal and Jack left the ranch house through the back door and walked to the barn. Hal was still fuming but his anger wasn't directed at Jane. He was used to her haughty behavior. He wasn't happy because Ace took her side when she was the one who'd started the short war of words. After all, he was the one who had created the plan to keep Ace from hanging. It had worked perfectly, and while he admitted that Jane had played her part very well, Ace would have still been on his way to Lewiston if it hadn't been for him. He could have just taken control of the boys and given Jane to Jack, but he'd been loyal. And this was the thanks he got for all he'd done. What made it even worse was that Jane hadn't even had to ask Ace to make him apologize. Ace wanted to please Jane even if it meant humiliating the one man who kept him from climbing the gallows steps.

As they entered the barn, Jack asked, "Are we takin' the same horses?"

"Might as well. We ain't gonna push 'em. I just hope that Frog didn't find the woman already. He shoulda been back by now and that's the only reason for him bein' late."

"Maybe the sheriff wasn't dead and killed Frog."

Hal threw his saddle blanket over his roan and said, "C'mon, Jack. You saw him fall after Ace blasted all those slugs through the driver's seat."

"But Ace said that there wasn't any blood on that side."

"So? Think about it. He opened fire and by the time we heard the gunfire, the sheriff was already on his way to the ground. The other side had all that blood 'cause the driver stayed on the seat just bleedin'. The boss ain't gonna miss from four feet away, Jack."

Jack huffed as he continued saddling his horse. He wasn't as sure as Hal was that Frog had found a dead or even wounded Sheriff Ward. But even if the sheriff plugged Frog, Jack figured that he'd head to the way station to let them know what happened. He wouldn't dare face four dangerous men, especially in the dark. Just finding them would be almost impossible.

They finished saddling their horses and led them from the barn. They mounted and set their mounts to a slow trot as they passed the front of the ranch house.

———

Mitch hadn't seen them leave the house or the barn, but as he watched the light coming from the ranch house's windows, the one on the right side flickered on and off as the two men rode by. He waited until they passed the second window to find out how many were coming before he trotted around the side of the boulder.

He set up with his left shoulder pressing against the rock. He'd let them get within thirty yards before he opened fire unless they spotted him sooner. He pulled back Goldie's hammer and waited for them to get close enough so even the weak moonlight would be sufficient to mark them clearly.

Mitch listened for their hoofbeats but before he detected the distinct sound, he heard their voices. He didn't know what they were talking about, but the subject didn't matter. By the time he picked up the sound from their horses, he already had a good estimate of the range.

———

Hal and Jack were still discussing Frog's absence as they headed for the rocks. If the sun was up, they would have just angled to the road, but they didn't want to risk letting their horses snap an ankle by stepping into a gopher or prairie dog hole.

They were about two hundred yards from the end of the access road when Hal said, "I swear, Jack, if Ace wasn't so good at plannin' those heists, I woulda let that sheriff take him to Lewiston to get hanged."

Jack snickered then said, "No, you wouldn't, Hal. I reckon you're just as good as he is at plannin'. It's just that he's the boss and we're part of his gang. We're makin' good money at it, too."

"I suppose you're right. But I think Jane is gettin' too big for her britches."

Jack guffawed before saying, "You ain't never seen her in britches, Hal. If you did, then you'd know she needs a little more meat on her backside to fill 'em out."

Hal's sour mood vanished as he laughed then said, "I'd sure like to see that Jew woman in a pair of britches. I reckon she'd fill 'em out real nice."

"I never got a good look at her. Is she really that pretty with a good figure to match?"

"She's a lot more than pretty and I reckon she'd look a lot better if she dressed like Jane. That's why I wanna find her."

They were passing a hundred yards as Jack said, "Now I gotta see her too, and I wanna see all of her."

Hal just grinned but didn't say another word. He was beginning to think that maybe he should tell Ace that he deserved his own woman for saving his hide. He wasn't concerned if Esther didn't want to become his personal bedmate.

———

Mitch had been able to hear smatterings of their louder conversation as they drew closer, and those few words erased any moral concerns he may have had about shooting two unsuspecting men. To Mitch they stopped being men a long time ago.

He brought Goldie level and waited. He could make out the two shadowed riders but wanted them closer to ensure that he got them both. His heart began thumping, so he tried to calm his excitement. He didn't want anything to throw off his aim.

They were sixty yards out now, then…fifty…forty…thirty.

Mitch had his sights on the shorter man and squeezed his trigger. Goldie popped against his shoulder as he shoved the loading lever forward.

Hal was still thinking about having Esther in his bed when Goldie's muzzle flashed in front of his eyes. The Winchester's sharp report arrived at almost exactly the same moment that its .44 ripped into the center of his chest. The bullet drilled through his sternum, shattering the flat bone before it tumbled through the soft tissue, ripping apart his right lung and blood vessels. He could only gasp before rocking once and falling off the right side of his saddle.

Jack was stunned for a few seconds, so by the time he reached for his Colt, he saw a second flare of light then felt Mitch's second shot hammer into the lower left side of his chest. The slug wasn't deflected like the bullet that hit Hal, but after splintering his ninth rib, it passed through his heart as if it didn't exist. The spinning missile then exited through Jack's back before eventually ending its deadly flight by burying itself into the ground twenty yards behind him.

Jack didn't wobble but dropped onto his horse's neck. Mitch brought a fresh cartridge into Goldie's chamber and was about to fire again when Jack slid from his horse and plowed face first into the ground.

Mitch lowered his Winchester and quickly trotted toward their skittish horses. He just administered quick kicks to the two dead men to verify their condition before walking to the horses and taking their reins. He hurriedly led them down the access road but checked behind him to see if anyone exited the ranch house.

Ace and Jane didn't hear a thing as they were heavily engaged and making enough of their own noise to mask the distant gunfire.

Joe was in the kitchen cleaning up after supper and as he scrubbed out the pot that he'd used to heat the beans, he thought he heard something outside and stopped. Sudsy water dripped from his fingertips as he listened. If Mitch had taken that third shot, Joe would have realized that someone was firing a Winchester. After another thirty seconds of silence, Joe shrugged and returned to cleaning the pot.

Mitch led the horses around the boulder and tied them to Frog's horse. He didn't release Goldie's hammer as he trotted back to the access road and watched the light coming from the distant ranch house. He had expected the house to be dark by the time he reached the access road and was surprised to find the windows were still illuminated. He expected Ace would blow out the lamps at any moment.

As he focused on the house, he wondered if Ace and his lone male supporter would wait in the dark for him to show up, or if they'd leave and try to find him in the dim moonlight. The smart thing to do would be to stay inside. One could sleep while the other kept watch. They could even use Ace's girlfriend to take a shift. By the way Esther had described her, she would probably be just as dangerous with a Winchester or a pistol.

After five minutes of waiting for the lamps to be extinguished, Mitch finally released his Winchester's hammer. He couldn't imagine why they hadn't reacted to the gunfire. They had to have heard it. He began to believe that they might be trying to lure him close enough to let the light from the windows give them an idea of where he was. But even that was risky because those lamps would let him know where they were long before they discovered him.

He was so puzzled by the well-lit ranch house that he didn't know what he should do next. Mitch continued watching for more than forty minutes when the flames from the lamp wicks finally began to die. One by one, the windows joined the dark night until the house was almost invisible.

He exhaled, then turned and walked back to the horses to decide how to deal with the survivors. By the time he reached the three saddled animals he began to feel drowsy. He slid Goldie back into its scabbard and leaned against Frog's horse.

He guessed it was somewhere around ten o'clock, but he'd been up before dawn. It didn't even seem as if it was the same day anymore. It felt as if he'd helped Aaron load Ace into the stagecoach a week ago.

He sighed and began unsaddling Frog's gelding. He'd been ridden for most of the day and was more in need of rest than the other two. After stripping the animal, he began removing the saddle from Hal's horse. He relied on the wanted poster's accuracy about Jack McFarland's height to identify his horse.

Twenty minutes later, the horses were all clear of their tack, and were grazing on a patch of prairie grass or nibbling on the bush.

He spread Frog's bedroll onto the ground, then took off the outlaw's hat and tossed it aside before laying down. He still wore his jacket with its two older model pistols and the box of .44s. He knew he needed sleep more than anything else right now. He'd try to stay awake as long as he could in case Ace, or the other outlaw came looking for Hal and Jack. He hadn't moved their bodies for a couple of reasons. He didn't think they deserved respectful treatment and if Ace did ride down the access road, he'd stop to look at the carcasses. If he did, Mitch was sure that he'd release a loud expletive which should act as an alarm just in case he was still asleep.

He didn't realize that he didn't need to stay awake at all and could have drifted into a deep sleep as soon as he was on his back. Ace and Jane were already clinging to each other as they slept in their birthday suits and after Joe finished his cleanup, he blew out the lamps and headed for his room. He wasn't worried about Jack and Hal. He figured that they probably found the woman and Frog, so they wouldn't be back until morning.

Sheriff Mitchell Ward was the only one on the ranch who was still awake as the new day arrived at midnight.

_____

Esther had fallen asleep much earlier. After Maggie closed her door, and Esther finished her prayers for Mitch's safety, she spent a few minutes trying to imagine where he was and what he was doing. But even her vivid imagination wouldn't have come close to what had actually happened while she slept. Before she entered her dream world, she shifted her thoughts to what her life would be like when Mitch returned. She'd never been inside his big house, but it wasn't the house

214

that filled her dreams. It was the man who made the large and unnecessary purchase just to share it with her at a time when he was unable to even speak to her.

CHAPTER 8

It wasn't Ace's discovery of the bodies that awakened Mitch, but they had been found. The pair of coyotes were now fighting over Jack's carcass rather than each of them having his own smorgasbord.

The loud snapping and yapping startled Mitch out of sleep as the gentle light of the predawn filled the sky.

He hopped to his feet and grabbed Goldie before he realized that he hadn't been disturbed by a human voice. He still walked to the access road and spotted the two coyotes at war.

He didn't cock Goldie's hammer, but pulled the .22 caliber Smith & Wesson from his left jacket pocket. He wanted to drive them off, but not wake up anyone in the ranch house.

As he cocked the small pistol, the coyotes called a truce and turned their eyes to the human intruder. They didn't snarl or even bare their teeth, but just stared at him. Mitch kept walking closer as he raised the Model 1.

Neither coyote shifted an inch as the man continued his approach. They knew the danger that humans posed but weren't about to give up the banquet.

When Mitch was just twenty feet away, he aimed the pistol at the larger animal on the right. At twenty feet, even the short-barreled pistol was accurate enough for his purpose. He squeezed the trigger and the .22 spat from its muzzle with a sharp crack. The coyote yelped when the small bullet struck his tail, then whipped to his left and ran off. His competitor didn't want to feel any pain, so he chased after his partner.

Mitch watched them until they disappeared before he slid his pistol back into his jacket pocket. He then dragged Jack McFarland's torn body back down the access road and after passing between the boulders, pulled the bloody corpse behind the eastern boulder. After leaving it, he returned to Hal Kingman's body and dragged it to join Jack's. When the two dead outlaws were lying next to each other, Mitch returned to the horses and slid Goldie back into its scabbard. He finally answered nature's call before taking Jack and Joe's slickers and heading back to their bodies. He covered them with the gray rubberized canvas, but it wasn't because he no longer wanted to see them. He needed to keep more scavengers away until at least until noontime.

Once they were under the slickers, he began collecting rocks and laying them on the slicker's edges to keep them down. He only needed enough weight to keep the wind from uncovering the bodies. When he was satisfied with his work, he walked to the access road, then stopped to check the distant ranch house for smoke. Nothing was visible, so he returned to the horses to have a jerky and hard tack breakfast.

He hoped that Ace and the last outlaw would soon head his way to look for Jack and Hal, but thought it was more likely that if anyone rode away from the ranch house, it would only be Joe Hobart. He was expendable.

———

It was almost an hour later when Joe left the ranch house, but it wasn't to saddle his horse. He scurried to the privy in the bright morning light before he returned to cook breakfast. After leaving the small house, he glanced down the access road. While it was still early, he was growing concerned. Even if Frog, Jack and Hal had all found the woman they should have returned before dawn. They hadn't brought any food with them, so after they finished with the woman, they could kill her and head back. Despite what Hal had told Jane, Joe couldn't imagine that he'd bring the Jew woman to the ranch.

He continued to the ranch with a grin on his face as he imagined the fireworks that would erupt if Hal tried to keep her in the same house with Ace's wildcat of a woman.

Joe entered the kitchen and opened the cookstove's firebox. He soon had a fire going and as he walked into the pantry, he heard footsteps coming down the hallway. He knew it was Jane and as he watched, he saw her rush past without a stitch of cloth covering her. He forgot his reason for being in the pantry and focused on Jane as she ran out the door. When she was out of sight, Joe shook his head and began to collect his fixings. It was one hell of a way to start a day.

Jane returned more slowly a few minutes later and was unashamed of her nakedness as she smiled at Joe and walked down the hallway. She was proud of her body and was still smarting over Hal's comparison with that Jewish woman.

About a minute later, when Ace passed through the kitchen on his way to the privy, he didn't seem to be remotely upset that Joe had seen Jane in the raw. Joe assumed it was because Ace saw him as a tool and not a man. It didn't matter to Joe. He was simply proud to be a part of Ace's gang.

When Ace reentered the kitchen, he asked, "Where are Hal and Jack? Did Frog get in last night?"

"Nope. I was just wonderin' about 'em. Even if they found that woman, they shoulda been back by now."

"Frog is still gone?" Ace asked with raised eyebrows.

"Yup. When I blew out the lamps, I figured he was with Jack and Hal. Now, I ain't so sure."

Ace nodded then walked back through the kitchen door and headed for the barn. He agreed with Joe that they should be back by now but wanted confirmation. He soon discovered that all of their horses were still missing. After what Hal had said to Jane about the Jew woman, Ace suspected that he might try to sneak her onto the ranch and keep her in the barn's loft or the old bunkhouse. Now he knew they were still out there somewhere, and he began to believe that none of them would ever return.

After leaving the barn, Ace stared down the empty access road for a minute before walking to the back of the ranch house.

As soon as he entered, he said, "Joe, I figure that I was right after all, and that damned sheriff didn't die before he fell off the coach. He probably got Frog, then took his horse and followed the tracks left behind by the stagecoach. Hell, a blind man coulda followed 'em. He mighta got Hal and Jack, too."

Joe stared at him as he asked, "Do you really figure he did all that, boss?"

"We can't risk that he didn't."

"What do you wanna do now?"

"Let me think about it."

As Ace began to mull his options, a fully dressed Jane entered the kitchen and asked, "Did I hear you right, Ace? You think Ward killed all three of them?"

Ace just nodded as he continued to figure out how to deal with the relentless lawman.

Jane didn't have to think. She just smiled at Joe and asked, "You can find them for Ace; can't you, Joe?"

Joe glanced at Jane before looking at Ace. He wasn't at all pleased with her question because Ace would probably accept it as more of an order.

Ace said, "I think that's a good idea. Joe, you don't need to do anything but scout around. As soon as you see somethin' movin', get back here and tell me what you saw. Okay?"

He reluctantly said, "Okay, boss," then when he glanced at Jane's smug face, he wanted to slap her silly, but that would be tantamount to suicide.

Ace put his hand on Joe's shoulder and said, "You're a good man, Joe."

Normally, Joe would be inflated with pride when Ace praised him at all, but this time, he thought it sounded more like a eulogy.

Joe didn't even nod before he turned and walked out the back door. He headed for the barn but kept his eyes focused on the access road as he walked. He decided that he wasn't about to take that route to leave the ranch. He'd ride diagonally before he reached the road. He soon entered the barn and began saddling his horse.

After his light brown mare was ready, he walked to the far wall and grabbed one of the Winchesters they kept on a crude rack. He cycled the lever to make sure it was loaded then released the hammer. After snatching the ejected cartridge from the floor, he wiped it clean before shoving it into the loading gate. He slid the repeater into the scabbard then led the mare out of the barn.

Joe then mounted and adjusted his hat. At least the sun would be at his back when he reached the road, so if he did run into that sheriff, he'd have that advantage. Joe felt he needed a lot more if they did cross paths. Any man who could outshoot Hal and Jack was a much better shot than he was. He preferred knife work. When he did have to use a Winchester, it was always when the other man wasn't looking, like that deputy in Lewiston. If he spotted Sheriff Ward, he wasn't going to risk trying to shoot him, even if he wasn't looking. He'd head back and let Ace deal with him.

———

Mitch had seen Joe enter the barn and when he led his saddled horse out, Mitch knew that Ace wasn't going to join him. He had already saddled Frog's horse and moved the other two across the road to small gully where he'd tied them down with his old rope. He kept watching Joe ride away from the barn and when he angled to the west, he knew he wasn't going to use the access road.

He quickly untied Frog's horse and led him closer to the western boulder. He mounted then pulled Goldie and cocked the hammer. He suspected that as soon as Joe came into sight, he'd check both directions. It was just a question of how far away he'd be when he reached the road.

He continued to sit quietly in the saddle waiting for Joe to appear.

———

Before he reached the road, Joe's head was already on a swivel. He saw the two boulders but nothing else. He was just a hundred yards from the road when he stopped looking to his right because he hadn't seen anyone on the eastern side of the boulders. Now the early morning sun that Joe considered to be his greatest advantage had become his biggest enemy. When he had checked the road east of the boulders, the harsh morning light had been blinding, but he was satisfied that the sheriff wasn't there. He now concentrated on the much more visible westbound road.

As he neared the roadway, he could see a good two miles west and was relieved when he didn't see anyone but realized that it also made it more likely that all of the others were dead. He was grateful that with the sun at his back, he'd see the sheriff long before the lawmen would be able to pick him out of the sun's glare.

Mitch spotted Joe just before he crossed the edge of the road about eighty yards away and started Frog's horse at a walk as he held Goldie in his right hand. He was waiting for Joe to look his way before he pulled his Winchester into firing position. But when Joe reached the road, he just turned west and set his horse to a medium trot.

Mitch was surprised but nudged the gelding into a slightly faster pace to close the gap. He could take the shot any time now but wanted to get as far away from the ranch house as possible, so Ace wouldn't know that he was alone with his witch woman.

Joe continued along the road and was growing more relaxed with each passing minute without seeing the sheriff. While the blazing sun kept him from checking his backtrail, if he had looked, Joe would be shocked to see Mitch just fifty yards behind him.

Mitch was beginning to wonder if Joe was just being used as bait, so he took a small risk and quickly checked behind him in case Ace was springing the trap. But the road was empty, so he returned his focus to the front and slowed the gelding to match Joe's speed.

They rode for another ten minutes before Mitch thought they were far enough from the ranch house. Because he had good light and was only facing one killer, Mitch decided to give Joe a chance to surrender.

He let his reins drop then set his sights on Joe before shouting, "Put up your hands, Joe! You're under arrest!"

Joe was beyond startled when he realized who had yelled at him. But he didn't know how close he was and wasn't about to face the noose. So, he dropped onto his mare's neck and set her to a gallop.

Mitch hadn't been surprised by Joe's reaction, so as soon as he dropped down and his horse accelerated, he fired. He'd aimed low, just above Joe's gunbelt, so even though his

Winchester's muzzle was bouncing, he was confident that he'd hit either a part of Joe or his horse's butt.

His .44 rocketed just four inches above Joe's saddle seat and ripped into his lower back, just to the left of his spine. Because Joe was bent over his horse's neck, the slug passed through his small intestines then after drilling through his stomach and diaphragm, it lodged in his heart's right ventricle.

It was difficult for Mitch to even know if he'd hit Joe at all as he prepared to take a second shot, but when he saw the reins drop from Joe's hands, he lowered Goldie and released the hammer before sliding it back into its scabbard. He took his reins and set the gelding into a faster pace to catch up to Joe's horse. While Joe may have been unable to hold his reins, he could still be alive.

Just before he reached the right hind quarter of the mare, Joe suddenly dropped to off the left side and bounced as Mitch rode past. He took control of Joe's horse and by the time he slowed the animal, Joe's inert body was already a hundred yards behind them.

Mitch turned the gelding around and led the mare to Joe. He tied the mare to his saddle then dismounted. He was going to just drag the corpse off the road but changed his mind. He lifted Joe from the ground and slid it over his saddle. He didn't bother tying it down because he only had to ride a couple of miles to reach the two boulders.

After setting Frog's horse to a slow trot, he began to plan how to finish the job. He was sure that Ace would be watching the access road now that he was alone. Then Mitch modified it to Ace being the only man in the ranch house. He didn't discount the danger posed by the blonde demon, but he expected that Ace would want to kill him more defiantly. Jane would choose her mode of murder depending on whether her boyfriend survived the expected gunfight.

He soon spotted the boulders in the distance and was grateful for the hills and rocks that hid the ranch house. If Ace was watching, he'd only have a small window to spot him on the road. He still hadn't decided what he'd do after he reached those boulders.

———

Inside the ranch house, Ace and Jane were still in the kitchen. Jane had cooked breakfast after Joe had gone and after eating, they were now just having more coffee.

Jane looked at Ace and asked, "You don't expect Joe to come back; do you?"

Ace slowly shook his head before replying, "Nope. I was just buyin' time. I figure that damned sheriff is gonna come ridin' down our access road soon enough."

"What are you going to do?"

"I ain't figured that out yet."

"You'll have to stop him before he gets here, Ace. You have to protect me. If you don't kill him first, he'll probably come in here and rape me for killing his deputy."

"You know he won't do that, Jane. He's more likely to either shoot you or take you to Lewiston to get hanged."

"So, you won't care if I get shot or hanged?"

"I didn't say that. I just said he ain't the kind who does what men like me do. That's all."

"Do you want to wait for him on the front porch or in the saddle?"

Ace looked at her for a few seconds before saying, "I'm gonna get a Winchester and stand out front. If you wanna be entertained, you can see which one of us dies."

Jane leaned across the table and kissed him before quietly saying, "I don't want to see you die, Ace. I want to watch that sheriff get shot and then die in a lot of pain."

Ace smiled at her then rose and said, "I'm gonna get ready now."

Jane smiled up at him before Ace turned and headed down the hallway. He kept his favorite Winchester in their bedroom.

After he left the kitchen, Jane finished her coffee then waited for Ace to leave the house through the front door before she walked into their bedroom and closed the door behind her.

––––––––

Mitch had reached the boulders and tied off Frog's horse before sliding Joe's body from his mare's saddle. As he dragged it past the access road, he glanced toward the ranch house, but Ace hadn't appeared yet.

After leaving Joe's body with his partners' covered corpses, he walked back to the two saddled horses and pulled Goldie from its scabbard. He then walked back to the gap between the boulders then stopped in the center of the access road where he stood with his Winchester's barrel resting on his right shoulder. He continued to watch the ranch house and only had to wait another two minutes before Ace stepped through the doorway.

While he stood in the morning light framed by the two boulders, Mitch began to plan how to deal with Jane, assuming he survived the gunfight with Ace. She was so unpredictable that he wasn't sure what to expect. If she was holding a gun, then he'd treat her no differently than any other outlaw. But he didn't know how good she was with a Winchester or even a pistol. She was less than three feet away when she shot Aaron and he was unconscious. He doubted that she would shoot it out, even if she was loyal to Ace. But after another minute, he recalled that she didn't know he'd found Esther. Jane might think that Mitch still believed she was the innocent Grace Dubois. While it might not make any difference, it was his ace in the hole.

Just thirty seconds later, he watched Ace step down from the porch. When he stopped and just stood in front of the house, so Mitch gave him a few more seconds to spot him before he slowly began walking down the access road. He let Goldie's muzzle drop toward the ground before he took that first step.

Ace had seen Mitch before he started walking, so when he noticed that the sheriff was heading his way, the gang leader without a gang began his own march away from the house. When he saw how the sheriff was holding his rifle, he cocked his Winchester's hammer and let its muzzle drop toward the ground.

The sun was on Mitch's left and Ace's right, so there was no advantage for either of them. The long gap between them closed slowly as neither man increased his pace. But as the distance diminished, each of them understood that it would be a battle of nerves as much as skill.

Behind the ranch house window, Jane was mesmerized by the drama unfolding in front of her. While she desperately hoped that Ace would kill that righteous lawman, she'd already made her contingency plans if the sheriff won the gunfight. She wasn't going to die if she could avoid it.

Mitch estimated that he and Ace were now about three hundred yards apart, yet their Winchesters' muzzles were still pointing straight down. It was a cool spring morning without a cloud in the sky and just a light breeze blowing from behind him. It was perfect weather and almost too pleasant for a gunfight.

Ace had his index finger on the trigger as he carefully strode toward the sheriff. He knew about Ward's reputation with his Winchester and wished this was a pistol fight. But it wasn't his call. He licked his upper lip as he watched the distance between them slowly decrease.

While he didn't notice that Ace had his finger already on his trigger, Mitch had his own reason for keeping his right index finger with the others as they gripped Goldie. He'd learned long ago the hazards of having it on the trigger of a cocked gun. He didn't want that first bullet burying itself into the ground at his feet. He needed to put it where it counted.

They were two hundred yards apart when Ace began to focus on Mitch's rifle. While the folks who made the Winchester placed the effective range of their repeater at one hundred yards, even he knew it could cause serious injuries at a greater distance. It may not be a killing shot, but it could do enough damage to end the gunfight before it started. Sheriff Ward might have enough confidence in his ability to take his first shot at any moment.

Mitch wasn't about to waste his first shot because he didn't want to take a second. He'd wait for Ace to initiate the action, but as soon as he began to move his Winchester, Mitch would turn clockwise ninety degrees before firing. It was his normal shooting stance and would make him a slightly smaller target as well.

When they passed the hundred-and-fifty-yard mark, Ace felt sweat beading on his forehead despite the cool air. He tried to shake his growing nervousness but knew it would only get worse with each step. *Why didn't Ward take his shot?*

Lemhi County Sheriff Mitchell Ward didn't fire but continued to focus on Ace's eyes rather than his Winchester. He knew he could hit Ace at this range, but he didn't want to just wound him because he had no idea where Jane was. If he had to stop to keep Ace from bleeding to death, she could use the opportunity to put a .44 into his back.

The two men passed into Winchester effective range yet continued without change. Ace was beginning to feel twitchy and knew he had to fire soon. He just wanted a few more yards to be sure. When they approached the eighty-yard mark, Ace was confident he could hit the sheriff and finally made his move. His right foot had just settled flat on the ground, and he was bringing his left foot forward when his right arm began lifting his Winchester. His left hand crossed in front of his torso to support the repeater's forearm.

As soon as he saw Ace's arms begin to move, Mitch planted his right foot and began to turn while bringing Goldie level.

Ace almost had his sights level when his index finger exerted just enough pressure to move the trigger and release the hammer. The firing pins struck both sides of the rimfire cartridge setting off the almost instantaneous chemical reaction inside the brass cylinder. The expanding hot gas blasted the lead bullet out of the firing chamber into the barrel where its grooves did their job. The .44 spun out of the muzzle at more than eleven hundred feet per second. It had to push the cool air out of the way and fight gravity's tug as it shot across the 235-foot gap. Less than a quarter of a second later it buzzed past Ace's intended target, missing his back by more than eight inches.

Mitch didn't know how close Ace's shot had been before he let Goldie's sights settle on Ace as he levered in a fresh round. He squeezed his trigger and just another quarter of a second later, Ace felt the hammer blow of the sheriff's .44 when it slammed into the left side of his chest. He only had time to gape at his killer before he dropped to his knees and let his repeater drop from his hands before falling onto his face.

Mitch had already cycled Goldie and had it aimed at the downed outlaw chief as he quickly crossed the eighty yards. He could see the ranch house a couple of hundred yards behind Ace's body but didn't know where Jane might appear or what she would do now that she was alone.

When he reached Ace, he didn't bend down, but just delivered a hard kick to his left shoulder. When he didn't move, Mitch released Goldie's hammer and lowered its muzzle. He didn't want to get any closer to the ranch house until he knew where Jane was hiding. It didn't take very long for her to reveal herself. It was what she did when she left the house that surprised him.

He was just staring at the house when the door flew open, and Jane rushed across the narrow porch and raced towards him. She wasn't holding a pistol and had nowhere to hide it, so Mitch began to walk toward the house to meet her.

Jane slowed down after just a few seconds and when he was close enough, Mitch soon noticed the flow of tears that was streaking down her face. He initially thought she was weeping for her boyfriend, but then realized it wasn't sorrow in her eyes. He was puzzled for another few seconds before he realized the scheme she was planning to use to avoid being hanged.

Jane stopped twenty feet away and as she wrapped her arms around herself, she exclaimed, "Thank God! You killed that bastard! Thank you so much, Sheriff. But be careful! There are four more of them somewhere."

Mitch stepped closer and just as he reached her, she opened her arms and threw them around him. He expected she might try to grab one of his pistols or plunge a hidden dagger into his back, but she didn't. She held him tightly as she trembled and sobbed.

He looked down at the top of her blonde head and asked, "What happened, Miss Dubois? Where is Esther?"

Jane lifted her damp blue eyes to him and shakily replied, "Didn't you find her, Sheriff? She escaped yesterday but I...I was too afraid to move. I'm so ashamed."

Mitch played his part and put his left arm around her and said, "I'm the one who oughta be ashamed, Miss Dubois. But don't worry about those other four men. I already killed all of 'em, so you're safe now. And maybe we'll find Esther on the way back, too. Can you tell me what happened? All I know is that the driver's seat began exploding and I fell off. Then I found the dead driver and my deputy. I figured I might never be able to find the stagecoach when the outlaw named Frog Bouchard showed up. I reckon Ace sent him back to make sure I was dead. I got him instead. So, how did Ace get himself free?"

Jane sighed and said, "I spilled some water on my dress and asked your deputy to close his eyes while I dried myself. I know now that I shouldn't have done that. After he closed his eyes and I was looking down at my chest as I dried myself, I heard a loud clink and a thump. When I looked up your deputy was already fallen to the side and the outlaw was taking his pistol. He threatened to shoot me and Esther, so all we could do was watch when he began shooting through the coach.

Esther was horrified when she saw you fall and I was, well, I was just terrified.

"Then all sorts of things started happening. The stagecoach raced away, and I thought we'd crash, but those four men must have been waiting to ambush the stagecoach, because they were able to stop it. Then…then…"

Jane closed her eyes before she buried her face in Mitch's chest and began sobbing again. He rolled his eyes as she wept and wondered how much longer he'd need to play his part in her well-performed drama. He suspected that she would continue just long enough to make him drop his guard, but he'd drop the final curtain before then.

Jane continued after her weeping pause, saying, "Then before he left the coach to drive it away, Ace shot your deputy and laughed. He laughed! Then he told us if we tried to leave the stagecoach, we'd be shot. We didn't even talk after that. I was so afraid, but Esther was sad because she thought you were dead and must have decided that she had to find you. I had my eyes closed when I heard the door slam, and she was gone. I thought they would shoot her, but they didn't."

Mitch quickly asked, "Do you remember where it was when she escaped?"

Jane shook her head and replied, "No. I'm sorry. But after we arrived at their hideout, they…they…each of them…"

She began shaking again and Mitch wished she had just rushed from the house firing a Winchester.

He patted her back and said, "I understand, miss. Nobody's gonna hurt you anymore."

"But…but what if I have one of their babies growing inside me? No man will want to marry me now. Not one!"

"Now, Miss Dubois, you're a very pretty young woman with a nice figure and I'm sure many men will overlook what happened to you. It wasn't as if you wanted them to do it. You're a victim, ma'am."

"Thank you for being so kind, Sheriff. But I feel so…so dirty and I don't know if I can ever have a normal life now."

There was a lot to do, and Mitch couldn't let this keep going, so he said, "Well, don't worry about anything now. I'm going to harness the team to the stagecoach, and we'll leave this place soon. Could you do me a favor?"

She looked up at him, wiped the tears from her face and replied, "I'm so grateful for saving me that I'd do anything for you, Sheriff. Anything."

Mitch had no doubt about what Jane meant by 'anything', but said, "Could you cook some breakfast for us while I harness the team? I'm really hungry."

She smiled then said, "Of course. I'll have it ready in the kitchen by the time you're finished."

"Thank you, Miss Dubois."

Jane released him and said, "Call me Grace, Sheriff. You certainly earned the privilege."

"Thank you, Grace. Call me Mitch."

Jane nodded then replied, "I'll do that, Mitch," before she turned to walk back to the house.

She hadn't taken two steps before she collapsed to the ground in a heap.

Mitch lowered Goldie, and as he looked down at her, he said, "That's payback for what you did to Esther, you blonde-haired bitch."

He left her lying on the ground as he jogged to the barn. Once inside, he hunted for some rope and was even happier to find a small spool of cord. He carried it out of the barn and after laying Goldie on the stagecoach's driver's seat, he opened one of the doors, put the cord inside, then hurried back to Jane. After lifting her from the ground, he carried her to the stage and slid her onto the coach floor. He stepped inside and lifted her into a sitting position before sliding his big knife from its scabbard. Ten minutes later, he exited the stage leaving a fully trussed Jane Newsome inside. It took him another twenty minutes to harness the team, but once they were ready, he climbed into the driver's seat and drove it to the back of the ranch house.

He clambered down and before he went inside, he checked the cabin and found that Jane was still unconscious or pretending to be. He might have hit her noggin a little harder than he'd planned.

Once inside the kitchen, he cut off a large chunk of ham then started his search for the gang's loot. They'd robbed the bank in Lewiston just a month ago, and most of that money should be somewhere in the house. There should be even more from their earlier jobs.

He started in the largest bedroom which assumed Ace shared with Jane. It took him less than a minute to find the express box under the bed. He opened the lid, saw the bundles of cash, then closed it again before finishing off the ham. He then carried it out of the house and slid it onto the stage's roof before climbing back to the driver's seat. He looked at the dark blotches of dried blood around the holes but still sat down. When he picked up Goldie, he noticed that the shotgun's stock was still sticking out of its holder. He pulled it free, set it in the footwell and slid his Winchester inside.

He turned the stage around and headed to the corral. After climbing down and opening the gate, he returned to the driver's seat and snapped the reins. The stage soon passed Ace's body with his Winchester lying on the ground next to him. He wasn't going to add his body or weapons to the stagecoach roof. This mess was in Sheriff Borden's jurisdiction and Mitch would let him clean it up. He'd give Lewiston their money back in payment.

When he reached the boulders, he had to stop again and found that Hal's horse had already wandered off, so after saddling Jack's horse, he tied the gelding and Joe's mare to Frog's horse who still carried his saddlebags. He then attached the gelding's reins to the back of the stagecoach. Each of the other horses held a Winchester, but he hadn't bothered checking the contents of their saddlebags. He could do that when he had the time.

As he drove west, Mitch knew his first destination would be the Ferguson ranch. By then, he was sure that Jane would be awake. That might present a problem for Esther if she had to share the cabin with the blonde killer. He'd leave Jane inside while he told her what had happened.

He drove for almost an hour when he spotted two riders coming towards him. While he didn't think that they were unknown members of Ace's gang, he couldn't take the risk. Not now. Those wanted posters hadn't mention Jane Newsome, either.

Mitch pulled Goldie from the shotgun's holder and laid it across his lap as he continued to watch the approaching riders. They were about a mile out as he tried to think of a reason for them taking the road at this time of day. He couldn't figure out how anyone could be there. Even if they'd stayed overnight at the way station, they would have had to be in the saddle before dawn.

Mitch was about to take Goldie from his lap when one of them waved his hat over his head which startled him. *Who were they?* It took him another forty seconds before he decided to leave his Winchester where it was. If they were some undocumented members of Ace's gang, they wouldn't be excited to see the stagecoach. He'd wait until he was able to see them more clearly.

That happened less than a minute later when he also understood why only one of them had waved his hat high. He pulled the stage to a stop, set Goldie back into the holder and climbed down.

He was grinning as Sheriff Lyle Borden and now Nez Perces County Deputy Sheriff Steve Finch slowed their horses and soon dismounted.

As they led their horses closer, Lyle said, "I was really happy to see you on that stage, Mitch. We weren't sure what to expect. Did you get 'em all?

"Yup. I left Frog on the road to Millersburg and the other four, includin' Ace are a few miles back lyin' on the ground near their hideout. They were usin' that abandoned ranch behind the two boulders."

"You're joshin' me! They were hidin' out in my county all this time?"

"Looks that way. I have the last member of Ace's gang inside the coach. She wasn't on any of their wanted posters, so I didn't even know about her. She was the one who killed Aaron and cut Ace loose."

Lyle pointed at the coach and exclaimed, *"You have that woman killer in there?"*

"You bet. I got her trussed up like a hog. She's probably more dangerous that any of those boys I killed."

"You got a hefty reward comin', you know."

"I didn't even think about it, Lyle. They killed Aaron. Oh, and I have their loot in an express box on top of the coach, too. Seein' as how we're standin' in your county, I'll let you handle the bodies and the money."

"Sounds like a fair trade to me. Are you takin' her to Lewiston for trial?"

"No, sir. She shot Aaron in my county. I'll bring her back to Salmon City with me. How the hell did you get here so fast, anyway? We're a hundred miles from Lewiston."

"When you wired that you were bringing him in on the stage, we were kinda worried about those other four. So, me and Steve were waitin' at the way station to help bring Ace in just in case they tried somethin'. When the coach was late, we got concerned but then two of Earl Ferguson's boys showed up and told us what happened. We returned with his ranch

241

hands, but it was late when we got to the ranch. Miss Cohen gave us all the details and kinda ordered us to come this way as soon as we could."

Mitch smiled as he asked, "How is she?"

"She seemed a might hobbled, but I reckon she was more worried about you than herself. How did that happen? I didn't even know you were visitin' her, and Steve was about ready to fall over when he figured it out."

"I'll tell you later. I need to get to the Fergusons and then head back south to pick up Aaron and Al Crenshaw's body to bring 'em home."

"They're probably already halfway to Millersburg by now, Mitch. Earl Ferguson had some of his boys take a wagon up there to take 'em to the mortician."

"I owe Earl for that. I need to get goin' so I can put Esther's mind at ease. Are you comin', or are you gonna ride to that ranch and check out the bodies to be sure?"

"We'll come with you to the main road, then Steve can head back to Lewiston. He can spend the night at the way station and let 'em know that you'll be takin' their coach back to Salmon City. They can wire Lewiston to arrange for our mortician to pick up those bodies."

"I don't care if they're left to rot where I left 'em, but the ranch might be worth a good search anyway."

Steve walked to the stagecoach, peered inside, then turned around and said, "She is one fine-lookin' woman."

Mitch stepped close to his recent deputy then said, "That's what got Aaron killed, Steve. She'd be smilin' at you while she plugs you with her Colt."

"I reckon that's what makes her so dangerous."

"Yup."

Steve headed back to his horse as Mitch looked inside the coach and found Jane's fierce blue eyes glaring at him.

He cheerfully said, "Mornin', Jane," before turning around and quickly hurrying up the side of the coach.

Steve and Lyle rode a few yards ahead as the stage rolled west. With the danger in the past, Mitch was finally free to spend some time thinking about Esther. He wasn't worried about woolgathering with the two lawmen out front. This was their jurisdiction anyway.

But after spending a few pleasant minutes letting Esther fill his thoughts, he reviewed Jane's behavior in front of the ranch house. It was possible that she was planning to lull him into complacency. But if she really believed that he hadn't found Esther, she might actually have been trying to convince him of her innocence. While she knew that her attempt had failed, she might still use her impressive acting talent when she faced a jury of twelve men.

243

She'd fooled him and Aaron before and he'd seen her believable performance after he'd shot Ace. Juries hated to convict women of any crime, especially one as young and pretty as Jane Newsome. It wouldn't be difficult for her to sway one or more jurors of her innocence regardless of his or Esther's testimony.

Then there was another issue. Esther had just returned to consciousness when Jane had confessed that she had been the one to kill Aaron. It wouldn't take a talented defense attorney to get her to admit to her confusion. Jane could testify that she had said something entirely different.

What made it worse was that by the time the stage stopped, he was on the ground a couple of miles away. All he had was the bullet holes and his testimony that the shooter was using two guns. Aaron only carried one pistol, so either Jane provided Ace with another one, or it magically appeared. But Jane could even accuse Esther of giving him the second pistol. He hated to admit it, but having a blonde woman point her finger at a Jewish woman might be more readily accepted than the other way around.

As they approached the main road, Mitch was beginning to believe that it was possible that Jane Newsome would never face punishment for killing Aaron. She wasn't about to confess, either.

He was becoming agitated with the lack of hard evidence when he suddenly realized that there was hard evidence to prove her guilt. It was probably back at their hideout, and he hadn't looked for it.

He softly cursed his error as they followed the southwestern road to the Ferguson ranch. By the time he remembered the purse, Steve had already taken the road to the way station, but he'd ask Lyle to find the purse that hopefully still contained the pistol Jane had used to shoot Aaron. He didn't know the model of the gun she'd used but was pretty sure that they hadn't been at the ranch house long enough for the pistol to be cleaned and reloaded.

———

After she'd rejoined the conscious world, Jane had been trying to loosen Mitch's knots, but gave up by the time the sheriff looked inside. Once the stagecoach started rolling again, she tried a different approach. She lifted her wrists to her mouth and began gnawing on the thin cord. She didn't have much time, but her tongue told her that her teeth were doing the job.

But she heard them talking and knew that the deputy would be taking the road to the way station and Sheriff Borden wasn't able to fire a gun because of his recent gunshot wound. That damned Mitchell Ward was her only serious problem and she knew that she could no longer use her best weapons against him. She needed a pistol.

As the coach rocked along the road, Jane chewed and ripped at the cord and after just five minutes, the line separated. With her hands free, she was able to quickly untie the cord tied around her ankles. She was rubbing her wrists while she looked outside. She wasn't sure where the other sheriff and his deputy were but didn't want to risk jumping. She had to wait for the right moment.

———

Esther had been relieved when Sheriff Borden and Deputy Finch had shown up late last night. She had remained in her bed as she told them what had happened before they retired for some much-needed rest.

After they'd ridden away early that morning, Maggie had brought her some breakfast and had stayed with her most of the morning.

Maggie was still sitting in the chair near the head of the bed as she said, "Don't worry, Esther. I'm sure that Mitch will soon drive that stagecoach down our access road and won't have a scratch on him."

Esther smiled and said, "That's what I've been praying to happen."

They hadn't discussed her relationship with Mitch since she'd arrived, and Esther appreciated it. But she did have one question she'd like to have answered before Mitch returned.

"Maggie, you and your husband have been very kind to me, and I am very grateful. I was wondering if you knew that I was Jewish?"

"I thought you might be, but it doesn't matter to me or Earl. Besides, our sheriff seems to place great store in you and that is much more important."

"I haven't experienced your level of tolerance in my life, and I wondered if it was more because of Mitch than me personally."

"I can't speak for other folks, Esther. I know a lot of so-called 'good' Christians don't think kindly of Jewish people or other non-Christians. The Protestants don't like the Catholics much either and the Catholics feel the same way about the Protestants. Have you asked Mitch about it?"

"No. Mitch could barely talk to me last week."

Her eyebrows shot up as she asked, "Really? How long has he known you?"

"Oh, he's known me for almost three years now. He just thought that I was too good for him. He only told me on Monday when he came to talk me out of coming with him on the stage. We've talked more in the past few days than the previous three years combined."

Maggie smiled and asked, "Has he kissed you yet?"

"Heavens, no! I think I still intimidate him a little."

Maggie laughed before she said, "I wish I still intimidated Earl."

Esther then quietly said, "Just before he left, he told me that the only reason he bought that big house two years ago was because he dreamed that I would share it with him."

"You will; won't you?"

"I hope so. I really hope so."

Just as Maggie was about to ask another question, Earl shouted from the front room, "Sheriff Borden is comin', and it looks like Mitch is drivin' the stagecoach!"

Maggie popped to her feet, then said, "You stay put, Esther. I'll send Mitch in as soon as he gets here. I'll close the door after he enters the room, too. Maybe he'll finally get the nerve to kiss you."

"Thank you, Maggie. But I won't wait very long for him to work up the nerve. I'll kiss him if he starts talking."

Maggie was grinning as she hurried from the room and headed for the open front door. She soon joined her husband on the porch and watched the stage roll down their access road with Sheriff Borden riding alongside.

Mitch had completely forgotten about Jane or the lack of evidence as he guided the team closer to the large Ferguson home. He wasn't expecting to see Esther on the front porch, so he wasn't disappointed. He waved to Earl and Maggie when he saw them, and they waved back.

He leaned back on the reins pulling the team to a stop then left Goldie in the holder as he hurried down the side and trotted to the porch. He never looked back at Lyle.

When he hopped onto the porch, he shook Earl's hand and said, "Thanks for all your help, Earl."

"You're welcome, Mitch. Did you get 'em all?"

"Yes, sir. All but the blonde killer. She's wrapped up inside the stage. I'll take her back to Salmon City for trial."

Maggie said, "Mitch, Esther is waiting for you. She's been worried sick since you left."

"I got back as soon as I could to let her know I'm okay. Where is she?"

"Follow me, Sheriff. After you talk to her, I suggest that you take a bath and shave off that crop of stubble."

As Mitch walked behind her into the house, he replied, "Yes, ma'am."

He was much more anxious now than he'd been a few hours ago when he and Ace had their Winchester confrontation.

When Maggie turned into Esther's bedroom, he took off Frog's hat and followed her inside where he found her deep brown eyes smiling at him. He passed Maggie who then quickly left the room and closed the door, but Mitch didn't notice.

He slowly stepped to the chair and as he sat down, he said, "I'm okay, Esther. I didn't get a scratch and all five of the gang are dead."

Esther quietly replied, "It's what I prayed for, Mitch."

He wanted to tell her about Jane, but those dark eyes drove any thoughts of Jane and her blue eyes into the ether. He sat in admiring silence for twenty seconds before he leaned forward and gently kissed her.

Esther may have been wishing that he would, but when she felt his lips on hers, she was stunned by her unexpected and overwhelming release of emotions. All she could do was to take her right hand and put it behind his neck to make sure he didn't stop.

Mitch had intended to just kiss her gently and quickly because he was still concerned that he was being too forward. But when he felt her fingers behind his neck, he realized that Esther wasn't going to be satisfied with quick or gentle.

Their first kiss lasted more than thirty seconds, and when the need for air dictated that it should end, Mitch sat back in the chair and smiled.

"I guess you figured out by now that I love you, Esther. I've loved you for a long time but was too much of a coward to even talk to you."

"You weren't a coward, Mitch. You just thought too much of me and too little of yourself. I wanted you to call on me for years but had concerns about my heritage that prevented me from letting you know. It wasn't until you told me why you didn't talk to me that I realized how much I'd grown to love you. So, now can we dispense with all of our silly obstacles?"

"Yes, ma'am. I hope you're not plannin' to go to Lewiston now."

"I'd much rather take that stage back to Salmon City with you. You have an empty house waiting for us."

Mitch smiled as he said, "It'll never be empty again, Esther."

After a short pause, he asked, "Do you have to get married in a synagogue?"

She laughed before replying, "No. I don't even know where the nearest one is. I wouldn't object if you wanted to travel to Rome and get married by the pope."

"I've never been on a ship before, so I reckon we can get hitched in the county courthouse. Is that okay?"

"That's better than standing in front of a pope and listening to some choir chant in Latin."

Mitch laughed then said, "I told you I shot all of five of Ace's gang, but I captured Jane. She's tied up in the stagecoach right now. I want to bring her back to Salmon City for trial, but you'll have to share the coach with her. Can you do that?"

"You captured her? How did you do that?"

"Well, after I shot Ace, she came runnin' out of their ranch house and pretended that she was an innocent victim. I let her tell me her make-believe story then asked her to make me some breakfast. When she turned around, I smacked her on the head with Goldie's barrel. It was kinda payback for what she did to you. I thought about punching her knee with Goldie's butt, but figured you did that to yourself. I got her all wrapped up after I put her in the stage. So, can you stand sittin' across from her for a few hours?"

"I can do it, but may I ask for one favor?"

"You don't have to ask, Esther. Just tell me what you want."

"Can I have the gun you offered me before we left Salmon City?"

Mitch grinned as he pulled the small Smith & Wesson from his left pocket.

As he offered it to her, he said, "It only has six cartridges because I didn't bring any spares. I haven't even removed the empty brass or cleaned it. But I think you won't need more than one or two to keep Jane in line."

She accepted the revolver and asked, "What did you shoot with it?"

"I had to drive off a couple of coyotes before dawn. I didn't want to make 'em mad, so I just shot the big one's tail and they ran off."

"When are you planning to leave?"

"I didn't get that far ahead yet. I needed to talk to you first. Maggie said I need a bath and I gotta shave off my stubble before it turns into a beard, too."

"I noticed the beard, but I don't think you're that dirty."

"Now you're just bein' polite. Let me go talk to Lyle. Then I'll come back and let you know when we'll be headin' back."

"You still need to tell me what happened, too."

"I gotta tell you a lot more than that, Esther. I didn't even propose proper."

"No woman ever received a better proposal than when you told me why you bought the house."

"I just wanted you to know in case…well, you know."

"I understand. Go and have your chat with your brother sheriff and tell me what you decide."

He stood and said, "I'll be right back."

She smiled and asked, "And?"

He took a deep breath, then leaned down and kissed her again. He wasn't going to let his protesting lungs interrupt this one.

When their even longer kiss ended, Esther settled back onto her pillow and sighed as Mitch walked away. After he opened the door and left the room, she closed her eyes. She wanted to relive every second of his return which had been more thrilling than she ever could have dreamed.

———

After hearing the two lawmen leave, Jane was initially relieved that they hadn't even looked inside. She'd arranged the cord as best she could to make it appear as if she was still securely bound, but it hadn't even been necessary. Then Jane couldn't believe she was this lucky and suspected it was a trap so they could shoot her as she tried to escape.

But after a minute of silence, she tossed the cord aside, leaned her blonde head out the window, saw no one, then hurried around to the back of the coach and almost giggled when she spotted Frog's horse saddled. She hurriedly untied the gelding and climbed into the saddle. Her feet didn't reach the stirrups, but she didn't care. She turned the horse back toward the access road and set him to a walk for the first fifty yards then nudged him into a slow trot.

When she reached the end of the access road, she turned right and looked back to the ranch house. She smiled and kicked her heels into the gelding's flanks. As the horse raced along the road with the two horses trailing behind, she noted that each of the ones behind her had Winchesters in their scabbards. While she preferred her small Colt, she could fire a Winchester reasonably well.

Mitch was still talking to Esther as Jane neared the main road. She would soon reach the intersection then follow the busier highway before reaching the eastbound road to Elk City. She kept checking her backtrail and grew more confident that she'd successfully escaped when she didn't see anyone behind her.

———

Mitch soon entered the front room and found Lyle talking to Earl and Maggie.

When they heard him enter, they turned their eyes toward the hallway and waited for him to take a seat.

He looked at Lyle and said, "I need to get Jane to Salmon City and Esther doesn't mind join' her in the coach. I can get to Millersburg by sunset, but I'd rather leave in the mornin'. What do you think?"

"I figure you should get some sleep, Mitch. I ain't much use with this bum arm, so maybe I'll come along myself."

"Before you make the offer, I need somebody to get out to their hideout and find Jane's purse."

"Why do you need it?"

Mitch explained his concerns about Jane's trial and his hope that the pistol was still inside and hadn't been reloaded.

When he finished, Lyle said, "She could always claim that you fired it to frame her, Mitch."

Mitch sighed before saying, "I reckon she might try that, but I still wanna go back and find it. It can't hurt. What really gets my goat, is that if she was a man, I'd just have to point at her and say that she killed Aaron. The jury would find her guilty in ten minutes."

Lyle nodded then said, "Let's get her outta the coach before we do anything else, Mitch."

Mitch turned to the Fergusons and asked, "Where can we put her for the night, Earl?"

Maggie replied, "We don't have any locks on any of the bedrooms and each of them has a window."

"That's okay. I'll let her loose then after she uses the privy, I'll tie her up again. I'll keep an eye on her, too."

"Then you can use the bedroom near the kitchen."

He stood, said, "Thanks, Maggie," then waited for Sheriff Borden to get to his feet before they headed for the door.

When they stepped onto the porch, Lyle snickered and said, "I reckon you're gonna have to explain to your girlfriend why you're spendin' the night with blondie."

"I'll tell her I'm keepin' Jane safe from her. I gave her my Smith & Wesson Model 1, so she'd probably wanna put the last six rounds into Jane's pretty face."

The two sheriffs were grinning as they stepped to the ground then noticed that all of the trailing horses were missing.

Lyle said, "They musta got loose."

Mitch replied, "I hope so," as he began trotting to the stage.

When he yanked open the door, he looked inside, saw the clump of cord piled on the floor then slammed it shut.

C.J. PETIT

He snapped, "She's gone! It looks like she chewed through the cord."

"There were Winchesters on two of those horses; weren't there?"

"Yeah. I still have Goldie on the stage, but she has Frog's pistol in his saddlebags, too. She's a well-armed killer now but she couldn't have gone that far. I gotta get a horse saddled and run her down."

"You can take my buckskin. He's a solid horse. I'd offer to help, but I'd just be a target."

"Okay. Thanks, Lyle."

As Mitch walked to Lyle's horse, Sheriff Borden hurried to the ranch house to let them know of Jane's escape.

After mounting the buckskin, Mitch walked him closer to the stage and lifted Goldie from the shotgun holder. He pulled Lyle's Winchester, laid it on the driver's seat and slid his trusted repeater into the empty scabbard. He didn't set the gelding into a gallop or even a canter to begin his chase. He was pretty sure that he knew where Jane would be going but would still have to pick up her trail. He assumed that she still had the two other horses trailing Frog's animal.

He hadn't even turned off the access road when he was able to confirm that Jane hadn't untied the other two. It gave her a real advantage if she spotted him. She could ride Frog's hard until it was winded, then change to a second one and then the third. She was also about eighty to a hundred pounds lighter than he was.

Mitch kept the moderate pace as he looked ahead with occasional checks of the tracks to make sure she hadn't left the road to ride cross-country. He soon reached the intersection and continued following the tracks. He expected that when he reached the next turnoff, he'd see them take the eastbound road. He was sure that she was headed to the hideout, so it was just a question of how far ahead she was. He'd left her on her own for more than thirty minutes, so she could be five miles away by now.

———

Jane was indeed heading for the hideout, but she was no longer riding Frog's horse. She had noticed that the gelding was already winded, so she pulled up, then untied Joe Hobart's mare and climbed into the saddle. She didn't bother taking Frog's horse because she believed it would slow her down and it didn't have a Winchester anyway.

She soon had the mare moving at a faster pace as the gelding wandered off the road to graze. Jane hadn't even checked the gelding's double set of saddlebags in her haste to continue her escape.

———

Mitch still hadn't spotted Jane and suspected that she was increasing her lead. While he didn't know if she was proficient with a Winchester, he wasn't about to ride into an ambush. He no longer thought of her as a woman. She was nothing more than a cold-blooded killer who wouldn't hesitate to shoot him if he gave her a chance.

He scanned the landscape as he rode and was grateful that she hadn't turned south into Lemhi County. If she had gone that direction, she'd soon enter a world populated by good ambush sites. There were a lot fewer on the southern edge of the Camas Plains.

As he rode, he was actually pleased that she'd escaped and hoped that she didn't just put her hands in the air when he found her. Her escape also meant that she didn't realize that her best chance for freedom was to enter the courtroom and smile at the jury.

————

Esther looked at Lyle and said, "I'm actually more worried about him now than when he rode after Ace and the others. Jane is as devious and unpredictable as she is vicious."

Sheriff Borden was sitting in the chair beside her bed as he replied, "I'm sure that he'll be okay, Esther. He was kinda worried that a jury might let her go, so this might be the only way Aaron gets justice."

"I suppose it would make me seem heartless if I said that his deputy was almost as guilty for what happened inside the stagecoach as she was."

"How's that?"

"When I saw her spill that water onto her blouse and then ask him to close his eyes so she could dry herself, I thought she was flirting. But he had a job to do and even if he only shut his eyes to be polite, it was still a mistake. He should have told her that he had to keep an eye on his prisoner, and she couldn't have pulled the pistol."

Lyle nodded but said, "It's always easy to figure out what shoulda happened after it's over. But if you tell Mitch what you just told me, then I can tell you what he'd say. He'd say that he shoulda trained Aaron better or that he shoulda checked her purse himself before she boarded the stage. He'd say that we all make mistakes, and I'm sure Mitch already told you about some of his now that he's talkin' to ya. Besides, even if Aaron hadn't closed his eyes, she coulda cocked that pistol and pointed it at him to take control and nothin' woulda changed."

"You're probably right. If I hadn't been so irritated with her flirting, I could have watched what she was doing and maybe stopped her."

"That's not likely, ma'am. She probably woulda shot you if you tried. But all of that is water under the bridge. Mitch should be back in a few hours, and he'll finally take that bath and shave."

Esther laughed then asked, "Could you get my travel bags from the stagecoach boot, Sheriff?"

"Yes, ma'am. I'll have Earl bring 'em in 'cause I've only got one workin' arm."

"Thank you."

Lyle stood and headed out the door to find Earl. He'd have the strongbox moved into the house, too. Until he'd listened to Esther's worries, he hadn't a single doubt that Jane wouldn't survive until sunset. As he entered the front room, he began to share her concerns.

———

When Mitch spotted Frog's gelding ahead and off the side of the road, he pulled Lyle's buckskin to a stop to scan for Jane and the other two horses. The only place that would provide enough cover was more than six hundred yards past the saddled horse, so he set the gelding to a medium trot. He thought that Frog's horse might have gone lame after being ridden so much yesterday but was surprised when he noticed that his saddlebags were still lashed above Frog's.

Despite the open ground, he was still alert for a possible ambush as he approached the peacefully grazing animal.

Five minutes later, he dismounted and took the horse's reins and walked him in a small circle watching his gait. He didn't notice the slightest sign of an injury before he stopped and checked the two sets of saddlebags. While he was sure that Jane wouldn't bother taking anything from his bags, he was surprised when he found Frog's gunbelt.

He switched Goldie to Frog's horse because it carried his spare ammunition, then tied Lyle's buckskin to the saddle before he mounted and returned to the road. He was almost six miles behind her when he resumed the chase.

————

Jane was pleased with her decision to switch horses as she was keeping a faster pace and had a Winchester just a few inches from her right leg. She made a point of checking her backtrail every couple of minutes, but when it remained clear, she began to wonder if the sheriff still hadn't noticed that she had escaped.

"Maybe he's in bed with his Jewish whore," she said aloud before she laughed.

But even as she enjoyed the thought, she recalled Hal's rude comment when he said that she wasn't as pretty or as well-figured as that dark woman.

She loudly said, "Well, you're dead, Hal. And I'm not only still alive, I'm also pretty enough and my figure is impressive enough to snare another man who will do whatever I tell him."

She angrily kicked the horse's sides with her sharp heels and Joe's mare shot forward, yanking Jack McFarland's gelding forward.

––––––

Now that he had a spare mount, Mitch picked up the pace. Even though the road's surface was now heavily marked with all of the recent traffic, he still found the tracks left by the two horses. Once he spotted them, he no longer bothered following the trail. Hunting for a possible ambush made better use of his sharp eyesight.

He guessed he would spot the two boulders in another ninety minutes and by then, Jane should already be in the ranch house and would probably be waiting for him to pass between the two rocks.

Mitch had no intention of riding down that access road. He wasn't facing Ace Carr this time. He may have been an outlaw and a killer, but Jane Newsome had no sense of fair play at all. He'd have to approach from a different direction, which meant that if he didn't see her before he spotted those boulders, he'd leave the road and ride south for a mile or so. Then he'd turn east and pass behind that small hill that hid the ranch house from the road.

––––––

When Jane spotted the giant rocks on the eastern horizon, she smiled, checked behind her again and after seeing an empty road, she began to giggle. While she was still worried about that the sheriff might soon arrive, she was looking forward to having a delayed lunch.

Before she reached the entrance road, she spotted Joe's exposed body and assumed that Jack and Hal were under the slickers. When she reached the boulders, she didn't even stop before turning toward the ranch house. It was just a few seconds later that she noticed Ace's body sprawled on the ground. But it wasn't alone. Two coyotes were ripping at his carcass which made her queasy and vultures were circling overhead. She didn't look down as she passed the snarling coyotes and wasn't about to try and scare them off. Ace had served his purpose.

She rode into the barn before she dismounted. She didn't unsaddle the horses but slid the Winchester out of Joe's scabbard before walking away. As Jane stepped quickly toward the back of the ranch house, she looked through the narrow gap toward the road. She didn't see anyone but didn't expect to. If she wanted a good view, she could always climb to the top of the nearby hill but wasn't about to waste the time. Aside from the strenuous climb, she didn't want to expose herself if that sheriff did show up.

Jane soon entered the quiet ranch house and hurried to the bedroom she'd shared with Ace. She knew that Ward had found the strongbox, but she hoped he hadn't taken her purse. When she spotted it lying on the dresser, she exhaled, stepped across the room and picked it up. After finding her

Pocket Colt, she slid it into her dress pocket. If it had a slightly longer barrel, it wouldn't have stayed there. But the cloth held and made an almost perfect holster.

She walked to the front of the house, looked through one of the windows to make sure the access road was still empty, then headed back to the kitchen to make a fast but filling lunch.

———

As soon as the boulders appeared, Mitch turned Frog's horse to the right and rode directly away from the road. He kept his eyes to the east but knew he'd get no more than a brief glimpse of the ranch house and barn before it disappeared behind the hill. Once it slid out of sight, he changed direction and headed directly toward the hill.

It was possible that Jane had continued riding east to Elk City, but it wasn't likely. It was already well after the noon hour, and she'd have to ride another five hours and cross the Clearwater River. He couldn't picture Jane setting up a campsite.

He reached the hill fifteen minutes later and turned Frog's horse south to circle around behind it. Once he had the ranch house in sight, he'd pull up and just watch for a little while. He wanted to verify that she was there before he decided when and how he would approach the house.

———

Jane had made her lunch selections but when she saw the half-full coffeepot, she decided to take the risk of starting a fire in the cookstove to heat it up. She believed she had enough time but once the coffee was hot, she'd douse the fire.

She soon had flames crackling inside the firebox and closed the door. After sliding the coffeepot onto the hot plate, she picked up the sharp butcher's knife and began to cut thick slices from the last of the ham.

As she prepared her lunch, she remembered that the wounded sheriff had sent his deputy to the way station to arrange for somebody to come to the hideout to pick up the bodies. So even if Sheriff Ward might still be back at that other ranch enjoying his reunion with the Jewess, it wouldn't be long before more lawmen arrived at the ranch, and she'd have to be gone by then. *But where should she go?*

There was only one direction she could take that wouldn't have the risk of running into a lawman who knew about her. She had to ride to Elk City tomorrow morning. While Ward had taken the strongbox with all of the gang's loot, she still had her own cache. It was more than three hundred dollars, which should be enough. Once she reached Elk City, she could take the eastbound stage. Just a couple of hours later, she'd be in Montana Territory and within a day, she could stay in Missoula. She was confident that she could make full use of her feminine arsenal to start a new and very profitable life after she arrived.

With her future taking shape, Jane smiled then laid the two thick ham slices onto her plate before adding two biscuits and some cold beans. After setting her plate on the table, she opened the cutlery drawer and placed a fork and table knife neatly beside her plate.

She walked to the cookstove, touched the side of the coffeepot, then yanked her fingers away before they blistered. She grabbed a towel and picked up the pot and filled the largest cup to the brim. Then she opened the firebox door and doused the flames with the last of the coffee. As it hissed, the cloud of steam blew into the kitchen which made her laugh. She closed the door and after setting the empty coffeepot on the back of the cookstove, she walked to the table, took a seat and picked up her utensils.

———

Mitch had just rounded the hill and after seeing the barn, the ranch house slid into view. He pulled up then dismounted. He detached Lyle's buckskin and tied him to the low branch of a Ponderosa pine. After remounting, he continued walking Frog's horse closer to the ranch house. He might not have spotted the smoke as the northern wind was carrying it quickly away, but just as he began to search for any sign of Jane's presence, the blast of steam shot out of the cookstove pipe. He was startled by the sudden silent blast and wasn't even sure what it was at first. He soon realized that it had come from the cookstove exhaust pipe and expected more smoke to follow. But nothing more poured from the iron pipe after that one sudden cloud. He still didn't know what it was, but it didn't matter. Knowing that Jane was probably in the kitchen was all that was important.

He couldn't believe that she'd be so careless as to light a fire in the cookstove and wondered if she was setting a trap. But even that seemed ludicrous. He sat in the saddle for another five minutes just watching the house. None of the kitchen windows faced the hill, so he knew she couldn't see him if she was still in that room.

He finally tapped the gelding's sides and let him walk toward the house. As he drew closer, he pulled Goldie from the scabbard but didn't cock the hammer. He still had more than eight hundred empty yards before him and hoped that she'd leave the house to watch the access road.

———

Mitch was still four hundred yard out when Jane finished eating. After placing the plate, cup and flatware in the sink, she walked down the hall to take another quick look down the access road. She stopped before the closest window and stared toward the twin boulders for a minute or so before wheeling around to return to her bedroom. She needed to pack for tomorrow's journey to Elk City. Her travel bag was still in the stagecoach's boot, but she could use Ace's larger bag.

When she entered what was now just her bedroom, she decided to take some of his clothes as well. Not that she

269

wanted to preserve his memory, but she might need to present a more rural appearance when she reached Elk City.

———

Mitch pulled up again when he was about three hundred yards away from the house. He'd give her a free shot if she was foolish enough to take one at this range. He thought that she probably had left the kitchen by now and wasn't sure where she was. The smartest place for her to wait would be the front room. It had windows on all three of its exterior walls and she would be able to see him unless he rode around the barn. If she'd gone to the bedroom to look for the strongbox or her purse, she wouldn't know he was here. But he wanted her to see him. Then he'd react to whatever she did.

If Jane had even taken a glimpse out of the western window before she left the front room, she would have seen Mitch, but as he sat watching the house, she was calmly packing Ace's travel bag.

Mitch's patience was growing thin after he'd remained in place for another ten minutes without a sign of Jane. He started walking the gelding closer and soon approached Winchester's effective range but didn't pull up. He was about forty yards from the west wall when he stopped yet again. After cocking his Winchester's hammer, he raised Goldie's muzzle and set his sights on the stone chimney at the front of the house.

Jane was setting one of Ace's flannel shirts into the travel bag when she heard the sharp Winchester report followed almost immediately by the sound of a ricochet coming from the front room. She jerked upright and grabbed her pistol before hurrying to the bedroom door where she stopped to listen for another shot. She didn't have to look out a window to know who was firing the Winchester.

After her panicked reaction, she realized that the sheriff didn't know where she was and thought that he had tried to scare her into running outside into his line of fire.

She huffed and said, "I'm not that stupid, Ward."

But even if he was close to the house, she knew she wouldn't be able to put a bullet into him with her small pistol. She needed a rifle and slowly began walking back to the kitchen where she'd left Joe's Winchester. She stopped at the end of the hallway and looked through the kitchen's only window but didn't see the sheriff.

Once she knew the coast was clear, she glanced to her right and saw the Winchester as it leaned against the wall waiting for her. She hurried to the west wall and quickly snatched the repeater. Now that she was armed with an effective weapon, she felt safer and believed that she now had the advantage. She was convinced that the sheriff didn't know where she was. So, if she stayed far enough from the windows, she'd be able to target him and then take time to ensure that she didn't miss. She'd heard Ace and the others talking about Sheriff Ward's marksmanship with his rifle, so she wasn't about to give him a chance to take a single shot at her.

She tiptoed closer to the kitchen's south facing window, and as her angle of view widened, she still didn't see the sheriff. Jane then turned and hurried to the front room. The report from the sheriff's Winchester had come from the west, so she didn't bother looking through the east-facing bedroom windows as she passed by.

Once she reached the end of the hallway, she stopped. Now she faced a dilemma. The sheriff might have fired then immediately moved, so she had to allow that he might be in front of the house by now. Then she remembered the coyotes and smiled. The sheriff wouldn't risk letting the wild animals broadcast his location. It was as if Ace was protecting her.

More confident now that Ward was still on the west side of the house, she stepped into the main room, turned left and slowly approached the one window in the house that faced in that direction. She saw the distant hill first then continued to deliberately approach the window. She cocked the Winchester's hammer as more of the outer world revealed itself.

———

Mitch had expected an almost immediate response after his warning shot. But when she hadn't fired, even though he was giving her a target, he decided that he'd head to the barn and wait. He even slid Goldie into its scabbard to add even more temptation for Jane to react. He was about to turn the gelding to his right when he figured that he may as well ride around the house leaving a hundred-yard gap in the hope that it would inspire her to action.

He pulled the reins and just as the gelding's head turned, the front room's window was shattered by a .44 which then struck the top of the horse's skull and ricocheted away. The horse screamed and reared, almost throwing Mitch from the saddle. But he had both hands on the reins and was able to avoid being tossed to the ground.

Jane thought she'd hit him, but after her first shot, she realized that she had probably shot Frog's horse instead. She quickly cycled in a fresh round as the horse continued to wheel and buck. But while the horse's erratic motion made it difficult for the sheriff to calm the injured animal, it also made him almost impossible to hit. She held her fire for just ten seconds before she understood that she didn't have to shoot him, at least not right away. She barely let her sights settle on the horse's chest when she fired again.

Mitch had just begun to get the gelding under control when another shot blasted out of the broken window and the horse suddenly stopped bucking and collapsed beneath him. Even as he fell with the horse, he knew he was in trouble. Before the gelding toppled on top of his legs, he pushed himself from the saddle and rolled away.

Jane was ready to fire again when she was startled to watch the horse fall over. She shifted her sights to find the sheriff but the gunsmoke in the room and the dust cloud around the dying horse blocked her view. She wasn't sure if the sheriff was trapped beneath the horse, but if he wasn't, he'd know where she was now.

Rather than wait for the smoke and dust to clear, she hurried back to the hallway and hurried to the kitchen.

Mitch had expected more gunfire to erupt from the window, but when she hadn't fired after a few seconds, he ripped Goldie from the scabbard and scrambled to the windowless wall forty yards away. He didn't even look at the window as he raced to the protection of that wall.

He was almost to the side of the house when Jane reached the kitchen, and she had to decide whether to go through the back door or wait for the sheriff to try something else.

When Mitch reached the wall, he plastered his back to the wooded surface and gulped for air. He looked back at the fatally wounded horse and wished he could go back and end his suffering, but he had to stay out of Jane's gunsights. After just ten seconds of more silence, he began to doubt that she'd remained in the front room. She probably knew that she had failed to kill him, but he believed that she thought he was wounded or trapped by the dying horse. He expected that she might soon leave the ranch house to finish the job. When she did, he'd have to be ready. But if she didn't come into the open within a couple of minutes, he'd go find her.

But it was no longer a long-range shootout, so he leaned Goldie against the wall and pulled his Model 3 from his holster. As he stood with his pistol's closed hammer touching his right shoulder, Mitch faced a moral question. While he realized that Jane was probably more filled with evil than any of the men that he had killed over the past two days, he wasn't sure if he'd be able to shoot her even if she was pointing her pistol at him. He'd see her blonde hair and blue eyes and was worried that he might hesitate too long before pulling his trigger.

Then he let his mind leave the blonde woman waiting to kill him to visit the dark-haired woman waiting for him at the Ferguson ranch. She wanted him to return without another gunshot wound. It didn't take long for him to decide that he would rather deal with his moral qualms over shooting Jane than disappoint Esther.

With his mind set, he turned and began slowly walking to the back of the house. His left shoulder was just a few inches from the wall as he approached the small porch. He'd still wait a little while in case she did suddenly appear, but with each passing second, he began to believe that she was waiting with her pistol cocked for him to enter the house. It was now just a question of which door she expected him to use.

Inside the kitchen, Jane had understood that the sheriff wasn't going to make himself a target again. She laid the

275

Winchester on the table and pulled her small Colt from her dress pocket. She pulled out a chair from the table and turned it to face the back door before sitting down. If the sheriff came through the front door, she'd have time to change position.

She thought he was still laying on the ground expecting her to start firing the Winchester but when he felt safe, she was convinced that he would try to sneak in the back door. She cocked the Pocket Colt's hammer and aimed at the open doorway.

Mitch reached the back corner of the house then stopped. He wasn't going to pull his hammer into the firing position until he entered. It would only add a fraction of a second to his first shot, but he wasn't going to be facing a talented gunfighter. He did want her to have her pistol in her hand, so he decided to wait to give her more time to find it and prepare her firing position in case she wasn't ready yet.

His decision to postpone his entrance had an unintended effect on Jane. She had been mentally counting the seconds after she'd cocked her pistol. She visualized Sheriff Ward staring at the shattered front room window through the dust. Then when it settled, she imagined him scrambling to his feet from behind the dead horse and grabbing his Winchester. She didn't think that he'd use a pistol because his reputation was built on his ability with his rifle.

Her mental clock kept going until she was sure that he had to burst through the kitchen door at any moment, but everything remained quiet. The silence was becoming unnerving, and Jane almost shouted to make him come through that door.

As each second ticked by, she became more nervous. After two minutes without a hint of what the sheriff was doing, she started to get fidgety. She needed some way to calm her nerves, so she studied her Colt as a distraction. Ace had given her the pistol last summer. He had kept it well maintained and handled the reloading. She wasn't even sure how many bullets it held which was almost embarrassing. She knew that she'd fired one to kill the deputy, but now began to wonder if she had four or five shots remaining.

She turned the Colt's muzzle to count the number of charged chambers, found the one that didn't have a lead ball and had to take a few seconds to let her eyes circle the cylinder until she understood that she had four shots remaining. She had almost forgotten why she was sitting in the chair with a cocked pistol when she looked at the front sight. She wondered why the Colt company bothered putting it on a gun with such a short barrel.

Mitch had stepped past the porch and seen the open door, so just as Jane wished Ace was there to tell her why the metal tab was there, he leveled his Smith & Wesson and hopped onto the back porch.

Jane was startled by the loud sound and as she jerked, her index finger yanked the trigger back just far enough to release the hammer. The front sight which had piqued her curiosity was already turning clockwise away from her face or she would have shot herself between the eyes.

Mitch had just crossed the threshold when the .31 caliber bullet shot from its muzzle just four inches from her cute nose. The lead missile grazed her forehead just above her left eyebrow barely breaking the skin. But the half-inch wound caused by the bullet, while already gushing blood, wasn't nearly as bad as the damage created by the powder burn that exploded into her face. The tiny pieces of discharged bits of paper from the wad added to facial injuries when they blasted into her left eye. She screamed in pain before she dropped the pistol and covered her burned face with her hands as blood poured from her forehead.

Mitch hadn't been shocked to find her in the kitchen or even that she'd been about to shoot him, but he couldn't understand what had happened. He didn't know where her bullet had gone, but the moment he saw her, he realized that she was no longer a danger. He rammed his pistol into his holster and hurried toward the screaming woman. He couldn't see her face behind her hands but saw the stream of blood sliding across the left side of her face. He stopped, then snatched the towel she'd just used to hold her coffeepot from the counter before he approached Jane.

He looked down at her Colt on the floor wondering if a neighboring chamber's percussion cap had ignited when she fired, but it only took a second to realize the pistol was undamaged. He still kicked the Colt down the hallway before stretching out the towel in front of Jane's face.

"Take your hands down, so I can see how bad it is."

Jane didn't even know Mitch was standing just a couple of feet in front of her until he spoke. But the moment she heard his voice, the pain from her damaged face was overshadowed by her rage.

She dropped her bloody hands and screamed, "You bastard! You shot me!"

Mitch was stunned when he saw her face, but not because of the amount of blood. Head and face wounds bled profusely, and hers wasn't that bad. It was the massive powder burn that almost made him recoil. The black powder had not only burned the skin but had created a large triangular tattoo starting just on the right side of her nose and expanding until it was four inches wide near her temple. He was sure that her eye, which was in the center of the reddish black powder burn was badly damaged as well, but it was covered in blood so he couldn't tell.

His revulsion only lasted a couple of seconds before he placed the towel across her face and said, "I didn't shoot you, lady. You did. And here I always figured that only men could do somethin' that stupid. Now hold the towel to your face to stop the bleedin'. The wound ain't that bad."

Jane suddenly recalled looking at her pistol and realized that he wasn't lying. Her rage dropped to mere anger as she pressed the towel to her face.

"I suppose you're going to drag me back to your town thinking that I'll hang for shooting your deputy."

"Nope. I figure that I'll just leave you here."

Jane thought he was lying, so she snarled, "You aren't going to let me go. You want to see me hang!"

"I don't lie. I have better things to do than be your nanny. I don't want Esther to worry anymore. And I promised my fiancée that I'd take a bath and a shave when I got back."

Jane realized that he wasn't lying and couldn't understand why the sheriff was going to let her go, but that's not what interested her when she heard his reply.

Despite her confusion and pain, she asked, "Your fiancée? You're really going to marry her? I guess even a Jew is good enough for the likes of you."

"Even a homely Jewish lady beats a blonde bitch all to hell. But she's far from homely and I reckon with your face lookin' the way it is, you'll be lucky to find work as a two-bit whore."

As Mitch was reaching for the Winchester laying on the table, Jane yanked the towel from her face and screamed, "*What do you mean?* You just said it wasn't a bad wound!"

Mitch picked up the Winchester and replied, "The bullet wound ain't bad, but I wouldn't go lookin' at myself in a mirror if I was you."

Jane was about to ask him what was wrong with her face when she realized that she could only see out of her right eye. She thought her left was still covered with blood, so she began rubbing it with a dry part of the bloody towel.

By the time she realized that she might be blind in her left eye, she shouted, "I can't see out of my left eye! How bad is it? Tell me!"

But Mitch had already walked out of the house and by the time she demanded that he tell her how badly she'd been disfigured, he was already stepping off the porch. He heard her asking about the extent of the damage to her face, but he'd let her make that discovery on her own.

He soon reached Goldie and picked up his own repeater. He walked to the downed horse and heard his labored breathing when he was still ten yards away. When he reached the suffering animal, he laid Goldie's forearm on the saddle then quickly cycled the lever on Jane's Winchester. He didn't close his eyes as he pointed the muzzle just a foot from the side of the gelding's head and fired. His hoarse breathing stopped, and Mitch tossed the repeater to the ground near the dead gelding's head. He stepped to the saddle, untied his saddlebags and had to spend almost a minute of hard tugging to free them. He hung them over his shoulder then picked up Goldie before walking to the barn.

Once inside, he wasn't surprised to find both horses still saddled, so he walked to Joe's mare and slid Goldie into its empty scabbard. He untied Jack's gelding's reins and mounted the taller horse rather than sit in the same saddle that Jane had used. He tied off the mare's reins to Jack's saddle and walked him out of the barn.

He headed southwest to retrieve Lyle's buckskin. As he rode, he was certain that his decision to leave Jane at the ranch house was right but now he began to think about the men who would be coming to retrieve the dead outlaws' bodies tomorrow.

After adding the buckskin to Joe's mare, he headed back toward the ranch house. He had no intention of getting within Winchester range even though he didn't believe that Jane was in any condition to fire a gun of any type. He suspected that she was probably already rummaging through her purse for her hand mirror. He couldn't imagine a woman like Jane Newsome not having one. When she finally looked at her hideous reflected image with her only working eye, she might finally understand what he'd told her. It was also the reason he made the almost instant decision to leave her on the ranch.

He gave wide berth to the two coyotes who were trying to feed on Ace's remains while fighting off some brave vultures. The more patient birds were still circling overhead, but he knew that they'd be landing near the gelding's body soon now that no humans were nearby.

He rode down the access road until he passed through the boulder guards. Once on the other side, he dismounted and walked to the three bodies he'd left on the road just a few hours earlier. The vultures must not have spotted them yet in the rock's shadow but was surprised that no more coyotes or wolves had found them.

He dragged Joe's corpse around the boulder and left it in the open about ten feet behind the eastern boulder. He then returned and pulled off the slickers and grabbed Jack McFarland's ankles and pulled his body onto the access road and left it on the open ground behind the western boulder. After pulling Hal Kingman's body beside Jack's, he returned to the front of the road and grabbed the slickers. He rolled them into a ball and carried them to the nearer boulder and wedged them beneath the bottom edge.

After mounting Jack's gelding, he spotted Hal's horse grazing about four hundred yards away. He guessed that the gelding wasn't about to return to his home barn while those coyotes were busy. He was going to leave him on his own, but when the horse lifted his head, Mitch noticed that he still wore his bridle. So, he rode to the horse and after reaching the unsaddled animal, he took his reins and led him back to the road. After dismounting near the rest of Hal's tack, he tied off Jack's gelding using the same bush he'd used before. Ten minutes later, he was riding west trailing three saddled horses.

———

Esther sat on the edge of the bed and said, "I want to try, Maggie. I know it looks bad, but I don't think I can make it worse by walking. It's just a matter of putting up with the pain."

Maggie looked at her with a measure of concern as she replied, "You're the nurse, Esther. But I'll be close enough to catch you if you fall."

Esther smiled and said, "I won't fall, Maggie," then leaned forward and slowly stood.

Once on her feet, she carefully stepped away from the bed and soon developed a stiff, awkward gait that minimized the pain. As long as she didn't bend her knee, it wasn't bad at all. She soon stepped into the hallway and made a circuit around the front room before returning to the bedroom as Maggie watched.

When she stood with her back to the bed again, she said, "This might be a trifle more painful," then slowly sat on the mattress.

Once she was seated, she smiled and said, "That wasn't nearly as bad as I expected."

Maggie asked, "Do you really think that Mitch will let you ride next to him on the driver's seat all the way to Salmon City?"

"It would be better than riding inside with that...that woman. Even though Mitch gave me his small pistol, I won't feel safe even if she's wrapped in rope from her blonde head to her toes. She'd probably just burn them off with fire from her eyes."

Maggie laughed then asked, "Is she really that bad?"

"She may not be able to throw lightning or flames from her eyes, but she might be the most despicable person God ever placed on this earth. I know Mitch is worried that she might not be convicted for murdering Aaron, but even if she is found guilty and hanged for her crime, I don't think it would be sufficient punishment."

"I guess we'll just have to leave her final punishment in God's hands."

"He created her, so He can pronounce her final judgement."

"Amen to that."

Esther nodded and wondered if Mitch had already found her. If he had, that created a library of possible outcomes, yet she couldn't think of any that were satisfactory. Her biggest worry was that even if Jane began shooting at him, he would be unable to return fire until he'd been shot. But despite the large number of possible outcomes, not one was even close to what had already happened twenty-one miles east of the Ferguson ranch.

———

Sheriff Borden was in the barn with Earl. He had expected Mitch to return within three hours and he'd already been gone almost six. There was still another three hours of daylight, but while he wasn't worried, he was growing anxious because he didn't know what had caused the delay.

Lyle was leaning on the fence of an empty stall as he asked, "If he's not back in a couple of hours, can I borrow a horse to go lookin' for him?"

"Sure thing, Sheriff. I'll even come along if Maggie lets me."

The sheriff chuckled before asking, "You really don't need to ask her permission; do ya?"

Earl grinned as he replied, "I do unless I feel like sleepin' in the loft."

"I'm just wonderin' what Mitch is doin'. I reckon that he already found that murderin' mare, but I don't know if he'd be able to shoot her no matter what she did. She was a pretty handsome witch, and I might have a problem pluggin' her myself."

"I'd hate to be in Mitch's shoes if she decided to fight it out. But I'd be kinda surprised if she just gave up."

"So, would I. I hope we don't need to saddle our horses to find out what happened."

"Well, at least the Overland's team is havin' a good rest and fillin' their bellies."

"You know, after I sent Steve to the way station, I figured that the stage from Lewiston was probably already more'n halfway there. I reckon that he'll tell the driver what happened before they get the telegram, so they might be payin' us a visit tomorrow mornin'."

"If they do, what do you think Mitch will do with his prisoner?"

"I'll ask him when he brings her in. Maybe I won't have to ask if he rides in alone."

"I reckon that would be better for everyone."

"Except for that pretty blonde murderer."

Earl nodded before they turned and left the barn.

———

As Lyle and Earl walked to the porch, Mitch spotted the first intersection. He hadn't seen any traffic all day which was a mild surprise, but not out of the ordinary. He guessed it was around five o'clock, but he felt as if he'd been awake for days. But seeing the main road ahead pushed aside much of his exhaustion. He'd see Esther in another hour or so but asked Jack's gelding for a little more speed to cut a few minutes off of his arrival time.

287

He soon reached the road, but rather than turning north, he continued straight ahead going cross country. He'd shave another ten minutes from the last part of the ride by making his own shorter trail to the southwest road. Soon after he reached the road to White Bird, he'd spot the Ferguson ranch.

While he was still anxious to see Esther, he still had to avoid obstacles and dangerous ground as he guided Jack's gelding closer to the ranch. He may have been trailing three other horses but didn't want to have to shoot another one just because he wanted to save a little time.

He soon reached the southwest road and picked up the pace when he saw the Ferguson's barn rise above the horizon.

Earl and Lyle had turned the stagecoach to face the road and were sitting on the driver's seat of the horseless stagecoach looking to the northeast. Lyle had Earl move the strongbox into the cabin when he'd brought Esther her travel bags. Just a few seconds after Mitch saw the barn, they spotted the line of horses trotting quickly down the road.

As they stood, Earl asked, "Is that Mitch?"

"It sure looks like him, but I don't see the blonde. Do you?"

"Nope. He sure has a lot of horses with him, though."

"I reckon he's got a good story to tell us when he gets here. Let's climb down and I'll go tell Esther that he's comin'."

"I'm gonna stay up here 'til he reaches the end of the access road."

Lyle replied, "Good enough," then clambered down the side of the stagecoach and hopped to the ground.

He half-jogged and half-walked to front of the house and jumped onto the porch. The front door was still open, so he quickly entered the front room. He didn't see either Maggie or Esther, so he pulled off his hat and headed for the hallway.

When he reached Esther's room, he tapped on the door jamb before stepping over the threshold.

Esther and Maggie had heard him coming, so before he even rapped on the side of the doorway, they were both watching the open door.

He stopped when he saw them looking at him, then grinned and said, "Mitch is comin', Esther."

Esther felt her heart skip a beat or two as she smiled and quickly asked, "Is he alone?"

"I think so. He was pretty far out when we saw him, but all we could see trailin' behind him were a few empty horses. I'm sure he'll let us know what happened."

She nodded then not-so-carefully stood and said, "Let's hear what he has to say."

The sheriff said, "Yes, ma'am," then turned and hurriedly left the room to rejoin Earl. He expected that Mitch would reach the access road within five minutes.

———

As Mitch approached the access road, he hoped that Esther would accept the sentence he'd given to Jane. He may have had much longer conversations with her over the past few days but knew that he still didn't understand her well enough to be able to predict her reaction. Yet he trusted that her kind heart and gentle nature would allow her to at least forgive him for what many might see as insufficient punishment for her crimes.

He turned his short parade onto the access road and spotted Earl and Lyle standing near the stagecoach waiting for him. He hadn't expected to see Esther outside as he believed that she was still unable to walk on her injured knee. He'd delay telling the others what had happened until after he'd talked to Esther and listened to what she thought of his benevolent decision.

He soon pulled up and as he dismounted, Earl and Lyle stepped close.

Sheriff Borden asked, "What happened, Mitch?"

"I'll let you know in a little while, but I need to talk to Esther first."

"She's waitin' in the main room, Mitch. She walked there on her own and said you can tell us all at the same time."

Mitch tied the gelding's reins to the stagecoach's front left wheel and without saying another word quickly strode past Lyle and Earl. They trotted quickly behind him and followed him onto the porch.

Mitch pulled off his temporary hat as he walked into the house and after a momentary search, found Esther sitting on the couch looking at him with her wonderful, smiling brown eyes. He was all smiles himself as he stepped across the room and sat down beside her.

He quickly said, "I need that bath a lot more now, Esther."

She laughed before asking, "You don't have any fresh wounds that need to be repaired; do you?"

"No, ma'am. But I reckon you and everybody else wants to know what happened. I was hopin' to tell you first, but I guess I'll just go ahead and let everyone else hear the story at the same time."

"Why did you need to tell me privately?"

"I reckon it doesn't matter now, so I might as well get on with it."

Lyle asked, "Did you have to kill her, Mitch? Is that what's got you kinda ashamed? You don't have to feel bad about it if that's the reason. She was probably already shootin' when you returned fire."

"No. I didn't kill her. Let me tell you what happened. I was pretty sure that I did the right thing when I was out there, but you can tell me if you think it was wrong."

He turned his eyes back to Esther to watch her reaction, then began his story.

Telling about the chase only took a few minutes but when he reached the point where he fired at the chimney, he needed to provide many more details. He expected that now he'd be interrupted by a lot of questions and wasn't wrong.

"Her first shot through the window hit the top of the gelding's head that I was ridin', and I had to fight to keep him from throwin' me. I was just gettin' him to stop twistin' around when she shot him in the chest, and he collapsed from under me. I got off the saddle before he hit and thought she'd keep shootin'. So, I hunkered down behind the horse for a little bit until I figured out that she was probably already movin' to another room."

Lyle asked, "Were there any more windows she coulda used?"

"Not on that side of the house. After I figured out that she was probably runnin' to a different room, I grabbed Goldie and ran to the wall and waited for her to show up. She didn't, so I leaned Goldie against the wall and pulled my Model 3. I figured that she was probably waiting in the back of the house in the kitchen, so I headed that way. I waited for a while to see if she came out or made some noise. But after a few minutes, I had to take a look. When I passed by the porch, I saw the door open and was sure she was sittin' inside with her Winchester ready to fire."

Earl quickly asked, "Was she?" which caused him a sharp look from Maggie for interrupting what she expected to be the most interesting part of the story.

"She was waitin' alright, but not with her Winchester. She had that Pocket Colt she used to help Ace escape. Now, I don't know exactly what happened when I rushed through that door, and she fired her pistol."

Lyle took his shot at incurring Maggie's wrath when he asked, "She musta missed, so what was so confusin'?"

"It took me a minute or so to figure out, but even then, I never understood what she was doin' before I showed up. It was almost like she didn't know where the bullet came outta the gun. She musta been checkin' the load with the hammer back and her finger on the trigger when I crashed into the room. As stupid as that was, it's the only thing that made any bit of sense. Anyway…"

Lyle exclaimed, "*She shot herself?*"

"Yes, sir. At first, I figured she had another chamber go off. She screamed and already had her hands on her face when I first looked at her, so I didn't figure that out right away. Blood was rollin' down her face, so I grabbed a towel and told her that I needed to use it to stop the bleedin'. She must not have known I was even there, 'cause as soon as I told her to drop her hands, she screamed at me and accused me of shootin' her. When her hands were out of the way, I saw the big powder burn coverin' most of the left side of her face then figured out that she musta shot herself.

"She was still pretty mad at me like it was my fault, but when she put the towel over her face, I was tryin' to figure out how to tie her down and bring her back when we had a few words. She didn't seem worried about a trial in Salmon City. I reckon it was because she figured that she was still a pretty blonde woman. But she was pretty scary lookin' already, so I told her that she wouldn't want to look at herself in a mirror. Then she dropped the towel to yell at me again, but she got mad again when she couldn't see out of her left eye. After she began using the towel to wipe her eyes, I grabbed her Winchester and just walked outta the room."

"You just left her there?" Maggie asked, breaking her own rule by interrupting.

"Yes, ma'am. If you saw her face, you'd understand why I figured it was a better sentence than any judge could pass down. I even left her with her pistol and Winchester but took all of the horses from the place. She probably has some money hidden away, but I didn't care much."

Earl asked, "Don't you think she'll escape and start more trouble?"

Mitch shrugged then looked at Lyle and said, "It's not in my jurisdiction, but I reckon that ranch will turn into the Jane Newsome Prison. Remember I asked you to have somebody go out there to pick up the four bodies?"

"Steve should have sent the telegram to Lewiston by now."

"Well, it's your call, Lyle. But I moved 'em all off the road before I left, so folks ridin' by wouldn't see 'em. There were already coyotes and buzzards fightin' over Ace's remains by the time I got back there. With the carcass of Frog's horse just outside the house and now three more bodies near the access road, I don't figure Jane will be goin' outside for a while. If you wanna send somebody out there, it's up to you. She's got enough food for a month or so and by then, she can use her Winchester and Ace's that was lyin' next to his body to do some huntin' if she wants to keep from starvin'."

Esther finally asked, "Was she so disfigured by the powder burn that she wouldn't be able to convince some passing rider to help her?"

"Her face was pretty bad, but I reckon she might be able to tempt some feller to look past her face and get him to take her outta there. But she'd know that she couldn't stay in the territory now because she'd be easy to spot. I'll tell you later what I told her she could do."

295

Lyle said, "I don't figure you'll say anything that would offend our civilized ears, Mitch."

Mitch nodded, but then passed over Jane's comment that had inspired his reply and said, "I told her with the way she looked, she'd be lucky to get work as a two-bit whore."

Maggie asked, "She was that bad?"

"Yes, ma'am."

He then looked at Esther and said, "I was kinda worried that you might be disappointed in what I did. If you are, just tell me and I'll ride out there in the mornin' and arrest her."

Esther took his hand as she replied, "It was a judgement worthy of King Solomon."

Mitch smiled and said, "I reckon you oughta know, Miss Cohen."

She wanted to kiss him but had to settle for just patting his hand. She hadn't been so proud of being Jewish since her father died.

Lyle then said, "I reckon I'll be headin' back to Lewiston in the mornin'. I figure the stage to Salmon City might show up with a spare driver to take their stage back. I might take advantage of that and ride in the one with the holes in the driver's seat so I can relax all the way home."

"We need to get your buckskin and the other horses unsaddled, Lyle. I'll let you and Earl handle that while I'm takin' my bath."

Earl snickered then said, "I'll have some of my boys take care of 'em, Mitch. Are you gonna take the outlaws' horses back to Salmon City with you?"

"Nope. I don't care what happens to their horses or their guns. I know we're in my jurisdiction now, but I found 'em in Lyle's county, so he can figure out what to do with everything. I need to get my saddlebags and Goldie before you take care of the horses."

Lyle said, "I'll bring 'em inside, Mitch. You need to get cleaned up. I reckon you're a might hungry, too."

"I need my clothes from my saddlebags, so I'll need to get 'em before I get cleaned up. But I could use a bite or two."

Maggie stood and said, "That's my department, Sheriff Ward. You head to the bathing room and make good use of one of those bars of soap while I start cooking. It's almost suppertime anyway."

Mitch smiled and said, "Thank you, Maggie," before she walked out of the room and soon disappeared into the hallway.

Earl and Lyle stood, then left the house and walked out the door leaving Mitch and Esther alone on the couch.

He quietly asked, "Do you really think I did the right thing to let her stay on the ranch?"

"I wasn't exaggerating when I told you I thought it was a judgement worthy of King Solomon. I can't imagine a more fitting punishment for a woman like her. Almost as soon as I met her, I could tell that she was proud of her appearance and the way she could manipulate men. I imagine that after she sees her new face in the mirror, she'd wish that you had shot her. Is it possible for her to wash that gunpowder stain from her face?"

"Nope. I've seen a few men who got too close to a blast of powder and not one was able to get rid of it. The difference was that most fellers seemed proud to show off the damage 'cause they figured it made 'em seem more manly. The rest of us figured it made 'em look more stupid than we were. When I noticed the burn on Jane's face, I even told her that I only thought men were stupid enough to shoot themselves.

"But it's more than just a big tattoo across her face, Esther. She'll have a good-sized scar just on top of her eyebrow from the bullet and her left eye was already swellin' up before she told me she couldn't see. I was kinda jokin' when I told her she'd be lucky to get work as a two-bit whore, but it wasn't far from the truth. I don't know what she's gonna do out there, but I'm not about to head that way just to find out."

"Now that the whole Carr gang is gone, and you seem to be less concerned that I might correct your grammar, can we spend more time getting to know each other better? After all, you did propose to me. Well, almost."

Mitch grinned then said, "I reckon we can do that if we get to ride inside the stagecoach back to Salmon City and I can propose to you proper. But I guess that you won't be goin' to Lewiston now."

"I don't need the job at St. Anne's anymore. I have a house waiting for me in Salmon City."

"I just hope I don't need you to be a nurse anymore."

She smiled then Mitch asked, "Can I ask you somethin' that I already answered myself when I was lookin' at Jane's face?"

"Of course."

"If I brought her back, would you have fixed her up as best you could?"

"I wouldn't be happy about it, but yes, I'd do what I could to help her. From how you described the damage, all I could do would be to suture the wound on her forehead and apply cold compresses to her face."

Mitch smiled as he said, "That's what I figured you'd do. Even after all she did, I knew you would still take care of her. It's because that's who you are, Esther. You're not Jewish or even a dark-haired, beautiful young woman with incredible brown eyes. You're a warm, compassionate person, and you gotta remember that's what matters.

"Folks like Earl and Maggie aren't different than most folks. I reckon that some of 'em might figure you're not as good as they are 'cause you aren't Christian. But those are just the ignorant ones who figure they're better than everybody else. They also seem to forget that Jesus was a Jew and so were all of the first Christians. But folks like that don't just dislike Jews, either.

"I've met some Baptists who don't like other Baptists and Lutherans who figure Baptists are close to bein' heathens. There are Protestants who reckon that Catholics wear horns and have forked tails while some Catholics are sure that it's the Protestants who are headed for hell. There are Christians who call the Jews Christ murderers while there are Jews who say they're the chosen people and everyone else is wrong. All of those religions preach that they should love God and their neighbors, but too many of 'em don't see it that way.

"Now I don't know what Arabs or Orientals believe and folks down in Australia could worship kangaroos for all I know. But I reckon everybody is entitled to believe whatever they want, and they oughta treat others kindly no matter what's in their hearts. Most folks are like that, Esther. It's not just about religion either. Folks sometimes think they're better than others just 'cause they're different.

"For most of my life, I didn't talk much 'cause I didn't want folks to think I was stupid. You showed me different. But until I started talkin' to you, I didn't know that you felt that way about bein' Jewish. I reckon that if you stopped expectin' that folks don't like you before you even talk to 'em, you'll meet a lot more people like Earl and Maggie than ignorant ones like Doc Brandt."

When he stopped talking, he grinned sheepishly and said, "Sorry for preachin'."

Esther stared at Mitch for a few seconds before quietly saying, "It wasn't preaching. It was the truth. I have been too quick to judge people after my parents died. I was alone and had some bad experiences that made me believe that everyone thought ill of me. I promise that I'll stop prejudging people from now on. For a man who considered himself to be less intelligent than others, you are nothing less than the most incredible man I've ever met, Sheriff Mitchell Ward."

Mitch blushed slightly then said, "I may not be stupid, but I sure am filthy. I need to take that bath and shave. My fiancée asked me to do that before I rode off and I wouldn't want to disappoint her."

She smiled as she replied, "You can never disappoint me, Mitch. But you definitely need a bath and a shave."

He laughed just as Lyle entered the house with his saddlebags and Goldie.

He set the saddlebags on the floor near his feet and laid his Winchester on the center table before saying, "The leather is lookin' pretty sad, Mitch. You might use some of that reward money to buy a new set."

"Maybe."

Esther asked, "You get reward money?"

"Yes, ma'am. I don't know how much, but Lemhi County lets me keep any rewards. That's how I was able to buy our house."

She smiled and said, "More than two years ago when you had barely been able to speak to me."

"I'll make up for it from now on."

Lyle said, "After I got your wire, I added up the wanted posters and it came out to twenty-three hundred dollars."

Mitch looked up at him as he said, "That's even more then I figured. I reckon I had old posters. I don't suppose any of those new ones mentioned Jane; did they?"

"Nope. We woulda noticed. But we did find the one for Joe Hobart this time."

"Are you gonna send anybody down to that hideout after a while?"

"Probably a lot sooner. I reckon I'll have Steve or Jimmy head over there in a week or so. I figure that she'll stay put with all of those wild critters outside. But when they're gone, she's gonna be so mad that she won't care who sees her. You didn't leave her a horse, but she could use a Winchester to shoot some rider and take his. She might even come after you."

Esther quickly said, "I still believe that Mitch did the right thing to leave her there to wallow in her misery. And I doubt if she'll chase after anyone."

Mitch was about to suggest that he ride back out to the ranch again when Lyle said, "I think she'll keep for at least a couple of weeks. But it's my jurisdiction, Mitch. So, I'll handle that…woman."

"Alright. I just hope she doesn't cause anybody any harm 'cause I didn't bring her back."

Esther asked, "Would you feel better if you watched her hang, Mitch?"

"No, I reckon not."

Lyle said, "Let it go, Mitch. Go get cleaned up so we can breathe easier."

Mitch snickered before he rose, picked up his saddlebags then looked at Esther and asked, "How is your knee?"

"It's stiff and still painful, but it's getting better already, and I only notice the bump on my head when I brush my hair."

"That's good to hear."

He left Goldie on the table before he turned and walked down the hallway.

———

Mitch was scrubbed and clean shaven when he joined everyone for supper. While he'd been removing his crust of Idaho, he had begun to question his decision. He should have at least taken all of the guns from the place when he left so she couldn't shoot any passersby.

He didn't realize that he added little to the dinner conversation. Esther noticed and didn't believe that he had returned to his lifelong silent behavior. She was convinced that he was regretting his decision to leave Jane alone. She didn't ask him or even mention Jane but would wait to broach the subject until they were on their way back to Salmon City.

Mitch still had those misgivings when he turned in for the night. He was exhausted and should have fallen asleep in less than a minute, but the image of a disfigured Jane Newsome shooting an innocent rider as he passed the two boulders wouldn't leave his mind.

It was still troubling him when sleep finally overtook him.

CHAPTER 9

After breakfast the next morning, Mitch left the house with Lyle and Earl. Sheriff Borden was going to have one of the ranch hands saddle his horse so he could ride to the way station. He expected to meet Steve and the scheduled southbound stagecoach before he got there. Mitch and Earl were going to harness the coach, but Mitch promised Lyle that he'd stay on the ranch until midmorning. It was only a six or seven-hour drive to Millersburg, so there wasn't any rush.

Lyle waved before he rode his buckskin down the access road. The three outlaws' horses were already mingling with some of Earl's remuda in the corral.

The stagecoach was ready to roll, and Esther's travel bags were sitting on the roof with his saddlebags and Goldie when Mitch returned to the house. Earl still had a ranch to run, so he rode out to the herd with most of his ranch hands.

After entering, he smiled at Esther as she looked at him from the couch then walked across the room and sat down beside her.

"The stage is ready to go, so now we'll just have to wait a little while to see if they send the other one this way."

"And if it doesn't show up, where will I sit when we leave for Millersburg?"

"I sure don't want you tryin' to climb up top with your bad knee. I'll help you inside before gettin' up top."

"I'll be pretty bored not having anyone to talk to, Mitch. Of course, if we were sharing the driver's seat, I'm not sure that it would be much different. You're second-guessing your decision to leave Jane alone on the ranch; aren't you?"

He nodded as he replied, "I shoulda taken all the guns with me. She almost shot me through a window at forty yards with her Winchester. If she set up to ambush some innocent rider, she wouldn't miss. She's an evil person, Esther. Somebody might die 'cause I didn't do my job."

Her smile vanished and her eyes flared when she snapped, "Don't take one step down that road, Sheriff Ward! I told you it was a perfect sentence and haven't changed my mind. You still think of her as an outlaw more than a vain young woman. Unless you exaggerated the damage to her face, she'll be so horrified when she discovers her new, hideous appearance that she wouldn't want anyone to see her. I've met other pretty young women like her, well maybe not as evil as she is, but the ones who lived for compliments. She'll stay in that house long after the vultures and coyotes have retreated."

"She's still gotta eat, Esther."

"She'll turn into a scrounger rather than let anyone see her. When one of Sheriff Borden's deputies goes there, he may not even find her. But as he told you yesterday, it's his jurisdiction and he will decide what to do. You need to focus your attention on our future, not hers."

Mitch looked at her fierce brown eyes and smiled as he replied, "Yes, ma'am."

Esther's face softened again before she said, "I don't want to hear her name again and I hope we get to share a seat in a different stagecoach when we leave. Then we can finally have a normal conversation about things like marriage and children."

"We sure have gone pretty far in just a few days; haven't we?"

"That, sir, is an understatement," then she picked up her purse and said, "I forgot to ask if you wanted your small pistol back now. I'd hate to accidentally shoot myself."

"So, would I, especially after seein' Jane's face. But I reckon you're too smart to look down the barrel of a loaded pistol with the hammer back and your finger on the trigger."

Esther shivered at the thought, then opened her purse, pulled out the small Smith & Wesson and handed it to him before setting her purse on the couch. Mitch slid it into his jacket's left pocket and reminded himself he had to clean and reload the pistol and Goldie when they returned.

Maggie entered the front room and smiled as she sat down in a chair facing the couch.

Esther said, "You have very good timing, Maggie. I don't suppose that it was just coincidental."

"I'll let you figure out if I was eavesdropping. Are you going to get married as soon as you return to Salmon City?"

Esther looked at Mitch and waited for him to answer the question.

Mitch took the hint and replied, "I sure wouldn't want her to move into the big house before we were hitched, so I reckon we'd better avoid the gossip and visit the judge the first day we're back."

Then he looked at Esther and asked, "Is that alright?"

"I was hoping we'd find a justice of the peace in Millersburg, but I suppose I can wait until we reach Salmon City."

"I need to arrange for Aaron's burial, too."

"He wasn't married; was he?"

"No, but he was visitin' Annabelle Gruber, so I reckon that I'll have to tell her. He was gonna propose to her, but I had a feelin' that he mighta been disappointed if he did. I knew her since she was just a young girl and a lot longer than Aaron did. Annabelle was one of those women you were talkin' about who liked to have men tell her how pretty she was. I never told him. I figured it was personal. I'll still tell her, but I reckon she'll just move on."

"What about the stagecoach driver. Did he have family?"

"Nope. He was a lifelong bachelor and enjoyed bein' on his own. That was why he liked drivin' the stage."

"You'll have to hire another deputy."

"I was already short one deputy after Steve left to work for Lyle, so I'll need two more. But after we get back and I have our undertaker take care of Aaron, we can see Judge Whitlock about gettin' married."

Maggie said, "I might be able to help you find a new deputy, Mitch. One of our ranch hands who went on the wagon to take Aaron and the driver's bodies to Millersburg always wanted to be a lawman. He's a very dependable young man and I'm sure you'd be able to train him to be a good deputy."

"Have I ever met him?"

"I'm sure that you have because whenever you stopped by, he dropped whatever he was doing just to talk to you. His name is Ryan Grady."

"Is he about three inches shorter than me with reddish-brown hair and blue eyes?"

Maggie laughed as she nodded and said, "That's him. I'm surprised that you remember meeting him. He said that you barely even nodded when he introduced himself."

"I reckon it musta seemed kinda rude, but Esther already made me mend my ways. I'll either see him on the way back or find him in Millersburg and we'll talk a bit."

"I'm sure he'll be very happy to hear what your voice sounds like."

"After we've been back for a week or so, I reckon the whole town is gonna figure I was a doppelganger sheriff."

Esther said, "You'd just have to show them some of your scars to prove your identity. Of course, there is that one in a private place that was too embarrassing to show to the nurse who was suturing your wounds."

"It's not 'cause it was in a private place. It's just that it's pretty ugly."

"If we're going to be married in a couple of days, I'm going to see it anyway; aren't I?"

"Yes, ma'am. Maybe you oughta see it before we get married. You might be scared off."

Esther laughed then said, "I promise it won't scare me off. You can show it to me when we're in the privacy of the stagecoach, so you won't have to worry about it."

"I suppose I might as well get it over with before we get back. I'm gonna wait on the porch for a while. Do you want to join me?"

"Of course, I do."

He helped her stand but just held her hand as they walked out of the room. Once on the porch, he waited until she was sitting in one of the rocking chairs then slid the second one closer and sat down himself.

Esther looked west and asked, "We can't see the intersection with the main road from here; can we?"

"Nope. But if we see a rider instead of a coach, I figure it'll be Steve Finch comin' to tell us about the stage."

"Then we'll wait here until it shows up?"

"No, ma'am. If Steve tells us that it's on its way, we'll let him drive us to the intersection in the damaged stage and we'll wait there. They'll most likely have passengers, so if we meet 'em on the main road, it won't add more time to their trip."

She smiled as she said, "And when we're riding to the intersection, you can show me your hideous scar. I'm sure it's not nearly as bad as you believe. I've seen some pretty bad ones over the years."

Mitch nodded and was about to contradict her when Maggie stepped onto the porch with Esther's purse and handed it to her.

Esther smiled and said, "Thank you, Maggie. I forgot that I'd left it on the couch."

"I hope there's nothing valuable inside."

"Not valuable to anyone else, but I have a small book of poetry that means a lot to me."

Before Maggie turned to leave, Mitch popped to his feet and walked to the edge of the porch and stared at the road. He had spotted a rider and immediately recognized Steve Finch's dark brown horse.

Esther and Maggie both looked in that direction and Esther asked, "Is it Steve Finch?"

"Yes, ma'am. He'll be here in about five minutes or so."

They continued to watch until he turned down the access road. Mitch then hopped to the ground and walked to the stagecoach where he stopped and waited.

Steve soon pulled his dark gelding to a dusty stop, dismounted and grinned as he led his horse closer to Mitch.

"The stage will be comin' in about thirty minutes. They were really happy when they got my telegram about what you did, Mitch. I reckon the bank will be even happier to get their money back. I ran into Lyle about halfway between here and the way station and he told me what happened. I'm surprised you didn't shoot her. She was tryin' to fill you with lead."

Mitch shrugged then asked, "Are you goin' back with this stage, Steve? The strongbox is inside."

"Yup. Sheriff Borden is waitin' for me back at the way station. There's a married couple takin' the southbound coach, but I never met 'em before."

"Did you know their names?"

"Nope. I didn't ask."

"I reckon it's not important. Go ahead and tie off your horse behind the stage and get in the driver's seat. I'll help Esther get inside and we'll wait for the regular coach at the intersection. Okay?"

"Alright, Mitch."

As Steve led his horse to the back of the coach, Mitch leapt onto the porch. Esther had already risen from her rocking chair, so he took her hand and smiled at Maggie.

"I really appreciate your hospitality, Maggie. When Earl gets back, tell him I'm grateful."

"I'm sure he already knows, Mitch. Besides, he wound up with three more horses, three sets of tack, and more Winchesters."

"I might be takin' one of his ranch hands to balance that scale. Ryan will let you know when he gets back with your wagon."

Maggie then kissed Esther on the cheek then gave a short peck to Mitch before he helped Esther down the porch steps.

They both waved to Maggie before Mitch helped her into the coach. He glanced up at Steve who already had the reins in his hands then climbed inside. He hadn't even turned to sit down when the stage lurched forward, and Mitch almost fell onto the strongbox at the other end of the floor.

After dropping onto the leather seat beside Esther, he grinned and said, "I almost needed you fix me up again."

"Speaking of that, now that we're alone, you can show me your mysterious scar."

"Okay, but don't say I didn't warn you."

Esther laughed lightly as Mitch opened his jacket, slipped off his gunbelt and set it on the opposite seat. As she watched he unbuckled his belt and unbuttoned his britches and shirt then folded the left sides of his jacket and his shirt behind him.

As he watched her eyes, he pulled down the side of his pants and underwear exposing the side of his torso to eight inches below the top of his pelvis.

Esther may not have believed it could be that bad but when she saw the long, poorly repaired scar, she almost gasped.

She quietly asked, "How did that happen, Mitch? It looks more like a bad burn than a gunshot or knife wound."

As he pulled up his britches, he said, "You're right about the burn, but it was a gunshot wound first. I was still a deputy sheriff in Oregon City and was chasin' two brothers named John and Joe Goodfellow. They weren't exactly good fellers and had just stolen four horses, which was a hangin' offense. I tracked 'em for almost a day when I spotted 'em ridin' down this narrow valley. It was more like a rocky tunnel than a real valley. They saw me and hid behind a tangle of rocks. Now I was still young and cocky and what made it worse was that I just bought a new Henry. It was my first repeater and I figured that I was king of the hill. And once those boys knew I could rain a bunch of .44s down on 'em, I figured that they'd just throw up their hands.

"So, after they hunkered down, I tied off my horse, grabbed my new Henry and began climbin' those rocks until I could shoot down on 'em. I had a box of spare cartridges in my pocket, so I wasn't worried. I kept climbin' at an angle to get closer. I was about two hundred yards out and was lookin' at the spot I figured would be perfect to start shootin' when the brothers opened fire. I never even checked where they were."

He was buckling his gunbelt around his waist when Esther asked, "Is that when you were hit?"

315

"Nope. I heard both of their bullets ricochet off some nearby rocks. That's when I made my second big mistake. I figured I had another fifteen seconds or so while they reloaded their rifles and just started climbin' faster. I only got about ten more feet when they both fired again. One of 'em hit me, but I knew I couldn't stop now 'cause I was so close to where I wanted to go, and I'd be able to hide. They fired again just before I tumbled into the small patch of level ground behind those rocks. I sat down and pulled my knife to cut away my britches to check the wound. I remember how surprised I was to find that the bullet had passed beneath my knife.

"Anyway, when I cut open the cloth, I knew I had to stop the bleedin' fast. So, I began piling some dry grass and then tossed some dry twigs on top. I took a match from my shirt pocket and set the grass on fire. Then I held my knife over the flames until it was startin' to glow and, well, you saw how I stopped the bleedin'. It took me a couple of minutes to settle down and I figured that the Goodfellow brothers were using the time to reload their Spencers.

"Once I thought I could start to return fire, I didn't just pop over the top of the rocks and start shootin' like a nervous Nellie. I crawled up the hill until I was layin' close to the edge and could see 'em behind their rocks. I was kinda surprised when I noticed that they were just talkin' as if I wasn't even there anymore. I reckoned they must have seen their hit and they'd were just waitin' for me to bleed out. When I proved otherwise, Joe was hit right off and couldn't return fire. John took two more shots before he fell. It took me a while to get their bodies back to Oregon City. When I got back, Sheriff Croaker was so proud of me that I didn't even tell him that I was shot. Other than me, you're the only person who has ever seen it."

"I'll admit that it's pretty ugly. But are you telling me that you haven't been with any women since that injury?"

Mitch's distressed face answered her question before he replied, "It's a hard thing for a guy to admit, but I've never been with a woman at all."

Esther was more than mildly surprised as she asked, "Why not? It's quite obvious that you like women."

"Why would you think so?"

She smiled as she replied, "Each time I was suturing your wounds, I observed that you were…um, inspired when my hand was touching your bare skin. And that was when you were in pain."

"I was hopin' that you didn't notice. At least you didn't laugh."

"Trust me, Mitch. Laughing was the last thing on my mind. I'll tell you what was on my mind on our wedding night. So, why haven't you ever been with a woman? Not that I'm complaining, mind you."

"I was kinda afraid of girls after leavin' the work farm and then I was too busy learnin' how to be a lawman. I didn't want to do anything that might make Sheriff Croaker think I was immoral, either. I was gettin' pretty interested in ladies when Abe Croaker died, and I left Oregon City. After I got settled in Salmon City, it took me a while before I finally figured it was time to find a wife. But then you showed up and I stopped lookin'.

Esther was ready to kiss him when he quickly asked, "What was the worst wounds you had to sew up?"

She suspected he was still embarrassed about his virginity, so she smiled and said, "My father did most of the really bad ones and my mother assisted. I only observed until I was thirteen or so. I suppose the worst ones that I had to suture on my own were yours. When I was working in Boise, I wasn't allowed to do much more than bathe patients and empty their bedpans."

"Tell me about Boise."

As the stagecoach rolled toward the intersection, Esther told Mitch of her indifferent treatment by most of the staff at the hospital. The exception was when some of the doctors and male nurses expressed their interest in a liaison but nothing more.

Just before they reached the main road, Steve pulled the stage to a stop, set the handbrake and climbed down.

Mitch looked at Esther and said, "Just relax while I wait with Steve for the scheduled stage."

"Okay."

Mitch quickly left the coach but stayed near the door.

When Steve stepped close, he said, "That stage will be showin' up pretty soon."

Mitch nodded as he looked north and replied, "I reckon so."

Steve grinned as he said, "When I met Lyle on the road a little while ago, he told me what happened when you found that blonde. That musta been pretty strange."

"I gotta admit that it was pretty queer."

"I was kinda surprised that you didn't shoot her after she fired a few rounds at you. I woulda been so mad by then that I wouldn't care one bit about killin' her, no matter how good-lookin' she was."

"I reckon you would at that."

"Lyle said he'd send me or Jimmy out there in a week or so to check on her. I hope he sends me. If she tries to take a shot at me, I'd be bringin' her body back to Lewiston."

Mitch hadn't been surprised by Steve's comment. It was one of the reasons he was glad that he had gone to Lewiston. While Pete and Aaron were both young and still learning the job, he thought that both of them were already better lawmen than Steve would ever be despite his almost ten years of experience. He was too quick to react and prided himself on his prowess with his Colt. But there were other, less obvious facets of Steve's character that hinted at a darker nature.

Rather than explaining his reason for not shooting Jane, Mitch just grunted and said, "Here comes the stage."

Steve turned around and said, "I'll help gettin' your things down from the roof."

"Let's do that."

Steve clambered to the driver's seat and handed Mitch Goldie and then his saddlebags. Mitch hung his saddlebags over his shoulder then leaned his Winchester against the front wheel before Steve lowered Esther's travel bags into his waiting hands.

Steve then sat down and watched the approaching stage while Mitch stepped back to the window and looked at Esther.

He didn't have to ask if she'd overheard their brief conversation after seeing the curious look in her brown eyes.

He smiled and said, "Later."

Esther nodded and asked, "Do you know the driver and shotgun rider?"

"Yes, ma'am. The driver is Will Dooley. His first name is Wilson, but nobody calls him that. The shotgun rider is Jim Branford. I'm just kinda curious about the other passengers. I figured that if they lived in Salmon City, Steve would have recognized 'em. They could be just passin' through, but maybe they're just visitin' a relative."

"We'll find out soon enough."

Mitch smiled then looked north again. The stage was less than a mile away and Will Dooley had it moving fast. He must have heard the whole story from Lyle and wanted to get more details. Mitch would be happy to provide them, but not until they arrived in Millersburg.

When the fully manned stagecoach pulled to a stop before the intersection, Jim Branford climbed down and hurried to where Mitch stood.

As he snatched Esther's travel bags, he said, "Lyle told us a lot of what happened, so I reckon you and your lady are kinda anxious to head back."

"You're right about that, Jim. I'll be right behind you. Oh, and tell Will that if he sees a wagon heading north, to pull up and if one of the two fellers is named Ryan Grady. I need to talk to him."

Jim replied, "I'll let him know, Mitch," then walked to the boot behind his coach.

Mitch picked up Goldie before he opened the door. He helped Esther step down and continued to hold her hand as she walked to the other stagecoach with only a slight hitch in her step.

She said, "I heard him call me your lady, Mitch. I guess our secret is out."

"And here I was plannin' on sneakin' you into the house without anyone knowin'."

She laughed, and just when they reached the scheduled stage, the door suddenly sprang open courtesy of the gentleman passenger.

Mitch assisted Esther inside and after she sat down, she thought he'd climb in behind her, but he didn't. He stood beside the open door even as Jim trotted past after storing her travel bags in the boot then climbed back to his position on the driver's seat.

Will looked down and was about to ask Mitch why he wasn't boarding yet when Steve drove past and headed north. Mitch watched the departing coach for another ten seconds before climbing into the cabin and closing the door. Once inside, he set his saddlebags on the floor before he sat down beside Esther. After wedging Goldie's stock into the edge of the seat and leaning the barrel against the seatback, Jim snapped his long reins, and the team yanked the stage forward.

Esther wondered why he had delayed entering the coach and added it to her earlier stored question about Steve's comment about what he would do if he'd encountered a gun-wielding Jane Newsome.

After ensuring that Goldie was secure, Mitch smiled at the couple sitting across from them. He guessed that they were in their mid-forties and judging by their wardrobe, he thought the man was a successful businessman. He was dark haired without a hint of gray and sported a well-trimmed beard. He wore a dark gray wool suit and had his jacket unbuttoned because it was probably too warm already. He had a bowler hat on the seat beside him and a gold watch chain stretched across his dark gray vest. His wife's light brown hair was properly styled even after a day's journey. Her blue eyes were expressive, and Mitch thought they were a well-suited couple.

After his almost instant evaluation, he said, "Good mornin', folks. I'm Lemhi County Sheriff Mitch Ward and this is my fiancée, Miss Esther Cohen."

After a short pause, the husband replied, "Good morning, Sheriff. I'm Reverend Ralph Berthold and this is my wife, Elizabeth. We'll soon be the newest residents of Salmon City. I've been sent by my bishop to replace Reverend Summers."

"I heard that he wasn't feelin' well and even missed a few services. Is he gonna stay in Salmon City?"

"No. He's going to return to Portland to recover."

"I hope he gets better. I'm sure that you'll be welcomed by the congregation and the other folks in Salmon City. It's a peaceful town and I'm sure you'll be happy there."

Elizabeth Berthold had been looking at Esther but then turned her eyes to Mitch as she said, "Deputy Finch told us about your horrible experience when you tried to transport a gang leader to Lewiston. I pray that it was a unique situation."

"Yes, ma'am. They won't be causin' any more trouble."

She then looked at Esther again and said, "The deputy told us that you were in the stagecoach as well and had been knocked unconscious when the gang freed their leader. He said that you managed to escape which must have been very frightening. Thank God that you weren't violated."

Esther replied, "I did thank God for His deliverance. Then I thanked Mitch for finding me before they even knew I was free."

Elizabeth asked, "How long have you and the sheriff been courting?"

Esther glanced at Mitch before smiling and replying, "Almost three years."

Mitch suppressed a laugh but still grinned before he looked out the window. Just a few seconds later, the eastbound road passed before his eyes. After passing the turnoff, he knew that they'd soon be climbing into the mountains and then pass where he'd left the bodies. That made him wonder what they did with Frog's remains. He hoped young Ryan Grady and the other ranch hand didn't add the outlaw's body to the wagon alongside Aaron and Al's.

Reverend Berthold then asked, "Sheriff, wasn't there a young woman involved in the brazen plot to free that gang leader? I thought you'd be taking her back to Salmon City as a prisoner after eliminating the others."

"Well, Reverend, I did bring her back, but she escaped."

"Really? Did you chase after her or let her go?"

"I kinda did both. We've got to fill the time to Millersburg, so I might as well use up some of it by tellin' you the story."

Esther listened as Mitch told the reverend and his wife about the confrontation with Jane Newsome. Even though she'd heard it more than once before, she was still transfixed by the tale and listened for any new details. It also reminded her to ask him about Steve Finch's claim of what he would have done if she'd fired at him.

After he finished the story and answered their many questions, they asked him to tell the entire story of Ace's escape and his takedown of each of the gang members. Esther had to explain what Mitch hadn't seen and answer questions that he couldn't.

By the time the storytelling ended, they'd emptied one of the canteens. Ten minutes later the stagecoach slowed, and Mitch knew that they weren't close to Millersburg or one of the streams, so he suspected that he was about to talk to his prospective new deputy.

When it pulled to a stop, he turned to Esther and said, "I'll be right back," then opened the door and hopped out.

When the door closed, Elizabeth pointed to Goldie and exclaimed, "The sheriff forgot his rifle!"

Esther smiled and replied, "He's just interviewing a young man who wants to be one of his deputies."

As his wife looked out the window to see where Mitch was, her husband said, "I hope this doesn't delay our arrival in Millersburg."

"I doubt if he takes more than a minute or two. He's a very decisive man."

"How can he make such an important decision so quickly?"

"Mitch has the wisdom of Solomon. And I should know."

Elizabeth turned her eyes back to Esther as she said, "Yes, I can imagine that is so. Is the sheriff Jewish as well?"

"No, he's a Catholic."

She and her husband both seem startled by her answer before she said, "Oh. My husband and I are Methodist. Of course, the sheriff would know that as he will be replacing Mister Summers."

Esther was about to reply when Mitch climbed back into the cabin. After he sat beside Esther, the coach began rolling and as the wagon heading north passed, he waved at the two ranch hands.

He looked at Esther and said, "Ryan will be comin' to Salmon City next week. I told him to have Earl give him one of those three horses, a set of tack and one of the Winchesters. He said the Millersburg mortician already sent Aaron's and Al's bodies to Salmon City this mornin'."

Reverend Berthold asked, "Did you know the young man long?"

"No, sir. I only met him a couple of times before but didn't talk to him."

"Then how did you know he was a good candidate for a deputy?"

"I just asked him a couple of questions."

"I assume one was how proficient he was with firearms."

"No, sir. I can always train a new deputy to shoot. I asked him if he could read and write first. After he told me he had eight years of schoolin', I asked him what was more important, the law or justice. He said justice right off. I was gonna offer him the job right then, but then he kinda confessed that he just did a bad thing, and I oughta know about it before he made the trip to Salmon City. He said that after he and Eddie Stubbins put my deputy and the driver's bodies in the wagon, they rolled the outlaw's carcass down the side of the road into a deep crevice. I told him it was the right thing to do, and I was hopin' that they didn't load it onto the wagon with the good men."

Elizabeth asked, "You don't believe that all men deserve a Christian burial?"

"I didn't bury the ones I left at the ranch either, ma'am. To me, those fellers weren't even men. If God wants to forgive 'em, it doesn't matter where He finds 'em."

Esther then asked, "Did you know the other ranch hand?"

"Not much more'n I knew Ryan. But he asked me if he could come to town with Ryan, so I could interview him for my last openin'. I reckon I'll probably hire him, too. He and Ryan seem to be good friends and that's important in this business. He seems to be an honest young man, too."

Elizabeth asked, "How can you tell?"

"For one thing, I stared into his eyes ,and he never looked away. And he's been workin' for Earl Ferguson for four years and Earl isn't the kind of man who tolerates bad behavior. I was impressed that they didn't even ask what happened to the rest of the gang even though they musta been anxious to know about it. I reckon they didn't want to keep the stage waitin'. That shows patience and it's important in a lawman. Besides, if I hire 'em, I can always send 'em packin' if they don't work out."

Esther looked at Mitch and said, "Like Steve Finch."

Mitch replied, "I didn't send him packin', but I was kinda glad when Steve went to Lewiston. And to answer the question you didn't ask yet, I was kinda worried he might drive that wagon east after we left, so I waited 'til he headed north to the way station."

"Thank you for answering the first of my unasked questions."

Elizabeth smiled and said, "It's quite obvious that you have been spending a lot of time together during your long courtship. I can't imagine there is anything that you don't know about each other after three years. Have you finally set a date for your wedding?"

Mitch replied, "Yes, ma'am. We're gonna tie the knot when we get back to Salmon City."

"Will you be married in the Catholic church after Miss Cohen converts?"

Mitch glanced at Esther who didn't help him one bit when all she did was smile.

When his eyes returned to Mrs. Berthold, he replied, "No, ma'am. We'll be married by the county judge."

Elizabeth looked at Esther but didn't say anything.

Her reverend husband then moved away from the topics of marriage and religion and asked Mitch about his choice of guns. It was a wise decision and kept the conversation safely away from delicate subjects for the rest of the trip to Millersburg.

But even as he explained his affection for Smith & Wesson revolvers, Mitch wondered why Mrs. Berthold had not only believed that he was Catholic, but that Esther would convert. He'd ask her when they were alone.

————

It was late afternoon when the stage pulled into Millersburg and Mitch helped Esther leave the coach after Reverend Berthold assisted his wife from the cabin.

Esther only needed to take one of her travel bags. So, after Jim Branford handed Mitch her overnight bag, he and Esther walked to the hotel where they'd stayed just a few nights earlier.

As they approached the desk, Esther said, "It seems like it was ages ago since we left this hotel."

"We weren't gonna get married when we were here the last time either."

When they reached the desk, the clerk who seemed indifferent at best the first time they'd checked in, smiled and said, "The whole town is buzzing about all that happened to you and Miss Cohen since you left, Sheriff."

He replied, "I reckon so," as Esther signed the register and the clerk handed Mitch two room keys.

Mitch knew that Ryan and Eddie had left the Ferguson ranch before he'd even ridden east to find Ace and the others, so the clerk must have only heard about the escape and his pursuit. He expected that the clerk was expecting him to tell him more details but wasn't about to spend twenty minutes standing at the desk. He was pretty hungry and knew that Esther was probably just as anxious to have supper as he was. He hadn't dipped into his saddlebags' store of jerky during the ride because he wasn't sure he had enough for everyone. He also doubted that Mrs. Berthold was a fan of the tough salty meat and suspected her reverend husband would also decline an offer. He was pretty sure that neither of them would dare be so crude as to eat with their fingers, especially in mixed company.

When Esther finished writing, he exchanged her key for the pen and added his name to the register. He picked up her travel bag then started walking to their rooms as the Reverend and Mrs. Berthold entered the lobby carrying three travel bags.

Mitch glanced back before they entered the hallway and asked, "Do you think I shoulda asked 'em to join us for supper at The Widows' Kitchen?"

"I'm sure we'll meet them again shortly. You can answer my other question about Steve Finch while we're having our dinner."

"And you can tell me why the reverend's wife asked me if we were gonna get married in the Catholic church after you converted to bein' Catholic."

Esther laughed as she opened the door to her room and Mitch followed her inside where he set her travel bag on the floor near the chest of drawers.

After leaving Goldie and his saddlebags in his room, they left the hotel without seeing the Bertholds and walked to The Widows' Kitchen.

They had barely taken their seats when Mary hurried to their table with Alice trailing a few feet behind.

Mary smiled as she said, "Welcome back, Mitch."

Alice then added, "And we're glad to see you as well, Miss Cohen. We heard about that gang leader's escape, and we were so relieved to hear that you both were safe."

Mitch asked, "How did you even know we were comin', Alice?"

"Sheriff Ward sent a telegram from the way station to Marshal Thompson letting him know that you'd killed all of the Carr gang and would be returning on the stage with Miss Cohen. It was a long telegram, but I'm sure that it left out a lot of details. We're not going to bother to ask about them because we're sure that you're both exhausted from your ordeal and in need of a good meal, too."

"I appreciate your consideration, Alice. And yours too, Mary. I'll let you decide what we'll have for supper as usual."

Mary said, "We'll be right back," then she and her sister bustled away.

Mitch said, "I was wonderin' how word got out. That means that my only deputy, Pete Carter knows most of it by now, and he'll be able to arrange for Aaron's burial before we get there."

"You'll still have a lot to do; won't you?"

"Yes, ma'am. But one of 'em won't be askin' Father O'Neill to marry us. Can I guess that you told the reverend's wife that I was Catholic?"

"I suppose I might have mentioned it. Ward is an Irish name; isn't it?"

"I reckon so, but I never knew anything about my parents or where they came from. And I sure wasn't baptized a Catholic or anything else that I know about, either."

"I hope I didn't cause you any embarrassment."

Mitch snickered then said, "Not a bit. It was just a might confusin' for a few seconds."

"Now you can tell me why you didn't say a word after Steve Finch almost bragged about wanting to shoot Jane."

"It wouldn't have mattered if I did. Remember when I said that I'd probably hire both Ryan and Eddie because patience makes for a good lawman? Well, Steve didn't have any at all. He always acted before thinkin' and that was one of the biggest reasons that I was happy to see him go. I reckon it won't be too long before it gets him killed or even worse, he shoots somebody who didn't need a bullet."

"Did you always have patience, Mitch?"

"I kinda learned how important it was when I was at the work farm. But even then, it took a while."

"I'm glad that you learned patience, but even happier that you've discarded your vow of silence."

Mitch laughed then said, "It wasn't a vow, and I wasn't silent. But I'll admit I didn't talk much. It helped me survive that place but I shoulda figured out I didn't need it anymore after I ran off."

Esther was smiling when Alice and Mary arrived with two overfilled trays.

"That's a lot of food, ladies," Mitch said as he watched them move the loaded plates from the trays.

Alice said, "We knew that you and Miss Cohen needed it, Mitch."

"I appreciate your concern, but I don't know if we'll be able to finish all of it."

Mary replied, "Sure, you will," before they picked up the empty trays and carried them back to the kitchen.

Esther stared at her plate and said, "I'm famished, but I won't be able to eat all this."

"Well, it's sittin' in front of us, so let's see how far we get."

Mitch filled both of the large cups with coffee, then picked up his fork and knife and dug in.

They been eating for almost ten minutes when Mitch spotted the town marshal enter the diner and after their eyes met, he hurried to their table.

As soon as he stopped beside Mitch, he said, "I hate to bother you folks, but I just got a telegram from Sheriff Borden. He's still at the way station and was wonderin' where his deputy was. I didn't reply 'cause I figured I'd ask you first."

Mitch stared at Kent for a few seconds before saying, "I watched him headin' north before we started this way. He shoulda reached the way station about two hours ago."

"Do you reckon some friends of Ace Carr met up with him?"

"Nope. I figure Steve decided to be a hero and drive the stage to their hideout to face down Ace's girlfriend."

"Lyle is waitin' for my answer, so I'll let him know what you said."

"Kent, tell him to head to the intersection but wait for me there. He's in no shape to deal with any problems. I'll need the use of a good horse for a few hours."

"You're gonna ride down there right now? You'll be gettin' there after dark."

"I know. Go ahead and send the telegram and find me a horse. I'll meet you at your office in a little while."

Marshal Thompson said, "Okay, Mitch," then turned and quickly left the diner.

Mitch looked at Esther and said, "It could just be that somethin' broke on the stagecoach, but I need to be sure. I've gotta go, Esther."

"I know. I'll stay here until you return."

"Alright. Do you have enough money?"

"I'm fine."

"Um...about the house and all my other stuff..."

She interrupted him when she snapped, "Stop! I don't want to hear any talk about what I should do if you don't return. I don't care how evil that woman is, she won't stop you from coming back to me."

"I'm not worried about her as much as I am about Steve Finch."

Esther was surprised but didn't ask why he was concerned about his old deputy. She knew he needed to eat quickly before he rode north.

———

Since he started driving the stagecoach to the way station, Steve had been thinking about the blonde woman that Mitch had left at the hidden ranch. He couldn't imagine that a powder burn would make that much of a difference in her appearance. And it wouldn't have changed her impressive figure at all. Without a horse, she was trapped and would be

337

pretty grateful to a man who arrived with a stagecoach and a saddled horse.

Then there was that strongbox of cash in the cabin just a few feet away. Mitch hadn't counted it, but Steve knew how much had been stolen from the bank. The rest of the gang's loot was probably inside, so he figured the total must be over five thousand dollars.

He drove more than halfway to the way station before he made a wide U-turn. He removed his badge from his jacket and put it in his jacket pocket. He knew he wouldn't get to the hidden ranch until sunset, but he wasn't worried. He'd wave his hat over his head when he turned down the access road to let her know he wasn't there to arrest her.

––––––––

Hours earlier, after the hated sheriff left her ranch house, Jane remained inside and didn't even watch him ride off through the front window. She avoided looking at her face in her mirror but collected the Winchester and her pistol and set them on the kitchen table. She then returned to her bedroom then laid on her bed with the towel across her face. She stayed there for over an hour letting her hate for Sheriff Ward simmer.

When she finally left her bedroom, she returned the kitchen and pumped water into the sink and carefully removed the bloody towel.

She soaked it in the cold water and gently began to clean her face. After the preliminary cleansing, she examined the towel and saw black stains in addition to the red blood. She smiled when she believed that the sheriff had been lying after all. She thought she'd wiped all of the burnt gunpowder from her face and now just needed the swelling to recede. She then touched her fingertips to her wound and while it was still oozing blood, it wasn't as bad as she believed. She still couldn't see out of her left eye, but thought it was only because of the swelling. She kept the wet towel pressed against the small gouge in her forehead as she took a seat at the table.

When she'd probed her wound, her sensitive, damaged skin told her the extent of the powder burn. But she was sure that the sheriff had only told her that it was hideous and permanent to hurt her. She knew that he couldn't shoot her and was confident that no jury of twelve men would convict her either. Ace had told her just last month that he was considering recruiting more handsome young women gang members just for that reason. Jane had convinced him that he only needed one.

Jane laughed as she began to believe that all she had to worry about now was to find a way off the ranch. She knew that she didn't have a horse, but she had enough food for a month. By then, her wound would be healed, and she'd be able to stop a passing rider to take her to Elk City . The swelling in her left eye should go down in a couple of days and she'd have her eyesight back.

Jane felt better about her situation, but still wasn't about to look at her face in the mirror. Not until she could clean all of the powder burn and look at her reflected image with both eyes.

She stood and walked to the front room to check outside. She saw the coyotes and vultures fighting over Ace's body, then walked to the shattered window and saw more vultures feasting on the dead horse. She was sure that more coyotes or maybe some wolves and bears would arrive later. She had yet to notice the three bodies near the boulders.

She walked back to the kitchen to make herself something to eat. If she had to go to the privy, she'd have the Winchester with her in case one of those four-legged scavengers decided that she would make a nice snack.

————

As Mitch escorted Esther back to the hotel, she asked, "Why are you worried about Steve Finch more than Jane? Is it because of his impatience?"

"Nope. I don't reckon Steve will try to shoot it out with Jane. Steve was one of those men who is still standin' at the fork in the road of good and bad. It won't take much to make him take the wrong direction. I was worryin' that he might head east and keep goin' after he found Jane."

Esther was surprised, but asked, "Then why would he share it with Jane? Didn't he believe you when you said she was seriously disfigured by that gunshot?"

"He saw her when she wasn't marked at all, so he probably figured I made it sound worse than it was. The added temptation of that strongbox full of cash makes me pretty sure that's where he's headed."

"Do you think he really might try to kill you if he gets a chance?"

"If he expects anyone to chase after him, he'll be lookin' for Lyle. He'll know that Lyle can't shoot a rifle, so he won't worry much. But it'll be dark when we find him, so even if he figures we're both comin', we'll probably see him first."

"I suppose I'll just have to get used to almost constant worry now; won't I?"

"Bad ones like this don't happen much, Esther. If I hire Ryan and Eddie, that'll give me three good deputies I can trust, so it'll be even safer."

Esther nodded as they left the boardwalk and entered the hotel.

After opening the door to her room, Esther turned and let her big brown eyes latch onto Mitch's strong hazels.

Mitch smiled as he wrapped her in his arms and kissed her.

Esther let him understand that this wasn't a goodbye kiss, but just a preview of their first night together in their big house in Salmon City.

After the kiss ended, Mitch said, "I'll see you tomorrow, Esther."

"I'll be waiting, Sheriff Ward."

Mitch smiled, then headed to his room where he retrieved Goldie and his saddlebags.

He was still smiling as he passed Esther who was still standing in her doorway with her arms folded. He was grateful that she hadn't tried to remind him once more about their wedding night. It was already uncomfortably difficult for him to walk back to the lobby.

Mitch hurried to the jail where he met Kent Thompson who was standing out front holding the reins to a tall black gelding.

As he accepted the reins, Mitch said, "He's a mighty handsome feller, Kent."

"He's my favorite, so bring him back healthy, Mitch."

Mitch slid Goldie into the scabbard then mounted before he replied, "I'll make sure of it, Kent. Blondie ain't gonna shoot your friend."

He waved then wheeled the big horse to the right then set him to a medium trot to leave Millersburg.

As he rode past the hotel, he wasn't surprised to find Esther standing outside. He waved as he passed and even though she smiled when she returned his wave, he could see the lingering concern in her big brown eyes. It made him more determined than ever to avoid being shot.

He turned onto the northern road and set the gelding to a fast trot. He wanted to reach the curve around Mount Idaho before the sun set and that was a tall order. He was pleased that Kent hadn't dragged out some nag from the back of the corral.

———

Thirty minutes after Mitch left Millersburg, Lyle Borden read the telegram from Marshal Thornton. He couldn't believe that Steve had gone to the gang's hideout but would still ride to the intersection to meet Mitch. He hoped to see the stagecoach off the side of the road with a broken wheel rather than not find it at all. But because Steve still had his horse tied to the back of the stagecoach, he had to admit it was more likely that Mitch was right, and his deputy had headed east to the gang's hideout. As he folded the telegram and stuffed it into his pocket, he still had no idea of Steve Finch's real reason for taking the stagecoach east rather than north.

He soon rode his buckskin out of the way station heading south at a medium trot.

———

Steve had made the left turn onto the eastbound road, then stopped and checked both directions on the main road before he continued. He expected that his new boss would be wondering where he was but wouldn't leave the way station until the morning. Besides, Lyle couldn't shoot with his bum arm.

Steve was much more concerned about his old boss. After working with Mitch for the past few years, Steve wasn't about to disregard the possibility that he might suddenly appear. While he believed that Mitch wouldn't know that he hadn't arrived at the way station until tomorrow morning, he still had a small measure of concern that Mitch was already headed his way. Then he grinned when he figured that the Jewish woman might be keeping him too occupied to even think about him or the stagecoach.

Despite that amusing image, as he drove east, Steve began to create an alibi for his decision to drive the coach east instead of returning to the way station in case Mitch did find him before he headed to Elk City with Jane and the strongbox.

———

Mitch had let the gelding drink from White Bird Creek before he continued riding and soon passed where he'd jumped from the stage. He quickly passed where he'd left Aaron and Al's bodies and noticed that his flag was still there. He soon spotted some dried blood on the ground where Frog bled to death. The curve was less than a mile away.

When he rounded the mountain, the sky was deep red, but the sun provided enough light for him to spot a rider approaching the turnoff to Elk City. He knew it had to be Lyle and asked the gelding for more speed as he began the long descent to the Camas Plains.

———

Jane was leaving the privy carrying her Winchester when she picked up something moving along the road to her left. She shielded her one good eye against the dying sun and spotted the stagecoach.

She snapped, "That son of a bitch!" then hurried into the house.

Once inside she continued down the hallway and entered the front room. She thought that Sheriff Ward had changed his mind and had decided to take her to jail after all. She wasn't about to let that happen and she wasn't going to miss this time.

She pulled a straight-backed chair close to one of the windows and after opening it as far as possible, she sat down and set the Winchester's barrel on the windowsill.

She smiled as she peered down the sights knowing that the temporary loss of vision in her left eye was now an advantage.

———

Steve spotted the boulders that Lyle had told him about then checked his backtrail. He smiled in anticipation of meeting Ace's girlfriend as he slowed the stage to make the sharp turn through the stone entrance.

He had his eyes focused on the ranch house, so he didn't see the bodies in the shadows as the stage started down the access road.

Jane had her sights on the stagecoach and wondered if the sheriff really believed she wouldn't shoot him again. Maybe he thought she had killed herself because he told her that she was hideous.

She giggled as she waited. The stage was about four hundred yards out now and soon Sheriff Ward would be a dead man.

Then just as the coach was another hundred yards closer, Jane was surprised when she saw the sheriff wave his hat over his head, almost challenging her to shoot him.

She kept watching through her gunsights as she said, "You're making a big mistake, Sheriff. I hope your Jew girlfriend satisfied you before you came back here."

Steve pulled his hat back on his head and slowed the team to a walk when he spotted the coyotes just a couple of hundred yard away. Then he pulled the shotgun from its holder to frighten them off. He let the stage continue to roll closer to the coyotes who didn't seem to care that a large human vehicle was heading towards them.

Jane had seen the sheriff pull a rifle and was certain he was holding his Winchester and waiting for her to fire so he could shoot at her muzzle flare. She'd let him see the flash, but only when he was so close that she couldn't miss.

Steve was approaching the ranch house just to the right of the porch so he wouldn't hit the team when he fired both barrels into the coyotes. He was just fifty yards out and had just cocked both hammers when he saw Jane's muzzle flash. He felt the .44 rip through the tip of his right shoulder making him drop the shotgun to the ground as the team bolted away from the house heading west.

He yelled more than screamed before he snatched the reins and tried to stop the coach from tipping over as it raced across the uneven ground.

Jane knew she'd hit him when she saw the sheriff drop his rifle but didn't know if it was a fatal wound before the stagecoach accelerated and veered away. She jumped to her feet, cycled in a fresh cartridge, rushed out the door and stopped on the porch.

Steve managed to get the team to slow slightly and turned them northwest toward the road.

Jane swore and fired a useless shot at the back of the stage as it disappeared into the growing darkness.

347

She shouted, "I won't miss if you come back, you lying bastard!"

After her short tirade, she was about to return to the house but remembered he'd dropped his Winchester, so she stepped to the ground and trotted to the fallen rifle. The coyotes had temporarily abandoned their meal because of the gunfire. When she was close, she realized that it was a shotgun and not a repeater.

As she picked it up, she snapped, "That lowlife lawman was going to try to kill me with both barrels!"

She set her Winchester down, then aimed the cocked scattergun in the direction of the access road where the coyotes had been before she opened fire. Jane had never fired a shotgun before, so when she squeezed the trigger, the enormous kick from the two barrels knocked her to the ground.

She cursed then left the shotgun on the ground as she rose to her feet. As she leaned down to pick up her Winchester, she felt a sharp pain in her right shoulder from the unexpected, almost violent kickback.

Jane muttered a low curse as she returned to the house and her seat by the window. She didn't think that the sheriff would return after being shot, but she would keep watch for another half an hour or so.

———

After he regained the road, Steve Finch pulled the coach to a stop, set the handbrake and tied off the reins. After carefully stepping to the ground, he walked back to his horse and flipped open his left saddlebag's flap. He stuck his hand inside and let his fingers find his spare flannel shirt then yanked it out.

He knew he had to stop the bleeding first, so he held the clean shirt in his useless right hand and used his left to extend the tear in his bloody shirt exposing the wound. Once he thought it was big enough, he began stuffing his clean shirt over the wound. Satisfied that it would slow and eventually stop the bleeding, he walked back to the front of the stage and awkwardly climbed to the driver's seat.

Steve didn't take the reins after he sat down. He knew he needed to have the gunshot wound closed but wasn't sure which direction he should go. Elk City was about thirty-five miles behind him, but he'd have to cross the Clearwater River at night. He still wasn't sure where he'd stop when he untied the reins and released the handbrake. His right shoulder screamed when he snapped the reins, so he soon was only holding them in his left hand as he started driving west to the north-south road between Lewiston and Salmon City.

———

The two sheriffs had met at the intersection and as they rode east, Mitch told him why he'd been concerned enough to wait until Steve was driving north before getting into the stage with Esther.

"You watched him head north? He musta turned around after you were outta sight. I was hopin' to find the coach broken by the side of the road, but I knew it wasn't likely 'cause he had his horse with him. Damn! I wish this arm worked better!"

"I shoulda taken her in, Lyle."

"Nah. If I was mad at you for anything, it's about sendin' Steve Finch instead of one of your other deputies."

"I didn't send him. He volunteered. But I gotta admit that I was happy he left."

"What do you think we'll find when we get there?"

"I guess we'll find out in another couple of hours. But I reckon Steve might have been hopin' that I exaggerated how bad Jane looked and he was plannin' to keep the strongbox and ask her to come with him to Montana."

Lyle's head whipped to look at Mitch as he exclaimed, "You're kidding! You figure he went bad?"

"Maybe. Ever since I knew him, I was waitin' for him to go that way. I guess he finally found somethin' that was too temptin' to ignore."

"I hope you're wrong. It's bad enough if he just figured to go out there and shoot it out with her."

"So, do I."

"We won't have much light by the time we find him. All we'll have is that skinny moon and a lot of stars."

"I reckon it'll have to do, Lyle."

Sheriff Borden grunted as they continued to ride at a fast trot.

———

It wasn't even forty-five minutes later when the two lawmen were surprised to see the oncoming stagecoach in the diminished light.

Lyle said, "I guess he finished her off like he said he would."

While Mitch hoped Lyle was right, he still didn't think that Steve would have just gone to the hideout, shot Jane and was now driving the stage back to the way station. But he could readily believe a very different reason for Steve to be heading their way.

"I don't think so, Lyle. I reckon that Jane plugged Steve and he's needin' to be fixed up."

Lyle stared down the road as he replied, "Maybe so."

Steve hoped the bleeding had stopped but didn't remove his shirt bandage to check. He let the horses follow the road as he tried to stay awake. He had decided to return to the Ferguson ranch to get help. He still hadn't come up with a cover story yet, but he believed he had enough time to invent one.

He was watching the rumps of the back pair of horses as they bulged and relaxed. It was almost hypnotic, and he let the rhythmic movement make the pain in his shoulder fade.

Just before the stage reached them, Mitch and Lyle spread to opposite sides of the road then pulled up and turned their horses to face each other.

They both watched the stagecoach as it rolled along and when the team was close, they each wheeled their horses to the west and Mitch took hold of the lead horse's bridle while Lyle rode beside the driver's seat.

It was only when the horses stopped that Steve realized they were there. He was dazed and didn't recognize the rider who had just dismounted was now climbing up to the driver's seat.

Lyle sat down beside Steve and sharply asked, "*What the hell happened, Finch?*"

Steve looked at his boss and in an almost drunken slur, he said, "She…shot…me."

Mitch had clambered up the other side and just as he reached the driver's seat, Lyle said, "He was hit in the right shoulder, Mitch. He's kinda loopy, but I don't think he's losin' any more blood. What do you want to do with him?"

"He's your deputy and we're in your jurisdiction, but I figure we should take him back to that hideout. After I take care of Jane, I'll fix him up. How's that?"

"Sounds good to me. Let's turn this coach around."

"You take care of the drivin', Lyle. I'll get back down and tie off your horse to the back. Then I'll ride ahead of you to the hideout. When you see those boulders, pull up and wait for me to fire three shots before you drive down the access road."

"Okay."

"Oh. And watch out for nasty critters. I left those bodies out there to keep her in her prison."

"They didn't keep Steve from visitin'."

"Nope."

Mitch quickly climbed down and after taking his borrowed gelding's reins, he walked around to the other side. After tying off Lyle's buckskin, he mounted and headed east at a fast trot while Sheriff Borden began to turn the stage around.

As he rode away, Mitch wondered how he'd deal with Jane this time. He was sure that he'd be able to approach the ranch house without Jane seeing him. But those coyotes had probably been joined by more sharp-toothed scavengers who might give her a warning. He'd just have to play it by ear.

He soon decided what he'd do when he had her under control. This time, he'd have no moral qualms about it, either.

———

Jane was satisfied that the wounded sheriff wasn't coming back, so she left her observation chair and walked to the hallway. While she may not believe that Sheriff Ward would return, she wasn't going to be foolish enough to light a lamp.

She returned to the kitchen and relit the fire in the cookstove to reheat the coffee.

———

Mitch didn't see the boulders before he knew he was getting close to the hideout. He was alerted to the ranch's proximity by the snapping chatter and yapping of the coyotes. He thought he also heard the deeper growl of a large wolf who probably brought friends with him. He angled the black gelding to his right and left the roadway. He continued heading toward the arguing canines as he focused ahead searching for the shadows of the ranch house or barn.

He walked the horse slowly for another five minutes as the sounds of the feeding frenzy grew louder, but he still hadn't spotted the shadowed buildings. He was finally able to figure out where he was when he saw the hill blocking out the stars to his right. Just a few seconds later, he spotted the barn's roofline and then the top of the ranch house. He pulled Goldie as the gelding continued carrying him closer. He didn't expect Jane to see him, but he was concerned about the coyotes and the maybe some wolves.

He was about four hundred yards out when the gelding began to get skittish, so he pulled up and dismounted. If the feeding scavengers didn't give him away, the gelding might. He led the horse to a nearby bramble and tied him off.

Mitch didn't cock his Winchester but pulled the Model 1 Smith & Wesson from his left jacket pocket. If he had any problems with the coyotes, he'd use the .22 to scare them off and hope that Jane didn't hear the small pistol. If he saw heard a wolf, he'd have to use the louder Winchester.

As he stepped closer to the ranch house, he was certain that Jane was still awake and alert. She'd still be nervous after her shootout with Steve. He didn't believe for a moment that Finch had the chance to shoot her.

———

Jane had finished her reheated coffee and was still sitting at the kitchen table. She was still seething about not knocking the sheriff off the stagecoach seat. But now she had more worries. She knew she wounded him and if he was able to make it to the way station, he'd send the Nez Perces County sheriff and a posse after her. She had to get away sooner than she'd expected but didn't have a horse. If only she'd killed Ward, then she'd have the stagecoach and its four horses.

She had her empty coffee cup in her hands as she sat in the dark trying to figure out a way to reach Elk City. At least she had two Winchesters and her pistol to keep the wild critters at bay when she left the house. If she left in the morning, she could start walking to Elk City. Maybe someone would come along, then she could ask for a ride and be there by tomorrow night. She may have convinced herself that her face wasn't nearly as bad as the sheriff told her. She still believed that he had lied, but now needed to be sure if she hoped to convince a stranger to help her escape. She knew that she had to look in her mirror to be sure.

She stood and walked to her bedroom and after lighting the lamp, she picked up her purse and sat on her bed.

Jane took a deep breath, opened her purse and took out her small hand mirror. She closed her right eye and held the mirror eighteen inches in front of her face. Then she slowly opened her eye and saw a gruesome face peering back at her.

She screamed and threw the mirror against the wall before she screamed, "I'm a monster!" then buried her disfigured face into her hands and began to cry.

———

Mitch had passed the coyotes without having to fire his pistol when light suddenly shone from the house. He froze and expected to see Jane moving inside, but after not seeing any signs of her, he started walking slowly to the porch.

Then he heard her chilling scream and knew immediately that she'd just seen her face for the first time. He didn't know why she hadn't looked right after he'd gone but didn't take the time to think about it. He quietly stepped onto the porch and carefully opened the front door and stepped inside. He slid his small pistol into his pocket and switched Goldie to his left hand. He pulled his Model 3 from his holster before tiptoeing across the front room. The light was coming from one of the bedrooms, and he could hear Jane's loud sobbing.

He maintained his stealthy approach as he entered the hallway and made his way closer to the bedroom door. Even though he believed that she didn't even know he was in the house, he had to assume that Jane was faking everything to lure him into her Winchester's sights.

Jane was so shattered by that one nightmarish glimpse her right eye had revealed that she wouldn't have heard Mitch if he'd marched down the hallway with hobnail boots and jingling spurs.

She was still loudly weeping into her palms when Mitch peeked into the bedroom. If she had been any other woman, he would have felt a surge of sympathy, but not for Jane Newsome.

He didn't see a gun anywhere close by but did see her hand mirror on the floor. He holstered his pistol and took Goldie in his right hand before he stepped to the opposite side of the bed where she was sitting.

He stopped and said, "Hello, Jane. I reckon you finally looked in your mirror."

Jane yanked her face from her wet hands and whipped her head to the left to look at him. Her despair was instantly replaced by rage and confusion when she realized who had spoken.

She exclaimed, "You! I shot you! How…where…" then she stopped and began to search for signs of blood with her one good eye.

Mitch said, "You didn't shoot me, Jane. You shot Deputy Sheriff Steve Finch. I reckon he was comin' here to take you away with him in the stagecoach. He still had Ace's strongbox inside, too."

She snapped, "You're lying!"

"Well, I admit I'm only guessin', so you can believe whatever you want."

"You came back to kill me; didn't you?"

"Nope. I just got to Millersburg when I got word that the stagecoach didn't make it to the way station. I figured Steve was headed this way, so I borrowed a horse to find him."

"What are you going to do now? Are you going to leave me here again or are you taking me back to your town so you can put me on trial for murdering your deputy?"

"Neither one. I'm sendin' you to Lewiston with Sheriff Borden so they can put you on trial for attempted murder of his deputy. If they don't send you to prison for twenty years, then I'll have Lyle bring you to Salmon City where I'll have you stand trial for murderin' Aaron."

If he'd told her his decision just minutes earlier before she had looked in the mirror, Jane would have welcomed the chance to face a jury of twelve men. But now, the thought of being in a full courtroom with everyone staring at her was horrifying.

She was still looking at him when she said, "I don't want to go to trial anywhere. Why don't you just shoot me now and save yourself the trouble?"

Mitch nodded, then cocked Goldie's hammer and aimed it at the wall three feet above Jane's head. Jane was stunned and dropped to the bed as he squeezed the trigger. She was still hugging the blankets as Mitch fired three rapid rounds through the wall.

After lowering his Winchester's smoking muzzle, he said, "I'm finished shootin'. That was just a signal to Sheriff Borden that he can drive the stagecoach to the house."

Jane slowly sat back up before she said, "You're a real bastard, Sheriff."

"You could be right. I never knew my parents. Now, I've gotta make sure you don't try to shoot me in the back, so lie down on the bed."

She laughed as she laid on the blanket then spread her legs apart and said, "Are you gonna pay me my two bits now, Sheriff?"

Mitch didn't bother replying as he walked to the dresser and began pulling out some of Ace's shirts. He set Goldie on the top of the chest of drawers then walked to the bed and used one to bind Jane's wrists before pushing her feet together and tying another one around her ankles.

He looked at her and said, "Go ahead and try to chew through those, lady," before he picked up his Winchester and left the room.

After lighting another lamp in the kitchen and leaving Goldie with the other two Winchesters and her Pocket Colt on the table, he walked back down the hall to the front room and lit a third. He then stepped onto the front porch to wait for Lyle.

As he looked down the dark access road, he said, "It seems I'm spendin' too much time waitin' on stagecoaches these days."

The stage rolled through the boulder gateway three minutes later and Mitch was soon able to spot the shadowy shape as it slowly rolled towards him.

Lyle had been surprised to see so much light streaming through the windows but soon spotted his fellow sheriff standing on the porch and wondered what he had done with the evil woman.

When he was close, Mitch stepped down to help Steve from the driver's seat and hoped that he hadn't already passed out.

Lyle pulled the coach to a stop and Mitch loudly asked, "Is Steve still with us?"

"Yup. But he's kinda wobbly, so I'll need you to help me get him down. You do have two workin' hands, don't ya?"

Mitch replied, "Last time I checked," then stepped closer to the coach.

Lyle helped Steve to his feet and guided him to the edge of the driver's seat. When he slowly began to climb down, Mitch grabbed both sides of his shirt and held on until Steve was standing beside him. He didn't say a word to his ex-deputy as Lyle dropped to the ground.

"Where's Ace's girlfriend?"

"I tied her up and left her on her bed. How bad is Steve's gunshot?"

"Let's get him into the house and some light to find out."

"Alright."

They half-carried Steve onto the porch, entered the main room and deposited him on the couch.

Mitch pulled out Steve's wadded shirt and inspected the damage as Lyle glanced at the wound before looking away.

Mitch said, "It's not too bad," then asked, "Do you want to take care of the team or clean his wound?"

Lyle turned his eyes back to Mitch and asked, "You wanna stay here tonight?"

"It's gettin' kinda late, Lyle. We'd be better off leavin' in the mornin'."

"I reckon you're right. I'll unharness the team and unsaddle our horses. Where's that black gelding that Kent let you use, anyway?"

"Oh. He's tied off a couple of hundred yards west of here. He was gettin' kinda twitchy because of the coyotes. Leave him there and after I take care of Steve, I'll go get him."

"Sounds good to me. I'll watch out for those coyotes, too."

"You might run into some wolves too, Lyle."

"I figured I might."

As Lyle walked out of the house, Mitch headed to the washroom. After finding some towels, he went to the kitchen and pumped some water into a bucket. He grabbed the one bar of white soap and returned to the main room.

As he entered the front room, he found Steve staring at him but wasn't about to ask him why he decided to drive the stagecoach to the gang's hideout. He was Lyle's problem now.

He set the bucket on the floor, dropped the soap into the water and began ripping Steve's shirt open. After soaking one of the towels, he worked in some soap to make a decent lather. He wasn't gentle as he scrubbed off the gooey blood. Steve grimaced and groaned as Mitch cleaned his wound. When he could see raw skin and open tissue, Mitch folded the dry towel and laid it onto the wound.

He looked at Steve and said, "It's clean, but it needs to be closed. Now I don't have any needles or thread, so you can wait until tomorrow or I can put some hot iron on there and seal it that way. It's your choice."

363

Steve whispered, "No…no burn."

"Okay. I'm gonna go get my horse. You stay put."

Mitch turned and left the room, but once outside he stopped near one of the windows and watched Steve to make sure he didn't head down the hallway. When his old deputy closed his eyes and curled onto his left side, Mitch left the window and trotted away from the house. He soon reached the tethered gelding, untied him, then mounted and rode to the barn. He didn't see any skulking shadows, but he was sure that the coyotes and wolves were nearby waiting for the humans and their loud guns to leave.

When he entered the barn, he wasn't surprised to find that since Lyle left the house, he'd just lit a lamp and managed to unsaddle his buckskin.

After he dismounted, he smiled and said, "I'll take over, Lyle. You can watch our prisoner and Steve."

"Thanks, Mitch. I just couldn't do much with Steve's wound."

"I know. Before you head back, we need to talk about Jane. I told her that you'd bring her back to face trial for attempted murder and if that didn't work, I'd bring her back to Salmon City and have her charged with murder. She almost begged me to stop her from bein' brought back to Lewiston. But it wasn't 'cause she was worried about the sentence. She was more scared about a bunch of men seein' her than she was about hangin'. I figure you could just offer her a deal where nobody sees her, but she'd go straight to prison for twenty years. What do you think?"

"If it's okay with you, it's okay with me."

"I'll ask her about it when I get back. What you do with Steve is up to you. But I reckon that it would be smart to play along with whatever he tells us until you get him back in Lewiston."

"That's what I was plannin' to do. He won't be wearin' that badge for long, either."

Mitch nodded then said, "I'll get these horses unsaddled and the team unharnessed. When I get back to the house, I'll have my chat with Jane."

Lyle said, "I'll look in on her before I sit in front with Steve," then turned and left the barn carrying his saddlebags.

Mitch had been impressed that Lyle had managed to get his horse unsaddled with his healing wound. Mitch knew that he had only offered to do the more physically demanding job to avoid dealing with Steve's bloody mess. If Lyle wasn't such a good lawman, he would have been laughed out of town because of his unease at the sight of blood.

As he quickly began stripping the horses, Mitch rehearsed the offer he'd soon give to Jane. He was sure that she'd quickly accept it but still wouldn't want to go to Lewiston where she would still be seen. It was why he had decided to leave her on her own in the first place. He had been the only one to have seen the damage done to her face. He'd also talked to her more than the others and expected that her dominating vanity would keep her in a prison of her own making.

But she obviously hadn't even looked into a mirror until after she shot Steve. He'd watch her reaction when he made the offer to decide what he'd do next.

After leaving all of the horses in the corral, Mitch blew out the lamp in the barn and headed for the house. Some of the coyotes had already returned and were busy, but he didn't pay them any attention.

When he entered the front room, he found Lyle sitting on a chair near a sleeping, curled up Steve Finch. He took off his hat and tossed it onto an empty chair and stopped next to Lyle.

Sheriff Borden looked up and said, "Jane didn't get loose at all, but she wasn't happy to see me when I looked in on her. And you didn't exaggerate about the mess that powder burn made one bit. That woman ain't close to bein' pretty anymore."

"I reckon she finally figured it out, too. I'll talk to her then I'll make us somethin' to eat. Okay?"

"I'd appreciate it. You know I can't cook worth a hoot."

"That's 'cause you got a good wife who can. I never did ask Esther if she could cook. But it doesn't matter to me if she can't. With all that reward money, I can hire a cook."

Lyle snickered as Mitch walked down the hallway then turned into Jane's room.

He was a bit surprised that she didn't curse him when she saw him, but figured she was glad he wasn't Lyle.

He pulled a chair close to the bed and sat down.

"Come to gloat?" she asked.

"No, ma'am. I'm here to make you an offer."

Jane didn't ask what it was but said, "I need to pee."

"I'll escort you to the privy in a minute. Here's the deal. If you'll plead guilty to the charge of attempted murder, I won't charge you with murder. You'll serve a twenty-year sentence and won't even have to go to trial."

Jane was surprised by the generous offer and suspected that Sheriff Ward would still charge her with murdering his deputy even if she accepted it. But that wasn't her biggest fear. She'd still have to go to Lewiston to meet with lawyers and a judge.

After almost a minute without hearing her answer, Mitch said, "You could wear a veil or somethin', Jane."

She exclaimed, "*Do I look like a bride?* That would be even worse!"

"Well, you think about it the offer. I'll untie you so you can use the privy."

She just stared at him with her right eye as he began untying the knots at her ankles. It was dark out there that she began to see a small chance to avoid having anyone ever see her face.

Mitch tossed aside the first shirt, then began untying the one binding her wrists. When he finished, he stood and waited as Jane rubbed her wrists.

He backed away from the bed when she began to stand and followed closely behind her as she left the room and turned to the kitchen. He hadn't pulled any of his Smith & Wessons as she entered the kitchen. She didn't even glance at the table covered with Winchesters and her Pocket Colt as she walked to the back door.

Jane opened the door and walked onto the small back porch with Mitch trailing four feet behind her. When she stepped to the ground, he stopped on the porch and watched as she continued to the privy about fifty yards away.

She didn't know he'd stopped until she opened the narrow door and looked behind her. She was startled when she saw him still on the porch and didn't even have a pistol in his hand. She had expected him to pick up one of the Winchesters.

After watching her enter the outhouse, Mitch just leaned against one of the porch support beams and looked at the stars. He'd give her another five minutes to make her escape through the back of the privy. The wood walls of the house was dry and the boards in the barn were not only worse, but many were already broken or missing. He suspected that the privy's back wall was about the same.

Jane hadn't even bothered to use the seat after she closed the door. She had often complained to Ace about the poor condition of the privy and had asked him to build a new one. But now she was grateful that he'd ignored her.

She quickly pushed one of the boards down and hoped that Sheriff Ward hadn't heard it hit the ground. She just shifted the ones on either side of the new opening to give her room to wiggle through. Once outside, she walked straight into the night keeping the privy between her and the ranch house.

Mitch heard the first board when it bounced off the ground but continued to watch to make sure she didn't head for the corral to take one of their horses. He would have been surprised if she did. If she was so ashamed that anyone might see her, she wasn't about to ride to Elk City.

Five minutes later, he turned and walked back into the house. He closed the door and opened the cookstove's firebox. After building a fire, he stepped down the hallway to tell Lyle that Jane had escaped again, if one could call it that.

———

In Millersburg, the woman he hoped would never escape was under her blankets and finding sleep difficult.

It wasn't because she was worried about Mitch, but rather something entirely different. After she'd waved goodbye and entered the hotel, she met Reverend Berthold and Elizabeth in the lobby.

After she told them that Mitch had ridden north to meet Sheriff Borden, the reverend had asked her if she was still going to continue to Salmon City. When she explained that she was staying in Millersburg until Mitch returned, Elizabeth had joked about it adding at least one more day to their long courtship.

Esther had laughed and suggested that maybe if they stayed in town, the reverend could marry them tomorrow so there wouldn't be any delay. She'd meant it as a humorous response, but neither the reverend nor his wife seemed to accept it as such.

Her words had barely reached their ears when Reverend Berthold had the look of a man who'd just come face-to-face with an angry, hungry grizzly bear.

He exclaimed, "No! No! I can't do that. I won't!"

Esther had been taken aback by his reaction and looked at Elizabeth expecting to see that she was still smiling. But she was far from smiling and wore the same horrified expression as her husband.

After she'd apologized and told them that she was just joking, the couple accepted her apology, but the atmosphere became much cooler. They soon left the hotel to have their dinner and Esther had returned to her room.

Now, as she lay in the dark waiting for sleep to arrive, she wondered if they had only been relatively pleasant to her because she was with the county sheriff. After two pleasant days with Earl and Maggie Ferguson, she'd begun to believe that Mitch was right about people. The reverend and his wife had added confidence to her newfound belief during their shared ride to Millersburg.

But as she lay awake, she began reviewing the conversations they'd shared with the reverend and his wife and soon discovered that they hadn't been nearly as friendly as she had first believed. She had been so happy to be with Mitch again, she had almost ignored them.

She knew she'd miss Mitch as soon as he'd told her that he had to leave to find the missing stagecoach. But now she desperately wished he was here. She needed to talk to him. She needed to hear him tell her that she was wrong.

———

Mitch and Lyle had returned to the kitchen after leaving Steve sleeping on the couch in the dark front room.

As Mitch cooked their late supper, Lyle asked, "Are you sure that she's not gonna take one of the horses?"

"Pretty sure. You had to hear her scream when she looked at her face in the mirror, Lyle. It was like a rabid wolf had walked into her bedroom. She actually yelled, 'I'm a monster!'. She broke out of the back of that privy rather than have to let anybody in Lewiston see her. Where would she go if she took a horse?"

"I reckon that you're right. Are we still gonna set up a watch tonight?"

"Yup. I'll let you get some sleep and I'll wake you up when I get tired. Okay?"

"Alright. You're not gonna leave her any guns this time; are ya?"

"Nope. I'm not even sure she'll come back to the house until we're long gone."

"Until I saw what she looked like, I figured your mighta made a mistake in leavin' her here in the first place. Now I understand. I wonder if she'll still be here in a couple of weeks."

"Maybe Steve did you a favor by comin' here early. Now you know."

"There is that. And I reckon that Jane did me a favor by showin' me what he was like and puttin' him outta action at the same time."

Mitch set their plates of Jane's warmed up leftovers on the table, took a seat and asked, "I wonder what Steve's story is gonna be?"

Lyle snickered and replied, "That might be kinda fun to hear."

———

After Lyle had gone to the bedroom, Mitch checked on Steve then walked to the back porch.

He wasn't very tired as he stared into the dark. He wouldn't be able to spot Jane if she did go to the corral. And with all the noise generated by the scavengers, he wouldn't be able to hear her even as she rode away. But he no longer cared what Jane did.

In a few hours, he'd harness the stagecoach, saddle the black gelding and ride away from this place and hopefully never see it again. He was already calculating how long it would take to ride to Millersburg. He could reach the main road in less than two hours, then there was another thirty miles to go after that. He should see Esther again in less than eight hours after leaving the hidden ranch.

As he stood guard, he wondered about the family that had built the place. He guessed it was almost twenty years old, but someone had spent a lot of time and money setting it up. He hadn't seen any evidence of livestock, so it must have been abandoned for some time. Maybe it hadn't been abandoned at all. Maybe Ace and his boys had simply taken it from the family and sold the cattle. It wouldn't have surprised him if they had. He'd seen it done before by other groups of ruthless men.

After standing on the porch for almost an hour, he reentered the house and closed the door. He carried the lamp into Jane's bedroom and as he sat on her rumpled blankets, he spotted her open purse lying on the floor. She must have just taken out her hand mirror and knocked it to the floor when she saw her face. He leaned over, picked it up and set it on his lap.

When he looked inside, he found a small container of lipstick, another slightly larger one of rouge, and an even bigger one of scented powder.

He whispered, "I imagine if I checked Esther's purse, I would only find her book of poems and a hair brush."

He was smiling as he continued exploring Jane's handbag. He soon found what he thought was her change purse, but it wasn't that heavy considering how stuffed it appeared to be. He took it out of the purse and when he opened it, he was surprised to find a wad of currency. He quickly counted the bills and came up with three hundred and forty-two dollars. He was going to return the money to the purse, then changed his mind and stuffed them into his pocket with his Smith & Wesson Model 1 that still needed cleaning.

He set her purse on the floor and left her bedroom to return to the kitchen. He figured he may as well use the time to clean Goldie and the small pistol.

So, for the next hour, Lemhi County Sheriff Mitchell Ward carefully cleaned and reloaded his Winchester then just cleaned the Smith & Wesson. He'd add the missing cartridge when he returned to Salmon City.

He let Lyle sleep longer than he had planned for no particular reason. He guessed it was around two o'clock in the morning when he snuck into the first bedroom and shook Sheriff Borden.

After Lyle rolled out of bed, he mumbled, "Is she still gone?"

"Yup. You can use the privy if you want to be sure."

Lyle chuckled and was surprised when Mitch turned and started walking away rather than climb into the bed. So, he followed Mitch out of the bedroom and soon joined him in the kitchen.

As he took a seat at the table, Lyle said, "I thought you were gonna get some shuteye."

"I will in a minute, but I gotta tell you somethin' now so I don't forget in the mornin'."

"It is the mornin' already; ain't it?"

Mitch grinned as he replied, "You know what I meant, Sheriff," then pulled the wad of bills from his jacket pocket.

"I found this in Jane's purse. I was gonna put it back, but I figure that when I get to Millersburg, the stage to Salmon City will already be gone. Esther can't ride a horse even if her knee wasn't banged up, so I'll need to buy a buggy or a carriage. If you want, you can take it out of the reward money. It's three hundred and forty-two dollars."

"I don't care, Mitch. Hell, I reckon that after the bank gets their stolen money back, there's another two thousand in that strongbox."

Mitch shoved the bills back into his pocket and said, "Thanks, Lyle. I'll get a few winks but wake me up when those stars disappear."

"I'll do that."

Mitch nodded before he stood and headed back to the recently vacated bedroom.

CHAPTER 10

Mitch waved to Lyle as he drove the stage down the access road. Steve Finch was inside the coach and probably was relieved that his boss had accepted his fable of why he'd gone to the ranch. It had been difficult for both of the sheriffs to keep poker faces as he'd spun his tale at the kitchen table.

He'd claimed that he had forgotten his saddlebags at the Ferguson ranch and had turned back to retrieve them. When he neared the intersection, he said he spotted a rider heading east on the road to Elk City and was worried that Jane would try to ambush him. But the rider was well ahead of him and moving fast, so Steve said he suspected that he might be another undocumented member of Ace's gang.

He was still about a mile behind the rider who had just reached the boulders. Steve said he heard Winchester fire, but Jane missed, and the man bolted away. He said he didn't want to risk having Jane shoot someone else. So, he pulled up and waited until the rider was out of sight before he approached the ranch with the shotgun in his hands. But the light was already fading, and he hadn't spotted Jane before she fired.

Lyle had told him that he'd done the right thing and Steve had gratefully accepted his praise. After hearing the story,

Mitch held his laughter until after he left the house to harness the team and saddle the horses.

As he watched the coach turn west on the road, he wished he could be in the room when Lyle fired his lying deputy. At least with his shoulder injury, Steve wouldn't be able to shoot anything for a while.

Mitch then mounted the black gelding and looked to the southeast for a glimpse of a blonde head but wasn't expecting to spot her.

He turned the horse to the northwest to go cross country and once he reached the road, he nudged the gelding to a fast trot.

————

As Mitch rode west, the stage to Salmon City left the depot in Millersburg with just two passengers. Esther was still sleeping in her hotel room after finally falling asleep in the wee hours of the morning. It was probably within five minutes of when Mitch had crawled into one of the hideout's beds.

When she did slip from under her blankets, she quickly dressed and hurried down the hall to use the bathroom. She was carrying her purse and her travel bag with a change of clothes. Jim Branford had carried her other travel bag to the hotel and left it at the desk when he learned that she wasn't going to be on his stage.

By the time she was leaving the hotel to have breakfast at The Widows' Kitchen, Mitch had already reached the intersection and was now making the long ascent into the mountains while Lyle had his stagecoach just twenty miles from the way station.

When she entered the diner, she expected Mary and Alice to be less friendly now that she was no longer with Mitch.

She walked to the same table they'd been sharing when Marshal Thompson arrived and took a seat in the chair Mitch had used.

Esther set her purse on the table and spotted Mary as she left the kitchen.

Then Mary saw her and smiled as she hurried to her table.

"How are you, Esther?"

"I'm fine, Mary. Mitch had to go back to find that stagecoach."

"I heard about that. Don't worry, I'm sure that he'll be fine. I imagine he's already making huge clouds of dust as he races back here."

"I hope so."

"What can I get for you this morning?"

"I'm not very hungry, so I'll just have some coffee and biscuits."

"Nonsense. Coffee and biscuits aren't enough of a breakfast. Let me decide what to bring you."

Esther said, "Thank you," before Mary hurried back to the kitchen.

When Mary returned a few minutes later carrying a tray with her breakfast, Alice was walking beside her with a full pot of coffee.

As they set their loads on the table, Mary said, "The next stage to Salmon City won't come through for another three days. Are you and Mitch going to stay here until then?"

"I don't know what we'll do."

Alice smiled and said, "Maybe you should get married here and enjoy a short honeymoon in Millersburg. I'd even bake a nice wedding cake for you."

Esther laughed before replying, "I'll ask him when he gets here. I know that if we wait until we return to Salmon City that the new Methodist minister who just left on the stage won't be performing the ceremony."

Mary's smile subsided as she said, "I don't think you'd want a man like that to do it anyway, Esther."

Esther asked, "Do you know him already?"

"No, but Fred McWhorter, the desk clerk, told us what he said to you. He said that you were smiling when that preacher almost shouted that he wouldn't marry you and Mitch. Fred was shocked at his rude behavior, but it wasn't his place to say anything."

Alice then said, "You should be grateful that you don't have to spend another six or seven hours in the stagecoach with him and his wife."

Esther was surprised at the sisters' reaction as she said, "I am."

Mary snapped, "Men like the reverend don't practice what they preach."

Esther smiled as she replied, "That's what Mitch would probably say."

Alice patted her on her shoulder and said, "Mitch is a good man, Esther, and he's also a lucky man to be marrying a good woman like you."

"I feel lucky, too."

The sisters waved then left her to her massive breakfast.

Esther was now more certain that Mitch, Maggie Ferguson and the sisters were right. It was men like Reverend Berthold and Doctor Brandt who were in the minority. When she looked at her loaded plate, she wondered if they expected Mitch to walk through the door to share her breakfast.

Esther laughed then began eating.

———

Mitch had watered Marshal Thompson's gelding in White Bird Creek an hour earlier and knew he was less than twenty miles from Millersburg. His only concern now was that he might have overextended the horse in his desire to see Esther again.

He may have been anxious, but he still didn't succumb to the sin of woolgathering. He even checked his backtrail every few minutes. After the twisting flow of events over the past few days, he almost expected to see Steve and Jane driving the stagecoach behind him.

But there was no trailing stagecoach as he gambled on the gelding's stamina by keeping him at a fast pace. He wanted to reach Millersburg by early afternoon.

As he passed along the familiar roadway, Mitch touched his face and said, "I reckon I need another bath and shave, Esther."

———

After returning to the hotel, Esther sat in the hotel lobby reading *The Millersburg Speaker* until she could quote it by heart. She spent another hour reading her book of poetry before she finally returned it to her purse then left the hotel to visit the jail. She knew it was unlikely that the marshal would have received a telegram from the way station but didn't think it would hurt to ask.

When she entered the small office, Deputy Marshal Tom Wilkerson popped to his feet and said, "Howdy, ma'am."

"Good morning. Is the marshal here?"

"No, ma'am. He's over at the Overland depot. I guess they're gettin' kinda anxious about their missin' coach."

"I imagine so. I was just wondering if he had any news about Mitch."

"Not that I know of. But I reckon Mitch oughta be showin' up pretty soon."

"How long have you known him?"

"Since he took over the job. I was kinda surprised that they gave him the badge 'cause he wasn't from here and he was a lot younger than the three deputies they already had. But it didn't take long for me and the good folks in the county to figure out we got lucky when he became our new sheriff."

"It seems that the only ones in Lemhi County who don't like Mitch are the ones who try to break the law."

"Oh, there are a few regular folks who have their own reasons for not likin' Mitch. I never met a feller who everybody liked, but our sheriff is as close as anybody can get."

"I hope they still think highly of him after we're married."

"Why would they change their minds? You must be a special lady to get Mitch to even talk to you. A lot of us figured he'd die on his lonesome."

Esther didn't answer his question but said, "I'll make sure that he isn't alone for the rest of my life."

Just as Tom was about to say something, Marshal Thompson entered the jail.

As he removed his hat, Esther turned around and asked, "Have you heard from Sheriff Borden or Mitch?"

Kent hung his hat then replied, "Not yet, Miss Cohen. But don't worry yourself. I'm sure Mitch will be ridin' into town soon enough. I just hope he doesn't break my gelding's leg tryin' to get back here so fast."

Esther smiled then said, "Well, I'll go back to the hotel and wait for him on the bench out front. I think I'll stop at the store on the way to buy a book to help pass the time."

After she left the jail, Esther stopped on the boardwalk and looked to the north end of town. She only saw normal street traffic, but it was early afternoon, so she didn't expect to see Mitch for a while.

She walked to J.B. Harrison & Son Dry Goods and Sundries to find something to read and decided to skip lunch rather than possibly miss Mitch when he rode into town. Besides, she had a very late and large breakfast just a few hours earlier.

She entered the store but didn't ask where to find the books. Instead, she wandered down the short, narrow aisles scanning the shelves for anything else she may need.

————

The black gelding was tiring but Mitch had been energized since he had first spotted Millersburg's buildings ten minutes earlier.

He soon entered the town and headed for the jail to return the horse before going to the hotel to see Esther. He expected that Kent Thompson would pepper him with questions, but he already had his short answers ready. His reputation for terse replies would help.

He rode past the hotel and was somewhat disappointed that Esther wasn't waiting on the bench but then thought he was just being silly. She wouldn't even know he was on his way back.

He passed the dry goods store and soon pulled up in front of the jail. He dismounted, tied off the exhausted horse, then removed his saddlebags and hung them over his shoulder. After taking Goldie from the scabbard, he hopped onto the boardwalk and entered the town marshal's office.

Kent and Tom were talking about what might have happened with the missing stagecoach when they heard the door open. As they turned and saw Mitch walk through the door, big grins exploded across their faces.

Marshal Thompson asked, "Did you find the coach?"

"Yup. Lyle probably has it all the way to the way station by now. I left your horse out front, but he's a bit tired. He did a good job and I appreciate you lettin' me borrow him."

"You're welcome. I'll have Tom take care of him. Did you have any trouble when you found it?"

"Not much. Lyle's deputy got kinda lost and ran into a .44. It got him high on his right shoulder, but he'll be okay unless it gets infected."

Tom Wilkerson quickly asked, "Who shot him?"

"Ace's girlfriend. The one I let go."

The old deputy marshal then asked, "Is she still there?"

"I reckon so, but I don't think she's goin' anywhere. This time, I didn't leave her any firearms."

386

Kent then said, "Your lady showed up a little while ago askin' about ya. She headed back to the hotel to wait on the bench out front but was gonna pick up a book at Harrison's on the way."

Mitch smiled then said, "I'll talk to you later," before he hurried from the jail.

Once on the boardwalk, he jogged past townsfolk and almost rammed Goldie's muzzle into Mrs. Lindell's backside. She smiled when she saw the sheriff rush past and didn't realize how close she'd come to having a Winchester bang her bustle.

Mitch slowed before reaching the store's entrance, then walked through the doorway.

He knew which aisle had the books and periodicals, so he waved to J.B. who was standing behind the counter as he strode to the back of the store. As soon as he turned down the aisle, he saw Esther with her head tilted as she read the titles.

He was smiling as he quietly stepped closer and when he was just four feet behind her, he stopped.

Esther was reaching for the copy of Wilkie Collins' *The Woman in White*, when she heard a deep voice close behind her and froze.

"Plannin' on wearin' white soon, Esther?"

387

She forgot about the book then whirled around and exclaimed, "Mitch! You're back!"

Mitch stepped closer and replied, "Yes, ma'am. I won't be needin' to go to that hidden ranch again, either."

She took his arm and said, "Let's go back to the hotel and you can tell me what happened on the way."

"Yes, ma'am."

They could barely manage to walk side-by-side down the narrow aisle. But before they even reached the front of the store, Mitch began telling Esther what had happened.

He had just reached the point where they bumped into Steve on the dark road when they entered the hotel lobby. Esther sat on the couch as Mitch set his saddlebags on the floor and leaned Goldie on the other side of the couch.

After he sat beside her, she asked, "So, what did Steve Finch do? Was it what you expected?"

Mitch nodded as he replied, "Pretty much. He musta thought that I exaggerated the mess Jane made of her face. He probably figured it was just like a small tattoo and it wouldn't bother him much. He had all the money in the strongbox, too. I guess he finally had enough of a reason to swing to the bad side of the law."

"At least he won't be wearing that badge much longer."

"Nope. And he won't be able to shoot at all for a while. Then even after the wound heals, he won't be a very good shot. He wasn't all that accurate when he was my deputy. He's gotta hope it doesn't get infected, too."

Esther agreed about the risk of infection before Mitch picked up the story from when they'd met Steve on the dark road.

Esther didn't ask any more questions until he finished talking.

He ended his narrative by saying, "And then I waved to Lyle and headed back."

When he finished, she only had one question remaining.

She asked, "What do you think Jane will do?"

"If I was a bettin' man, I'd wager that she'd just start walkin' into the wild country and let nature judge her. When I first saw her face after she shot herself, I told her how bad it was. I knew she didn't believe me, but I figured that after I was gone, she'd look in her mirror to see if I was lyin'. But must not have checked right away. I don't know why she decided to take out her mirror until after she shot Steve, but when she did, I was standin' on the porch and heard her scream."

"Do you know what she screamed?"

Mitch nodded and replied, "She yelled, 'I'm a monster!'.
Now it was pretty bad, but even I didn't figure it made her into
a hideous beast. After I talked to Lyle and then offered her the
deal to avoid goin' to court, I knew that she was terrified about
anybody ever seein' her face. That's when I decided to give
her a chance to escape again.

"After she broke out of the back of the privy, I watched for a
while but never even saw her shadow. I didn't see her the next
day before we left, either."

"Is Sheriff Borden going to send anyone to check on her?"

"No. ma'am. Neither one of us figured it was necessary."

Esther believed that Mitch was right about Jane but said, "I
can understand that she would be disturbed when she saw her
face, but I find it hard to imagine being so horrified that she
would rather die than let anyone see her."

"That's 'cause you aren't anything like her, Esther. She may
have been a bit ugly on the outside now, but she was a lot
uglier inside before she had her accident. Your face is
beautiful, but so is your spirit. Nothin' can damage your good
soul."

Esther took his hand as she smiled and said, "Ten days
ago, I never would have believed you to be a philosopher and
poet, Mitch. I can't imagine what else I'll learn about you after
we're married."

Mitch grinned and replied, "I'm only gonna go downhill from here, Esther. But before we get hitched, we need to get back to Salmon City. Now I don't wanna wait for the next stage, so I figured that I'd head over to Winslow's Carriages and see about buying one. You seem to be walkin' better, but I don't figure you'd be happy about ridin' all the way back."

"No, I wouldn't. Can I come with you?"

"You can if your knee doesn't object."

"I would ignore its protests anyway."

Mitch stood and after picking up Goldie and hanging his saddlebags over his shoulder, he took Esther's hand.

They left the hotel lobby and turned right to make the three-block walk to the carriage shop.

As they stepped along the boardwalk, Mitch explained where he found the money to buy the carriage and Esther thought it was only fair. After all, it had been Jane who had created most of the problems.

When they stepped into the large shop, Mitch waved to John Winslow who left his desk and walked towards them.

The carriage maker said, "I'm kinda surprised to see you back so soon, Mitch."

"I had to get back fast 'cause I was worried that Esther might meet a better beau while I was gone."

John snickered then asked, "What can I do for ya?"

"I need to buy a carriage or buggy, so we don't have to wait for the next stage to Salmon City. What do you have available?"

"Well, I have a couple of buggies, but I reckon you'd probably like the carriage we just finished last week. It's not fancy, but it'll ride better than the buggy and with two horses, it'll get you there faster, too."

"Let's take a look at it."

Mitch and Esther followed John through the shop and exited through the back door.

As soon as they returned to the sunshine, John stopped and pointed at the carriage.

"The canvas top is rubberized like a slicker, so it won't leak. It's easy to put up, too."

Mitch and Esther walked to the carriage and as Esther looked inside, Mitch turned to John and asked, "How much would it run me including a couple of horses?"

"I could let you have it for three-fifty. You can pick out the team, too."

"Sounds fair to me. I'll let you choose the horses. We'll be by in the mornin' to pick it up. Okay?"

John grinned as he replied, "I'll have it ready to roll."

Esther was smiling as she took Mitch's arm before they reentered the shop. She planned to ask him if she could drive part of the way as she'd never driven one before.

After paying for the new carriage mostly with Jane's money, they left the shop and headed back to the hotel.

Before they turned onto the main street, Esther asked, "Do you want to have an early supper again? I skipped lunch and I wouldn't be surprised if you hadn't eaten all day."

"I had a quick breakfast, but I'll admit that my stomach is close to standin' up and leavin' if I don't send somethin' along pretty soon."

They shifted direction and soon arrived at The Widows' Kitchen. Esther's second reason for asking about supper was to let Alice and Mary know that Mitch had returned safely. She suspected that they already knew by now, but thought they'd want more details from Mitch.

As soon as they stepped into the diner, it was Alice who spotted them first. She hurried into the kitchen while Esther sat at their usual table and Mitch set his saddlebags on the floor and laid Goldie's barrel on top.

The sisters almost exploded out of the kitchen just as Mitch sat down. When they reached the table, they pulled out the two empty chairs and sat down.

Mary then excitedly asked, "What happened?"

Mitch smiled at their enthusiasm and began telling them the short version. He hoped that they didn't ask many questions as he would rather be eating than talking.

When he finished, neither Mary nor Alice asked a single question, but after he said they could bring whatever food they chose, the sisters stood then turned to walk back to the kitchen.

But before they left, Alice looked at Esther and said, "What did Mitch think about Salmon City's new reverend and his wife when you told him how they behaved?"

Mitch looked at Esther as she replied, "I haven't mentioned it yet."

Alice glanced at Mitch before she and Mary hurried away.

Mitch was still focused on Esther when she said, "It wasn't that important, Mitch. It was just their reaction to something that I said in jest."

"What did you say that bothered them?"

Esther sighed then answered, "After I told them that I wouldn't be taking the stage to Salmon City, Mrs. Berthold jokingly said it would delay our long courtship. I said that they could wait with me. and Reverend Berthold could perform the ceremony when you returned to Millersburg."

Mitch interrupted her by saying, "I can imagine what the reverend probably said, so you don't need to tell me. I hope you didn't slap him when he insulted you."

Esther smiled as she shook her head and said, "No, I didn't even get angry. I'll admit that it hurt, and I began to doubt what you had told me how most people weren't like that. But after talking to Mary and Alice, I realized that you weren't wrong."

"I was just jokin' about the slap. I know you'd never do anything like that. I reckon I should have included a warnin' about how some folks pretend to be nice to hide what they're thinkin'. It's just another part of wantin' to feel all superior to other folks. What you gotta do is to let 'em pat themselves on the back and ignore what they say when they let expose what they're really thinkin'."

"How will I know who they are if they don't?"

"Assume they're all good folks until they prove otherwise. If you worry about who's hidin' bad thoughts, it'll drive you into a convent. Or whatever Jewish people have to hide their women away from all of the bad things in the world."

Esther laughed then said, "Like men."

Mitch grinned and replied, "Maybe."

Esther was about to ask about tomorrow's drive to Salmon City when Mary and Alice arrived with the now expected overloaded trays.

———

It was nearly sunset when they returned to the hotel and Mitch just waved to the desk clerk as he and Esther walked past and entered the hallway.

She could tell how tired he was, so when she opened her door, she smiled and said, "You get some sleep, Mitch. We can spend hours talking tomorrow when we're driving our new carriage to Salmon City."

Mitch nodded, but didn't even glance back down the hallway before he put his free hand behind her neck and kissed her. It lasted much longer than a typical goodnight kiss and by the time their lips parted, Esther almost wished he didn't go to his room.

But Mitch's long day was finally catching up to him, so he just smiled then turned and walked down the hallway to his room.

Esther waited until he went inside before she closed her door then walked to her bed where she sat down and closed her eyes. She set her purse on the blanket beside her and relived Mitch's unexpectedly passionate kiss. If he had arrived a little earlier, she might have asked him to take her to the justice of the peace.

———

Mitch set Goldie against the wall and lowered his saddlebags to the floor before tossing his hat onto the small dresser. After taking off his jacket and gunbelt, he sat on the bed and pulled off his boots.

He wished he could have spent more time with Esther, but knew he was in dire need of rest. He slowly stretched out on the bed and drifted into a deep sleep just three minutes later.

———

It was midmorning when Mitch drove their new carriage out of Millersburg with Esther sitting close beside him. On the floor behind them next to his saddlebags, was a large picnic basket filled with food and two Mason jars of lemonade courtesy of Mary and Alice. The carriage didn't have a scabbard, so Mitch let Goldie enjoy the comfort of the soft leather covering the back seat. Before they left town, Mitch had sent a telegram to Pete letting him know that he'd be arriving by midafternoon in a brand-new carriage with his fiancée.

As they left Millersburg behind, Mitch said, "Do you what's really kinda odd?"

Esther smiled as she looked at him and asked, "What hasn't been strange since we left Salmon City?"

"In a couple of hours, we'll be spot the stagecoach headin' north to Lewiston. It won't be the one we took when we left, but it's still kinda spooky."

397

"It's the same one we took to Millersburg; isn't it?"

"Yup. At least this time, it'll have a regular shotgun rider and no shackled gang leader inside."

"With no blonde witch waiting in Millersburg to free him."

"Nope. Maybe Reverend Berthold and his wife are inside after they decided not to stay in Salmon City. Imagine havin' a Catholic sheriff married to a Jewish lady livin' in the same town!"

Esther laughed then said, "You're never going to let me forget that; will you?"

"Maybe. But I reckon they're already talkin' to Reverend Summers about me by now. He's a good man and might give them an earful if they say anything bad about you."

"I never met him, but do you really think he'd do that?"

"Absolutely. I may not have been in his congregation, but I know him pretty well. He's not a fire and brimstone preacher even though of his flock wished he was. I'll introduce you before he leaves. If you asked him to marry us, he'd be more'n happy to oblige, even if I wasn't there."

"By the time you introduce us, we'll probably already be married; won't we?"

"I hope so, Miss Cohen. I'm lookin' forward to draggin' you into our big house and makin' good use of that big four poster bed."

Esther didn't reply before she leaned over and kissed him.

After settling back onto the seat, she said, "You are obviously no longer the least bit afraid of me, Sheriff Ward."

Mitch grinned as he handed her the reins and said, "I might get that way again if you can't figure out how to drive the carriage."

Esther smiled as she took the leather straps then turned her eyes ahead to watch the road. It was going to be a long drive to Salmon City, but she wished it was another hundred miles further away because she'd never been happier.

———

As Esther successfully navigated the roadway, their extended conversation included more details of their earlier lives and what they planned to do with their future lives together.

They pulled off the road to let the southbound stage pass almost three hour later and waved to Will Dooley and Jim Branford.

After the stage passed, Esther said, "They didn't seem surprised to see us. I thought they might stop to ask you what happened to the missing stagecoach."

"I reckon that pretty much everybody in Salmon City knows most of it by now."

"Even about our pending marriage?"

Mitch grinned as he replied, "I imagine that would be at the front of the gossip train."

Esther laughed. then snapped the reins letting the horses know it was time to start moving again.

They continued to talk until they stopped for lunch but were unable to finish all that Mary and Alice had packed. When they began rolling south again, they were less than twenty miles from Salmon City.

Two hours later as Salmon City appeared on the horizon, Esther said, "I'm almost surprised that we didn't get attacked by highwaymen or some other outlaws who decided to take advantage of your absence."

"I reckon things will quiet down a bit for a while. Pete's a good lawman already and after I hire Ryan Grady and Eddie Stubbins, we'll be fully manned for the first time in years."

"You seem to be pretty confident that they'll both work out."

"Time will tell, ma'am."

"When we arrive, I imagine that you'll have to spend some time with Deputy Carter. Can you drop me off at Doctor Walsh's house first?"

"You're driving, Esther. So, where we go is up to you. But you're right about my needin' a long jaw session with Pete. I might not get out of the office 'til after sunset. But I think you need some rest, too. So, how about if I stop by in the mornin' when I can, and we'll see about visitin' Judge Whitlock?"

"That sounds like a good plan, Sheriff. Just don't go riding off to Lewiston or somewhere else without letting me know."

"I hope I don't have to leave town again for a good while."

Esther nodded as the buildings of Salmon City grew larger. It had only been a week since they'd left the town and she suddenly had a creeping sensation of dread. She felt as if it had all been nothing more than a sequence of horrible nightmares and joyful dreams. In just a few minutes, she would return to the real world.

She surprised Mitch when she wordlessly handed him the reins, then after he had control of the team, she slid even closer before she put her arm around him.

Mitch glanced at Esther and even though she was still looking at the road ahead, he could see a touch of worry in her dark brown eyes. He didn't ask her what was bothering her because he knew that they'd reach Salmon City in just a few minutes. He hoped that Pete didn't have a lot to tell him, so he'd be able to spend suppertime with Esther.

———

Before they rolled onto Main Street, Esther slid a few inches away from Mitch. He assumed that she didn't want to add more fuel to the gossip train.

He waved to the folks whether they were on the boardwalk or passing traffic until they reached Third Street. Mitch turned the carriage and soon pulled up in front of Doctor Walsh's house.

After helping Esther down, he picked up her travel bags then walked with her to the house and onto the front porch.

She unlocked the door and waited for Mitch to carry her bags inside before following him into the foyer leaving the door open.

Mitch continued into the doctor's waiting room and set her bags down on the floor.

He turned and smiled at Esther who hadn't spoken since she'd handed him the reins.

"I reckon Pete's chompin' at the bit to ask me what happened, but I hope he doesn't have a lot to tell me, so I can take you to dinner."

Esther didn't smile as she replied, "I'll be all right, Mitch. Do what you need to do, and I'll see you in the morning."

Mitch put his hands on her shoulders and asked, "Are you okay?"

"I'm just tired. I'll be fine after a good night's sleep."

He nodded and felt that somehow an invisible wall had been built between them that he couldn't understand. Just an hour ago, she'd been laughing and cheerful and now she was acting almost as he did for the past three years.

He wasn't sure if it would help, but as he looked into her sad brown eyes, he said, "I love you, Esther. Tomorrow night, you'll be Mrs. Ward and we'll be together in our big house."

Esther finally smiled before she said, "It's all real; isn't it?"

Mitch was relieved as he replied, "You're damned straight it's real."

Before she could laugh, he pulled her close and kissed her.

Esther's nagging sense of unease evaporated as they shared the long, passionate kiss.

When their lips parted, Mitch said, "Now you get your rest and I'll see you in the mornin'."

Esther nodded and now wished that she'd agreed to have dinner with him, but still had a lot of things to do before she left Doctor Walsh's house tomorrow.

"I'll be ready whenever you show up, Mitch."

"Well, I reckon I've gotta head over to the jail and find out what kinda mischief happened in the county while I was gone."

He may have wished he could stay but was in a much better frame of mind when he turned and headed for the open door.

Esther was even happier as she picked up her travel bags and walked to her bedroom.

A few minutes later, Mitch pulled the carriage to a stop in front of the jail. After setting the handbrake, he grabbed Goldie from the back seat and stepped to the ground. He noticed the jail's door was open before he hopped onto the boardwalk and entered.

When he passed through the doorway, he found Pete sitting at the desk talking to the three county commissioners who all had their backs to him. They weren't the same men who'd hired him, but he knew each of them very well and was surprised to see them in the office. The newest of the three was Doctor Ernst Brandt.

As their heads all turned, Pete popped to his feet and said, "Welcome back, Mitch."

"It's been a helluva week, Pete. Anything bad happen that I need to know about?"

"Nothin' that can't wait 'til tomorrow."

Mitch then looked at Fred Smith, the head of the county commission and owner of the biggest lumber mill in the county.

Fred shook his hand and said, "We're all mighty proud of what you did to take down the dangerous Carr gang, Mitch. We already had Deputy Jackson and Al Crenshaw buried and no one blames you for what happened."

"I still shoulda stopped it, Fred. But I'm kinda surprised to see all of you fellers here on a Tuesday afternoon."

"Well, we knew you'd be returning today and expected that you'd come here to talk to Pete before you went to your house. We wanted to talk to you before you left the jail."

Mitch couldn't understand why they needed to talk to him this badly. He figured that while they must have known he was returning this afternoon, they wouldn't know exactly when he'd show up. They would have had to wait with Pete for a while and that seemed even stranger. Mitch had no idea what could be that important.

He took off his hat and asked, "Well, I'm back, so what do you need to talk about?"

Fred seemed uneasy and glanced at Harry Longstreet who stood beside him before saying, "Um, do you mind if we tell you in your office?"

Mitch was getting irritated but didn't show it as he nodded and walked past the three councilmen and headed down the hallway. Once inside in private office, he tossed his temporary hat onto his desktop then set Goldie next to it before he walked to his chair and sat down. There were only two other chairs in the office, and he wondered which of them would remain standing. He wasn't surprised when none of them took a seat.

Harry closed the door before Fred said, "Um, this is kind of a delicate matter, Mitch. We received word that you were planning to get married tomorrow."

Mitch instantly understood why Fred and Harry seemed uncomfortable but noticed that Doctor Brandt wasn't the least bit uneasy.

"Yes, sir. That's true. I woulda figured you'd be kinda happy that I finally decided to settle down and start a family."

"Oh, we are. We are. It's just that we were wonderin' why you had to get married right away. Maybe you should wait until after you hired a new deputy."

Mitch knew the real reason for their visit had nothing to do with new deputies but replied, "I'm interviewing two young fellers in a couple of days, but I'm sure Pete and I would be able to handle any trouble. It doesn't take that long to get married and I'm not goin' on any kinda honeymoon."

"That's good to hear, but well, we'd still appreciate it if you'd delay your nuptials for just a little while. You know, so the town could, um, get used to the idea. We didn't even know you were visitin' Miss Cohen until we heard you were gonna marry her."

"I reckon they can get used to it after we're married, Fred. She's a good woman and I'm one lucky cuss to be able to call her my fiancée."

Fred again glanced at Harry but didn't find any support as Harry was looking away.

Doctor Brandt finally revealed the purpose for their visit when he asked, "Didn't you know she was Jewish?"

Mitch was relieved when it was finally out in the open but was prepared in case that they actually confessed the true reason for their unexpected visit.

So, in apparent astonishment, he exclaimed, *"She's Jewish?"*

He watched a look of satisfaction appear on the doctor's face as he asked, "You didn't know?"

"How would I know? We don't have one of them Jewish churches in town. Does she have her Jewish rituals in private?"

Doctor Brandt replied, "They're called synagogues, Sheriff. I don't know what she does in behind those closed doors. I'm just surprised that you didn't even realize she was of Hebrew extraction for all this time. Even her name reeks of her Jewish heritage."

Mitch leaned back and scratched the stubble on the right side of his face as he said, "Now don't that beat all. And here I was thinkin' she was a good, moral woman."

Fred and Harry were even more surprised than Doctor Brandt had been that Mitch didn't realize Esther Cohen was Jewish. They had only wanted him to delay the marriage to soothe certain ruffled feathers. But after hearing his shocked reaction to Ernst's revelation, they began to believe that Mitch wouldn't marry her at all. That filled each of them with a deep sense of guilt. Both councilmen also believed that they had offended him so badly that he might even quit which would be even worse.

Mitch continued his charade for almost thirty seconds as he studied the three men standing before him. He then stopped scratching his face and looked into Doctor Brandt's blue eyes.

He quietly said, "I reckon it's not important to me. I still think she's a righteous woman and if I have to convert to the Jewish faith to marry her, I'll do it."

The doctor was startled and snapped, "You can't do that. You'd be…you'd…well, you can't!"

"Sure, I can. And I will, too."

Then he looked at Fred Smith and asked, "What made you fellers come here to keep me from marryin' Esther?"

Fred quickly replied, "It wasn't that we didn't want you to marry her, Mitch. It's just that some folks seemed kinda upset that you were marryin' her."

"Who were these folks? I imagine one of 'em is standin' right in front of me."

Before Fred could answer, Doctor Brandt replied, "Yes, I was one of them. If you marry her, you'll be just like her even if you don't embrace her faith. You won't be accepted as a member of this community any longer."

Mitch glared at Fred as he asked, "Is that what you and Harry think?"

Fred shook his head as he answered, "No. We just wanted to give those noisy folks time to get over it."

"Well, I don't think ignorant folks like that will ever get over it, Fred. And I ain't about to put off marryin' Esther. If you tell me that I have to wait, then you can have this."

He pulled off his badge and laid it on the desk next to his Winchester then stared at the head of the county council.

Fred and Harry knew that Mitch wasn't bluffing, so it only took a couple of seconds before Fred picked up the badge and held it out to him.

"You do what you think is right, Mitch. It's what you've always done since we hired you. I'm ashamed that we even showed up here. I'm also sorry we behaved like politicians and not men."

Mitch accepted his badge and pinned it on his jacket before saying, "Thanks, Fred. Sorry about the dramatics, but I wanted you to understand how important Esther is to me."

The frustrated doctor snapped, "But you didn't even know she was Jewish!"

Mitch grinned at the physician as he said, "I knew she was Jewish the day she stepped off the stage from Boise and she introduced herself."

"But you never even visited her once since she arrived!"

"Nope. I figured I wasn't nearly good enough to talk to her even when she was sewin' up my wounds. I even bought that big house a couple of years just 'cause I was dreamin' that she might help me fill it with young'uns."

"That's preposterous!"

"Maybe so, but she'll be movin' in tomorrow, and we're gonna start makin' babies. And those babies will all have some Jewish blood in their veins."

Fred and Harry were smiling as Doctor Brandt fumed.

As the doctor started to turn to leave, Mitch said, "By the way, I didn't have Esther fix my wounds 'cause I liked her. I did it 'cause she's better at medicine than you are."

Doctor Brandt just glared at Mitch before he spun away, opened the door and stomped down the hallway.

Fred was still smiling as he said, "I don't believe the doctor will be re-elected in November."

"I hope I didn't make him so mad that he leaves town. The folks still need a doctor and I reckon some of 'em wouldn't want to see Esther."

Harry asked, "Didn't you know?"

"Know what?"

"Doctor Walsh's nephew will be arriving next week. He's also a physician."

"Esther told me his nephew was takin' the house but not that he was a doctor. I wonder why she just didn't wait to see if she could be his nurse."

"His wife is his nurse and I imagine she didn't want to cause any problems."

"How come I didn't know all this?"

"We only found out when we met with Doctor Brandt yesterday. He used it as an argument to at least delay your marriage to Miss Cohen."

"Can I guess that another of those folks that protested was your new minister, the Reverend Berthold?"

"He's the one who talked to Doctor Brandt. I guess you must have mentioned it to him on the stagecoach ride to Millersburg."

"I mighta. Well, I need to talk to Pete for a while. If anyone else complains about me marryin' Esther, let me know."

"I don't think you will hear a peep. There will be some who'll be unhappy about it, but they won't say a word."

"That's okay."

"Do you mind if we sit out front when you talk to Pete? We'd like to hear all of the details about what happened after you and Miss Cohen boarded the stage a week ago."

Mitch grinned as he stood and said, "Well, you can hear the official part of the story."

The two councilmen understood what he meant and laughed as they left the small office with Mitch walking behind them.

————

The sun had set by the time Mitch finished his long tale and answered their many questions. He still found it difficult to explain his decision to leave Jane at the hideout, but neither of the councilmen nor his deputy asked for clarification. He even remembered to tell them about the possible addition of Ryan Grady and Eddie Stubbins.

But as soon as he finished, he looked out the barred window and said, "I reckon Nancy is gettin' a might worried, Pete. Tell her it's my fault and she'll probably forgive ya."

Pete grinned as he stood and said, "She's used to my bein' late, Mitch. I'll see you in the mornin' and man the desk while you and Esther get hitched."

"I appreciate it, Pete. But I'm gonna need a couple of witnesses, so would you and Nancy be willin' to do that for us?"

Pete nodded as he replied, "She'll be really happy to be there. We'll have Amy Flowers watch the children."

413

"Thank her for me. Now get your behind outta here so your supper isn't overcooked."

"Yes, sir."

Pete walked to the wall, snatched his hat and quickly left the jail as Fred and Harry rose from their seats.

They each smiled as they shook his hand then Fred said, "Congratulations on gettin' married, Mitch. You know you're breakin' a lot of ladies' hearts; don't you?"

"Nope. I only want to keep Esther from bein' disappointed."

Harry snickered before saying, "I doubt if that's possible, Mitch. We all know what a good man you are."

Mitch didn't argue as the councilmen pulled on their hats and left the jail.

He stayed sitting behind the desk as the kerosene lamp flame danced just a couple of feet away.

He wasn't sure of the time but expected that Esther might already be in bed by now. Even he was tired after the strenuous week, and he hadn't been hurt either. It was only after he blew out the lamp that he remembered he had a carriage and team waiting out front that needed care.

He didn't return to his private office for the hat and Goldie but pulled his keys from his pocket as he walked to the door.

Once on the boardwalk, he locked the office then climbed into the carriage.

He released the handbrake and took the reins before saying, "Sorry I forgot about you boys. I promise it won't happen again…or at least I'll try not to let it happen."

He cracked the reins and had to make a U-turn to head back to Meadow Street. He had only used the nice carriage house in back for Homer, his dark gray gelding. It had seemed almost as bad as living alone in that big house whenever he left the horse in one of the four stalls. Now his horse would have company and as he made the turn onto Meadow Street, he wondered if he should name the two horses pulling the carriage.

He was still smiling as he turned into number eighteen's drive and pulled up in front of the carriage house. He stepped down and slid the two wide doors open before entering.

He knew that Pete would have taken care of Homer in his absence, but still made sure he had enough oats, and his trough was full before patting Homer's side and leaving his stall. After filling the next two stalls' oat boxes and dumping a couple of buckets of water into each of the small troughs, he left the carriage house to unharness the team.

Twenty minutes later, he entered his big home, lit one of the four lamps in the parlor and walked to the grandfather clock.

He checked the time and then wound it for the next week before walking to the kitchen.

He set the lamp on the table and was thinking about lighting a fire in the cookstove but didn't want to bother cooking. He hung his jacket and gunbelt over their usual pegs before going into the cold room to pick up something he could eat cold.

As he set his selections on the counter, he suddenly realized that there weren't any biscuits in the kitchen. He'd been so focused on either the Carr gang or Esther that he'd totally forgotten about Donna Brown.

He sat at the kitchen table eating his thick slice of cold smoked pork with its side of cold beans as he thought about the widow who had kept the house clean and baked him biscuits since he'd bought the place. He'd never told her why he'd bought it and she'd never asked. He knew she needed the ten dollars a month and was loath to end her employment for that reason alone.

By the time he finished eating, he decided to ask Esther about it in the morning. He cleaned his almost dry plate before walking to his bedroom and sitting on the edge of the four-poster. As he pulled off his boots, he was already imagining what it would be like when he was no longer sleeping alone.

———

Esther was already asleep when Mitch was yanking his feet out of his boots. She had hoped that Mitch would be able to join her for supper, but when the sun set, she quickly ate and cleaned up before going to her small bedroom.

She changed into her nightdress and after sliding beneath the blankets, she wondered just what it was like inside Mitch's enormous house. He said that there was a big four-poster bed in the main bedroom but wasn't sure if he was serious. She'd find out tomorrow night, if not earlier.

With that pleasant image in her mind combined with the wonderful memory of their last long kiss, Esther drifted off to sleep.

CHAPTER 11

Mitch checked on the team and decided to saddle Homer to give him some much-needed exercise rather than just walk to the jail. He knew he'd have to use the carriage when he went to Doctor Walsh's house to bring Esther and her things back, but he needed to get some more things done before he returned to harness the team.

After he saddled his gelding, he mounted Homer and walked him out of the carriage house leaving the doors open. He hoped to find the jail empty when he arrived. When Pete showed up, he'd do his rounds and talk to Esther before he returned to the office. He wanted to ask her about Mrs. Brown and the new Doctor Walsh but wasn't sure that he'd mention the councilmen's visit. At least not until after they were married. He didn't want to give her an excuse to change her mind. He had to remember to buy a set of wedding bands, too.

He soon reached the jail and noticed that the door was already open even though it was barely seven o'clock. He dismounted, tied off Homer and stepped through the doorway.

Pete grinned when he spotted his boss but didn't leave his seat.

Mitch smiled as he walked to the front desk and said, "You're here early, Pete."

"I figured you might want to get out of here pretty quick."

"You got that right. Did you talk to Nancy?"

"Yup. And I didn't even have to ask her about bein' a witness. When I said you were still gettin' married, she volunteered right off."

"I reckon you heard most of what the councilmen said in my office."

"Yup. They were talkin' kinda loud. I told Nancy and she was pretty angry. I was just glad she ain't never been that mad at me."

"It's like I kept tryin' to tell Esther. Most folks aren't like Doctor Brandt or our new reverend and his wife. Did you know that Doc Walsh's nephew was a doctor, too?"

"Not until you did. Do you want me to make the rounds while you go talk to Esther?"

"Nope. I'll talk to her after I do the rounds. But I'll need to wear Frog's hat that I left in my office for a while. I need to pick up a new one sooner or later, but I gotta buy a set of wedding bands right away."

"You got time. I don't think Judge Whitlock will be in his office for another couple of hours anyway."

419

Mitch tapped Pete on the shoulder before walking to his office and retrieving Frog's hat and Goldie.

After sliding Goldie into Homer's scabbard then walked west along the boardwalk to make his rounds. He wasn't expecting to find any trouble. Most of the businesses weren't open yet, but the shop owners were usually inside setting up for the day.

He was curious about the reception he'd receive from the townsfolk after hearing Doctor Brandt's claim that he'd be ostracized if he married Esther. He found it hard to imagine as most of the law-abiding residents had known him for a long time. The troublemakers didn't count. He could almost create a list of those he believed would be less friendly, but none of them mattered. They hadn't liked him that much because he wasn't a regular churchgoer. But the list of those unhappy citizens wasn't long, and he wouldn't care if those on it moved out of town.

As he walked along Main Street, he greeted the citizens he passed and received genuine smiles and congratulations for either stopping the Carr gang or his pending marriage. With each brief friendly reply, Mitch grew more confident in his trust in the basic fairmindedness of most people.

He soon circled to the opposite boardwalk and started walking east with the almost blinding sun in front of him. Only the boardwalk's roof allowed him to see clearly.

He was about to cross Third Street when he decided to go to Doc Walsh's house. Esther should be awake, and he wanted to talk to her before he returned to the jail.

As he made the turn, he looked at #21 and thought he saw a blonde head for a moment before it disappeared behind the house. He couldn't believe that Jane had somehow magically transported herself to Salmon City, but he still began jogging down the road.

———

Inside the house, Esther was collecting her things she'd be taking with her when she moved to the big house. Ever since her eyes opened two hours earlier, she'd been almost floating on air as she prepared for the big day. She'd taken a long bath then put on her nicest dress before she had a light breakfast. Now, as she moved her things to the waiting room, she kept glancing to the front door as she waited anxiously for Mitch to arrive.

She had just finished moving the last of her personal property to the waiting room and was heading down the hallway when she heard the back door open.

While she was surprised that Mitch would enter without knocking, she was still happy that he'd arrived. She hurried down the hallway but when she entered the kitchen, she didn't find Mitch standing there with a smile on his face.

She froze and stared at Annabelle who was glaring at her as she held a threatening, razor-sharp dagger in her hand.

Esther stared at the eight-inch blade as she quietly asked, "What are you doing here?"

Annabelle lifted the dagger before her and replied, "You helped that outlaw escape and almost got him killed. You're an evil woman."

Mitch had mentioned Aaron's misguided affection for Annabelle, but he made it sound as if she was just toying with the young deputy. If that was true, then it made no sense for Annabelle to threaten her with the knife just to get revenge for Aaron Jackson.

She didn't step back or show any sign of fear as she said, "I didn't even know what happened until Ace Carr was already free. You must have heard all the stories."

Annabelle glared at her as she growled, "They were all lies that you concocted to hide your crime. You even tempted Mitch to lie for you, but you're never going to marry him. Never!"

"And I suppose Sheriff Borden is part of this web of lies as well? Even he will tell you that Ace's pretty blonde girlfriend was in the stagecoach and flirting with Aaron before she knocked him out then did the same to me. When Ace's gang arrived, I thought they were going to kill me."

Annabelle laughed and asked, "Do you know how absurd that sounds? I'm not that stupid. I'm also the only pretty blonde woman in Salmon City."

"She boarded the stage in Millersburg. Why don't you drop the knife, and we'll have some coffee? I'll tell you the whole story and then you'll realize that I'm not lying, and neither is Mitch."

"You know I can kill you then tell everybody that you threatened to kill me because you were jealous."

As she studied Annabelle's fierce blue eyes, Esther knew that no amount of logic would be get her to change her mind. She was still very puzzled by Annabelle's reasoning. Even if she'd been devoted to Aaron, she could have just asked Mitch what had happened. *Why had she come here to threaten her rather than just going to the jail and asking Mitch?*

Annabelle wasn't about to sit down and share coffee or anything else with the woman. She knew the details of what had happened and didn't care about Aaron's death. She had a very different motive.

But just after she entered the kitchen and saw Esther's face, her rage and determination had started to fade. Even as she threatened the dark-haired woman with her dagger, her violent plan was evaporating. As she stared into Esther's brown eyes, Annabelle began to think of a way to just make her leave Salmon City.

423

Esther didn't know what Annabelle was thinking, but now wished she had Mitch's small pistol in her dress pocket. Without the revolver, she needed to quickly devise some other way to stop Annabelle. The kitchen knives were just six feet away, but she'd have to get past Annabelle just to grab one.

It seemed like hours as the two women stood facing each other in the silent kitchen, but it was less than thirty seconds.

During that half a minute, Esther remembered how Mitch had confessed his great fear of being sliced by a sharp blade and now understood his revulsion.

Just as she decided to take the risk of being stabbed and rush past Annabelle to grab the butcher knife, she saw a shadow in the open doorway behind Annabelle.

She didn't react because she knew who was about to quietly enter the room.

Annabelle was still glaring at Esther when she crumpled to the kitchen floor.

Mitch holstered his Model 3 then reached down and picked up the dagger.

When he looked at Esther, he said, "I hope that Annabelle's the last blonde I gotta conk on the noggin."

Esther stepped close to him then waited for him to toss the dagger into the sink before she took his hands.

"She sounded like a madwoman, Mitch. How much did you hear?"

"Enough to agree with you. I almost made a lot of noise comin' in but when I heard a woman's voice, I was confused and slowed down. Even after I figured out who was with you in the kitchen and heard what she was sayin', it didn't make much sense. I'm sure she didn't give a hoot about what happened to Aaron, and she had to know that you didn't have a thing to do with it."

"Are you sure that she didn't love Aaron? Why else would she be so willing to overlook the truth?"

"I got no idea. But do you want press charges?"

"No. There's no point; is there? Remember how you told me how difficult it would be to convict Jane of murder? I guess that trying to get your prosecutor to even think about charging a pretty blonde woman for threatening to stab a Jewish woman would be almost non-existent."

"I reckon so. I'll carry her back to the jail and have her father come to pick her up. It'll delay our weddin' again but not too long."

"I'm ready to move already, Mitch. I don't want to spend another night in this house."

"We'll make that happen soon. Before I take her away, I have a couple of questions for you. One is about Mrs. Brown, the lady who cleans the house. I don't want her to lose the ten dollars a month I pay her, but it's up to you whether I let her go. She does my laundry, too. That's a bonus."

"I know Donna Brown. She's a good woman and I won't mind if you want to keep her. What's your other question?"

"Did you know that Doctor Walsh's nephew was a doctor?"

"Of course, I did. I also knew that his wife was his nurse and they had four children. It was why I couldn't stay even if he was as nice as his uncle."

"I was just wonderin'."

Esther smiled as she asked, "Any more questions, Sheriff?"

"No, ma'am. I'll be back as soon as I can. Leave that dagger in the sink for now. If her father wants it, I'll pick it up later."

"You can pick up Annabelle first."

Mitch smiled as he dropped to his heels and scooped Annabelle from the floor and carried her out the back door.

When he stepped onto Third Street, he could almost feel everyone's eyes turn to look at him as he strode toward the jail. He wasn't sure what they were thinking as Annabelle's blonde head bounced against his right shoulder, but he doubted if any of them were close to being right. He wasn't sure how Carl Gruber would react when he told him what had happened but maybe he'd be able to explain why Annabelle had tried to kill Esther. He didn't think it was because she was Jewish. Even though he'd picked up Annabelle's dagger, he found it hard to believe that she would have actually used the sharp blade to hurt Esther.

When he carried her into the jail, Pete hopped to his feet as he exclaimed, "*What happened, Mitch?*"

"Let me lay her on the cot in the first cell and I'll tell ya."

Pete hurried to the cell and opened the door before Mitch entered and gently lowered her to the cot.

When he turned to leave, Pete asked, "Do you want me to lock the door, boss?"

"Nope. She just needs to wake up. I gave her a pretty good whack with my pistol, so it might be a while."

"Why did you do that?"

"I found her headin' into Doc Walsh's house and by the time I got there, I heard her threatenin' to kill Esther with a dagger. I ain't sure she woulda really done it, but she sounded pretty crazy."

Pete's eyes popped wide, and his eyebrows almost touched his hairline as he sharply asked, "She was going to kill Esther? Why would she do that?"

"It sounded like she was blamin' Esther for Aaron gettin' killed, but that didn't make a lick of sense to me. Does it sound right to you?"

"Nope. I figured she was just messin' around with Aaron."

"So, did I. Anyway, I'm gonna head over to Gruber's and talk to Carl. If she wakes up before we get back, see how she's doin', but keep her here."

"Okay, Mitch."

Mitch turned, left the jail and mounted Homer to make the short ride to Gruber & Sons Saddlery and Leathers. He thought that Carl would be shocked and confused, but he wouldn't be too angry. He just wasn't sure about Annabelle's brothers. Art and Jason weren't exactly model citizens and spent too much of their free time at Comey's Saloon and Billiard Parlor. They weren't noted for their skill at the pool table either.

He pulled up before the leather shop, dismounted and looped Homer's reins over the hitchrail. When he entered the business, he was a bit surprised to see Art at the counter talking to Billy Livingston. He didn't see Jason or his father, but assumed they were in workshop.

Art glanced at him before resuming his conversation with Billy.

But when Billy looked his way, he grinned and said, "Well, here's our sheriff already back in town. You did one hell of a job out there, Mitch. And I hear you're gonna be getting married today, too."

Mitch smiled as he walked to the counter and replied, "Thanks, Billy. It didn't work out like I expected, but at least I got all of 'em. I'm lookin' forward to tyin' the knot when I can, too."

He then looked at Art and asked, "Is your father in back?"

"Yeah, he's showin' Jason some trick about fixin' a tear in a saddle seat."

Mitch nodded then walked past the counter and opened the door to the workshop. As he entered, Carl and Jason both stopped working and looked at him.

Mitch asked, "Carl, can you walk with me to the jail? I got somethin' you need to see."

Carl stood, set down his awl and said, "Okay, Mitch," then grabbed his hat and followed Mitch through the open door. He was completely in the dark about the reason for the sheriff's request.

After turning onto the boardwalk, Mitch only walked fifteen feet to the nearest bench and took a seat. Carl was even more confused as he sat down and looked at him.

"What's going on, Mitch?"

"You know I'm marryin' Esther Cohen this mornin'; don't you?"

"Everybody in town knows that. I was surprised to see you when you walked into my workshop."

"How much do you know about what happened when I was takin' Ace Carr to Lewiston?"

"About the same as everybody else, I reckon."

"Did Annabelle know that it was Ace's girlfriend who killed Aaron?"

"Of course, she did. Why are you asking?"

"A little while ago, I was goin' to Doc Walsh's house to talk to Esther and saw a blonde woman walkin' down the drive to the back of the house. For a few seconds, I thought it mighta been Ace's girlfriend and hurried to the house. When I got close to the back door where she'd gone, I heard voices and knew it was Annabelle. Then I heard her threaten to kill Esther."

Carl exclaimed, "*She was going to kill Esther?*"

"That's what I heard, but I ain't sure she'd really go through with it. She sounded like she was outta her head. Anyway, I snuck through the open back door and saw her standin' in front of Esther with a dagger in her hand. I mighta figured she wasn't gonna use it but couldn't take the chance. So, I popped her on the head with my pistol and knocked her out. I carried her to the jail and she's probably awake by now."

Carl was stunned and didn't say anything for a minute.

Mitch stood and asked, "Do you want to come to the jail and take her home?"

Carl looked up and asked, "You're not arresting her?"

"Nope. Esther didn't press charges. We just can't figure out why she blamed Esther for Aaron's death."

Carl stood and said, "I think I might know. Let's go to the jail and if she's awake, I'll talk to her."

Mitch left Homer at the hitchrail and as soon as he and Carl started walking, he asked, "Why do you figure she wanted to stab Esther?"

"I think it was because she didn't want you to marry her."

"Because she's Jewish?"

Carl glanced at Mitch as they strode along the boardwalk before replying, "No. I think she didn't want you to marry anyone. At least not until she got your attention."

Mitch laughed then said, "That's just plain silly, Carl. I knew Annabelle when she was just a stick of a girl. Hell, I'm almost as old as you."

"She's almost worshipped for a long time now. Do you remember when you visited the school a while back? You told a story about confronting an outlaw dressed like an Indian."

"That was a long time ago, but I remember tellin' the young'uns that story. It was just a yarn I made up real fast."

"But the real stories about you since then have almost turned you into a legend in the territory. My wife and I both knew she had a schoolgirl crush on you, but many of the other girls and women in town had similar fantasies. So, Ellie and I didn't say anything and figured it would fade away as the boys started paying attention to her.

"When she started flirting with them, we thought she was over her crush. We were a bit surprised when she started seeing Aaron because, well, we were just surprised. Now I'm beginning to think that she was just seeing him as an excuse to talk to you more often in the hope you'd see her as a woman and not a girl."

Mitch was knocked completely off balance by Carl's explanation. He hadn't heard all of what Annabelle had told Esther in the kitchen, but he'd ask her later. He hadn't even noticed Annabelle's more frequent visits to the jail until Carl mentioned it. He still hadn't spoken very much to her and assumed her flirtations were just part of her personality.

As they approached the jail, Mitch asked, "Do you mind if I talk to her first, Carl?"

"Not at all. I don't know how you'll be able to put an end to her pursuit. She's a very stubborn girl."

"Just don't get mad at me when I try."

"I'll just watch as long as you don't shoot her."

"Fair enough."

They soon walked through the jail's open doorway and found Annabelle sitting on the cell's cot beside Pete.

When she saw them enter, Annabelle wasn't sure what was going to happen. She had been confused when she found herself lying on a cot in a jail cell and Deputy Carter hadn't told her how she'd been brought here. She recalled facing Esther with her dagger and then the next thing she knew, she was waking up in the jail.

Carl stopped near the desk as Mitch walked into the cell. He looked at Pete who shook his head to let him know that he hadn't told Annabelle anything.

"I need to talk to Annabelle, Pete."

"Yes, sir."

After Pete left the cell, Mitch sat down beside her and said, "I'm sorry I tapped you on your head to put you down, but I had to stop you from hurtin' Esther. I didn't want you to ruin your life, either."

Anabelle wasn't the least bit angry that Mitch had hit her with his pistol because he was sitting beside her and talking to her.

"You knocked me out? How did I get here?"

"I carried you from Doc Walsh's house."

"You carried me through the streets?"

"Yes, ma'am. But I need to know why you were gonna stab Esther?"

Annabelle exclaimed, "I didn't try to stab anyone! I was just talking to her, and she pulled a knife! She's an evil woman and you can't marry her, Mitch."

"She's the best person I've ever met, Annabelle. I've just been kinda stupid for not tellin' her that a long time ago. I even bought that big house hopin' she'd marry me."

She looked at him with pleading eyes as she snapped, "You can't marry her! You can't!"

Mitch realized that Carl was right, and Annabelle's motive wasn't what either he or Esther had suspected. It also changed his mind about how he would convince her that he was more like a father to her than a boyfriend. He had planned to turn Annabelle across his lap and spank her behind like a little girl, but now he thought he'd take a much different approach.

434

He asked, "Why can't I marry her, Annabelle?"

Annabelle hesitated before quietly saying, "You just can't."

"I love her very much, Annabelle. I'll never love anyone more."

"You just don't know her at all. You never even talked to her."

"I reckon that's so, but I never talked much to anybody before I got to know Esther better. She made me understand that I was wrong to keep so quiet. I know her better than anyone else now and love her even more."

"But you…you don't understand!"

"I reckon I do. But can I ask you to do somethin' for me?"

"I'll do anything for you, Mitch."

"After I marry Esther, I'd like you to be our friend."

Annabelle just stared at Mitch as if he was asking her to confess to a murder.

After a few seconds, she asked, "You want me to be her friend?"

"Our friend. If you get to know Esther like I do, then you'll find that she could be the best friend you ever have. But you gotta remember that I'm old enough to be your father and there are a lot of good young men out there who are better than me.

"I reckon you were just kinda crazy when you let your heart rule your mind. But it's not you, Annabelle. I think you're a good person inside and once you just let that good woman push the flirty girl away, things will be a lot better. When you stop flirtin' and let those handsome young fellers see the real Annabelle, then you'll be a lot happier, too."

Annabelle didn't answer for thirty second before she touched the back of her head with her fingertips and asked, "Did you have to hit me so hard?"

Mitch smiled as he replied, "I didn't wanna hurt you at all. I hit Ace's girlfriend a lot harder, but I didn't care if I cracked her head open."

Annabelle looked at the cell floor and said, "I imagine you think I'm a lot like her."

"Not at all. She was an evil woman from her toes to the top of her blonde head. You're nothin' like that, Annabelle. If you were even a little bit like her, I woulda arrested you in a heartbeat."

She raised her blue eyes to look at Mitch as she said, "I'm sorry for all the trouble I caused, Mitch. Can you tell Esther that I won't bother her anymore?"

"I'll tell her when I see her shortly. But I'm sure she'd like to meet you without a knife in your hand."

Annabelle smiled but didn't say anything.

Mitch stood, then smiled at Annabelle before leaving the cell and stepping to the front desk.

He stopped before Carl and said, "You can help Annabelle home, Carl. I've got to go back to your shop and pick up Homer then see Esther."

Carl shook his hand and said, "Thanks, Mitch."

Mitch nodded then waved to Pete and headed out the door.

———

After Mitch carried Annabelle out of the kitchen, Esther walked to the sink, picked up the dagger then took a seat at the table. She set the knife on the tabletop and stared at the gleaming steel blade. She imagined what might have happened if Mitch hadn't arrived in time. She shuddered and decided that when he returned, she'd ask him for his small pistol. When they had time, he could show her how to use it properly.

But as she looked at the dagger, she replayed Annabelle's bizarre accusations. It was then that she realized that Annabelle hadn't mentioned Aaron's name a single time. She only seemed angry that Mitch was going to marry her. But she

437

assumed that it was because Annabelle didn't want him to wed a Jew.

She closed her eyes and wondered just how prevalent the distrust and hatred were in Salmon City. Since her father died, she had come to believe that it was almost universal. Then Mitch convinced her that she was wrong. Then she thought Reverend Berthold and his wife accepted her as she was until they revealed their true nature.

Now, just as she was beginning to reaffirm her belief that Mitch was right and the haters were just a small, but loud minority, Annabelle tried to kill her just because she was Jewish.

Her joyous anticipation of their marriage had been replaced by the terror of hearing Annabelle's threats as she stood facing her with her deadly blade. Now her fear was gone but she couldn't rediscover her earlier bliss. As much as she tried to regain that wonderful mood, Esther was unable to keep her depression from growing stronger.

She didn't cry but began to wonder if she was being fair to Mitch. *How would the community see him if she was his wife?*

Esther finally stood and walked to the waiting room where her belongings were stacked. She wasn't planning to return them to her room because the new Doctor Walsh would be arriving next week. She would wait for Mitch to return. Maybe he would be able to convince her that she was wrong one last time. As much as she prayed that he could make her change her mind again, she just didn't think it was possible.

———

Mitch was going to return to the big house to trade Homer for the carriage but changed his mind before he reached Third Street. He needed to tell Esther the real reason for Annabelle's visit. He thought she'd find it as silly as he did. While he wasn't totally convinced that Annabelle had readily accepted his suggestions, he knew that her parents would add their powers of persuasion to make sure she didn't bother Esther.

He pulled up before the house and dismounted. As he started down the walkway, he expected to find a happy Esther sitting in the waiting room with her personal things that she'd be moving to their new home.

He climbed the porch steps and didn't knock before opening the door and entering the house. He spotted Esther almost exactly where he'd expected to find her but could tell that she was far from happy.

She raised her sad brown eyes to him as he stepped past her belongings and sat beside her on the couch.

"It's all right, Esther. You don't have to worry about Annabelle. She won't bother you anymore."

She took his hands before she quietly said, "I'm not worried about her, Mitch. At least not about her trying to attack me again."

"Then what is bothering you? I thought you'd be happy when I got back 'cause we'd be gettin' married in a little while."

"Are you sure you still want to marry me, Mitch?"

Mitch was startled but quickly replied, "Of course, I do! Why would you think I changed my mind?"

"I know you wouldn't, but I'm concerned that everyone would think less of you for marrying me. I don't want that to happen."

"I thought you figured out that most folks are okay with you bein' Jewish."

"I did. But after you carried Annabelle away, I realized that she never even mentioned Aaron when she threatened me. She wanted to kill me to prevent you from marrying a Jew."

Mitch stared at her and asked, "Did she say that?"

"No, but what other reason could she have for wanting to kill me? It wasn't about Aaron; was it?"

"No, ma'am. It wasn't about Aaron, and it wasn't about you, either. Her father told me why she showed up in the kitchen, and I was kinda surprised myself."

Esther's curiosity overtook her sadness as she asked, "What did he say?"

"It turns out that Annabelle had been hidin' a schoolgirl crush for me since she was in school. I always saw her as that skinny girl even when she grew up. Her father told me that she didn't want me to marry anyone else and I reckon she was kinda surprised to hear that we were gonna get married so fast. It musta made her a little crazy, so she tried to stop it from happenin'. I talked to her in the jail with her father watchin'. I told her that I would only love you and after a while, she musta figured I was never gonna look elsewhere."

"You told her that?"

"Yes, ma'am. She seemed a lot calmer when I finished, and I reckon she sees me as an old uncle now. So, will you forget about the folks not likin' me 'cause you're my wife?"

"But even if Annabelle's reason wasn't what I thought, you don't know if they won't, Mitch."

Mitch smiled as he said, "That ain't quite true either, Esther. I wasn't gonna tell you about a meetin' I had with the three councilmembers yesterday 'til after we were hitched. But I figure you need to hear it now."

"Why did they want to meet with you?"

"They asked me to delay our wedding until the citizens got used to the idea."

441

Esther quickly asked, "Doesn't that prove my point?"

"Let me tell you what happened."

Esther nodded as Mitch resumed his explanation by saying, "One of 'em is Doctor Brandt, and I reckon he convinced the other two, Fred Smith and Harry Longstreet, that the folks wouldn't be happy about us gettin' hitched. When Fred asked me to postpone our weddin', I could tell he wasn't happy about it and Harry wouldn't even look me in the eye. Doc Brandt just kinda glared at me. He musta figured I'd give you up just to keep my badge. I'm sure that he was the one who brought up you bein' Jewish, so I figured I'd have a bit of fun."

"What did you do?"

Mitch grinned as he answered, "I pretended that I didn't know about it. I didn't think he'd fall for it, but he did. You shoulda seen his face when he figured he'd opened my eyes and I was gonna call it off. Then I made him mad when I said I was still gonna marry you and if the folks in Lemhi County didn't like it, then I didn't want to be their sheriff anymore. I even tossed my badge onto my desk."

Esther's eyes were wide as she asked, "Would you really have quit or was it just a bluff?"

"I never bluff, Esther. I figured if they were serious, then we'd move to Lewiston, and I'd be a deputy sheriff for Lyle. He's gonna be down to one deputy pretty soon."

"You're still wearing your badge. So, how did they react?"

"Fred and Harry almost panicked, but Ernst Brandt blasted outta my office like his britches were on fire. After he was gone, Fred apologized and said that he didn't think the doc would get many votes in November's election."

"Do you really believe that they represent most of the other residents?"

"Yes, ma'am. If they didn't, then I woulda left my badge on the desk."

Esther still wasn't convinced but did feel much better.

Mitch saw the sorrow fade from her eyes before he leaned over and softly kissed her.

"I'll ride back to our house and harness our team to our carriage. I'll be back to load your things and take you to the county courthouse in about twenty minutes. Okay?"

"Okay, but before you go, could I ask one favor?"

Mitch smiled as he reached into his jacket pocket, pulled out his Model 1 and handed it to her.

Esther wrapped her hands around the small pistol as she laughed then said, "You already know me well, sir."

Mitch returned her smile before he stood and said, "I'll be back as soon as I can."

Esther nodded and watched him hurry out of the waiting room. She stared at the pistol and wondered if she'd ever have to use it. She still wasn't sure about Annabelle.

––––––

Before he returned to the house, Mitch stopped at Robinson's Timepieces and Jewelry. He quickly dismounted, hopped onto the boardwalk and passed through the open doorway.

He barely crossed the threshold when Jim Robinson grinned at him and said, "I was expecting you to show up this morning, Mitch."

"I reckon so, Jim. I'll need a nice wedding band set."

"I already picked out a set that you'll probably like. I'm sure the large ring will fit your finger and have a good idea of Miss Cohen's size as well. Let me show them to you."

Mitch watched as Jim placed a small blue velvet box onto the thick glass counter and opened the lid.

"You did a good job, Jim. I like 'em and I'm sure Esther will, too."

He closed the lid and handed the box to Mitch as he replied, "You can pay me the eighteen dollars when you get a chance, Mitch."

Mitch plunged his right hand into his pants pocket as he said, "Hold on for a second."

After pulling out his few remaining bills, he counted out a ten, a five, and three singles then handed them to Jim. He jammed the last two one-dollar bills into his pocket before dropping the box into his empty left jacket pocket.

He grinned at the jeweler and said, "Thanks, Jim. I gotta get goin'."

Jim waved as Mitch hurried out of his shop and mounted his horse. When Mitch disappeared from view, he walked to the front, closed the door and locked it. After placing his 'CLOSED' sign in the window, he walked to the back of his shop and entered his residential area.

Mitch soon reached his house and as he turned down the drive, he realized that Mrs. Brown was probably at work inside the house. He walked Homer into the carriage house and after dismounting, he quickly unsaddled his gelding before leading the two carriage horses out and putting them in harness.

Once the carriage was ready to roll, he trotted to the back of the house and entered the kitchen.

Mrs. Brown had heard him ride in and was standing near the cookstove waiting for him.

When she saw him, she said, "I heard you were getting married today."

445

Mitch grinned as he replied, "Yes, ma'am. I was gonna ask you if you would still want to work for me. Esther could use some help to keep this big place clean and I'm sure she would appreciate your company while I'm out of town."

She seemed surprised and asked, "Have you asked her yet? I'd be surprised if she agreed with you."

"I did and she was pleased to know that she'd have another woman to talk to. She's a smart lady and so are you, Donna. So, is it okay?"

Donna smiled as she nodded and said, "Yes. Thank you, Mitch. And thank Esther as well. I think she's a fine woman and you couldn't do better."

"I knew that before I even bought this place. I just dreamed that she'd really be livin' here."

"Is that why you bought this house two years ago?"

"Yes, ma'am."

Donna laughed before saying, "I always wondered why you did, but never would have guessed that was the reason."

"Well, I need to take the carriage to Doc Walsh's house. I figure we'll be back around noontime."

"I'll cook you something and leave it warming, but I won't be here when you arrive. I think you and Esther will prefer the privacy."

Mitch chuckled then surprised her when he pecked her on the cheek before he turned and hurried out of the kitchen.

Donna touched her fingers to her cheek then sighed and walked to the cookstove to light a fire. She was happy for Mitch but still had a touch of regret.

————

Mitch pulled up before the jail, set the carriage's handbrake and hopped to the ground.

He opened the door, stuck his head inside and said, "I'm gonna pick up Esther, Pete. Can you and Nancy meet us at the courthouse?"

Pete shot to his feet and quickly replied, "We'll be there, Mitch."

Mitch turned and hurriedly climbed back into the carriage, released the handbrake and set the team moving toward Third Street. In his excitement, he wasn't paying the least bit of attention to the traffic or pedestrians.

He soon turned the carriage into the drive at #21 and yanked back on the reins when it was as close to the front porch as possible.

After locking the handbrake, he hopped out and trotted to the porch. The front door was already open, and he wasn't surprised to find Esther already standing next to her stack of possessions wearing a big smile.

Mitch quickly kissed her before he picked up her travel trunk and asked, "You haven't changed your mind since I left, have you, Miss Cohen?"

"No, Sheriff Ward. I haven't changed my mind or had any sudden regrets."

"Then grab what you can, and we'll load up our carriage before driving to the courthouse. Pete and Nancy will meet us there."

Esther was all smiles as she picked up two travel bags and followed Mitch out the door.

When they reached the carriage, he unfolded the baggage carrier at the back then loaded and secured her trunk. After placing her travel bags on the back seat, he helped Esther into the carriage, but had to make one more trip to the house to retrieve her last travel bag and a large canvas sack.

Two minutes later, he drove the carriage away from the house and turned toward Main Street. Esther was focused on Mitch, and he kept glancing into her big brown eyes to make sure she was no longer worried. Neither one paid any attention to their surroundings.

The carriage soon arrived at the old county courthouse. A new, larger brick building was almost finished, so Mitch figured they might be the last couple to be married in the original building.

He helped her out of the carriage and said, "I hope you aren't embarrassed 'cause I'm still armed."

She smiled and replied, "How could I be embarrassed? I have my own pistol in my purse."

Mitch laughed as they stepped onto the boardwalk and entered the courthouse. They were met by Pete and Nancy just after passing through the wide doorway.

Nancy smiled at Esther as she said, "We never thought we'd see the day when Mitch entered the courthouse escorting his bride instead of a vicious criminal."

Esther replied, "At least I'm not in shackles."

Mitch grinned and said, "I can go get 'em if you want to wear wrist cuffs and leg irons instead of a weddin' ring."

She smiled as she said, "I'll pass on the shackles, Sheriff."

Pete then interrupted the gay banter when he said, "Judge Whitlock is expecting us."

Esther took Mitch's arm and they walked down the hallway to Judge Bertrand L. Whitlock's chambers next to the courtroom.

Pete hadn't exaggerated when he said that the judge was waiting for them. When they entered the judge's outer office, he was already standing near his clerk's desk wearing his judicial robes.

He grinned as they entered and after shaking Mitch's hand, he looked at Esther and said, "Thank you for marrying our lonely sheriff, Miss Cohen. We thought he'd never settle down even after buying that mausoleum."

Esther returned his smile as she replied, "I'm very grateful myself, Your Honor."

"Call me Bert. Let's go into my chambers. We'll do the paperwork after the ceremony."

The judge stepped past his clerk's desk and Mitch and Esther followed. Their witnesses trailed behind. But after the door closed, the judge's clerk hurried out of the office leaving the paperwork on his desk.

Esther handed her weighty handbag to Nancy without advising her of its contents before taking Mitch's hand.

It was a typical wedding in the sparsely populated territory, with the notable exception that the groom was wearing a gunbelt. Esther was wearing her nicest dress, but it hardly qualified as a gown.

Mitch thought that Judge Whitlock seemed to be enjoying himself as he stretched the normally short ceremony with anecdotes and even asked a few questions. But it was still shorter than a fancy wedding.

When Mitch produced the small blue box, Esther's eyes misted as she watched him open the lid. He handed her the larger ring and took the smaller one before returning the empty box to his jacket pocket.

He carefully pronounced his vows without modifying any of the meaningful words as he slid the ring onto Esther's finger. He felt this was one time Esther would appreciate his proper annunciation.

Esther said her vows almost as slowly as she gazed into Mitch's hazel eyes then slipped the wedding band onto his finger.

Judge Whitlock pronounced them man and wife before Mitch took Esther into his arms and kissed her softly. He never heard him say, "You may now kiss the bride."

After their first kiss as husband and wife, Mitch and Esther accepted congratulations from the judge, Pete and Nancy before they left his chambers. Once in the outer office, the judge let Pete and Nancy sign as witnesses before Mitch and Esther filled out the rest of the forms.

By the time they completed the paperwork, Pete and Nancy were gone, but Mitch and Esther didn't even notice. Nancy had left Esther's purse on the absent clerk's desk.

After the judge shook Mitch's hand and gave Esther a peck on the cheek, the newlyweds finally left his office and stepped into the hallway.

They were holding hands as they slowly walked toward the open double doors. But just as they entered the bright sunshine, they froze when a large crowd filling Main Street exploded in loud applause.

Mitch and Esther exchanged a quick glance of stunned surprise before county commissioners Fred Smith and Harry Longstreet stepped away from the crowd and stopped a few feet before them. Harry was carrying a large bouquet of spring flowers.

When the applause ended, Harry handed the bouquet to Esther and said, "Congratulations, Mrs. Ward."

Esther was still so overwhelmed that she was barely able to say, "Thank you."

Fred Smith then shook Mitch's hand before saying, "We wanted let you know how happy the whole town and county is for both of you. And I don't think that you could have found a better wife, Mitch, even if it did take you a while to figure it out."

Mitch smiled as he looked at Esther and said, "I figured it out a long time ago. She's the reason I bought that big house, but I was a bit slow in lettin' her know."

The crowd laughed and tittered before Pete stepped past the councilmen and said, "Your carriage is ready, Mitch."

"Thanks, Pete."

He still held Esther's hand as they stepped off the boardwalk and the crowd parted to let them pass. When the carriage was exposed, it didn't look quite the same as it had when they'd entered the courthouse. The top was up, which wasn't that big of a change. But both horses were wearing a small bundle of flowers and ribbons on their heads and hanging over the side of the carriage was a banner that read 'CONGRATULATIONS MITCH AND ESTHER WARD' in large block letters.

Mitch laughed and waved as he opened the carriage door and helped Esther enter before climbing in behind her. Esther still hadn't recovered from the unexpected display as she sat on the leather seat holding her bouquet.

When Mitch took the reins and the carriage began to slowly roll through the crowd, he continued to smile and wave. Esther soon realized they were moving and smiled before she began to wave to the townsfolk.

They soon left the crowd behind, and Esther turned and asked, "Did you know about any of this?"

"No, ma'am. Especially not after my talk with the county commissioners yesterday. At least now I know why the judge seemed to be takin' his time. I noticed that Doc Brandt wasn't there, but I'm kinda glad he wasn't."

"Did you see Annabelle?"

"Nope. I reckon she's still at home with a sore behind. Her father wasn't too happy with her, and I don't think it matters if she's eighteen, either."

"I knew that you were popular, but I'm still surprised to see such a large crowd."

Mitch looked at her as the horses headed down Main Street and said, "I'm not the one who is holdin' a bouquet of flowers, Mrs. Ward. Those folks may not appreciate you as much as I do, but most of 'em respect you. You need to start seein' yourself like I do."

"I suppose you're never going to stop telling me that; are you?"

"I will unless you start feelin' sorry for yourself again. When you run into folks like Ernst Brandt or Reverend Berthold, just feel sorry for them instead. They're the ones who are ignorant and too set in their ways to ever change."

As Mitch turned onto Meadow Street she said, "I'll do my best, Mitch. But I've lived a long time believing everyone looked down their noses at me."

Mitch smiled as he replied, "And I, Mrs. Ward, have spent most of my life either not speaking or torturing the English language when I did. If you can change, then so can I."

She laughed as she said, "I reckon I won't be all that happy if you started soundin' like a schoolmarm."

Mitch laughed as he turned their carriage onto the drive next to their house.

As he pulled the carriage to a stop near back porch, he looked at the large house and wished he'd talked to Esther much sooner. But despite those lost two years, he was very happy that starting today, they'd share the house and their lives.

EPILOGUE

The Monday after the wedding, Ryan Grady and Eddie Stubbins arrived and Mitch hired them the same day. Earlier that day, Mitch had received a telegram from Lyle Borden informing him that after firing Steve Finch, the ex-deputy left Idaho Territory to find employment in Oregon City. Mitch figured that their sheriff deserved him.

Doctor Paul Walsh arrived with his wife and children on the fifth of June. When Mitch and Esther stopped by to welcome them to Salmon City, it was obvious that Edith Walsh would need a long break in her nursing duties until her next unborn baby was weaned. So, Esther resumed work as a part-time nurse for the new Doctor Walsh.

In early August, Esther was enormously pleased when she told Mitch that she was expecting. The timing was almost perfect as she'd have to give up her temporary nursing duties just after Mrs. Walsh was able to resume assisting her husband.

Donna Brown and Esther became good friends and spent more hours together than was necessary just to keep the house clean or bake biscuits.

Esther soon had another, unexpected friend. Annabelle showed up at the house one day when Mitch was at the jail and apologized to Esther. Of course, Esther being Esther, not only accepted her apology but invited her into the house to share coffee with her and Donna.

She then became a regular visitor and Mitch noticed that she had abandoned her flirtatious manner. Many of the young men in town were disappointed when she did, but one young man was very impressed with the new Annabelle Gruber. Mitch didn't believe it was another case of hidden motive when Ryan Grady began officially courting her in late September.

Ryan and Eddie were both learning quickly, and Pete helped enormously in molding them into good lawmen.

Doctor Brandt didn't win reelection in November. But it wasn't because he failed to receive enough votes. It was because he was no longer a resident of Lemhi County. He and his family moved to Boise in October after he accepted a position with the same territorial hospital where Esther had worked. Esther said that he probably would be well received.

Reverend Berthold's congregation began to dwindle, but not because of his dislike of Sheriff and Mrs. Ward. While his sermons weren't filled with fire and brimstone, they did offend a number of those who heard them. Those who stopped attending wrote a long letter to the bishop. By the first of December, he also moved south to Boise and was replaced by Reverend Summers who had recovered from his illness. When he returned, the entire congregation welcomed him enthusiastically.

On the afternoon of June 15, 1872, Esther and Mitch stood near the altar of Saint Michael's Catholic church as witnesses to Deputy Sheriff Ryan Grady's marriage to Annabelle Gruber.

Donna Brown was holding tiny David Solomon Ward in her arms as she sat in the first row. His first name was actually Mitch's suggestion, but Esther had chosen his middle name without having to provide a reason. He would be their only son. Over the next five years, Esther and Mitch would have three daughters: Rachel, Sarah, and Miriam.

Esther had never worried about her Jewish heritage since leaving the old courthouse. She didn't hide it nor was she in the least bit ashamed of it. She simply accepted it as part of her life but now her husband and children were a much larger part.

Over the succeeding years, the memories of the tragic events that happened during the stagecoach ride to Lewiston faded into legendary status.

The ranch that the Carr gang had used as a hideout was purchased two years after it was abandoned for a second time. The family that moved into the ranch house knew of its history but had been able to buy it for so little that it didn't matter. They turned it into a working ranch again and never saw a sign of Jane Newsome.

But they reported that every full moon, they would hear a chilling howl they swore sounded eerily human.

Author's Note

I thought I'd be able to end this one much earlier, but the characters wouldn't let me. I reckon they wanted to hang around a bit longer.

For those who visit the Facebook page that is run by my friend who does some of the audio books, I do appreciate it when you point out my mistakes. I've learned a lot since I started writing four and a half years ago, but I know that I still make errors beyond the typos. So, thank you for letting me know when I mess up.

For my Aussie readers, I apologize if anyone was offended by the worshipping kangaroo line. Maybe I should have used a platypus instead of a kangaroo because it's more believable. I probably know more about the southern continent than most folks living in the Northern Hemisphere. As such, I appreciate the well-developed sense of humor that still seems to thrive in the Land Down Under. I'm concerned that we're losing it north of the equator.

Anyway, I'm off to start number eighty. It's tentatively titled *The Saloon Lawyer*, but that might change. It may not even have a lawyer character by the time I finish.

Have a nice summer.

BOOK LIST

1	Rock Creek	12/26/2016
2	North of Denton	01/02/2017
3	Fort Selden	01/07/2017
4	Scotts Bluff	01/14/2017
5	South of Denver	01/22/2017
6	Miles City	01/28/2017
7	Hopewell	02/04/2017
8	Nueva Luz	02/12/2017
9	The Witch of Dakota	02/19/2017
10	Baker City	03/13/2017
11	The Gun Smith	03/21/2017
12	Gus	03/24/2017
13	Wilmore	04/06/2017
14	Mister Thor	04/20/2017
15	Nora	04/26/2017
16	Max	05/09/2017
17	Hunting Pearl	05/14/2017
18	Bessie	05/25/2017
19	The Last Four	05/29/2017
20	Zack	06/12/2017
21	Finding Bucky	06/21/2017
22	The Debt	06/30/2017
23	The Scalawags	07/11/2017
24	The Stampede	08/23/2019
25	The Wake of the Bertrand	07/31/2017
26	Cole	08/09/2017
27	Luke	09/05/2017
28	The Eclipse	09/21/2017
29	A.J. Smith	10/03/2017
30	Slow John	11/05/2017
31	The Second Star	11/15/2017
32	Tate	12/03/2017
33	Virgil's Herd	12/14/2017
34	Marsh's Valley	01/01/2018
35	Alex Paine	01/18/2018
36	Ben Gray	02/05/2018
37	War Adams	03/05/2018

RIDING SHOTGUN

RIDING SHOTGUN

Made in the USA
Columbia, SC
06 June 2021